DARK GATE ANGELS

DARK GATE ANGELS

DARK GATE ANGELS™ BOOK ONE

RAMY VANCE

MICHAEL ANDERLE

L M B P N

DISRUPTIVE IMAGINATION

THE DARK GATE ANGELS TEAM

Thanks to our Beta Team:
Jim Caplan, Theresa Holmes, Kelly O'Donnell, John Ashmore, Nicole
Emens, Larry Omans, Rachel Beckford

Thanks to the JIT Readers

Dave Hicks
Kathleen Fettig
Diane L. Smith
Dorothy Lloyd
Deb Mader
Veronica Stephan-Miller

If we've missed anyone, please let us know!

Editor
The Skyhunter Editing Team

This book is a work of fiction. All of the characters, organizations, and events portrayed in this novel are either products of the author's imagination or are used fictitiously. Sometimes both.

LMBPN Publishing
PMB 196, 2540 South Maryland Pkwy
Las Vegas, NV 89109

First US Edition, April 2020
Version 1.03, January 2021
ISBN (ebook) 978-1-64202-904-8
ISBN (paperback) 978-1-64202-905-5

DEDICATION

For Nora Stewart ... I'm damn lucky to have you as a mother-in-law.

—Ramy Vance

*To Family, Friends and
Those Who Love
to Read.
May We All Enjoy Grace
to Live the Life We Are
Called.*

— Michael

PART I

CHAPTER ONE

"There she is!" a photographer shouted, and the night was lit by dozens of cameras flashing simultaneously.

Anabelle Chase stepped from the limo. Her features were stunning, to say the least. She looked as though she had been carved from stone—a statue of a goddess whose time would never come to pass. Her hair young, punkish hairstyle was a striking contrast to her pearl-pink dress.

Anabelle's gown, hand-stitched by the last great dressmaker in Eastern Europe and flown in from Prague that morning, was an elegant throwback to the glory days of Hollywood while still adhering to modern sensibility in accentuating her curves.

The cameras continued flashing. They would have blinded most people, but to Anabelle, who was accustomed to the lights of the world, they were anything but dazzling. The bright lights of the red carpet, the hotels, and the paparazzi were mundane.

She had seen true lights before. Nothing would ever compare to those.

Anabelle scanned the paparazzi around her. It wasn't difficult to move between them. They all wanted the same thing.

A show.

They wanted to see into her life, to reveal to the masses that she was merely a regular human being, the same as everyone else.

And they were waiting for her to trip, to fall, to show a crack in the veneer of perfection. Anabelle couldn't help but smile. It wasn't going to happen. Perfection was what she had spent all of her training to attain.

Anabelle glided away from the limo, paying attention to every movement of her body as she sashayed between the flashing lights, occasionally stopping to smile or wave to one of the cameras. All her actions were a performance. Inside, she was cool and annoyed.

Not at the paparazzi; they were merely doing their job. Nor at her fans—they, much like Annabelle, were playing a role.

It was the *playing* that annoyed Anabelle. This wasn't her. She had said it in multiple interviews. Modeling was just a job. It wasn't what people made it out to be. There was nothing special about what Anabelle did. "I'm a glorified coat hanger," she had joked in an interview.

A hanger with thoughts and opinions rarely ever taken into consideration. Anabelle didn't know how much longer she could put up with this. She didn't know how many more of these events she could take before she finally threw up her arms and showed the world who she really was.

She strode to the entrance where security stopped the paparazzi from following her any farther. Inside, Anabelle approached the bar and took a seat. The young bartender's expression said he couldn't believe who was sitting before him, but to his credit, he kept his cool.

"What will it be?" he said, his voice cracking like that of a prepubescent boy.

OK, so he didn't keep his cool, she thought before saying, "A martini… shaken, not stirred."

The bartender chuckled and prepared the drink. Behind him, CNN was running another story on the 'impending war with the Dark One,' a phrase circulating in certain circles which news analysts attributed to an internet conspiracy.

Chett Baker, who the camera now focused on, believed the

supposed war was nothing more than "doom-mongering" used to sell video games.

On the screen, an image of Myrddin holding a copy of the immensely popular VR game, *Middang3ard*, popped up. "This game," Chett said. "The Dark One is the villain of the *Middang3ard* game and now Myrddin, the game's creator, is trying to tell you it's real. I mean, come on! The Dark One? *Dark One?* Seriously?" Chett said with an exasperated sigh. "Talk about a lack of creativity. Just a big, bad guy who no one knows anything about? They couldn't even come up with a scary name. Myrddin should hire some writers to help him with his apocalypse as we—"

The bartender put her drink down in front of her. She thanked him without taking her eyes off the TV. "If only you knew what you were talking about, Chett," she muttered.

"Excuse me?" the bartender said.

His question brought Anabelle back to reality. "Oh, nothing. Just watching the news. It seems all everyone talks about is Myrddin and the Dark One."

The bartender nodded. "No kidding. The news says this Myrddin guy is trying to recruit humans for a war or something? Sounds kinda like a scam to me. Something an old, eccentric billionaire would do. Kinda wacky, right?"

Anabelle laughed softly despite herself. "Yeah, it does seem that way, doesn't it?"

Coyness. Always the best deflection. But what Anabelle wanted was honesty. She wanted to tell the bartender how she felt about Myrddin. How Myrddin had wasted her time for the last thirty years.

Goddess, has it been thirty years already?

Anabelle could recall every mission Myrddin had sent her on. Not that her assignments were all that memorable. Always the same kind of thing. She'd been on Earth for thirty years, stealing government secrets, nudging politicians in the right direction, and playing in the background.

None of it had been any fun, either. She wasn't a spy like some of Myrddin's other agents. For the last thirty years, she had been a glorified socialite. Now she was a model and social media influencer. *Ugh. Could life get any more boring?*

Anabelle stared down at her drink as the bartender went on about his scam theories. She wished she could have talked to him. Honestly, talking to anyone would have been great. All of the pretending was starting to make her lonely.

Thirty years felt like forever.

A strange thought for a creature who would live forever.

Unless she died from boredom.

A beer was placed on the counter, interrupting Anabelle's thoughts. She glanced over her shoulder. Roy stood behind her, a beer of his own in his hand. He wore slacks and a collared shirt, both at odds with his scarred, dirty, and scruffy face. He would be more at home on a construction site.

Roy leaned close and said, "Beer?"

Anabelle glared at the drink in disgust. "Beer? You know I can't be drinking so many calories."

Roy grunted and gave a noncommittal shrug, then drained nearly half of his beer. "You don't have to drink it if you don't want. Also, cut the crap; I've seen you eat before. I got us a table." He pointed to the back of the room, retrieved her untouched beer, and walked off.

Anabelle followed Roy to a little private booth, away from prying eyes and ears. "It pays to keep up appearances," she said. "I don't want people to start spreading rumors that I have an eating disorder. That would be bad for my image. And you know, all I get to care about is my image."

"Speaking of which, did you get it?"

Anabelle reached into her purse, dug around, and retrieved a flash drive. She slid it over to Roy. "Easy enough."

Roy grabbed the flash drive and closed his hand over it, his good eye studying Anabelle from across the table. "Oh, yeah? How easy?"

"If you're looking for gross details, you might just want to read the report. It'll be a lot more interesting."

Roy finished his beer, then swiped Anabelle's. "Thanks," he said as he took a sip. "And no, I'm not looking for intimate details. But I was told the mark was going to be a difficult one. That he wouldn't part with this information without..." He paused. "Persuasion."

Anabelle leaned close and batted her gorgeous eyelashes. "Human men are human men. It doesn't matter how much money they have, what causes they care for, or how smart they think they are, they love to be flattered. They only think with one head. And most of them can't hold their liquor around a pretty woman."

Roy pocketed the flash drive and nodded as he guzzled the beer. "True. Very true. And thanks for this."

"The war effort thanks you," Anabelle muttered.

"No, I mean, *I* thank you. I really appreciate it. You have no idea how helpful this is going to be for the Mech Riders."

"Am I allowed to ask what's on it?"

"Of course. You're the one who swiped it. They're schematics. Our original design for the mechs had a few issues, and we've been outsourcing to different companies to help design past the flaw. The gentlemen that you stole this from stole our information from a rival company and started making improvements. He did some amazing upgrades. We let him work on it for a bit, and now we're taking it back. With interest."

Anabelle loved hearing what was actually happening with her missions. Other than Roy, no one told her anything. At least he had the decency to treat her as something more than a walking fashion billboard. "Roy, can I talk to you about something?"

Roy rose and held up his hand. "Hold on. I'm grabbing another round. Beer is weak as piss here. Every moment I'm here, I miss Middang3ard more." He left for the bar and returned with four more beers. "What were you saying?"

Anabelle accepted one of the beers and tasted it. Roy was right. The brew was weak compared to what the realm produced. "I want out of this assignment. I don't care who you need to talk to or what I need to do, but I want out. I can't take this shit anymore."

"Why would you want out? It's a cushy gig. You hardly have to do anything."

"And you think that's what I want? To spend the next forty years playing arm candy to whoever Senator Myrddin needs me to snuggle up to for political clout?"

Roy stroked his beard as he made a show of giving her words serious thought. "Doubt you would."

Anabelle tucked her hair behind her ears, which ended in points. Her skin shimmered, and the fairness of her elvish complexion shone for a second. "I'm nearly three hundred years old. This is a job for a teenager. Another two hundred years, and I'll be old enough to be a matron. I should be on the front lines."

Roy pointed at his ears until Anabelle covered hers with her hair. "How do makeup artists not notice them?"

"Seriously? *That's* what you're curious about? You want to know what spells I use to stay hidden. I'm—"

"Relax, relax." Roy raised his hands in mock surrender. "No need to start getting—"

"I've been trained in every elvish fighting style, sixteen orc styles, and every form of human martial arts. I should be out there. I *want* to be out there."

Roy sat back in silence, studying Anabelle as he slowly sipped his beer. She wanted to know what was going through his mind. This wasn't the first time she'd voiced her opinion to him. Hopefully, it would be the last.

Finally, Roy said, "I admire your zeal. Really, I do. But you have another talent that we haven't come across. Don't know if it's magic or just *you*, but there isn't anyone in any of the nine realms as charming as you."

Anabelle wanted to storm out of the bar right then, but she decided to wait and see what kind of hole Roy was going to dig for himself.

Roy scratched his beard nervously, his good eye scanning the bar. "You've been instrumental in prepping humanity for what's coming. Without you, Myrddin wouldn't have shit. You know that, right? I don't know how you do it, but you always get what you want."

Anabelle folded her arms and glared at him. "Yeah. Except this."

"Yeah. Except for this. I'm sorry, Belle."

"Fuck your 'sorry.' So? Which rich asshole do I have to entertain next week?"

"Well, since you brought it up..." Roy reached into his bag and pulled out a manila folder, which he slid over to Anabelle. Then he paused and scanned the bar. He sniffed the air and wrinkled his nose. "That's...not good."

Across the bar, the bartender had poured a few more drinks. He put them on a tray, headed over to their table, and placed the tray down in front of Roy and Anabelle. "Since it's a little slow, I figured these could be on the house." He winked at Anabelle.

She allowed herself to blush slightly, then lifted the corner of her lips up with just a hint of a coy smile. "Thanks," she purred before taking one of the drinks.

The bartender was grinning ear to ear, obviously beside himself. Then a loud crack sounded, as deafening as thunder, and the bar brightened as streams of electricity bounced around the room.

A portal ripped open in the middle of the bar, as though someone had torn apart the fabric of reality. The tables and chairs in the bar floated up to the ceiling, gravity ceasing to make sense before everything crashed to the floor.

The blast had flung the bartender through the air, and he landed behind the bar in a storm of broken glass.

Roy and Anabelle stared in horror at the portal as a group of orcs rushed through it. The creatures were armed and wore the insignia of the Dark One's rabid pack of assassins, a fist holding a dagger that dripped blood.

The orc captain, Jarok, pointed at Anabelle. "Her! She's the one with the drive," he shouted.

The room was quickly filling with orcs—more than Anabelle had ever seen before. *And to think they were once elves,* she thought, marveling at their obvious differences.

The orcs were gray creatures, tall, lanky, and extremely muscular. Their jaws stuck out a fraction, and their bottom fangs were almost long enough to touch their noses. Their brawny bodies were built for one thing and one thing alone—fighting.

Roy pulled his plasma pistol from the holster inside his jacket and fired a shot at Jarok, who deftly deflected it with his axe. Roy yelled at her, "You need to get out of here!"

She turned to run, but then she hesitated. Why the hell would she run and leave Roy alone to fight off all these orcs? She'd been running for so long. Running through different lives, running instead of actually taking what she wanted.

It stopped today. No more running.

CHAPTER TWO

Anabelle grabbed one of the fallen chairs and snapped off a leg. She brandished the piece of wood like a club and stood beside Roy. "I'm not gonna leave you here to get your ass torn open. You got any more guns?"

Roy snorted as he sized up the orcs in the room. "Nope. If you want a gun, or anything else for that matter, you're gonna have to rip it away from one of them. You ready for that?"

"I've been ready for thirty years."

Anabelle sprang forward, studying the movements of the orcs in front of her. It had been years since she had engaged in an actual fight —at least a hundred. And those had never been real combat, merely sparring lessons with instructors. Tonight she would find out how well muscle memory worked.

Three orcs fired their plasma rifles at Anabelle, but she dodged to the right, sliding across the floor to take cover behind an overturned table. *That was too close.* Anabelle grimaced. *Wonder if a stick is going to cut it?*

The orcs were firing again, and plasma flew above Anabelle's head before a blast tore through the right side of the table. She had to move, but she wasn't sure where to.

The air was hot and filled with the acrid scent of plasma. Another blast punched through Anabelle's table. One more shot and she was dead. She had to move now, and it didn't matter where.

One of the smaller orcs looked at Jarok, eyes troubled. Like any good orc leader, Jarok pointed at Anabelle and Roy and said, "To your last breath."

The smaller orc shrugged. "Yes, Master Jarok."

Anabelle decided not to wait. She leapt from behind the table as an orc came within arm's length of her. She sprinted to him and thrust her chair leg up against his chin with enough force to break his jaw. The orc stumbled away, and Anabelle dropped the chair leg. She grabbed the ax from his hand, spun around, and plunged it into his chest.

The creature fell backward, and Anabelle snatched his rifle. She flipped his corpse over as she fired at another orc, hitting him in the forehead.

Across the room, Roy had taken cover behind the bar. He was lining up his shots carefully, taking his time. He inhaled deeply and fired, his bullet ripping through an orc racing for him.

Anabelle tightened her grip on the orc's rifle and scanned the room for her next target. The bar was overrun with orcs, so it wasn't a question of finding someone to attack but rather of selecting the right one to tackle. And she had to get away from the horde bearing down on her.

Jarok was her target. Once she eliminated the captain, the orcs would fold. It would be easier than fighting them individually. But Jarok was nowhere to be seen.

That was going to be a problem.

A plasma blast ripped through the air, heading for Anabelle. Instinctively, she threw up an arm and cast a barrier spell. *Holy shit.* She had forgotten much of her training.

What had she been trying to accomplish by shooting orcs? Annabelle was a high elf, a Traveler trained by the Enclave of Alshiar. She tossed the rifle to the floor—such barbaric weapons were beneath her. She should have known better. If her masters could see her at this moment, they would be mortified.

It all came flooding back to Anabelle as though she were hit by a wave. Every lesson, every second spent undergoing soul-crushing training. She'd been turned into a weapon that had been sheathed for far too long.

Anabelle allowed her body to slip into the first stance. She couldn't remember the name of the pose, nor its purpose, but she knew she could trust herself, trust her training, her resolve. Tonight, she would remind Roy why she should be feared.

Anabelle surged forward, her hands glowing bright white. She slammed her fist into an orc in front of her, and he screamed in pain as her hand burned through his chest. She pulled her fist free and spun around, raising a shield instinctively to deflect an oncoming hail of plasma.

With hardly a breath between attacks, Anabelle dropped to a crouch, then sprang into the air. She flipped over the orcs racing for her and landed smoothly behind them. Her body hummed with manna discharges as she swept their feet out from under them.

Anabelle attacked with a glowing arc which sent a beam of light shooting across the floor, slicing through the legs of a couple of orcs.

At the bar, Roy was fighting off two orcs who were trying to over-power him. He grabbed one, snapped its neck, and ripped the gun from the creature's dead hand. Roy tossed the weapon behind the bar, punched the second orc, and shot it in the head.

He was about to look for more orcs to eliminate when he spotted the bartender curled up in a fetal position behind the bar. He went over to the guy.

Roy shook the bartender. "You better get up, kid. My occupation isn't protecting *people*. You want to stay alive? I advise you to keep yourself alive. What's your name, kid?"

"Th...Thani," he sputtered.

Roy grabbed the rifle he had pulled off the dead orc and thrown over the bar moments ago. "Thani, huh? You know how to use one of these?" He tossed the weapon to the kid.

Thani's eyes bulged as he caught the rifle and stared at it, his lips quivering. "No...I've never use—"

Roy grabbed the bartender by the shirt and pulled him up to look over the counter. He pointed Thani's rifle at one of the orcs and shouted, "Pull the fucking trigger!" Thani obeyed, and the orc dropped dead. "Good job," Roy exclaimed, slapping him on the back. "Now, don't forget, they're trying to do the same thing to you, so stay under cover, all right?"

And with that, Roy shoved Thani back to the floor, both narrowly avoiding a plasma blast.

Anabelle had slid back into her old ways. It was as though she'd stepped into a surging river and had submitted to the current, allowing it to take her where it saw fit. Her body was no longer hers to control. It belonged to the War Dance.

As Anabelle's body surged with manna, she tried to pull herself back together, remembering one of the first lessons she had received. Never get lost in battle. Never give in to the blood lust. Sometimes it was impossible to come back from such a place.

The manna in Anabelle's body was fading now. It had been years since she had used magic, but there were ways around this for an adept manna user, ways she had been taught. Anabelle slowed her breathing, focusing on fire instead of light.

Her eyes burned fiery red as she renewed her manna, and she sprinted toward an oncoming orc. She flipped over him and snatched his sword away. As she landed, she concentrated on the blade, on moving manna from her hand into the weapon and the steel of the sword melted, replaced by fiery energy. With the manna-infused sword in hand, Annabelle spun to face the orc, and with one slash of the blade, the creature burst into flames.

It was time to find the captain. By now, Jarok would have sensed how the battle was going. He hadn't been prepared for Anabelle to defend herself. *Typical.* Anabelle recalled her training. *Just like an orc to hide behind a shield of bodies.*

Anabelle directed her manna down into her legs. She wanted to end this fast.

Across the bar, Thani and Roy continued to fire at the orcs steadily pouring from the portal. The pair were making a reasonable dent in the numbers, but the orcs kept coming.

"How long is this going to keep happening?" Thani shouted.

Roy laughed as he pulled a grenade from his holster and threw it over the counter. "Ain't you ever been in a firefight?" he shouted. "This shit doesn't stop until everyone's dead. Us or them! Yippee-ki-yay, motherfuckers!"

The grenade exploded, sending orcs flying across the room.

Anabelle darted between them, not bothering to attack any. She moved faster than they were capable of seeing. The captain was the only one who mattered; once he was dead, the portal would close. If she failed, the orcs would keep pouring through.

"Ah, so you do remember the old ways," a voice whispered in Anabelle's ear as she ran.

She stopped and turned to face Jarok, who had been standing behind her. *How the hell is he doing that?*

Jarok assumed a traditional stance, one Anabelle recognized: Scourge of Life. The orc captain laughed at Anabelle's surprise. "Oh? Did you think your high-elf training is beyond the understanding of us simple orcs?" he taunted before springing forward to attack.

Anabelle was barely able to deflect his assault. The orc hit with the power of a freight train, and he was relentless. Attack after attack kept Anabelle on the defensive.

At last, Jarok stepped back. He inhaled deeply as his hands glowed bright white, then he struck, aiming for Anabelle's chest. She threw her arms up, blocking what would have been a fatal blow, but the force of Jarok's attack was still penetrating her defense. She'd dealt with the orcs easy enough, but now, fighting another adept, it became apparent how out of practice she was.

Fortunately, much to the irritation of past teachers, situations like these were where Anabelle thrived. She knew exactly what to do.

Anabelle imagined all of her manna leaving her body, surging out of her. As she envisioned the manna erupting from her in huge bursts, she felt it leaving, but if she lost too much, there was a good chance she would die. How convenient to have such a large pool of manna in front of her, ripe for the taking.

As Anabelle's manna left her body, she focused on drawing it from any source possible—mainly Jarok. He must have sensed her intent because he tried to back away, to withdraw his attack. That was all Anabelle needed. She lunged for Jarok, grabbing him by the throat and sucking him dry of his manna as she slammed him into the ground. Then she cut the connection and leapt into the air, focusing as hard as she could.

She hit the ground with the force of a grenade and obliterated Jarok's body, sending a shockwave through the bar. It threw every orc into the air, suspending them there for a few seconds.

Roy couldn't pass up the chance to do what he did best. He held his breath as he lined up his shots, then unloaded his entire clip faster than humanly possible.

By the time Annabelle's energy suspension ended, every orc in the bar was dead.

The portal closed, and Thani scanned the room, eyes suspicious. "Is it over?"

Roy vaulted over the counter and approached Anabelle. "That was an impressive show you just put on there."

"Impressive enough to get me off these bullshit assignments?"

Roy sighed as Thani approached. "If I had my way, yeah, sure. But it's not up to me," he explained. "Myrddin wants you to stay in the public eye."

Anabelle groaned as she threw her arms in the air. "Are you fucking kidding me?" she shouted.

Roy had turned his attention to the mess of orcs in the room. "We're going to have to call in a cleanup crew," he muttered. "Get this guy's memory wiped."

Thani's eyes went wide as he dropped his gun. "Wait, what do you mean, wipe my memory?"

Anabelle crouched among the dead orcs. "Fuck that."

She grabbed one of the orc's blades and, with one swift swipe, cut off the creature's head. Before Roy could say anything, she stormed to the bar window and kicked it down, sending glass flying everywhere.

A handful of paparazzi had hung around outside the bar, waiting for another glimpse of her. They turned to take their photos of her, all freezing when they saw what was in her hand.

Everyone stood there in shocked silence, staring at the orc's head until someone shouted, "What the hell is that?"

Anabelle pulled her hair back, revealing her elf ears while her skin lost its human dullness and returned to its shining elvish glory. "My name is Anabelle Chase," she shouted. "I am an elf from the realm of Elliyral. War is coming to you humans. Here is proof, and I'm the one who's going to save your asses."

CHAPTER THREE

Roy and Myrddin dragged their chairs across the floor, creating a shrill shriek that made Anabelle's pointed ears twitch.

"The stunt you pulled at the hotel was childish and shortsighted." Myrddin's dark blue eyes were unflustered, a calm sea.

Anabelle hated that about the wizard; it was impossible to tell what he was thinking. He even spoke with an air of mystery, as though he were only telling you half of the truth. Every statement was a riddle.

"We're fighting over here, and it's time for the humans to wake up to that fact," Anabelle shot back.

"And a few pictures with a model carrying an orc's head will... what? Wake them up?" Myrddin straightened his tie, his blue eyes twinkling. "You don't change the entire course of history through a couple of ham-fisted public appearances. Anabelle, you haven't had a chance to see the news yet, but the press is much more concerned with the nature of your relationship with that bartender than with the head of the orc you were holding."

Anabelle couldn't believe what Myrddin was saying. Could humans really be vapid enough to care more about a potential relationship than the head of a creature they'd never seen before?

"I should fire you," the wizard said.

Anabelle stood, preparing to launch into a tirade, but Myrddin lifted his hands and cast a spell that made her sit down. What was more, she was now mute. "I should fire you, but I won't. I won't because of this man." He nodded in Roy's direction.

"That fight was something else," Roy said. "I've never seen an elf use magic like that. Heard about it, you know. But from what I gathered, the magical martial arts weren't practiced anymore. Things tend to get a little messy."

Anabelle remembered the lectures she'd received from her various masters. Always talking about self-control. Keeping the battle within from seeping out into the real world. It was why elves had moved to wands for battle.

"I'm glad to see you're still keeping the tradition alive. Roy, I trust you can take it from here?" Myrddin said as he got to his feet. The wizard strode to the door, then stopped to ask, "Should I unmute her, or do you prefer her this way?"

Roy stroked his chin before saying, "She does like to yell, but unmute her. I'd like her participation in this conversation."

Myrddin waved a hand, and Anabelle felt her voice returning. But she didn't say anything.

As soon as Myrddin was gone, Roy leaned forward. "You were like a force of nature in the bar. And I think you'll be happy to hear you're getting what you want." He pulled out an envelope and handed it to her.

"Are you saying that I can finally stop telling the whole world what I'm eating and how often I work out?"

Roy tapped the envelope as he stood and headed toward the door. "Try not to screw this up, all right?"

She opened the letter and read the first few lines. By the time she looked up, Roy was gone. Anabelle turned her attention back to the letter. She smiled wider.

CHAPTER FOUR

Abby pulled out a bandana, putting it on as she ascended the stairs leading to the top of the barn on the Crookins farm. She'd been working in the fields all day and was exhausted, but tired or not, there was more work to be done. She entered the barn and closed the door behind her.

Most of the family had learned by now that when the barn door was closed, it was best not to bother Abby. None of the Crookins family could be said to have a temper, which was one of the reasons some folks suspected Abby might have been adopted. The other reasons tended to be less polite.

The inside of the barn was well lit by a series of lights running along the entire ceiling of the barn. There was hardly a shadow in the place. You also had to look hard to find any tools. Probably the least barn-like barn in the county.

A dozen or so tables were scattered around the space, most of them covered with the guts of computers, cords and cables, CPUs and RAM boards, the barn giving the impression of being the ghost of a RadioShack.

The floor wasn't any better. There was no sense or planning to the technology mess dominating the barn. That didn't seem to bother

Abby. She stalked through the maze of terminals, monitors, and technojunk until she reached her worktable.

Grabbing her welder's mask and rod, she got down to business. Sparks flew as she worked on a drone.

It was roughly the size of Abby's torso, and she was a tall girl for her age. The device looked like something out of the future, unlike the drones she had seen flying over the different farms throughout the county. She had based the design on old science fiction pulp covers, and it had an alien flair to it.

Abby had worked on the code for nearly three months now, trying to get everything perfect.

Building the mechanical parts of the drone had been easy. The code was where the art was.

Abby pulled up her mask and studied the drone as she ran her fingers over its blackened steel casing that was barely visible in the dark metal. "Hopefully, this'll work," she muttered as she hurried over to the computer monitor.

The computer booted up fast, flashing a green DOS programming screen. Abby typed in her credentials and collapsed back into a rickety rocking chair.

Her pa couldn't see how she worked like this, surrounded by junk and old things. But it was the way Abby loved it.

A knock sounded on the door. It creaked open, and Pa shuffled into the barn. He was a tall man, face chiseled with age and weathered by time. He kept his hair short, but he let his beard grow wild and gray. When he laughed, his eyes seemed to darken.

"Working hard, huh?"

Abby left the computer and approached him. She didn't want him to have to make his way through the mess. His sight was beginning to go, and he didn't stand as straight as he used to. A bad fall could put the farm out of business for a couple of weeks.

"Tinkering, you know," Abby answered.

"Come out with me. It's brighter in here than in the fields."

Abby chuckled as she followed her father out of the barn to where he sat on a nearby bale of hay.

Pa picked at the straw. "You finish those fields yet?"

Abby crossed her arms and stared at her dad. "You really come up here, banging on doors and all that, just to ask me about the fields?"

Pa laughed as he stuck a piece of hay in his mouth and began chewing. "Nah. I didn't. Came to see how you were doing. Missed dinner yesterday. And breakfast this morning. I'm assuming you'll be skipping lunch too."

"Might be. Got a lot to work on."

"Any of that work on them fields?"

"Why you on at me about the fields? You know I always get 'em done. What is it that you're always saying? 'Don't come at me cross-eyed?'"

"Yeah, but the phrase ain't quite what you're thinking of."

"Stand by it. Don't cross-eye me, Pa."

Pa chewed on the piece of hay as he chuckled. "Just worried about you is all." He finally sighed. "Skipping meals and working the hours you are ain't the healthiest. Some would say it was markedly unhealthy."

Abby stood and stretched, reaching down to touch her toes before cracking her knuckles. "It's just for the day. I'll be in for dinner and start eating you out of house and home bright and early tomorrow."

Pa rose and patted Abby on the head before scooping her up in his arms and hugging her tight. "That's what I like to hear," he said before dropping her back on her feet. "I love you, Abs."

Abby smiled as she shoved her father away. "I love you too, Pa. Now you best get back to work before Ma gets after you."

Pa waved Abby's concerns away as he headed toward the house. "I'd be more worried about you," he joked. "Last time I saw her, she said she was coming in to check and see if you'd cleaned that barn yet. I'll tell her you have. Give you a week's head start."

Abby watched Pa amble back to the big house, watched his slight limp, and the way his spine angled forward. Then she went into the barn and sat back in front of the computer.

It took Abby the better part of an hour to finish proofing everything, but by the time she finished, the code was perfect. Or as perfect as Abby was going to get it. She shut off the computer and cleared her throat. "Bobby," Abby commanded. "Operate."

The drone jiggled a little before something inside it clicked. Then it lay still.

Abby sighed as she stalked over to it. "Oh, dang," she muttered. "Here I was, thinking you were ready to get to work."

The drone's lights suddenly came to life and it floated into the air, a collection of tools and contraptions dangling from its body. "Hell, yeah!" Abby shouted. "Bobby, pack your stuff."

The tools hanging from the drone were sucked up into its body.

Abby slapped her hands together and jumped into the air. She felt like she could dance, but she had never been one for it. Now would have been as good a time as any. Maybe after the final tests were done.

"Bobby, follow me," she commanded. The drone beeped and whistled as it followed Abby, who had pushed open the barn door. "All right, Bobby, it's showtime. Get working."

Bobby floated out toward the hay bale Abby and Pa had been sitting on. A pair of claws fell from the drone's torso and clasped the bale. She held her breath as she watched Bobby lift it and take it over to the truck parked outside the barn. The drone dropped the bale and returned to her.

Abby couldn't help herself; she broke into a brief jig, kicking her feet up as she pumped her fist. "Perfect!" she shouted before running back into the barn, Bobby following behind her like a puppy.

She sat at her computer and started typing. After a few seconds, she hit enter. A loud buzz rang throughout the barn as the lights flickered. Once the power stabilized, two more drones rose from different tables and joined Bobby.

Abby, beaming from ear to ear, stood before the drones. "Bobby, Robby, and Gertrude. Start your chores."

The drones chirped enthusiastically and flew out of the barn. Abby went outside and crouched in the dirt, careful not to let her butt rest on the soil. She watched the drones mowing the hay, bundling it up, and piling it onto the truck. At the rate they were going, she could take care of every field in a day or two.

"Well, I'll be damned to hell and back," a woman shrieked.

From her right, Abby's mom was approaching. She was a woman thick with corded muscle. She wore a hat that must have been picked out with a sense of dark irony. Her plum lipstick and theatrical eye shadow had remained untouched by the heat or the intensity of her workday.

Ma jogged over and tossed her arm around Abby's shoulder. "You gotta be kidding me, girl," she exclaimed. "That is amazing! How did you do this?"

Abby bit at her thumb as she considered her answer. "I started around January, and I've been doing most of the coding after school. Throwing it together wasn't hard. The coding was the shit part."

"Language, young lady. Just because we're celebrating, it don't mean you get to talk like one of those foul-mouthed, heavy-drinking, hard-living scientists."

Abby burst out laughing as Ma winked at her, chuckling. "Seriously, Abby-Lynn, this is amazing. God damn amazing."

"Ma! Language."

"Hush it. I'm in awe. Can hardly contain myself."

Abby and her mother stood there for some time, watching Bobby, Robby, and Gertrude work as the midday sun shone over the farm, the sky beginning to soften into the dark envelope of evening.

At dinner, Abby sat next to her sister Margie, across from the baby twins Kelly and Mandy. Pa was singing in the kitchen while Ma read lazily through an almanac. Abby couldn't believe both of her parents still used those things. It was like they were trying to ignore the internet.

After a while, Pa came in with a steaming platter of pulled pork. Next, he brought in the mashed potatoes, mac and cheese, and collard greens. He placed them on the table with more than a hint of pride.

"All right, dig in," he said as he took a seat.

Most of the conversation centered around the drones and how

amazed everyone was.

"They do everything themselves?" Margie asked.

"Everything I tell 'em to."

"Even take a pee?" Margie laughed hard at her own joke.

"You hush," Ma said, playfully tapping Margie with a wooden ladle. "Robots don't pee."

Maybe they don't, but they do need to charge, Abby thought, wondering if the drones had returned to the barn after they had finished their task. It would be more than a little embarrassing if the machines did something stupid like cut down crops that weren't ready.

"I have to go check on something," Abby said as she stood.

Pa pointed to her plate and shook his head. "Not with that full plate, you ain't."

Abby checked her plate. It was mostly empty, with a spoonful of collards left, if that. "Gotcha, Chief!" she said as she scooped up the collards and downed them. "May I be excused now?"

Pa shrugged and went back to his food.

As Abby passed the dining table, a bright flash lit up the entire room. "Was that lightning?"

Pa was already on his feet, going to the window to take a look. "Shouldn't be lightning. It's not set to rain for the next couple of weeks, right, Ma?"

"Right. Supposed to be dry until the beginning of next month."

Abby went to stand beside her father. As she peered through the window, another flash of white lit the night. "It's not raining," she murmured. "There's no thunder, either."

Pa grabbed his coat and cane and went out the front door. Abby followed as Margie rose from the table, curious. She and Ma hurried to the door and watched as Pa and Abby walked into the darkness.

Pa stuck his hand out and stopped Abby. As they stood there together, she sniffed the air. It didn't smell like rain at all and she nearly always could tell when a storm was coming. The air didn't smell like lightning either.

Another flash brightened the night, and a bolt of white lightning cracked in front of Abby and Pa, scorching the earth two feet ahead of them. Abby fell to the ground and covered her head as more lightning flashed and the earth began to tremble. Pa edged closer to her.

The air above the ground where the lightning had struck had turned gray and thin, as if it were being stretched, then reality tore open. Abby felt like she was looking through a painting with its canvas ripped apart.

Something moved behind the tear, then a gray hand with long, knobby fingers pushed through the opening. Another hand followed, this one holding a glowing ax. Next came a head, long with drooping ears, drool dripping from its slack-jawed mouth.

The strange creature stepped through the tear. He stood, puffing his bony chest out as he sniffed the air. Then he turned and motioned toward the portal, and three more hideous creatures emerged. They stared around, clearly trying to get their bearings.

The first monster waved his hand, and the portal closed. He pointed at the house where lights were shining brightly. "There wasn't anything about a house being here." He grunted. "It's supposed to just be land, right?"

The second creature coughed and spat. "Doesn't matter. It'll just be humans. Killing them won't take too long. We can still bring the forces here. Might even be better if they got a place to hide. I'll go ahead—" He stopped talking when he spotted Pa and Abby, and his lips turned up in a sneer. "Guess we found the humans," he growled as he drew a pistol and aimed it at Pa.

There was a flash of light, not nearly as bright as the lightning or the brightness when the portal had opened but bright nonetheless.

Pa collapsed beside Abby, his eyes staring, wide and surprised. It was the kind of face he would make when they played hide and seek. She almost didn't notice the smoking hole in his forehead.

Abby heard someone screaming far away, and she frowned. Why were they screaming? They sounded scared. The person was also wheezing, struggling to breathe.

That was when she realized *she* was the one making the noise. She was screaming, "Run! Run! Run as fast as you can."

CHAPTER FIVE

Be careful what you wish for, Anabelle thought as she was dropped with a team of twelve human soldiers into the canyons of Zion National Park.

If the landscape had appeared otherworldly before, from her current position, it felt as though she were in an entirely different dimension.

Unfortunately, Anabelle had no time to enjoy the bizarre beauty.

She was too concerned with trying to move. The exoskeleton hanging from her body proved much more uncomfortable and unwieldy than she had expected upon first seeing them. The weight and slight delay in movement, despite being connected to her spinal nerve, irritated her.

But humans needed the exoskeleton to fight, and Annabelle had been given command of a small detail.

So, for their first mission, she had decided to dress the part.

The soldiers didn't seem to mind the extra weight. None of them were complaining, but each had at least twenty pounds of muscle on Anabelle.

Then there was the HUD.

Anabelle couldn't get used to such a heavy helmet. Roy had

explained the importance of the piece of tech to their missions, but she believed the whole system was outdated and asinine.

Anabelle called her HUD—which was executed with a single thought—and contacted Roy as she tapped her foot impatiently.

Roy's face blinked into view. "What's up, Chase?"

Anabelle waddled over to a boulder and struggled to seat herself. "Roy, this is fucking ridiculous," she grumbled. "What the hell are we doing out here?"

"You read the briefing. You should damn well know what you're doing there."

Anabelle grunted. "All it said was Dark One activities were sighted on Earth. But here? In the middle of nowhere?"

Roy gave her a sly smile. "Hey, the Dark One does what the Dark One does. Don't hate the game, hate the playa."

Anabelle rolled her eyes. "Fine. Then what about the plan? What are we supposed to be waiting here for?"

"Finally, a reasonable question. We've detected electromagnetic anomalies in the area. They have the same signature as the portal that opened up at the bar. It hasn't gotten to the same energy spike yet, so we're assuming it'll be opening up soon."

"Why the hell would it be opening up here? There's nothing here."

Roy took a ragged breath, the rough sound an indication of his growing irritation. "There's been reports of the Dark One's forces around where the energy spikes are happening. Even some reports of humans being abducted. Only men for some reason."

"So, what? The Dark One is opening Dark Gates to send a handful of minions at most through."

Anabelle's HUD screeched. She tapped the HUD a couple of times, but the feedback grew louder. Roy's voice distorted, then disappeared.

Around her, the soldiers scowled as they too tapped their HUDS, and the hair on the back of her neck stood on end. The smell of the crisp Utah air had disappeared, replaced with an iron scent similar to blood. Anabelle had gotten a whiff of this smell before—the last time she had seen a portal open.

The soldiers were unaware of what was happening.

"Hey," Anabelle shouted. "Something's coming. We need to get ready."

One of the soldiers, Private Lancaster, stepped forward. He was young, no older than twenty-one. Boyhood hope still shone in his eyes like Christmas decorations. "What do you mean? Our HUDS aren't giving any readings about anything."

The air crackled with an ear-shattering sound, and a loud boom rattled the bones in Anabelle's chest. Over a nearby ridge, a portal opened, splitting the fabric of reality, energy bursting from its edges.

CHAPTER SIX

nabelle ushered the soldiers away from the portal. Her sensors were going crazy, so she relied on her eyes. And right now, her eyes told her there were two Dark Gates—one right where her team stood, and one a few miles away, near a farm.

The soldiers' exoskeletons hadn't come back online yet, so maneuvering them was more difficult than it should have been. The humans were barely able to move, the simple act of walking more than a chore. And that was without taking their panic into account.

Most of the soldiers had begun to freak out the minute they'd seen the orcs.

Anabelle wasn't surprised, but she was disappointed. It hadn't occurred to her that Roy would have formed her squad using green soldiers. She had expected them to have at least seen combat, but here they were, behaving like they hadn't even come across a picture of an orc, let alone a platoon pouring out of a magical Dark Gate.

The soldiers stomped toward a series of boulders to take cover, helping others along the way. Their progress involved leaning on a partner and lurching forward in an awkward three-legged race to safety.

Anabelle didn't have as hard a time taking cover behind the boulders. Even though her armor was also defective, her elven strength helped her. She'd heard humans were stronger on Middang3ard than on Earth, though.

Convenient for everyone on Middang3ard, I guess, she thought. *Doesn't really help us here.*

Once Anabelle was certain the orcs above couldn't see her, she checked on the soldiers to ensure all were accounted for. No one was missing, but they were all easy targets should the orcs spot them.

Scratch that—when *the orcs spotted them.*

A private leaned over to speak with Anabelle. His eyes were wide and starting to tear up as he pulled at his exoskeleton. "What the hell are we supposed to do?" he asked.

Anabelle hadn't given much thought to what the humans were meant to do. They were, after all, soldiers. They should have been trained to take care of themselves in situations like this. They were not her responsibility. "I don't know, but you might want to figure it out."

The private stared at Anabelle in disbelief. "What do you mean, *I* better figure it out? You're our commander. You're supposed to, you know, command us."

Anabelle leaned against the rock and allowed the gravity of his statement to settle in. She hadn't been under the impression that the lives of the human soldiers were in any way related to her own. Now she had discovered that they were her responsibility.

There was that word again.

Irritation flushed Anabelle's cheeks as she kicked herself for only skimming the dossier Roy had left her with, not that it would have changed anything. The file hadn't provided any suggestions in case their exoskeletons malfunctioned. Or maybe it had. Either way, trying to recall what had or had not been said in the file wasn't helping.

"Any backup plans for the suits?" Annabelle asked sharply.

The private tried to lift his arms, groaning with the effort before allowing them to drop back to his side. "None that we were told of," he reported. "As far as I know, these are supposed to be top of the line. The best tech we had to offer."

Anabelle hoped that wasn't true. What she'd seen of the exoskeletons so far left a lot to be desired. If that was the best Myrddin could do, he was talking a much bigger game than he had.

She popped her head up from behind her boulder to check on the orcs' activity. She didn't want to risk being spotted, but she also had to figure out where the enemy was moving. A hidden friend could still be an enemy—one of the first lessons her teachers had given her as a child.

Orcs were still exiting the Dark Gate. They weren't as many as Anabelle had initially assumed. Maybe she hadn't been too far off telling Roy her opinion on the limited numbers the Dark One could ship over at a time.

Or the Dark Gate could simply need time to send a large force through. Either way, there were still too many orcs for the humans to deal with. And with their malfunctioning exoskeletons, the humans were a pathetic group.

Anabelle ducked behind the boulder and wracked her brain, trying to come up with options. There didn't seem to be any. For now, she should probably get out of her exoskeleton. If the damn thing wasn't going to work, it didn't make any sense wearing it.

She forced all her strength into her arms, lifted the exoskeleton's shoulder pads away, and ripped out the cord attached to her spine.

Damn, that hurt!

She tossed the armor aside, relieved to have the weight off her body. Now all she wore was the sleek armor and the HUD left over from the exoskeleton.

The soldiers were also trying to take their exoskeletons off, with much less success. The suits were simply too heavy to remove fast; putting them on had taken nearly half an hour and required the help of two robots.

Anabelle watched the humans struggle, gauging how much effort it would take to undress them all versus how much help they would be in a fight. Even if the soldiers could remove their exoskeletons, they were still human. And what's more, their weapon systems were part of those exoskeletons. Rail guns, heat knives, missiles, grenades...all required the suit's power to function.

Anabelle turned to the private she had spoken to earlier. "All right, so if you get these things off, can any of you fight? Or are you just going to sit here and shit your pants?"

The private was now more composed. "Of course. We'll be able to take care of ourselves. But taking care of those orcs is an entirely different question. We don't have any—"

"Weapons. I know. But what if I could get you some?"

The private smiled, which caught Anabelle off-guard. Maybe this human wasn't as defenseless as the rest. "If you get me a gun, I'll make you orc soup," he said with a grin.

Anabelle peeked from behind the boulder, counting orcs and gauging how far they were from her and the soldiers. "Good. Then I'll get you a gun."

Abby didn't remember running from the monsters or leaving her father lying there dead. Nor did she remember racing to the big house. She simply had to keep moving. Keep the monsters...no, "monsters" wasn't right. They looked like those creatures in *Lord of the Rings*. Trolls...no, orcs. That was it. Orcs.

But she was inside now, which was all that mattered. She found Margie and forced her toward the back door, scooping up the twins as she went.

She scanned the room and spotted Ma, who stood frozen on the threshold of the front door, staring out at the portal. "Ma! We have to go," she whispered as loudly as she thought was safe without drawing the attention of the orcs to her.

The woman turned to stare at Abby. Her eyes were empty. Her gaze was focused someplace else, her jaw slack. She looked almost like an old painting, worn and tired. "Rick..." she whispered.

"He's dead," Abby hissed, giving Ma a desperate, pleading look. "He's dead. Come on!"

Ma snapped back to reality as though hearing those words had breathed life back into her, the life Pa no longer had. She raced through the living room and picked Margie up without breaking her stride. They ran out the back door together.

When they reached the cellar, Abby whirled around, checking if any orcs had followed them or were trying to cut them off. She didn't see anything. Ma opened the door and ushered Margie down the stairs. Then she took the twins from Abby's arms.

Then Abby heard the sounds of leaves crunching and heavy plodding. She didn't pause to think. She met her mother's haunted eyes peering out from the darkness, pressed her finger to her lips, and shut the cellar door.

One of the orcs turned around the corner of the house. He smiled at Abby. "Found her," the monster shouted.

Abby spun and sprinted toward the stable, her heart racing as she tried to think of what to do. The only option that seemed reasonable was running. She had to keep the orcs away from the cellar. As long as Ma and the kids were safe, she'd be okay.

The stable was unlocked, and Abby threw the doors open. She ran to the back where the Crookins family kept Sergeant, an old mare who rarely wanted anything to do with people. Abby sprinted to the horse and dove into the hay. She was glad she had cleaned the stables earlier that day.

From beneath the hay, Abby watched the open doors, waiting for the orcs to find her. Only one came. He strolled through the stable, taking his time. Was he trying to draw this out? Either that, or he had no idea where she was.

A pitchfork lay beside her, and Abby grabbed it, holding it close as she tried to disappear. This had to be a nightmare. None of this was really happening. She was going to wake up any minute and come downstairs to have breakfast with her family. Pa would...

She fought back her tears. This was real. She knew it was. And Pa was gone.

The orc was close to Sergeant's stall—about an arm's length away from the horse, who was already neighing irritably about having to share a stable with Abby.

Abby slapped Sergeant's hindquarters, and the horse neighed loudly before rearing. The mare kicked her front legs out, catching the orc in the chest. The creature went flying and hit the ground with a heavy thud. He struggled to sit up, holding his ribs as he attempted to catch his breath.

She sprang from the hay, holding the pitchfork high above her head, and brought it down on the orc's throat, driving it deep into the ground. He sputtered blood and reached up, trying to grab the pitchfork from Abby, who gritted her teeth and pushed down harder, pinning him to the floor.

He wheezed and thrashed as he choked on his own blood. Then he was still.

Abby approached the stable doors as quietly as she could, checking over her shoulder every couple of seconds in case the dead orc had moved. She peeked out from behind the door, searching for the other orcs.

A pitchfork wasn't going to cut it if she wanted to get out of this alive. She needed more firepower.

Once Abby was satisfied that the coast was clear, she made a beeline for the back door to the big house. She slipped inside as fast as she could and locked the door before going upstairs to her parents' room.

A box sat on her father's nightstand. Beside it lay a card which said, "Happy Anniversary." Abby opened the box. This had been the last part of her gift—a timepiece that could control the drones from afar.

She had only tested it a handful of times, but if the drones worked, the watch should as well. But it still needed to be calibrated to the drones.

As Abby turned to leave, she spotted the shotgun hanging above the mantel. Neither Ma nor Pa was huge on locking guns up. Instead, they had been adamant about the kids receiving extensive gun and safety training.

Abby seized the shotgun from the mantel and searched under her parents' bed for the ammo. She loaded and racked the shotgun before looking down the sights, refreshing herself on handling the gun. It was something to focus on because if her thoughts wandered...

A vision flashed in her mind's eye; Abby saw Ma and the kids lying in a pool of blood, their heads bashed in.

Focus. Stay focused!

Abby shook away the thoughts and double-checked that the shotgun was fully loaded. She would have to make her way to her barn and link the watch to the drones. That was the only way to ensure that Ma and the kids didn't end up dead.

She tried to control her breathing as she descended the stairs to the living room. It felt like the world was peeling away around her. She couldn't tell if the walls were real or not. Her chest hurt from the pounding of her heart.

She gripped the shotgun tightly and crossed the living room.

The front door rattled. Shadows moved behind the stained glass in the door. The handle jiggled.

Abby froze. Then she raised the shotgun and pointed it at the door just as it opened. An orc entered the room, his eyes searching the place for her.

She didn't wait to be seen. She fired.

The round hit the orc and tore his stomach open. The creature slumped against the wall, blood staining the wallpaper.

Abby ran up to the orc, pressed the shotgun against its head, and pulled the trigger. Blood splashed on her face. It was warm, almost comforting, but she had to focus.

That shot was going to give away her position—first rule of hunting.

Abby sprinted to the back door. She would run through the cornfield, swing along the back of the barn, stay out of sight. She raced across the backyard and into the cornfield. She kept to the outskirts of the field, careful not to go so far that she would get lost. The barn came up fast enough, and she slipped in through the back, keeping the lights off and working from her spatial memory.

Finally, Abby made it to her drone table. The drones had finished their tasks and returned to their stations. Abby switched her watch on, hit the sync button, and raised it to get a better signal.

A soft green light glowed on Gertrude. Abby's watch emitted the same hue. It would only take a few moments for the watch and drones to link up.

A high-pitched scream pierced the night—a scream Abby recognized. *Margie.*

Abby sprinted toward the cellar.

CHAPTER SEVEN

The orcs continued to exit the portal as Anabelle watched. Some of the creatures were now exploring the area around them. That was the only chance she would have to grab some weapons—separating a few orcs from the pack.

Stealth had been part of Anabelle's training. Stealth: one of the Three Roads of Halal-Elforaim, or the Path of Least Resistance. The path had been passed down from elf generation to generation for thousands of years. Each practitioner was kept secret from the rest of elvish society, the teachers of the path choosing one student from the most ancient bloodlines to carry on the tradition.

Anabelle had been that Wanderer, as they were called. It was an honor beyond honor. But her training had been squandered for the last hundred years, wining and dining corrupt politicians and vapid millionaires. And there was still so much Anabelle had learned that she simply couldn't remember.

The fight at the hotel bar a few days ago almost felt like a fluke now. Muscle memory of her fighting positions had come back, but that was a different Road of her path. The three Roads were Force, Silence, and Lost. Anabelle had reawakened the Road of Force, which wasn't going to help her now.

The Road she needed to travel was that of Silence. And, at the moment, Anabelle's mind was too loud. She was under too much pressure. This wasn't the place, or the time, to focus on Silence. Yet Silence was where all of her memories resided. Somewhere in the quiet places of her mind.

To live as long as elves did, it was necessary to forget. It was not a conscious decision. Nor was it one which brought them pain or sorrow. It was a natural aspect of their existence, much like the dreams of humans or gnomes. As they grew older, memories that held no purpose slipped away.

The elves had learned to distill themselves down to the core of their existence. It was this distilling within Anabelle that now made it hard to remember. Her mind was filled with designers and dates, and a thousand other things she wished would have more quickly disappeared.

But there was one thing she did remember concerning the Road of Silence. All roads must be traveled if they are to be understood. How you traveled did not matter. Walk, run, skip, it didn't matter.

Only the traveling itself mattered.

Anabelle peeked from behind the boulder again, trying to ignore the anxious whispering of the soldiers still struggling with their armor. The orcs were multiplying—which was bad news. But they were also separating into groups, moving away from the Dark Gate, which remained open.

Different groups meant they would put space between each other. The most silent place in all the realms was space, the blackness where screams never echoed, where cries went unheard.

Perfect, she thought.

She slipped out from cover, quickly ducking behind another boulder, following the route she anticipated the orcs were taking. She moved in a roundabout fashion, making sure to avoid detection.

She did not make a sound.

Silence does not flow like water. Silence is constant. Unbroken. Untethered. There is fear in Silence. It must be used.

The memory came screeching back, nearly knocking Anabelle off of her feet.

She was a child. The ancient forests without names surrounded her, and she sat atop a stone. Her eyes were closed, and she was filthy from having not bathed in three months.

Anabelle's teacher—a wood elf far into his last years, a gnarled, sylvan creature not much different than the trees he dwelled among—came up to her. He snapped his fingers. The sound boomed in Anabelle's skull.

It was like thunder.

This was the last day of Anabelle's three-month journey on the Road of Silence. After the celebration feast, she would be allowed to speak again. Yet, she had no idea what to say. Such was the Road of Silence.

The Road stretched out in front of Anabelle now, memory after memory, shards of distant places and time, presenting themselves to her. There was a wealth of knowledge in her skull—separating and making sense of it would be the difficult task. Thousands of years of wisdom waited for her.

You'd think I would have figured out how to stop modeling sooner, Anabelle chastised herself, trying to rise above the odd sense of guilt her memories had illuminated. But there was a reason she needed the Silence: the group of five orcs moving East.

She peered around a boulder, memorizing the orcs' positions. They appeared to be doing reconnaissance, scoping out the area for some reason. Not that it mattered to Anabelle. There were only five of them. The Silence could handle five.

She needed a distraction, and the smooth stone beside her feet would be perfect. She grabbed it and felt the weight in her hand. Heavy enough. She leaned over the boulder and tossed it at the back of the closest orc's head.

The creature whirled, drawing his rifle, searching the direction the stone came from. He whispered something to the orc next to him, and three of the group strode toward Anabelle. Perfect.

She ducked down and pressed her spine against the boulder, felt the coolness of the rock as her body became weightless and thin as a shadow. She simply became part of the rock's shadow, silently watching as the orcs arrived at her hiding place.

They stomped around, searching for the source of the rock. They took their time. Anabelle watched them from inside her hiding space. Then she sprang forward, her torso leaning out of the rock, and snatched the two orcs closest to her. Annabelle pulled them back into the silent darkness she hid within.

The other orc drew its gun as quickly as it could, but it was too late. Anabelle slipped from the darkness again, this time flipping the orc over, sliding back into the Road of Force. She dropped to her feet and kicked its legs, manna traveling up to her hands, her fists bursting into flames as she incinerated the creature.

The three orcs lay dead, bodies smoking, and Anabelle scooped up their rifles. She checked to see if any other groups were heading her way. No one seemed to have noticed. She looked over her shoulder again to appraise her work. It was messy.

Huh, she thought. *Haven't cared about that in a long time.* Then she made her way back to the human soldiers.

Abby suddenly stopped in her tracks. Her dad's body lay crumpled on the ground, his cane next to him in a pool of blood. Margie screamed again, and Abby snapped back to reality, her grip tightening on the shotgun. Abby grabbed her father's cane and ran to the cellar.

Two orcs were waiting for her at the door. One of them held Margie in the air by her hair. The other stood behind Ma, who was on her knees, a strangely-made pistol pressed to the back of her head.

Abby aimed her shotgun at the orcs. "Let them go!"

The creature holding Margie tossed the girl to the ground and stepped on her throat. "Or what?" he asked. "I'll be damned if I let a human child deter me from my mission. This place is slated to be the Dark One's first conquest of the human realm. You should be honored to shed your blood here."

Abby racked the shotgun. "Let them go now!"

"Human, your weapon is woefully ineffective from that distance, and if you take a step forward, we will kill everyone. Or if you stay there. Either way, this place will be purged for the Dark One."

Abby's watch beeped, and she checked the screen. The sync was complete. She bent and whispered into her watch. "Drones…home defense mode."

A loud whirring emanated from the barn, though only one of the orcs bothered to pay attention. The drones burst out of the barn doors, rocketing toward the two orcs. Gertrude swooped over the one holding Ma and snatched up the creature as easily as she'd lifted the hay bale.

As the drone flew higher, the orc, in shock and panic, let go of Ma. Mistake, because he'd just lost his leverage, and the drone kept going up higher and higher, rising past the roof of the big house. Then her claws opened.

The orc splattered on the ground.

Bobby and Robby went for the other orc, who ran, attempting to escape into the cornfields.

The creature wasn't fast enough. Abby had already closed the gap. She took aim and fired.

Buckshot ripped through his leg, and he toppled over. As he tried to crawl into the cornfield, Abby came up behind him, her face and clothes smeared with orc blood. She raised her father's cane and brought it down on the back of the creature's head.

Abby lost track of time. There was only the rise and fall of the cane. The soft squish of the wood hitting the pulp of what remained of the orc. Ma and Margie had to pull her off the corpse.

Once she moved away from the body, Abby stumbled, lost in a haze until she dropped to her knees and vomited. Then the tears came.

They continued long into the night.

CHAPTER EIGHT

The Dark Gate was still open, but orcs had stopped passing through. Only the fifteen from the initial squad remained. They seemed to be interested in something on the ridge they had teleported to.

Distracted was how Anabelle liked her orcs. She moved back to her original position with the rest of her squad, and they hadn't noticed, even though she was carrying five jangling plasma rifles over her shoulders.

Most of Anabelle's squad were still fighting with their exoskeletons when she returned. The private had managed to get his exoskeleton off. Two other soldiers had succeeded as well and were now helping the others.

Anabelle handed them four plasma rifles, keeping one for herself. The private looked over his gun, probably trying to pinpoint any differences between the orc model and the ones the human military had developed. "So, what's the game plan?"

Anabelle slumped against the closest rock and scratched the back of her head. "Well, there would have been a plan if I had more than four combat-ready humans," she grumbled. "But you're all I got, so I guess we're going to have to find a way to make it work."

"I've been watching the orcs since you left. That, and trying to help the rest of the guys get their suits off. That shit is unbelievably heavy."

"What about the orcs?"

"While the rest of the squad were taking off their suits, I did some recon. Best I can tell, the orcs have been going back and forth between the Dark Gate and another point about a half a klick south. They're now coming toward us over fairly easy terrain. They're getting closer. If we can't get anyone moving, the orcs are going to be on us eventually. That doesn't leave us many options."

The private was right. There were only two options with the current state of things. First was wait for the orcs to arrive and try to defend the position. If Anabelle decided on this one, the humans would have some decent cover, but the orcs still outnumbered the combat-ready soldiers by a noticeable margin.

Option number two would be attacking the orcs head-on. Anabelle leaned more toward this plan, but she also could see the obvious flaw. Only four of her soldiers were armed. But dealing with fifteen orcs seemed within the realm of her abilities. There had been more at the bar.

But the human soldiers were a major concern. If Anabelle took them with her, she had no idea how they would do in battle. They could end up dead. Without their exosuits, they were defenseless. All it would take was one stray plasma shot.

The private cleared his throat to get Anabelle's attention. "Whatever you decide to do, Commander, we're with you," he said. "Gotta show you that humans can hang too."

The sentiment tickled Anabelle. She didn't understand why these humans would want to prove themselves to her. Nothing but disdain had come from her mouth since they had arrived. She chalked it up to human resilience.

If anything, they don't know when to quit.

Anabelle peered over a boulder. The squad of orcs was moving toward her position. The Dark Gate was still open, but the orcs appeared to have other business to attend to. They hadn't taken battle formation yet. It was likely they still didn't know the human soldiers were here.

She turned to the private. "All right, how much combat experience do you have?" she asked. "I need to know what you're all capable of."

The private answered quickly, showing his military experience with his tone. "Three tours with the US Marines," he barked. "Might not be used to shooting at orcs, but I'm more than comfortable with the shooting part. We won't hold you back if that's what you're afraid of."

At least this one isn't oblivious, Anabelle thought. "All right, then this is what we're doing."

The private and the other able-bodied soldiers leaned in as Anabelle explained how they were going to get out of this mess.

The orcs were returning to the Dark Gate. Whatever had interested them enough to leave the Gate must have turned out to be inconsequential. Remaining by the portal seemed to be their priority at the moment.

Anabelle and the four soldiers were sneaking around the back of the ridge where the orcs had posted up. Once in position, she tossed a rock behind her, toward a soldier armed with a plasma rifle who was set up against a boulder, halfway between Anabelle and the rest of the men. He, in turn, grabbed the rock with his free hand and chucked it toward the soldiers behind him.

The bulk of the soldiers were grouped together, and when the rock landed at their feet, they sent up a loud shout of agony, whooping dramatically, trying to call as much attention to themselves as possible.

It worked. The orcs atop the ridge came to the edge in search of the origin of the noise. As they prepared to investigate the source of the commotion, Anabelle and the humans began to scale the ridge. They worked fast, scrambling up the side of the hill, not at all worried about noise since the yelling from the other soldiers gave them enough cover.

Once Anabelle arrived at the top of the ridge, she checked the orcs' positions in case they had heard her and her team coming. From what she could see, they were already descending the hill and moving toward the rest of her squad. She quickly turned to help the private and two other soldiers up.

When the small fireteam was all atop the ridge, Anabelle gave the signal to the private, who aimed his plasma rifle at one of the orcs. At the last second, the private pointed the gun at the largest orc and fired five shots at the creature, felling him. "One down," he muttered.

The orcs whipped around, drawing their weapons. Down in the valley, the soldier who had relayed the rock message aimed his rifle. He fired, the shot tearing through one of the orcs, who fell off the ridge, dead.

Anabelle and the soldiers took cover behind a set of boulders closer to the Dark Gate. The private nodded at her and then saluted before breaking cover and opening fire.

The air quickly erupted into a blistering-hot volley of plasma blasts from the human soldiers. The orcs were caught off-guard for a second time by the assault from the rear, a few of them slumping over, dead from the attack.

Anabelle slipped in among the chaos, the words of her trainers reminding her not to lose herself on the Road. That was always the danger. Each battle brought you ever closer to losing yourself. She had heard of Travelers of the Road being consumed by a bloodlust to rival the most insane berserker's.

An orc aimed his plasma rifle at Anabelle and fired. She had been so caught up in her thoughts that she barely managed to deflect the attack with a small barrier. Since she was already up in her head, she reminded herself to pay attention to how much manna she was using.

The benefit of a wand was manna conservation. The tradeoff to not using a wand was the ability to manipulate more magic in its rawest elemental form. Anabelle may not have been able to call down a thunderstorm, but the lightning in her kicks would be more focused. And lightning is lightning.

"Cover me," Anabelle shouted as she dashed forward, pulling manna into her legs for more speed while also infusing a small electrical storm around her body. She zipped in between two orcs, kicked one in the head, flipped over the other, and brought her knee down hard into his face.

The remaining orcs scrambled below the edge of the ridge, hiding from the human squad at the summit, who were still firing. The orcs turned their attention to Anabelle, who was backing away, sizing up her next point of attack.

There was hardly any time for planning. The orcs opened fire, ignoring the humans crouched behind the rock, focusing all of their attention on Anabelle.

Which wasn't what she had expected. She'd thought the orcs would have chosen to destroy the weaker foe—the humans. Instead, they'd concentrated all the energy on the person who was most likely going to kill them.

One of the orcs reached into his satchel and pulled out a grenade. He lobbed it at the group of armed humans. A second passed before the grenade exploded, throwing the soldiers into the air, where they floated, suspended and vulnerable.

The orc who had thrown the grenade peeled off from his squad. He must have believed he didn't need any help dealing with the humans. Anabelle agreed with him, all too aware that if she didn't intervene, the soldiers were dead.

She tossed up another barrier as she ran toward the humans. The orcs fired, and she extended the barrier so she didn't have to pay attention to each blast.

The soldiers, unable to move, floated lazily, their eyes wide as the orc approached them. He had probably intended to savor these kills, or he would have fired from afar. He must have wanted to be close, to feel their blood spill across his hands.

The orc unsheathed an ax and swung it cheekily as he approached the soldiers.

Anabelle came up behind him, her hands flaming, momentarily dropping the shield. She swiped the orc across the neck, slicing his head from his shoulders. It flew through the air in a burning arc.

Plasma shots came from behind her. Anabelle barely turned in time to deflect the first three. The plasma went careening into the sky and burned out.

She positioned herself between the humans and the orcs. A good number of orcs still remained, but Anabelle's brain hadn't yet kicked into fighting gear. All she could think of using was her elemental magic. Once more, a crushing sense of guilt washed over her. Thousands of years of wisdom wasted on her. Any of the old masters could have handled this in their sleep.

But Anabelle wasn't one of the old masters. She was an elf who still didn't know herself. That was what the Road was for, though. The Road was how Travelers found themselves.

Anabelle spread her barrier out, thinning it so that it was more like a piece of magical sheet metal. She grabbed it and rushed toward the orcs. As one of the creatures raised his gun, she turned the barrier on its side and tossed it at him.

The barrier flew at her target and sliced the orc in half. The other orcs saw their chance and opened fire.

Anabelle pulled the barrier back and whipped it around, knocking away the plasma blasts, though one penetrated the barrier and singed her cheek.

One of the orcs moved in close, choosing his fists over his ax. He sprang, arms raised, and fell upon Anabelle with a ferocity she'd never seen in her sparring partners.

The orc punched her in the face, and her vision blurred. As she tried to raise her barrier back up, he brought his fists down on her chest.

With the wind knocked out of her, Anabelle thought she was going to pass out right there. But if she did, she was dead. Still, the darkness did call loudly.

And in the Darkness, is Silence, Anabelle thought as she studied the orc's long shadow. She leaned forward, headbutted him, and leapt into the shadow, where she flattened herself and effectively disappeared.

The orcs stared around, confused, and alarmed at Anabelle's sudden disappearance. She held her breath, waiting quietly. The orc, whose shadow she was attached to, spun in circles, trying to figure out where the elf had gone.

When the orc's shadow fell on a second orc, Anabelle reached out, filled her two fingers with manna, and struck the creature in the forehead. He dropped to the ground, dead.

Another orc, having caught a glimpse of Anabelle, opened fire.

She sprang from the shadow, back into the light world as the orcs turned and gunned down her former host.

The moment of surprise was all Anabelle needed. She drew her manna into her chest and surged into the air, where the power passed to her hands. She dropped to the ground, slamming both fists into the earth, sending out a shockwave of pure manna that incinerated the orcs surrounding her.

As the smoke cleared, Anabelle sprinted over to the suspended soldiers, waving away the barrier holding them in the air.

The private rushed over to the remains of the orcs. "Holy shit, that was amazing," he mumbled as the other soldiers joined him.

Anabelle wasn't paying attention to their praise. She was extremely low on manna and ready to pass out. The fight shouldn't have been so strenuous. If she was going to keep this up, she had to get better. At the rate she was going, she would be unable to fight more than once a day.

The private, having finished praising Anabelle's work, turned and pointed to the Dark Gate, which was still open. "Should we take care of that?" he asked.

Anabelle cast a glance back at the human as she tried to fix her hair. "And you know how to close Dark Gate?"

"I mean...no. But I'd be willing to try and figure it out."

Even if Anabelle was unable to admire the human for his battle prowess, she had to admit the little guy was a well of pluck and positivity. "Human, what is your name?" Anabelle asked.

The private clicked his feet together and saluted Anabelle, barking, "Private Thomas Blackwell!"

"Well, come on, Blackwell. Let's figure out how to shut this thing down."

Anabelle and Blackwell hiked over to the ridge where the Dark Gate stood. A weird humming came from the Gate. There didn't seem to be any discernible mechanism for the portal. It merely hung in the air.

Blackwell walked around the portal, scanning it. "Huh, doesn't seem to have an off switch. Hey! You should come check this out!"

Anabelle came around the side of the portal to where Blackwell was pointing. She leaned in to get a closer look. What she saw surprised her.

Through the portal, a scene played out in front of her. A small female human stood over an orc, bashing its brains in with a cane. The orc appeared to have been dead for some time.

Anabelle leaned back and activated her HUD. The portal was fading of its own accord, and her HUD was working again. She quickly reached through the portal and selected a command to remember her position. "Now, that's the kind of human that knows how to fight. That's a rage that I can work with."

The funeral for Abby's father was small. The farmers nearby showed up. A few people from town. Whoever heard attended. Ma and Abby thought it best if the news didn't spread, though.

The pastor of the nearby Lutheran church shared a few words, a quick, dry sermon, and was on his way. Just the way Pa would have liked it. Ma spoke longer, but Abby could barely hear her words.

Abby stayed for some time after the mourners left. She remained there after Ma and the kids left as well. She promised to be back by supper.

There was nothing to say. Abby wished she could have thought of something. Instead, she stared at the mound of dirt her father had just been lowered into.

"You must have loved him dearly," a man said from behind her.

Abby turned to face an old white-haired man dressed in a suit that looked to be the finest to have ever been made. The man's eyes danced with an energy Abby had never seen before. "What would you know about that?"

The man sat beside Abby. "Anger is the way you grieve," he said. "I can see it in your eyes."

"Who are you, and what you here askin' about? Ain't got nothing better than to bother a girl grieving her daddy?"

"The creatures with the gray skin—the ones that came to your farm—they're called orcs."

Abby looked at him for the first time since he'd taken a seat. Her eyes narrowed, and when she spoke, her words were slow and deliberate. "What you getting' on about what happened at the farm?"

The old man straightened his tie as he smiled sadly. "You did quite the number on them. And your drones...genius is the only way I could describe them."

"Would have done more if I could have."

There was a long silence between them before Abby turned to the man and asked, "Who is the Dark One?"

Myrddin lifted a curious eyebrow, "Where did you hear that name?"

"One of the orcs said it while...you know." She gestured to the coffin.

Myrddin, the old wizard, leaned forward, cocking his head to the left so that he could look Abby in the eye. "Abby-Lynn," he whispered. "What if I told you that you could? What if I told you that the creature who sent the orcs, the Dark One, is dangerous and real, but also someone very killable. You want revenge? It's him you need to direct it at."

Abby clutched her father's cane, which rested at her side. "The Dark One. You know where he is?"

Myrddin stood and brushed off his pants as he looked down at the

51

freshly turned earth. "There is a war going on, Abby," he explained. "Someone like you could do a lot of good, protect a lot of innocent lives. Your tech skills, your passion. I know it's cruel to try to recruit you at this moment, but the war effort needs you. What do you say?"

Abby stood, leaning on her father's cane, her brow as dark and as furious as a storm. "Take me to 'em," she whispered. "I'll kill 'em. I'll kill 'em all."

Up above, in the fading afternoon, the sky swelled with the fiery color of blood. It would be night soon, but evening had yet to come to pass.

CHAPTER NINE

Meanwhile, somewhere else, far from concerns about orcs and Dark Ones and the war, Terra Spartan stood in front of her bathroom mirror. She held a pair of clippers in one hand, and in the other, her bright red hair, bundled up so that it wouldn't cascade down her back to her hips. It had taken her nearly ten years to grow out her mane, as she called it.

Obviously, anytime you cut off this much hair, you had to psyche yourself up to finish the job. She grabbed her hair by the roots and snipped. Then she put the chopped bundle on the toilet seat and continued.

After the locks were cut away, Terra took the clippers to her head. When she was done, she wet her skull and applied shaving cream. She removed her father's straight razor from the cabinet and scraped the cold blade over her scalp as she had seen him do thousands of times.

Once Terra was satisfied with her gleaming bald head, she ran the hot water and put her head under the faucet, relishing the sensation of water against her skin. The mirrors had steamed up by the time she turned off the faucet. Then she applied the aftershave.

The Morning After—the only aftershave her father had ever used. Terra's mother had once told her it was the greatest smell in the world. It smelled strong. Confident. Powerful. Terra couldn't disagree. She had grown up with that scent, the scent that had soaked into the weight room she had shared with her father. It was strong, just like Terra.

Terra wiped her head off one more time and studied her reflection in the mirror. She hardly recognized herself. Most people never saw past her bright red hair. Now that it was gone, what would people see? How were they going to remember her?

Abby stood in front of a glass skyscraper. The building looked unreal. The glass seemed thin, and there were no discernable girders. How did the building manage to keep from being blown away in the wind?

Earlier that morning, a limo had arrived at her house. Four really short guys—who Abby swore looked like garden gnomes—had emerged from the vehicle and informed her that Myrddin had sent them to help keep the farm running while she was gone. A deal she had made with the wizard—she'd only join his army if her family was taken care of.

Seeing how industrious these little guys were, Abby realized Myrddin's word was good.

She turned to say goodbye to Ma and Margie. Margie gave her a quick hug and then retreated inside so as to not reveal she was crying. Abby knew, and she wanted nothing more than to go inside and comfort her sister.

"She'll be all right," Ma said. "I'll see to her."

An uneasy silence fell over them. Abby had never been very good at showing her emotions. So, the pair simply stood next to each other in silence until Ma nodded in the direction of the four gnomes. "Seems that Myrddin is good to his word. Those guys, weird-looking as they may be, are already hard at work. Almost as industrious as your drones."

"Yeah," Abby said. Then a rush of regret and worry washed over her. "I can stay, Ma. Help here. I don't have to go."

Ma gave Abby the look she always did when she knew the right thing was hard to do. "Yes, you do. You have to go. You have to help them with their war efforts by doing what you were meant to be doing...building those amazing robots of yours. They need you."

"But *you* need me."

"We do, honey," Ma said, pulling her close. "But they need you more. We'll be fine. We got help. And we got Facetime, Zoom, Skype, Whatsapp, and a whole slew of other ways to stay in touch. Go, do what you need to do. We'll be fine. And if we're not, I'll call you home. Don't you worry about that."

"You promise."

"With all my soul."

Abby hugged her ma and strode off the front porch toward the limo. She turned for one last wave goodbye. Margie was outside now, holding Ma and waving to Abby so vigorously that Abby felt like her heart was going to break with love. Then she remembered Pa and what those bastards did to him.

With one last wave goodbye, she climbed into the limo, which took her to a small airport where a sleek private jet waited. The logo on the plane's side was one Abby had never seen before.

Abby slept through most of the plane ride. She had tried to stay awake, but anxiety and sleepiness had gotten the best of her. She had managed to keep her eyes open for the first few minutes as the plane ascended through the clouds.

The takeoff wasn't something she would easily forget. It was, after all, her first plane ride.

When the plane landed, the limo driver woke her up and ushered her to another limo. Abby slept in the backseat. The blurred white lights of the city around her had lulled her back into slumber. She'd slept curled in a ball, hugging her knees tightly, crying softly.

By the time Abby had arrived at the glass skyscraper, she was as rested as she could possibly have been. Though it hadn't changed the fact that she still felt exhausted. It was as if a heavy blanket had been thrown over her shoulders. A slight, yet noticeable, weight.

The limo driver guided Abby up the glass stairs to the entrance of the building. A guard stood at the door—a young man with a smooth, easily likable face. Abby only noticed it in passing as he opened the door and motioned for her to follow.

Here, the driver said goodbye and returned to his limo, leaving Abby with more questions than answers. Myrddin hadn't explained much at the funeral. The extent of their conversation had revolved around the prospect of revenge. Which was all it had taken to sign her up.

Now, as Abby entered the building, she wished she'd asked more questions. Not that she would have known where to start. The tragedy on the farm seemed like a distant memory, a story someone had told her a long time ago. She hardly felt involved at all.

She glanced up as she crossed the threshold. The lobby was a sprawling, nearly empty space. There were no desks or tables or decorations, yet the room buzzed with energy.

People on floating glass platforms zipped back and forth in the air above Abby. It was hard to tell what they were doing, but it gave the whole building the feel of an elongated glass beehive encased in a cathedral.

"What is this place?" Abby asked, still staring bewildered at the scene above.

The guard chuckled as he beckoned for Abby to follow him. "This is Myrddin's HQ," he explained. "It's his home away from home, you could say. Most of Myrddin's plans are concocted here. Thus, the business. Takes a lot of people to see if stuff will work."

"Is Myrddin here?"

The guard approached an elevator and extended his hand. A glowing pad on the wall registered his palm print, and the elevator door opened. "No one really knows unless Myrddin wants them to know," the guard answered. "Grunts like me hardly ever know. And I like to keep it that way. If Myrddin wants to see me, that probably means I've screwed something up."

Abby and the guard entered the elevator, which was also made of glass. They ascended, and she watched as level after level whizzed past her. She lost count eventually, but she hoped she'd get a chance to see each level up close. The brief glimpses had piqued her interest.

Finally, the elevator stopped, and the door opened. This level was not made of glass.

The guard exited the elevator, and Abby followed, trying to keep up with his long gait. She couldn't quite match his speed. It didn't help that she was distracted by all the doors lining the walls. Loud explosions echoed from behind some of them. "How come this floor ain't transparent?" Abby asked.

The guard turned a corner. "Necessity. This is mostly a research and development wing. There's a series of magical charms placed on the floor to keep people from being able to see in. You never know who is a spy. Or who they're spying for."

Abby did a double-take at the word "magic." She waited for the guard to offer a clarification, but when he remained silent, she assumed his joke had gone too far. She wasn't stupid. "Magic, huh? Don't try to kid a kidder."

The guard tossed a look over his shoulder. "I'm sorry, Miss, but you don't seem like that much of a kidder."

"My way of saying I ain't stupid. Nothing about this is anything like a card show. How come you think I'd fall for a sad sack lie like that?"

"No lie about it. Just safety protocols. You have magical clearance to see this floor. When I say clearance, it's a—"

Abby stopped and interrupted the guard. "All right, you just hold on there a second. There's that word again. What exactly are you trying to say when you say *magic*?"

The guard chuckled again. "When I say magic, I mean just that. Magic. Spells. Wizardry. Witchcraft in some situations. The kind of stuff you read about in fantasy books. This whole place is magical."

Abby was starting to get annoyed. She didn't take kindly to being treated like a child, and only children still believed in magic. That was on par with the Tooth Fairy or Santa Claus. But orcs were also on the list of other magical creatures.

And Abby had definitely seen an orc.

The guard had walked off again, and Abby jogged to catch up with him. "It's usually hard to wrap your head around at first," the guard went on. "I didn't believe any of it when I got assigned here. Trust me, it only takes a couple of hours. You feel kinda stupid trying not to believe at that point. But you got eyes. You'll get the picture eventually."

The guard stopped in front of a door and knocked twice.

From inside came the shuffling of chairs and a loud crash. Once the noise settled, a voice shouted, "Come in, come in. But close the door fast."

The guard smiled politely at Abby. "This is where I'll leave you. Have a good day."

The voice from behind the door shouted, "If you're going to come in, come in already!"

Abby opened the door and stepped inside.

A goblin was hunched over a steel workbench. He turned to face Abby as she came in, his spectacles nearly falling off of his hooked nose as his batlike ears twitched. "Oh, it's you, Ms. Crookins," he chirped as he leapt off of his chair and ran toward Abby.

She backed away instinctively, bumping into the closed door behind her. "Oh, hi," she managed to murmur as the goblin thrust his hand at her.

He peered over his spectacles, "I'm Creon...and please, please excuse the mess. I've been at it for days without a break. I kept telling myself, I'll clean up before Ms. Crookins gets here, I must make sure to make this place tidy. But you must know how it gets to be in the middle of your thoughts when the idea is just rushing at you, and you have to get it down on paper."

Abby grunted a noncommittal reply as she stared at the goblin. She couldn't register what was standing in front of her. Same as when she had seen the orcs. The only real difference was that Creon didn't appear to want to kill her.

Quite the opposite. Creon seemed positively delighted to see her.

As Creon walked around Abby, the four-foot goblin looked her up and down. "You're much younger than I thought you'd be," Creon finally said. "From your work, at least. Your programming. We have geezers here who could hardly touch your code on their best days."

"Oh...thanks," Abby murmured.

She managed to move away from the door, and she studied the room. Creon had been exaggerating about how messy the place was. The workroom was not neat by any standard. But it was much cleaner than Abby's.

Creon returned to his workbench and started tossing gears and rivets to the ground. "I imagine all this is a lot to take in," he called over his shoulder. "You aren't one of Myrddin's recruits from *Middang-g3ard* VR, are you?"

"'Fraid I don't know what it is you're talking about."

"That's what I figured. First time seeing a magical creature before?"

"No. I've seen orcs before. Once."

Abby suppressed the image of an orc towering over her dead father. She pushed it deep down to a place she hoped to forget.

Creon turned back and smiled sadly at Abby. "I am sorry to hear about that," he whispered. "Let's turn our minds to other business. Come, I'm to be giving you a tour. To show you the kind of facilities that you'll be allowed to work in."

The goblin jumped down from his workbench and waddled to a steel double door on the other side of the room.

Abby still clung to the wall, staring at Creon. She wasn't frightened of the goblin. Not exactly. She was frightened of everything the goblin represented. A world outside of the one she knew and understood. One filled with a source of power she had no understanding of.

Creon tapped on the double door, then spun around and pushed up his spectacles. "Come now, we got a little bit to see before we get down to work," he exclaimed.

Abby pulled herself away from the wall, glancing at the contents of Creon's worktable as she walked past. The table was filled with mechanical tech. Even if the goblin was magical, it seemed he was much more interested in the mechanical.

Abby, still as confused as she'd been on her arrival, now joined Creon at the double doors and asked, "Are you, uh, magical?"

Creon smiled crookedly, which was surprisingly charming. "Oh, of course," he replied. "Different kind of magic than an elf or a gnome, or human, of course. It's not the sort of thing you can see on the surface for most goblins."

He raised his hands and spread out his spindly fingers. "You see, the magic is all in these elegant digits," he explained. "Dwarves might lay claim to smelting and smith work, but us goblins are unrivaled in tinkering. Something that I've heard you have an exceptional hand at."

Abby was growing less and less wary of the goblin. She nodded and allowed herself a smile. "I guess you could say that," she admitted. "Don't have a lot to go comparing myself to, though. But I do make what I got to work with usually work. More or less."

"Modesty as well as skill. You're going to go far here. Come, let me introduce you to the rest of my workspace."

CHAPTER TEN

The double doors opened up to what appeared to be a giant metalworking facility. It was the largest working area Abby had ever seen before. Nowhere near the size of her barn, the scale of the area was closer to that of her family's wheat fields.

Creon waved his hand, and two transparent platforms zoomed over to them. He stepped onto one, prompting Abby to climb aboard her own. The platforms rose, and she stared skyward, surprised that the facility also used up nearly all of its vertical space.

How is there so much room for this? She had only descended a couple of floors on the elevator, but this room appeared to be almost the entire height of the glass skyscraper.

Creon pointed at the right side of the facility. "We'll start over here," he droned. "This is the T.E.M., or Technology-Enhancing Magic laboratory. I figure this is a good place to start since you don't have much experience with magic."

The two platforms rose higher and headed to a door Creon indicated. The lab was encased with glass, much like the rest of the building.

As they arrived, a glass door slid open, and Creon stepped off his floating platform, appearing to walk on air. Merely an optical illusion, though. The floors were made of glass as well. Abby, against her better judgment, also stepped off the platform, thanking God that there was solid glass under her feet.

Creon ambled through the lab, rattling off the different projects they were working on. Abby hardly heard a word. Not for lack of paying attention but because she was thoroughly entranced by everything around her.

An elvish scientist was wielding a fireball while another ran scans on it. A third came over and placed a visor on the elf, who smiled before splitting the fireball into hundreds of smaller balls.

At another station, a group of gnomish scientists wrestled with a yeti who was growing, shrinking, then growing again, at an alarmingly fast rate. A dwarfish scientist rushed into the room with a fire extinguisher just as the yeti's fur burst into flames. After the smoke and jets from the fur extinguisher disappeared, the yeti was left sitting in the middle of the station, hairless and laughing hysterically.

A much larger third station held two human scientists, one holding a wand and the other wearing a Kevlar vest. The wand-wielding human held up his hand and counted down to zero before blasting the other man, who went flying across the station, eventually landing in a pile of pillows.

Creon stopped at a more serene station where a handful of scientists walked around, working quietly. "This is where we've been working on the HUDs." Creon waved a hand at the room. "It was our first foray into using technology to improve how one uses magic."

Abby stood on her tiptoes to see what the scientists were doing. "And what exactly is this magic? I ain't ever seen anything like this."

"It's because humans have been cut off from magic for years. You don't show it often. Thus, the HUDs. These allow humans to use magic. Though there are a number of loopholes. Nothing you'll need to worry about. Just thought you might be interested."

"I am. It's fascinating. Got anymore?"

Creon rewarded Abby with his warm, crooked smile. "Of course, follow me."

He led Abby back to the floating platforms, and they soared to the left side of the room. "This is our M.E.T. or Magic-Enhancing Technology lab—the reverse of the other side. Here we try to find ways to improve technology through magic."

After they disembarked from their platforms, Creon led Abby through the lab, indicating different stations where scientists tinkered with ancient tomes, fusing them to generators.

At one station, a scientist tossed what appeared to be a grenade. The device detonated, and a horde of mini dragons burst from the center of the explosion.

Creon stopped in front of one station and peered through the glass. A scientist wearing an augmented-reality suit was running through a projection of the world. "This is a revamp of the tech we used for our VR recruiting program." Creon grinned proudly. "A personal pet project of my own. It has its own problems, though."

Abby was almost too engrossed in the activity around her to respond. Then she blinked. "Wait, this all seems like good work. I'd be tickled pink if I could cobble up something like this."

"Oh, the problem isn't with the tech. The VR program only brings a certain kind of recruit to us. Take yourself, for instance. Amazing creative skills and brains. But you don't play videogames. We almost missed out on you entirely. Now come, we have one more lab to see."

They hopped aboard their floating platforms and headed for the lab in the middle of the facility where Creon led Abby through a laboratory, empty save for a variety of equipment.

"Which one is this?" Abby asked.

Creon sat in a floating glass chair. "This, my dear, is our lab."

Abby spun around, unable to believe that these were going to be her working conditions. She barely knew what any of the equipment was. How did they think she would be able to keep up with what the other scientists were developing? All she had ever made were her drones.

Creon pointed at a worktable that had just shimmered into existence. Abby's three drones rested on the table. "Granted, if you need anything to work, all you have to do is let me know. We can requisition it, and it'll most likely be here within the day."

Abby sat in the glass chair behind her. This was all a lot to take in. She still couldn't believe she was going to be working in this lab.

Creon hit a button on his chair, and both their seats floated to the workbench that held Abby's drones. "Myrddin informed me of your work. I know that the originals are still at the farm helping your family. But I took the liberty of looking at their schematics and reconstructed your creations here."

Abby stood and approached the new drones. Well, *new* was a stretch. Creon had created exact replicas, down to the dings and dents her own drones had received in the fight on the farm.

They were also perfect replicas. "Thanks. Much appreciated."

Creon bent and pulled something from under the table. "And, as a welcome present, I cobbled something together for you." The goblin held three glowing tubes.

Abby recognized the tubes instantly. They were the length and shape of the lithium batteries she used to power her drones.

Creon handed Abby the tubes. "These are some reverse-engineered batteries. You won't have to worry about charging those drones for the next two hundred years or so. My way of saying welcome to the team."

Abby could hardly contain her excitement. She wanted to drop the batteries into her drones immediately. "Do you mind if I put these in? No one's ever given me something like this before."

"Please do. I'd love to see how they work."

Abby went to the Gertrude replica and flipped it over. She pulled out the battery rig she had created and replaced it with the one Creon had given her. A jolt of energy ran through the drone, and it blinked to life, rising into the air and spinning in a circle before obediently floating above the other drones.

Creon came up behind Abby, circling her to get a better look at the drone's performance. "Seems to be working about right."

Abby turned Gertrude off, and the drone returned to the bench. "And you're saying this, all this here, is where I get to work?" she asked. "Not often something like this comes without a catch."

"The only catch is that your work and your skills will be implemented to help defeat the Dark One."

Abby's eyes darkened at the sound of the Dark One's name. "The wizard...Myrddin. He told me I'd get a chance to avenge my father."

Creon fidgeted, then looked away as he drifted over to a computer console. "And you will. What you will help create here will avenge your father. But as for the front line, you're not trained, and I highly doubt the front line is for one like you."

So *that* was the catch. Abby could see it now. She'd spend all of her day behind glass walls while the weapons she worked on would be used to burn the Dark One away. Which wasn't what she had wanted. *Abby's* finger was the one that deserved to be on the trigger.

Abby hid her disappointment from Creon as best she could. She was used to throwing up a smokescreen to distract from her sulking. Pa had always told her she was the sullenest child he'd ever seen. Sullen and stubborn. Attributes Abby had learned to cherish.

Creon must have noticed the silence in the room because he cleared his throat awkwardly to cover it. "At any rate, we'll have to get you all set up. Come on over here. We can get your credentials and everything processed. Then you can let your creativity run wild."

Abby trudged over to Creon's desk. It shouldn't be too bad. Even if she had to spend all of her time in Research and Development. Abby had a lot of ideas floating around inside her head.

This facility was the ideal place to turn those ideas into realities.

CHAPTER ELEVEN

Myrddin and Roy sat in the War Room. The wizard was drinking tea, blowing steam from the rim of his cup while Roy leaned over a holographic projection of the Dark Gate, which had opened up in Utah, chewing on a cigar that hung limply from his lips.

Neither spoke for some time, Roy still staring as he hoped to receive a message from the map. He got nothing, though. He switched the map off and kicked the chair next to him.

Myrddin glanced up from his tea. "Something wrong?"

Roy righted the chair he'd kicked over and plopped onto it, hanging his head as he placed his cigar on the rim of the holotable. "I got nothing. Absolutely nothing," Roy grumbled. "Two Dark Gates open in the same state, only a few miles apart from each other. Nowhere else in the country."

Myrddin's eyes glinted from behind the steam. "Yes, go on."

"You'd think they'd have something in common. But nothing. Absolutely nothing. I can't see one thing that Abby's farm and the Zion National Park have in common, other than that they're both in Utah. That makes no sense. If it were going to be an invasion, why the hell would the Dark One pick somewhere out in the middle of nowhere? Or a hiking trail?"

Myrddin waved his hand, and the holomap came to life again. "Those are good questions. But we have found through the last few years that the Dark One's strategies are often far beyond what we are expecting. I'm assuming you read the report sent by the Mundanes?"

Roy grabbed his cigar and chewed on it again. "Which one? That kid Suzuki sends a new one out every five hours or something."

"Hardly. The squad is meticulous and thorough, something you could learn to incorporate into your team."

"I'll ask him for notes if I ever meet him. Did you bring him up just to hand me a passive-aggressive insult?"

"No. Merely to call attention to the point of the Mundanes' reports. They discovered how the Dark One was influencing the minds of his captives, where the bulk of his army had come from. A sophisticated form of mind control. Something far beyond what we'd seen before. All that is to say, whatever the Dark One is planning, it will most likely look like nothing we've ever come across."

Roy crossed his arms and leaned back in his chair. "Great. Not only is the Dark One relentless, but he's also got a creative bent," Roy complained. "Could it get any better?"

The door of the War Room slid open, and Anabelle marched in, her eyes red with fury. She had barely crossed the threshold when she shouted, "All right, you both have some explaining to do, and I expect you to start really fucking quick!"

Roy jumped at the sound of Anabelle's voice, fear flickering briefly across his face. "Whoa, who gave you clearance to come—"

Anabelle raised her hand. "*You* did, you idiot," she spat. "And not another word from you. Not a peep. I know *you* don't have the answers." She sat in front of Myrddin, leaned forward, and locked eyes with the wizard. "*You* have the answers. So, start talking."

Myrddin took a measured sip from his tea. He studied Anabelle with the focus one would expect from a warrior engaged in a duel. "It would behoove you to be a tad more specific in your inquiry," he said softly.

If there was one thing Anabelle hated, it was people putting on airs. She'd seen it millions of times over the last hundred or so years.

Back a person into the corner, and they start speaking with fake accents or magically expanded vocabularies. It was a petty tactic, and it drove her crazy.

Anabelle inhaled deeply. She'd also learned the only way to deal with such people was to play their game. Shouting and revealing how pissed she was would work with Roy. Myrddin would simply sweep her under the rug as he'd done before.

Using all of her self-control, Anabelle spoke slowly and deliberately, maintaining the same regulated cadence as though she were at a job interview. "Most of the troops you sent me with were woefully undertrained. The equipment you sent was faulty as well. If I hadn't been there, they would have all been dead now."

"Lucky for them that their commander was there. Glad to see you aren't the type of leader who abandons their post."

Anabelle tried to understand the meaning behind Myrddin's words. The wizard often spoke in riddles, barely saying anything of import while still expecting others to work it out. "So, what was that? Some kind of test?"

Myrddin smiled pleasantly. "No casualties. Not even a scratch. An entire orc platoon eradicated. No, it was not a test. But if it had been, you would have passed with flying colors, and I would be very proud of you." He pointed to the holomap and magicked his teacup away. "The recruits were trained specifically with their exoskeletons. The malfunctioning of the equipment was due to an EMP pulse generated by the Dark Gate, a variable we had not foreseen. We are working on the suits to ensure that nothing like that happens again. I apologize for placing you in danger."

Anabelle had already had her response prepared, but at Myrddin's apology, she choked on it. He had never apologized for anything before. Was this another trap?

"Uh, it's okay," Anabelle replied, her tone deflated.

Even Roy was staring at Myrddin in confusion.

Myrddin waved at the holomap, and the view changed, now revealing a closeup of the Dark Gate. "Our working relationship has been strained for far too long, Ms. Chase. You were right about your field qualifications. With that in mind, I'd like to offer you a more specific role in our fight against the Dark One."

Anabelle was interested. It still felt like a trap, though. "All right, I'll bite. What are you thinking?"

"Sending soldiers who are not on par with your skills is dangerous for you *and* for them. Instead, I'd like to place you in charge of training a new squad to tackle any Special Ops missions suited to your talents."

Anabelle stood, anger flushing her cheeks. She knew what Myrddin was up to. Stick her in some barracks and put her on drill sergeant duty. "If you think you're going to keep me off of the field, you have—"

Myrddin raised his hand. "Quite the contrary. I would like you to train a group of field agents to accompany you on missions. One of the last living Travelers must have something to offer a young pupil."

Heat crawled up to Anabelle's throat. Even if Myrddin wasn't trying to trick her, he still wasn't pulling his punches. She didn't enjoy thinking about what had happened to the rest of the Travelers. Nor did she want their legacy to fade away.

Roy sat up, finally taking an interest in the conversation. "Honestly, that's not a bad idea. Even if you aren't training new Travelers, you have more theoretical knowledge than anyone else here," he admitted. "You could probably rustle up some good recruits. Get them ready for a fight like only you can."

Myrddin nodded as he stroked his long, white beard. "True. You would be an ideal leader of the S.W.A.M.R.R.T."

Anabelle covered her mouth and tried to stifle her laugh before erupting in insolent guffaws. "What the hell does that stand for?"

Myrddin's cheeks turned the lightest shade of pink. "Special Weapons and Magic Rapid Response Team," he murmured.

Anabelle slapped her knee, still laughing loudly. "Oh, man, I've heard bad names before, but that is *awful*. Aren't you a wizard? Isn't naming things, like, one of your hobbies or something? The acronym doesn't even spell anything."

Roy, who was obviously stifling his own laughter, said, "How about you come up with something better?"

"All right. K.T.D.O. Rolls right off the tongue."

Roy nodded as he considered the name. "What does it stand for?"

Anabelle shrugged as if she'd already lost interest in the conversation. "Kill the Dark One," she offered. "That's what we're trying to do, right?"

Roy stood and shook his head. "No, no, that's not going to work. We got to have something with, you know, a little more snap. Something that catches you. You hear it, and you think, goddamn, I don't wanna fuck with that."

Myrddin rubbed his brow as he sighed. "Our realms are fighting for their very survival, and you two have this much energy to care about a name? Perhaps our efforts should be concentrated on something a bit more important."

Myrddin pointed at the holomap, which had changed again. A hadron collider schematic filled the screen. "Our agents on the gnome world have informed us that the Dark One has gotten his hands on a hadron collider."

Anabelle had seen news reports about the hadron collider over the last few years. It hadn't interested her much. Theoretical physics had never been one of her hobbies. She was surprised to hear Myrddin mention it, though. Physics was typically a nonmagical endeavor.

"So, what's the big deal?" she asked.

The image on the holomap changed, this time revealing a large facility with a collider. Elves, humans, and gnomes walked along scaffolding erected around the collider. "We have one as well," Myrddin said. "It is a tool we use for slipping between realms with nonmagical folk."

"Why would the Dark One need a collider? Most of his forces use magic, don't they?"

Myrddin nodded as he waved away the holomap. "True. Many of his followers have the ability to use magic. But we have noticed the Dark One has a tendency to rely on technology instead of magic. Perhaps it is because we find it harder to track. It has surprised us multiple times."

Anabelle stood, stalked over to the holomap, and leaned against it. "That makes this easy enough, doesn't it?" she asked. "We just need to find where his collider is, blow it up, and I'll buy the first round of drinks. Except for Roy's. He's got to pay for his own."

Roy looked wounded. "Wait, why just me?"

"Because you have unnecessarily expensive taste. Trust me, I've paid $2,000 on bottle service before. You'd be an expensive date."

Myrddin cleared his throat until Roy and Anabelle were silent. The holomap blinked on, displaying a galaxy. Thousands of bright lights flickered. Planets and stars. "Each of those lights is a potential place the collider could be. And that's all we have to go off at the moment."

Anabelle studied the map. Now that she could see the possibilities laid out before her, the mission seemed much more daunting. "All right, what are we doing then? Checking out each one?"

Myrddin shook his head as he removed a speck of dirt from his suit. "No, that would be impractical. We are going to deal with these Dark Gates as they arrive while we wait for our spies to deliver more intel. That will give you time to assemble and train a team as well."

He handed Anabelle a dossier. She took the datapad and scrolled through the list. There were hundreds of candidates to consider. This was going to be a bigger pain in the ass than she had expected. "All right, I'll get on it," said Anabelle at last.

Abby was hooked up to a VR simulator. A heavy VR headset rested on her head, and her body was covered in electrodes. A screen behind her displayed what she saw.

Creon walked back and forth, monitoring the video, then Abby's vitals and back again.

Abby held a set of controllers, which she used to guide Gertrude as it flew through the glass halls of the research and development facility. Abby was taking it slow, trying to get the hang of how the drone handled when it wasn't automated.

The invention was extremely new. Abby had only suggested it to Creon a few hours ago. After they had brainstormed for a little bit, they got to drawing schematics and wondering what they could throw together, whether or not it would be practical.

Abby had never worked alongside someone so smart before. Not that her family wasn't. They were just smart in a different way. If Abby was honest with herself, she'd never met anyone who was the kind of smart Creon was.

The goblin only seemed to think in terms of technology. He helped Abby move from daydreaming to planning to construction in the amount of time it had taken her to write down the idea for her drones. It was exhilarating to get a glimpse of what working for Myrddin was going to be like.

Abby guided her drone around a corner, then pulled back suddenly. An elf was walking into the hallway. This would be a perfect chance to try one of the upgrades Creon had suggested. A stealth mode.

A button somewhere on Abby's controller would activate the stealth mode, but she was having a hard time finding it. She pulled off her headset, located the button, and tapped it.

She placed the headset back on her head and checked for the icon indicating stealth mode had been activated. She peeked through the wall first to make sure the elf was still in the hallway, then guided the drone around the corner.

The elf was scowling at the datapad in her hand and shaking her head. And there was one way to find out what had annoyed her. Get closer.

Abby maneuvered the drone forward, hoping her tweaks to the stealth mode had muffled Gertrude's exhaust.

The drone hovered closer. The elf didn't seem to notice.

But suddenly, she whipped around, her eyes bright with anger. Her hands shone as though they had caught fire, and she brought them down onto Gertrude.

Abby's display went black, and she jerked off her headset. "Someone attacked Gertrude," Abby shouted. "Where is she?"

Creon pulled up the GPS system they had attached to Gertrude and pointed to the floor where the drone had blacked out.

Abby didn't wait for instructions from Creon. She studied the map, ran to the floating platform, and leapt onto it. As the platform ascended, she counted the floors until she reached the right one, rode the platform to the main doors, and jumped off.

The only thing Abby was concerned about was the damage to her drone. Gertrude was the first one she'd built, the culmination of months and months of hard work, a physical manifestation of her own faith in herself. And now it could be reduced to a piece of scrap metal.

Abby ran down the hallway, familiar now from the feed she'd gotten from Gertrude. She turned the corner in time to see the elf crouched over the drone.

"Whoa, now hold on," Abby shouted as she sprinted to her fallen drone.

As Abby raced toward Gertrude, the elf stood and watched her, recognition flashing in her eyes. "Is this thing yours?" the elf asked.

Abby knelt beside Gertrude and began poking around the exposed wires. "Yes, it is, and I'd take it kindly if you didn't go ripping my drones apart," she hissed.

"And I'd *take it kindly* if you would refrain from spying on me."

Abby blushed and brushed her hair from her eyes. "I wasn't spying. Just testing out my drone. Didn't mean to invade any privacy."

The elf crouched beside Abby. "Hey, you...you're the girl from the field. The one with the white cane. The one Myrddin brought in, right?"

Abby jumped to her feet and backed away from the elf. "Why's it of interest to you?"

Anabelle turned and opened the door across from her. She entered the room and beckoned Myrddin and Roy, who followed her back into the passage where she waved at Abby.

"Ahh, my human recruit is finally here," Anabelle said with a devilish grin.

CHAPTER TWELVE

"SWARMMT? That is a stupid name."

Abby and Anabelle were in the changing room designated for the obstacle course. They were sitting near the lockers, talking quietly while the other potential recruits prepped themselves.

Anabelle pulled her hair back into a ponytail, removed her earrings, and placed them in her locker. "Exactly!" she exclaimed. "That's what I was saying. Terrible name. Utterly terrible."

Abby giggled as she scrolled through the different options of her watch that controlled her drones. "We could be called something like, I dunno know, KTDOF," Abby offered. "Kill the Dark One *First*. Straight and to the point."

Anabelle leaned over and pinched Abby's cheek, making the girl giggle again and blush for reasons she didn't quite understand. "Thought there was a reason I liked you. Other than the murderous rage in your eyes. I like that too. I'd drop the 'First,' though. Otherwise, great name. Myrddin won't go for a swear word in the name, but if I had to pick one, yours wins, hands down."

Abby focused on her watch again. "Thanks," she said awkwardly.

Abby and the elf had spent some time with each other the night before, after Anabelle had announced she wanted Abby on her team.

Anabelle had explained the situation, and Abby had agreed as soon as she understood she'd be out on the field.

But getting Abby field-ready still required a lot of foot- and paper-work. The first step was completing an obstacle course. All new recruits were expected to pass an obstacle course tailored specifically to the kind of field operative they were training to be.

Recruits from *Middang3ard* VR, espionage teams, and Dragon Riders all had separate requirements they were expected to fulfill. Abby wasn't certain what the obstacle course would entail, and she was worried she wouldn't be able to handle it.

Anabelle had been nothing short of encouraging to Abby. It helped a little bit. But Abby was very aware that Anabelle didn't have to complete the same course at all. Nobody was going to help her out with this, and she still had no idea what she was doing.

Abby watched the elf retelling an anecdote, only listening with half an ear—not that she didn't find Anabelle interesting. In fact, it was quite the opposite. Abby was enamored with the class and charm Anabelle exuded. She wondered if all elves were like Anabelle.

Across the locker room, the other recruits were getting geared up. They wore an updated model of their old exoskeleton suits. There hadn't been time for a complete overhaul, but the suits had been given some tweaks.

Still, the exosuits hadn't grown less bulky. They didn't look capable of offering the increased speed and mobility they promised. Abby figured at best, they would increase strength. But she couldn't be sure until she saw them in action.

Abby also considered the various tweaks she could make to the suits if she could get her hands on them. Creon hadn't worked on them. She'd seen his work already; it had a certain elegance the exosuits lacked.

Abby abandoned her thoughts as Annabelle held out a HUD, a sleek visor that fitted comfortably over Abby's head. "Missions come with headgear too?" Abby asked.

Anabelle shrugged as she checked herself out in the mirror. "Don't know. Word is you have to wear it though. Something about increasing your survival rate."

"And you don't?"

"Kid, I increase my own survival rate."

Abby couldn't get enough of how Anabelle talked. Everything Anabelle said was steeped in confidence.

Anabelle shook the HUD at Abby, who accepted it before sliding it over her head. She turned the HUD on and flipped down the visor. She was immediately greeted with a startup screen displaying a variety of information she didn't understand.

"All these squiggles are supposed to keep me alive and not distract me?" she muttered.

Anabelle clapped Abby on the back. "I'm just happy I don't have to wear one. Doesn't go well with any of my outfits."

Abby flipped the HUD back up, hands shaking. She sat on a bench and tried to calm her breathing.

The elf must have noticed because she sat next to Abby. "Hey, you doing all right?"

Though her breath was haggard, Abby managed a quiet, "Yes. I'm okay."

A loud bell went off, sending a jolt of anxiety racing down Abby's spine. She jumped to her feet, searching for the source of the noise.

Anabelle rested her hand on Abby's shoulder. "Hey, hey, calm down. That's just the bell for getting out there," the elf said. "You sure you're okay?"

Abby nodded, which was a lie. But it didn't matter if she felt okay or not. This was merely one step toward getting what she wanted.

Revenge.

The other recruits were now heading toward two double doors where a pair of guards were posted. Abby managed a weak smile for Anabelle, then followed the other recruits.

CHAPTER THIRTEEN
TERRA

Terra tossed a bundle of thick red hair onto the table.

"What the fuck did you do to your hair?" Jack asked, his face screwed up in confusion. In all likelihood, he probably hadn't recognized Terra until she had sat at the table with him. "You look like a dude."

"Figured one of us probably should. And I thought you might want to hold onto it," she said. "Since you love my hair color so much."

Jack picked up the bundle of hair, grimacing as he studied it. He tried to hide his disgust, but it was difficult to tell what repulsed him more, the pile of hair or Terra's bald head.

Terra figured it out, but it made no difference. Either way, he was disgusted by something stupid, which he should have been adult enough to deal with.

Jack put the bundle of hair back on the table and cleared his throat before taking a sip of his drink. "Thanks for meeting me tonight. I didn't think you were going to make it."

Terra grabbed Jack's whiskey and Coke and downed it in one gulp. "Me? Miss our weekly drinks?" she asked. "The very foundation of our relationship? If I didn't see you at the bar, I don't think I'd ever fucking see you. So, you know I have to make it to these."

Jack laughed uncomfortably as he stared at the bundle of hair. "Are you just going to leave that there?" he asked. "Don't you want to do something with it?"

"It's your hair now. You can do whatever the hell you want to do with it."

Jack scowled at the pile of hair as though it were a rotting animal. He reached out to grab it again but then thought better of it. Instead, he just watched it from afar as though afraid it would jump up and attack him like some sort of feral zombie hairpiece.

Terra ran her hand over her bald head. "You know, the funny thing about red hair is that there are different kinds," she said. "Everyone thinks it looks the same. Unless you have red hair. Then you start to see the differences. Differences other than just being bright or dark."

Jack leaned back in his chair, waving for another drink. His face was creased with confusion as if he was trying to put together a puzzle in his head that he didn't quite understand. "Really?" he asked. "What kinds of red hair are there?"

"Cherry Coke, auburn, red sand, brick red, merlot… I think the hair I found in our bed was merlot. Mine is more of a red Coke. Very bright. Not nearly as sedate as merlot. Or unnatural. I'm pretty sure you have to dye to get a merlot."

"Uh, you found a merlot hair in the bed?"

A waiter came over and put a drink down in front of Jack. Terra grabbed the drink and tossed it back. "*Our* bed. Yeah, a couple. And not just in the *bed*. The bathroom was filled with them when I got back from my work retreat. Guess the drapes match the carpet." Terra dropped the empty glass on the table as she glared at Jake. She said quietly, "Most people don't bother dying their crotch as well. Whoever the lucky lady is, she's consistent."

Jack shook his head as he scrambled for excuses. "Hey, I don't know what you're trying to imply, but—"

"I'm not trying to imply anything, Jack. I know you fucked someone else while I was gone. The most I was expecting was for you to man up and admit it. Grow some fucking balls for a change."

"Hey, I feel like we should talk about this at home or some other—"

Terra slammed her fist into the table, and everyone in the bar stopped talking for a second and looked over at them. "No," Terra said firmly. "We're talking about this right now. Unless you want to cut and run like you always do. But if you do, you're not coming back this time. Got it?"

Jack sat there quietly, avoiding Terra's eyes. Finally, he stood, grabbed his coat, and left the bar. Terra remained there for some time by herself before she went to sit at the bar counter.

Fred, the bartender, an older man with soft brown eyes and a beer gut, came over to Terra. "Can I get you something?"

Terra sighed. "Maybe a renewed faith in the human male."

"Not sure if I can provide that, but I can give you something to forget that they exist."

Terra raised two fingers. "Gimme a double of your cheapest whiskey. Actually, make it a double of a double."

Fred grabbed a large glass and a bottle of whiskey. He tossed in a couple of ice cubes and poured more than a reasonable amount. "You look like you might need this," he said. "Now, you gonna tell me why you were making such a scene in my bar?"

Terra jerked her thumb in the direction of Jack's exit route. "That guy you saw just leaving with his tail between his legs and wrapped up around his cock? He tends to like red hair. But it doesn't really matter whose head it belongs to. Or whose legs it's between."

"Ah, a cheating bastard. Should have seen that one coming. Every time he's in here, he's talking to a different girl. Sorry to hear that you were the offended party. This one's on me. You know, I probably know who it was. In case you want me to find out."

Terra tossed back the whiskey and tapped the counter for another one. "Why the hell would I want to know who it was?" she asked. "I don't care about her. He's the one who was cheating on me. Hope she goes on to live a healthy and happy life. Him? Well, fuck him."

Fred poured Terra another drink. "We got a rule here. You find out someone's been fucking around behind your back here, you drink free for the night."

Terra raised her glass. "I'm drinking by myself?"

Fred nodded and smiled gently as he poured himself a double shot of whiskey. "To the never-ending pain that men cause."

"Fuck that. Let's toast to those who manage to walk away from shitty situations."

"Sounds much better."

Terra and Fred downed their shots. Terra let out a hefty burp as she tapped the counter for another one.

Fred did his duty and poured both himself and Terra another drink. He leaned against the back of the bar counter after handing it to Terra. "Hope you don't take any offense by this, but your asshole of an ex was kinda right."

Terra sipped at her whiskey, aware now that her vision was a little blurry. "What the hell are you talking about?" she asked.

"You do look a little...mannish, but I mean that in a good way. I mean, it looks good on you. Masculinity, that is. If that's what you were going for."

Terra laughed, then drained the last of her whiskey. "You know, I wasn't going for anything, but thanks," she said. "Glad it looks good on me."

CHAPTER FOURTEEN

Abby left the locker room with the other recruits, still uncertain whether or not she was capable of getting through the obstacle course. She had never thought of herself as an athletic person, and she'd never tried an obstacle course in her life. Sounded like something Olympians did.

Abby had received bits and pieces of encouragement from her ma and pa throughout the years. Now, she stitched them together to craft something helpful in the moment. It was only a jumble of words and smiles. That would have to do.

The four potential recruits reached the end of the hallway. They waited for a few moments while a red alarm rang above the door. When it opened, smoke from the other room poured into the hallway, making it difficult to see.

A voice boomed, "Begin!"

The three other recruits rushed forward, their exoskeleton suits whirring loudly as the gears spun. The exosuits made a lot of noise and didn't appear to be making their users any faster. But Abby didn't have time to study them at the moment.

She entered the room containing the obstacle course. It was difficult to see at first—even more smoke filled this room. Instinctively,

Abby pulled down her HUD. The visor automatically compensated for the fog and she could see again.

The obstacle course was a recreation of a city block. There were cars parked erratically in the streets, old buildings where people were hanging out on their balconies, smoking, and laughing, and even a couple strolling down the street holding hands.

If these were holographs, they were the most lifelike holographs Abby had ever seen. She watched the city block breathe around her.

What kind of obstacle course is this? And where are the rest of the recruits? Abby scanned the block. None of them were in sight. Had they completed the obstacle course already?

The ground suddenly trembled, and a thunderous sound shook the whole block. The couple dropped to their knees and covered their heads.

In the middle of the street, a Dark Gate opened. Just like it had on the Crookins farm.

Abby grabbed her throat as her heart raced. Her hands trembled, and her chest was growing tighter and tighter. Running was obviously her only option. Yet her feet remained rooted to the ground. No matter how much her brain told her to move, her body refused to respond.

Abby saw the burning hole in Pa's forehead, saw his eyes staring unfocused as if he were staring at something she couldn't see.

Abby's stomach clenched, and she turned and ran to hide behind a car as sweat beaded her forehead, her throat closing. She gasped for air before leaning to the side and vomiting, her whole body convulsing as she tried to block out her memories.

Orcs were walking through the Dark Gate, each armed with an ax, a vibrating energy blade, and a plasma rifle. One orc, much larger than the rest, marched to the front of the group. He roared loudly, sending a wave of panic down Abby's spine.

She pressed her back against the car and imagined her body floating away. She could be in any other place but here. Any place would be better. She couldn't get the image of her father's lifeless eyes out of her mind.

The orcs had just killed him. For no reason. They had tried to kill her family. To kill *her*.

Abby's stomach still burned, but her throat opened at last. She could breathe again.

The orcs had come to her farm. The orcs had killed her family. For no reason.

Abby peered around the car, studying the orcs who were leaving the Gate. Myrddin must have been using the term obstacle course very loosely.

As she watched the orcs shouting at the humans on the street and wrangling them together, she felt the panic fading from her body. Her panic was quickly replaced by something else—a seething hatred that quieted Abby's body and steadied her hands.

If this was an obstacle course, none of this was real. That didn't mean Abby couldn't get hurt. Nor did it mean she didn't still want to kill these orcs. But more importantly, obstacle courses had goals. She needed to figure out what to do.

The most obvious option was to kill the orcs. But that would be too simple. If Myrddin wanted to see how good a shot Abby was, he could have simply taken her to a firing range with the other recruits. No, there had to be something else.

Across the obstacle course, one of the recruits leaned out from behind cover and opened fire on the orcs. The creatures roared in retaliation, grabbing one of the humans and throwing her into the line of fire. The human screamed in horror as she fell.

Abby's heart sank. Even if this wasn't real, it *felt* real enough. Then she had an idea. She activated her HUD and started scrolling through the menus. She quickly found the backend DOS program. After a quick search, she located the priorities for the obstacle course.

The list of goals was encrypted, or written in a language Abby couldn't understand. "Damn," she muttered. "Gotta be something here I can use."

Abby glanced at her watch. Not only had she programmed it to run her drones, but she'd also included a few programs that allowed her to access other OS programs, and to infiltrate networks.

It took a few seconds, but Abby managed to link her watch to the HUD. She opened her watch's virtual assistant, a hacked version of one of the larger brands, and asked, "Show me the goals for the obstacle course."

The assistant hummed for a moment, something Abby had never heard it do. Then it said, "Obstacles in order of importance as follows: Keep civilians alive, destroy the Dark Gate, eliminate threats."

Again, Abby checked the area from behind her cover. The other recruits were still firing at the orcs. No other hostages had been lost, but no headway was being made. "Any suggestions?" she asked her assistant, only partly joking.

The assistant hummed again, and this time whistled. "Orcs are superstitious. Their tribal necromancers use a combination of fear and real magic to keep some tribes subservient. Perhaps this can be used to your advantage."

"Uh, didn't know thoroughness was your strong suit," Abby murmured.

The assistant made a noise that sounded like a long, uncomfortable groan. Then it said, "There are several holographs loaded onto your HUD that will likely terrify the orcs. Would you like to project them?"

Abby activated her HUD and focused on the orcs. "Yes, sir, I would," she whispered.

A light on her HUD turned on, projecting an image of a ten-foot zombie orc on the wall of one of the buildings. All the orcs caught sight of it at about the same time. They screamed and scattered, leaving the hostages behind.

Abby hit her HUD's communication module and patched herself into the other recruits. "Hey! Most important part of the mission is saving hostages. Y'all do me a favor and sweep on in and get heroic with those folks over there?"

"Who the hell is this?" one of the recruits shouted.

"The person helping you score some points. Please and thank you, goodbye."

Abby disconnected, wondering if the other recruits would actually give her a hand. Much to her surprise, they snuck out from their cover and grabbed the hostages, leading them to safety.

Abby checked the list of goals on her HUD. Rescue hostages had disappeared. "All right, now we just need to close the...Dark Gate or something," she murmured.

The virtual assistant chirped, or it whistled. Abby couldn't tell what the noise was. "Your HUD is picking up a strong electromagnetic pulse coming from the Gate. It is likely that disrupting the electromagnetic current would effectively destroy it."

"Okay, and how exactly am I supposed to do that?"

"The plasma weapons you are equipped with can be reverse-programmed to fire a radio wave which counterattacks EMP's."

Abby checked her watch. Her assistant had never been this helpful before. Something had changed. She'd have to figure out what later, though. "All right, let's try that one out," she finally said as she selected the rifle from her HUD.

The plasma rifle appeared in Abby's hand. She leaned out of cover and aimed at the Dark Gate. The orcs were nowhere to be seen. Abby squeezed the trigger.

She saw no visible signs of the radio waves, but the portal did turn off. She checked her HUD, and one more goal had been crossed off. "Perfect," Abby muttered. "Last one is self-explanatory."

The assistant said, "I've accessed the cameras in the obstacle course. The orcs are located in the westernmost corner. They are currently organizing for a strike. The right side of their formation is susceptible to flanking."

Abby patched herself into the other recruits. "Uh...so, the orcs are preparing to attack. Figure we could cut them off before they come on over here," she suggested.

She didn't receive an answer immediately. Then one of the recruits asked, "All right, what's your plan?"

"We go in on the right side. Right? That sound good?"

The recruit sighed. "You're the one calling the shots. How am I supposed to know?"

Abby realized she hated giving orders. "All right, whatever. Just get over here, and we'll head over on the right side."

The recruits moved from their cover, slowly crossing the city block until they reached Abby's side. "Okay, let's go," she whispered as she motioned toward the location her virtual assistant had highlighted on her map.

The block was small, and in a couple of minutes, the recruits and Abby arrived at a spot to the right of the orcs. They didn't waste any time. Abby fired first, and the others were quick to join in. After a few minutes, they had wiped the orcs out.

Abby activated her HUD's menu. All of the goals had been achieved.

A voice came on over the intercom. "Congratulations. Power down and prepare to be debriefed."

CHAPTER FIFTEEN

Abby returned to the barracks while the other recruits went to the locker room to remove their exosuits. The barracks weren't too far, and Abby was amazed at how much space Myrddin's HQ had. It was like a little world all in itself.

The barracks felt like they were on the other side of the building, but Abby knew it was because she only really knew where the R&D department was. Once she reached the barracks, she pressed her hand to the security panel and let herself in.

Abby had been given a private room. A space all to herself. She had never had a place to herself before. She'd always shared a room with a sibling. Pa had told her that sometime soon, she would have her own room.

The memory of her father brought tears instantly to Abby's eyes, but more than that, she felt like the wind had just been sucked out of her. All of a sudden, she was dizzy, and she stumbled over to one of the beds to take a seat. There she sobbed hot tears, grateful the barracks were empty.

Once her tears dried up, Abby composed herself as much as possible. Pushed the memories of her father, his words, his lessons, as far away as possible. Dwelling on her pain wasn't going to help. She had to stay focused on what was in front of her.

Unfortunately, she had nothing pressing to turn her attention to. Just an empty barracks with flickering lights. "Ain't no reason for a light to be flickering," Abby muttered, unable to avoid thinking about her father's lessons on electrical wiring.

Abby scanned the room for something to stand on. She grabbed a chair and dragged it over to the defective light fixture. She climbed onto the chair, undid the light's cage, covered her hand with her shirt sleeve, and unscrewed the light bulb. Then she pulled out her trusty pair of needle-nose pliers and got to work.

As Abby tinkered with the light fixture, the door of the barracks opened. The three other recruits entered, talking to each other softly. They were followed by Anabelle and Roy. When Abby spotted the crowd entering the barracks, she finished her task as quickly as she could and jumped off of the chair.

When Roy saw Abby, he said, "Good that you keep yourself busy. Very good quality to have."

Unlike Roy, Anabelle didn't appear to be in anything remotely like a good spirit. Her anger radiated off her like a nuclear cloud. Abby hoped *she* was not the target of that anger.

The other recruits lined up across from the beds. Abby took that as her cue and jogged over to them, falling in line at the end of the row.

Roy paced up and down the line, studying each recruit, shaking his head in an almost theatrical fashion. Abby had seen this scene multiple times in old war movies. Roy must have been a fan of the genre. "So, you all passed the obstacle co—"

Anabelle stormed over to the recruits, cutting Roy off before he could speak again. "Passed the obstacle course?" she shouted. "That's one way of putting it. What I saw was an entire squad being carried by one person. Hm…I wonder if this feels familiar to any of you?"

Abby stared at her feet, keenly aware of how the other recruits must be feeling. She didn't want her efforts singled out at all. They'd all finished the requirements of the obstacle course. Wasn't that good enough?

Anabelle was still pacing, shaking her head. "On paper, you four have the best score of any squad going through that obstacle course to date," she lectured. "How you got it, I have no idea. For the most part, it looked like you were content to hide behind cover and hope you hit something. Explain yourselves. Now!"

One of the recruits stepped forward, a short human with bright red hair and a little bit of a beer gut. "Excuse me, ma'am. We—"

Anabelle's eyes shot daggers at the recruit and she shouted, "'Ma'am' is reserved for the elderly and your commanding officer. I am not elderly and I'm not sure if any of you are going to make it far enough to call me *your* commanding officer. Now get on with it."

The redheaded recruit coughed nervously and glanced at the others before speaking. "We were having technical difficulties," he explained. "Our exosuits malfunctioned...or, they didn't perform as we thought they were going to."

"What did you think your suits were going to do?"

The recruit shifted his weight awkwardly as he tried to come up with an answer. "Well, we were told that they would improve our combat abilities," he went on. "But well, it turns out they're really hard to move in. They're very heavy."

Anabelle leaned forward and got up in the recruit's face. "It sounds like what I'm hearing is that if your equipment malfunctions on the field, you're completely defenseless. What I saw out there was utterly pathetic. No forward movement. Content to wait for the enemy to regroup and deal with *you.*"

"Ma'am...I mean sir...uh...what should I call you?"

Anabelle straightened and gave a sigh of exasperation before walking away. "Address me as Ms. Chase. Go on," she barked.

"We've only been trained to fight with our exoskeletons. We haven't received any other training. When the suits don't work, then—"

"Are you telling me you've only been trained with faulty equipment?"

Roy stepped in, putting himself between the recruits and Anabelle.

"You're gonna need to rein it in a little bit," he suggested. "You're going to have to learn to work with humans."

She bit her lip and turned bright red as she tapped her foot furiously. Before she could open her mouth, Roy grabbed her by the arm and pulled her aside. "I know how to work with humans." Anabelle spat. "My entire career has been working with humans."

Roy shook his head as he scratched at his beard. "No, your entire career has been manipulating humans. Those are two different things. You need to speak to them like you respect them."

"First off, I don't respect them. Secondly, I've been working with you for years. We've never had a problem. Which means I can work with humans who are worthy of my respect."

Roy chuckled as he folded his arms. "You respect me?" he asked. "I always thought you were waiting for me to be replaced."

"You? Of course not. You're my favorite person in the department. Handsome, smart, and you know how to fight. Occasionally a good joke, but don't let it go to your head."

"Okay, your obvious admiration for me isn't the point of this conversation. These are your recruits. They passed the course. You're going to have to figure out how to work with them, or you aren't going anywhere. Got it?"

Anabelle's stern demeanor faltered, and inside she transformed into a young elf, younger than she ever let on. "These guys are going to get killed," she whined. "The only one who was capable of anything was Abby. She was the one who scared off those orcs and..." Anabelle stopped mid-sentence, her jaw hanging for a second before she caught herself and resumed her regular, hard persona. "How exactly in the nine hells did she do that?"

Roy tossed a glance over his shoulder at Abby, who appeared to be trying to shrink behind the other recruits. "You know, I didn't even stop to think about that. She was hiding just like the rest of them. And that radio wave thing...how'd she know about that?"

Anabelle approached Abby with Roy at her side. "Hey, Abby," Anabelle asked, the bite of her voice fading. "How did you manage all that out on the course?"

Abby jumped at the sound of her name, lost in her own thoughts and concerns. "Wait, huh? What part?" the girl asked.

"All of it. You hardly moved until you organized the strike."

"Oh, that." Abby raised her wrist, revealing her watch. "I hacked into the system with my virtual assistant. But once it connected to my HUD, it started acting...odd, you know. Ain't ever gotten answers that specific before."

Anabelle grabbed Abby's wrist and turned it over, attempting to see what made the smartwatch so special. There were no obvious clues. "All right," Anabelle said, taking a deep breath. "Let's try this again. Explain to me what went wrong out there, and we can work through it while we figure out what your strengths are."

The recruits responded well to Anabelle's change of approaches. This time they were much more forthright with the issues they experienced. For one, there hadn't been any clear-cut leadership until Abby made her suggestions.

Second was the equipment. The recruits expressed irritation over being given untested equipment and having all of their training dependent on whether or not the equipment worked. All three of them were frustrated.

Abby was the only one who remained quiet during the conversation. Roy noticed and nudged her. "So, what do you think we could do to improve this shit show?"

Pulled from her thoughts, Abby stumbled over her words at first, trying to find the right thing to say. When she was greeted with silence, she cleared her throat and started again. "Well, my Pa used to always say you can only punch a wall so many times. It ain't the way you bring down a building."

"A very rustic anecdote, but I fail to see how it applies to this."

"I ain't the toughest kid out there. So, I figured if I can't beat 'em, gotta outsmart 'em. When you're wrangling cattle, you ain't trying to wrestle each one of 'em. You figure ways to outsmart 'em. Spook 'em with a heel-nibbling dog or get one of the steers to come after a bell. Don't make no sense to be pushing and pulling on them. Just gotta find a way around it." Anabelle was studying Abby as she spoke. Abby sensed the elf's eyes skimming over her, and it made her extremely uncomfortable. "That's what I did with my assistant," Abby said. "Didn't think I'd be taking down fifteen or so orcs. So, I just started asking questions."

Roy asked to see her smartwatch. She removed it and handed it to him. "Doesn't sound like a typical virtual assistant, though," Roy said. "You said it gave you detailed responses and performed its own search queries?"

Abby nodded as he returned the watch. "Yeah, 'bout two all on its own. Never seen anything like it since I been poking around in its digital guts," she admitted.

"Now that's a scary premise. You said you worked on this assistant yourself?"

"Yep, tore it down and built it back up all by myself. Even added a couple of new protocols and such. Trying to make it smarter and the like."

Roy sat across from Abby and crossed his legs. "Don't want to alarm you at all, but what you described sounds like the beginnings of an AI. Looks like you might have stumbled onto something there."

Abby's heart raced, and she had to keep from screaming with joy. That made total sense. She might have already been pushing her virtual assistant into the realm of AI.

Anabelle clapped her hands together. "All right, we'll let's go with what worked and didn't. Obviously, your exoskeleton training isn't holding up. So, we're heading back to the field and starting a new training regimen. Abby, you're hitting the lab."

Abby picked nervously at the lint on her pants. "What for? How come I'm not getting any training?"

"I'm not as versed on tech as Creon might be, but I know an AI is a huge deal. I want you to talk with the goblin, figure out how to push this thing into full AI. And then I want you to structure it and get it ready for these idiots to use. Think easier than a smartphone if you can. A smartphone for your grandma. All you got that?"

The recruits barked out a "hurrah" that Abby only managed to catch the tail end of. Then the recruits marched out of the barracks, leaving her alone with Anabelle and Roy. "Y'all serious about this AI thing, huh?" Abby asked tentatively.

Roy stood and headed to the door. "AI isn't an easy thing to come across. Sounds like you're close, which frankly, is unbelievable. Anabelle's right. That's where you need to be putting your focus."

Abby nodded. She wasn't sure how she had stumbled upon AI, but she intended to figure out how to finish the job. Sounded fun.

CHAPTER SIXTEEN

Fred rang the bell for last call. Most of the bar had already cleared out, but a handful of regulars and folks hung about, probably looking to hook up. Everyone jumped when they heard the bell and Fred's shout over their conversations.

Terra was still at the bar, staring down the bottom of her shot glass. She had no idea how long she had sat there, but she didn't care. She'd had a fun time shooting the shit with Fred. The guy had some wild stories to tell. And he hadn't wanted to focus on how bad Terra must have been feeling. That was the most important part.

Fred poured Terra one final shot for the road as the last of the patrons left the bar. "You're welcome back anytime," Fred said. "And I'll make sure that your ass of an ex isn't. Sound good?"

Terra leaned forward drunkenly and gave Fred a high five before turning to stumble away. "That sounds good to me, Red. Do people call you that? I'm going to call you that if it's okay."

Fred shrugged as he wiped down the bar. "Call me whatever you want the next time you come in," he said. "Just make sure to make eye contact, so I know you're talking to me."

Terra staggered to the exit. She concentrated on placing one foot in front of the other. It appeared very likely that the ground might flip from under her. Concentration was absolutely necessary. By her own observation, she was faring better than most of the other late-night barflies.

Terra made it outside and leaned against the side of the bar as she fumbled in her pocket for her phone. Tonight was definitely going to be a taxi night. She could come back and pick up her car the next day. Maybe grab another drink. Lord knows she was going to need them to get through the week.

Someone in the parking lot up ahead shouted, "Hey, what the fuck is that?" The man was pointing at the sky.

Terra stared up but couldn't see anything. She was surprised that there weren't any stars out. And the moon was gone. Terra knew for a fact that there was a full moon out. She had seen it when she'd first arrived at the bar. There also hadn't been a cloud in sight.

Now the sky was dark. Darker than she could ever imagine it being. Almost as if there were no lights on anywhere in the world. Just the deep void stretching out in front of her. "It's the booze," she muttered as she tried to focus on the screen of her phone.

A flash of green lit the sky. It was bright enough to set the whole sky emerald and jade. The green light began to morph and take shape, as if a tear had ripped the sky open—a tear that was deepening and stretching.

Terra stared up at the burgeoning portal as green mist leaked from it. Then a loud boom erupted, and a cigar-shaped spaceship was floating above the bar. The ship appeared to have been made from a sleek metal with no discernible windows or parts. It was just one long piece.

Terra had seen enough horror movies to know what was going on. She turned to run back into the bar. But as she moved, her legs gave out. She hadn't fallen, though. It felt like something had grabbed her by the shoulders and was lifting her up.

All around Terra, beams of light were firing from the spaceship while creatures crawled from invisible cracks in the shape. The creatures dropped to the ground and made their way to the humans who were caught floating above the ground.

The creatures—hunched-over gray monsters with tusks and elongated, muscular arms—were grunting to each other. To Terra, they resembled the orcs she had seen in fantasy game drawings.

One of the orcs near Terra grabbed another and pulled him close, snarling loudly, "We're only here for males. Double-check them. I don't want to be explaining any more fuckups tomorrow."

Terra was suddenly aware that these were not aliens. They were something else.

An orc hurried over to Terra and studied her closely. He sniffed her, then coughed loudly. Then he signaled to the ship above, and Terra felt herself flying upward so fast she blacked out.

CHAPTER SEVENTEEN

Terra's eyes snapped open, and she tried to jump to her feet. Her movement was restricted, though. As her mind woke up, she became aware that her hands and her feet were shackled. *Huh. That is fucking weird.*

Again, Terra tried to stand but to no avail. Not only was she shackled, but the chains were connected to the wall behind her. Which was about all she could make out. It was too dark to see anything. The only light came from what appeared to be a walkway.

Even though it wouldn't make a difference, Terra strained against the shackles. At least it gave her something to do. She wasn't sure how long she'd been out for. After a while, she wasn't certain of how long she'd been awake, either.

Time became less abstract. Terra had the vague sensation that her body was being stretched by an outside force. And not just her body. Everything around her. Reality was growing thin and tight, ready to snap at any moment.

Sleep and awake ceased to have any meaningful distinction. Terra slipped between both states without knowing the difference. She couldn't tell if her dreams were real; if reality had seeped into her nightmares or vice versa.

Jack's face kept floating in front of Terra. She wanted to reach out and punch it. As she tried, his face turned dead and gray, great big fangs forcing themselves out from under his overbite. Now Terra really wanted to deck Jack.

A voice roused her from her sleep. Or brought her deeper into it. She didn't know which. "Hey," the voice repeated. "You here? Hey. Talk to me."

Terra answered groggily, "Don't know who you think I am, but I'm here. What's it to you?" She peeled her eyes open. The room was lighter now. She could see people shackled to the wall alongside her.

The man next to Terra appeared to be in his mid-forties. He had a scruffy-looking face and a badly maintained beard. His eyes were those of a broken man. It was hard to tell how long ago he had cracked. "Doesn't matter who I think you are," he replied. "We're both here. Together. All of us are."

Terra strained her eyes to see in the dark. "And where exactly is here?"

The man struggled to sit up, fighting against his shackles. "Another world. Not space. A whole other realm. Another plane of reality, of existence."

Terra laughed as she hung her head in her hands. "You hear yourself, man? You sound fucking crazy."

"Do you remember how you got here?"

Flashes of the abduction fired off through Terra's memory. The bearded man took her silence for an answer. "You gonna tell me I'm the crazy one?" he asked.

Terra still wasn't ready to swallow the man's bullshit hook, line, and sinker. "So, what exactly are we doing on this plane of reality? Those guys didn't look like any Gray aliens, I've seen."

"Not Grays. Worse. You ever hear about *Middang3ard* VR? The world within a world?"

She frowned. The name sounded familiar, but she had never cared about video games. Her sister may have been into the game. Fantasy bullshit wasn't for Terra, though. She dealt with the here and now. Fairies and gnomes were for kids.

But telling the bearded man she thought he was full of shit wasn't going to help. It would just end the conversation. "No, don't think so. What is it?"

The man's eyes suddenly lit up, almost brighter than the lights of the walkway. "It's a VR simulation. People think it's a game, but it's real. I mean, it's a picture of something that's real. There's a war going on. Across the nine realms. A great evil is coming. It's trying to devour everything."

Terra tried to keep from sighing and rolling her eyes. She couldn't believe that of all the people to get stuck next to, it had to be a crazy nerd. "Oh, yeah?" she droned. "A great evil?"

The bearded man continued, "The Dark One...he's coming. He's going to swallow up everything. That's what's happening. He's coming."

Something about the silence that followed after the man's statement chilled Terra to the bone. He sounded crazy. But he also sounded sincere. "Is there anyone trying to fight against...the Dark One?" she asked.

The man nodded, staring off into the dimness of the room as he pulled at his chains. "Yes, there's a wizard. An old wizard named Myrddin," he whispered. "He's trying to convince us, to let us all know. To warn us. To warn us all."

The man had just finished speaking when a door opened. Light poured into the room. "What the hell is all the noise in here?" someone shouted.

Terra spoke before she realized her mouth was moving. "Hey, fucker! What's the Dark One want with us?" she shouted.

An orc stepped into the light, his eyes narrowing at Terra as he pulled out an ax. He pressed the blade to her throat. "You lot?" he asked. "You're probably going to the camps. All the best males go to the camp."

The orc leaned in closer, studying Terra's face. "Hm...you look...a little soft for a male," he murmured.

Terra leaned forward and headbutted the orc. "Who the hell are you calling soft?" she spat.

"Hm, maybe your balls haven't dropped yet?" The orc scrambled to his feet and pulled out a scanner. A green hue floated over Terra's body. "Not a male. How the hell did we miss you?"

"Probably because none of you knows the difference between a dick and a clit."

The orc threw his ax at Terra. The blade hit right above her skull, nicking the crown of her head. Blood trickled down her face. "Not-males go to the games," the orc barked. "Consider yourself lucky. At least your death will be entertaining."

With that, the orc left the room. Terra tried to flick the blood off her face, but the ax was still embedded in the wall above her, which meant anytime she moved, she cut her skin a little more.

"You know anything about the games?" she finally asked the bearded man.

He convulsed and shook his head. "They talk about it in Middang3ard," he said after a long silence. "The orc blood games. An arena, a tournament. Slaves battle monster after monster. There are no heroes, only victors. Only champions. Only the Blooded."

Terra tried to get comfortable. It was impossible. A sharp piece of metal was slicing the top of her head open. "Great," she muttered. "Blood games. Sounds fucking great."

CHAPTER EIGHTEEN

Abby spent the next few days locked in the Research and Development department by no one's choice but her own. She had explained her goal to Creon, who countered with the very accurate point that Anabelle knew nothing about the complexities of artificial intelligence.

In short, Creon believed it was impossible. That was until Abby had shown Creon her virtual assistant. The goblin couldn't help identifying there was something slightly odd about the way the assistant performed its tasks.

Which was the only encouragement Abby required. She called it in early that day and woke up the next morning at 5:30am—old farm habits die hard, she had joked—and had begun running tests on the virtual assistant.

At first, Creon believed Abby was thinking in circles. The first day was host to a selection of repeating experiments, which she refused to take the time to explain to Creon. He didn't mind. A part of him still believed she was wasting her time. "Let her waste it," he muttered under his breath. "Some of the best science is just a mistake."

On the second day, Abby made her mistake. "Creon," she'd shouted. "You have to see this!"

Abby had realized that her virtual assistant only operated differently when linked to a specific program running through the HUD. It was the program used to run the obstacle course. The program Abby had hacked into by accident.

Figuring out *why* was the difficult part of the experiment, which was what Abby and Creon found themselves working on the most. Abby had never worked with anyone before. She had assumed it would be unbearable.

As it turned out, Creon was the best company she had ever experienced. The goblin wasn't only sharp; he was also unbelievably inquisitive. He didn't seem interested in teaching her anything. Instead, he asked questions, probed her mind, and pushed her in a multitude of directions.

By the third day, Abby couldn't imagine having done anything else with her life. Creon hardly talked about the project other than in a vague, abstract, conceptual sense. She sometimes wondered if he remembered they were working on an AI.

On the fifth day, Creon came into the lab around ten, carrying two plates of food, both standard goblin fare. A small scoop of *bahjar*, a thick black paste with kernels of something similar to nuts, and a large slab of raw vrosk heart. Abby had discovered she was a huge fan of goblin food.

Creon placed a plate in front of Abby, and she absentmindedly grabbed the slice of raw heart and bit into it. "Did you try talking to it yet?" he asked.

Abby glanced up from her workstation as Creon mimed wiping his face to Abby, who quickly cleaned the vrosk blood off her chin. "What do you mean, 'ask it a question?'"

Creon pointed at her screen. "We keep just running search questions to the program and taking notes on how it's processing information. But that's not what we do to each other. If we're trying to crack intelligence, maybe we need to treat it like an intelligent creature."

Abby finished off her vrosk heart and played with the pile of *bahjar.* "That's not a bad idea," she mused. "Wouldn't hurt to find out. I got an idea."

She whirled over to the other side of the lab, grabbed a holoprojector, and tossed it onto the floor. Then she uploaded her assistant into the projector, closed every firewall she had open, and turned the assistant on.

Creon stood behind her, watching her work. "Why did you turn off the firewalls? That's not exactly the wisest decision. There's a lot of classified information on our servers."

Abby got up from her chair and approached the holoprojector. "Trust deserves trust," she offered. "Gotta get off to a good start. You know, proper introductions and all. 'Sides, we already broke into the system. If we're getting fired, we already earned it."

Creon chewed the gristle off of his vrosk heart and spat a piece of fat into his *bahjar.* Abby hadn't picked up that particular goblin habit yet. "Makes sense," he murmured as he went back to his seat and watched the projection. "I believe you should have the honor of greeting our guest."

Abby turned back to the holoprojector, where two digital eyes had just opened. "Uh, hi. Name's Abby-Lynn, what's yours?" she asked.

The eyes closed for a second. Then they disappeared, to be replaced by the answer, "I don't know. I don't think I have one yet. Should I have a name?"

Creon's jaw dropped as he scooted his chair closer to the holoprojector. "And there we fucking have it," he whispered, in awe of what stood before him.

A human girl from the farms of Utah and a goblin who had managed to escape the orc slave mines had created the first form of non-organic life.

Neither Abby nor Creon had time to celebrate the advances in artificial intelligence they had stumbled upon. The next day, Anabelle called for her team to assemble in the barracks. Something had come to her attention that needed to be addressed.

Abby was told to bring the AI if it had been finished. She loaded the program back onto her smartwatch and took it with her to the barracks.

The three recruits were waiting with one other recruit named Blackwell. Abby didn't see Anabelle anywhere and figured it was about time she started with the introductions. They would be working together, after all.

Abby strolled up to Blackwell, extended her hand, and repeated the gesture with the other three: Stinsons, Pablo, and Sam. All of them were scanning the barracks for Anabelle, though Blackwell didn't appear agitated. Abby suspected he'd be the best one to keep talking to.

She sat next to Blackwell and asked, "So, what's all this about? Didn't get many details when I got the call."

Blackwell glanced at the clock on the wall. "Hm, guess there wasn't time to give us any real details. I have no idea. Got the call and came as soon as I did. We'll probably be briefed in a few minutes anyway.

Just then, Anabelle stormed into the room, dressed like she had just stepped out of a military fashion show. Abby had no idea how the recruits and Anabelle were wearing the same uniform. Anabelle rocked it in a way the others didn't. Probably something that came from years of being a model.

"All right, everyone here?" Anabelle barked.

Blackwell and the recruits jumped to their feet. When Abby slowly stood, she peeked around the queue of soldiers to wave at Anabelle.

The elf couldn't resist a small smile in Abby's direction as she strode past the other recruits. "Looks like we finally got something," Anabelle informed them. "We have reports of the same energy disturbance that accompanied the two Dark Gates we've already witnessed."

Abby remembered the way the air had felt when the Gate opened on her farm. Like something hot and evil had stripped the life out of the air. She wanted to make sure another Gate like that never opened up again.

Anabelle was still talking, and Abby kicked herself for zoning out. "We're trying to find its exact location at the moment, but until then, I'm going to need you all to get geared up," Anabelle commanded before turning her attention to Abby. "Did you finish the AI?" she asked.

Abby pointed at her watch, grinning. "Yeah, we finished working on it a day or two ago," she said, feeling a rush of excitement. "All I have to do is upload it to their exosuits and HUDs."

"To both of them? Isn't that redundant?"

Abby shook her head as she hurried over to the exosuits in the corner of the barracks. Anabelle and Blackwell followed while the other recruits hung back timidly. "That's what I thought at first too, but me and Creon got a chance to peek at them suits and found a couple of issues overlooked by Roy's boys."

A sly, triumphant smirk spread over Anabelle's face. "Oh, *Roy's* department missed something?" She sneered. "That's good to know."

"No offense, but whoever's messing around with these suits ain't looking too hard. There were tons of tweaks to get these babies running smoothly. And they installed a neural compensator to help that no one ever turned on. Anyways, that's what we're hooking the AI up to."

Anabelle kicked one of the exosuits lightly. "Sounds kinda dangerous to let an AI connect to anything concerning neurons, right?" she asked.

"Nah, he's an all right guy. 'Sides, neural compensator's just a fancy way to say 'electric jolty thing that makes sure you don't fall over.' Anyway, 'bout time you guys met our new friend. Get over here."

The recruits left their safe space by the beds, looking around uneasily when they joined with the rest of the team as Abby held her smartwatch up for everyone to see. She hit a button and a holographic display popped up. A 3D image of a paperclip with large eyes, holding a coffee cup shimmered into existence.

"Meet Martin."

Anabelle stared at the paperclip, which matched her stare,

although with a noticeably more annoyed expression. "A paperclip?" she asked.

"You said to make it user friendly."

"And *Martin?*"

Abby shrugged as Martin sipped from his cup of coffee. "Myrddin did a survey, and people felt safe with the name. Don't ask me. Big boss says name him Martin, it's the least I can do. I'm just a programmer."

Blackwell came up to Martin and took a long look at the paperclip. "And this...paperclip is going to help us?" he asked.

Martin drained the last of his coffee, held his cup out, and a French press appeared to pour him another cup. "Uh, last time I checked, I was a computer program that processes information that *your* brain takes a decade to dream of, within a fraction of a nanosecond, so, uh, yeah, I think I can help." Martin yawned.

"Huh. He's a little...rough around the edges."

Abby closed the holograph using her watch. "Oh, sorry, he's still trying out personalities," she explained. "Though he seems pretty settled on arrogant, crotchety drunk genius. He's a sweetheart deep down, though. Anyways, let me get him all uploaded."

She swung down her HUD and started typing away on a keyboard projected from her watch. "All right. Martin's live," she said.

Anabelle jerked her thumb at the exosuits. "All right, everyone get loaded up. We got a Dark Gate to shut down."

CHAPTER NINETEEN

Abby, Anabelle, and the recruits sat quietly aboard the helicopter taking them to the location of the Dark Gate. Anabelle was attempting to rally the troops, but it seemed as though nobody was taking notice. Nerves, most likely. Other than Blackwell and Anabelle, the other recruits hadn't seen combat before.

As silence fell within the copter, Anabelle stood and pulled out a large canvas bag. She dug inside and retrieved a glowing cylindrical battery. "Surprise time," she said. "I know that your suits have been reconfigured to deal with the Dark Gate, but just to be safe, we have some special batteries for you. Proton packs. Slam these in if your suits go down, and you'll be back on your feet. Also, the batteries and mods on your suits should allow a lot more movement, but make no mistake, they're still cumbersome."

Blackwell took the proton pack and weighed it in his hand. "Not a bad idea."

Anabelle snatched the proton pack back and handed it to one of the other recruits. "Of course, it's not a bad idea. It's my idea. Better to be safe than sorry."

A loud knock came from the front of the helicopter. Abby's eyes widened as she stood. "Great, we're almost there. Everyone get ready for the jump."

The recruits were in their exosuits, and Anabelle was relieved that it only took them a couple minutes to get in and out of them now—a task that was much less arduous than before. Less arduous, but still not easy.

Abby observed the recruits as they prepared, wishing she had something to do instead of watching everyone else. All she wore was a light armored suit that reminded her of SWAT team gear. Granted, she was meant to stay far from the action and monitor the situation with her drones, but still, an orc could break through the line and get at her. She really wished she had something a bit more meaty on her.

But she had her drones. They sat ready for use on the floor of the helicopter.

Anabelle was noticeably excited. Her eyes had lost her usual droll, businesslike veneer. She had fight in her, a want for combat.

Another knock came from the front of the helicopter. "Jump time!" Anabelle shouted as she opened the side door.

Abby stared around frantically. Everyone else had exosuits for the jump. She was the only one who didn't have a parachute. "How am I getting out of this thing?"

The other recruits were already at the door. Blackwell jumped out, shouting loudly, his voice quickly cut off by the wind. The next recruit took their place and jumped.

Then Anabelle came up behind Abby and wrapped her arms around Abby's stomach. "You ready for this?" she asked.

Abby's eyes went wide as her heart started thumping harder. "Wait, are you serious?" she shouted.

Anabelle didn't answer. Instead, she picked Abby up and ran to the door, leaping out, laughing maniacally as they flew through the sky.

Abby couldn't hear herself screaming over the wind thundering in her ears. There was only panic. She was going to vomit. Then she heard Anabelle chuckling softly in her ear. Once the elf stopped laughing, Abby heard only the whipping of the wind.

She stared out in front of her. The whole of the earth stretched out before her eyes. Around her was nothing but blue skies and clouds. It was surprisingly tranquil. She was reminded of the early mornings on the farm before anyone else had risen when there was only crisp air and the sound of silence.

Before Abby knew what she was doing, she was laughing. A laughter she had not experienced since her father had passed. She felt free. Truly free for the first time in a while.

Anabelle, hearing Abby's laughter, grabbed the girl tighter and spun around, sending the both of them twirling through the air like insane ballerinas, plummeting toward the ground. When the two of them stopped spinning, Anabelle leaned forward, sending them rocketing faster toward their impact.

As the clouds passed them, Anabelle called a reasonable amount of manna to slow their descent.

Around Anabelle and Abby, the recruits and Blackwell activated their parachutes, ballooning up, and slowing down. Anabelle and Abby didn't slow. They continued toward the ground.

Abby gritted her teeth, ready for the breaking of her bones against the ground. Maybe she had made a mistake trusting the elf this much.

Anabelle situated herself so she fell with her feet toward the ground. Abby screamed because there was nothing else to do.

Anabelle amped up the manna, slowing her descent so she landed on the ground as if she had simply stepped off a low ledge.

Abby moved out of Anabelle's arms, and because of the magic used, she was unhurt. Shaken, sure, but in one piece.

She walked around a bit, trying to get used to being back on solid ground again as Anabelle stretched her legs. "You planning on bringing the drones with you?"

The question surprised Abby. For a second, she had forgotten she was on a mission. The drones were as necessary as she was. "Oh, yeah, of course," Abby said as she used her watch to call the drones to her. "Should be here soon enough."

The other recruits slowly landed beside Abby and Anabelle, detaching their parachutes and trying to regain their equilibrium.

Blackwell was the first to free himself of his parachute. "Damn, forgot how fun that is!" he exclaimed.

Anabelle, who was still excited, clapped him on the back and said, "You're going to have to try that without a parachute once. There's nothing that beats it."

Without missing a beat, Anabelle's face returned to its serious façade. "Okay, we need to get moving. We have the coordinates. Let's get to it."

The squad waited for a few minutes for Abby's drones to arrive then headed West.

The helicopter had dropped them off in what appeared to be a desert. From Anabelle's briefing, they weren't too far from where she had come across her first Dark Gate. Myrddin didn't know what interest the Dark One had in Utah, but it seemed to be where he was applying most of his focus.

The SWARMMT squad started their trek through the desert. Blackwell passed Abby a canteen of water to make sure she was hydrated. The sun beamed down on their heads as if intent on punishing them for attempting to thwart the Dark One's plans.

They hiked for almost twenty minutes before cresting a hill that provided them with the lay of the land. Anabelle pulled out a pair of binoculars and peered through them. She handed the binoculars to Abby, who glassed them as well, and, in turn, passed them to Blackwell.

When Blackwell was done, he returned the binoculars to Anabelle and said, "So, that's where we're headed?"

Anabelle pocketed the binoculars. "Yep. That's where the Gate is supposed to open. Hopefully, we get a jump on them before they realize what's up."

A caustic voice came through on all of the squad's comms. "It's not rocket science to surprise them," Martin said. "It still wouldn't be rocket science to get into positions that would let us take care of them easier."

Abby blushed when she heard Martin's voice. Part of her wished he would have chosen a more amicable personality. But wasn't that the point of AI? The little paperclip got to be the type of person he wanted to be.

Anabelle wasn't bothered by the AI's suggestion and readily agreed. "Martin, what's the best place for us to post up?" she asked.

There was no immediate answer, just the sound of loud slurping and then a burp. "Split up," Martin suggested. "There are four small hills around here. Set a sniper on each one. You take point at the exact coordinates. Use the drones to flush out the rest. Sound easy enough?"

Anabelle's eyes narrowed at the point where the Dark Gate was supposed to open. "Yeah, that sounds doable."

CHAPTER TWENTY

S WARMMT split up across the various hills surrounding the coordinates where the Dark Gate was to appear. The recruits posted up, ready to take aim at whatever came out of the portal.

Abby stood next to Blackwell, waiting to see what was going to happen. Adrenaline was pumping through her veins, and she felt like crawling out of her skin. She wasn't sure when the Dark Gate would arrive, but she knew it would be there. And she felt like she wasn't going to be doing enough about it.

The air turned acrid. Abby could smell it. The same scent from on her farm. Above them, the sky turned crimson as swathes of lightning cut through the blackening clouds. She glanced across the valley and met Anabelle's eyes, which were nearly the color of the red flashes of lightning.

In the middle of the valley, a rip in space and time occurred. The same as Abby had seen before. From that tear, a shape began to materialize, slowly taking form, the outer lines of the Dark Gate coming into existence as its portal expanded and solidified.

An orc stepped through. Anabelle considered sniping him, but the disturbance from the Gate made getting an accurate shot off almost impossible.

The orc roared upon entering Earth, raising his ax, his shout echoing through the still valley. Another followed him, then another. Within seconds, twenty orcs had passed through the portal.

Martin's caustic voice came through the comms. "Uh, I'm pretty sure this is the part where you start shooting. If you're planning on staying alive or anything like that."

Blackwell took the first shot. He fired his plasma sniper rifle, and the bullet cut through the first orc who had arrived.

A cry went up from invaders as they drew their weapons, instantly scattering. The formation they assumed implied they were ready for an attack. They took cover nearby, behind a line of rocks, popping out and taking shots as they saw fit.

Although the orcs were ready for an attack, they weren't prepared for the sniping event they met. Orc upon orc fell, Blackwell and the recruits mowing them down as they came through the portal.

Anabelle's voice broke through the noise of the gunfire. She sounded annoyed as she said, "Looks like we already got them on the run. Great."

Abby could relate to the annoyance. She wouldn't have called it irritation, but rather, disappointment. The recruits were doing what Abby wished she was capable of. Orc after orc was dying. The Dark One's minions. And Abby had almost nothing to do with it.

Anabelle was up on one of the hills next to a recruit. She was anxiously tapping her feet, waiting for something else to come through the Dark Gate, something worth her attention.

Then it happened. Just like she'd been hoping. The Dark Gate flashed bright white, and three trolls strode through the portal. "They're mine!" Anabelle shouted as she leapt to her feet and jumped off the hill.

A few orcs broke away from the group. Anabelle soared through the air, charging her arms with manna, flying into the fray of the orcs and trolls. She hit with the force of a small bomb, sending orcs tumbling through the air, the trolls pushed to the side.

Abby was still watching from afar, her eyes large with envy.

Anabelle was right where Abby wished to be. In the fray. Yet here she was sitting by, watching everything unfold around her.

The recruits were still firing, Blackwell taking the lead, lining up shot after shot. It didn't seem to be making a difference, though. For every orc that fell, another one came to take its place. Blackwell leaned back to take cover and reloaded his rifle. "How the hell are we going to do this?" he shouted.

Martin's voice crackled over the comms. "Were you just planning on shooting everything that came through the portal? Fucking stupid idea."

"Well, what the hell do you think we should do?"

"Obviously, shut off the Gate. Most reasonable thing."

Blackwell ducked out from under cover, taking a quick shot that blew through the head of an orc emerging from the Dark Gate. "And how the fuck do you suppose we do that?" he asked.

Abby used her drone's sensors to scan the area. "By shooting out its power source. I've highlighted the source for everyone. Check your HUDs."

Blackwell's HUD beeped loudly, and he glanced at the Dark Gate. Five points were glowing on the Dark Gate, one on either side, two at the base, and one at the top. "Holy shit," Blackwell murmured. "Abby, send this to everyone else."

"Already done. Hope you guys can clean this up fast enough."

Over at the Dark Gate, Anabelle was cutting through the orcs who were trying to ward off the fire from the recruits above. The trolls were attempting to catch her attention, but Anabelle was too fast for them. Lightning crackled around her as she sliced through whatever was in front of her.

Caught in the fury of battle, Anabelle had nearly lost herself. All she heard was the sound of her heartbeat and the screams of those around her. This was the Path of the Traveler. The path she had long since forgotten, the path she had craved.

A massive, furry hand wrapped around the back of Anabelle's neck and pulled her up into the air. Anabelle went flying, crashing against a rock, her vision blurring for a second as she tried to pick herself up and shake off the pain.

Two trolls stood in front of her, each holding clubs. One brought his club down so fast Anabelle could hardly see it move. She was barely able to roll out of the way as the troll cracked the earth in the spot she had just occupied.

The recruits fired at the points Martin had identified.

The Dark Gate shimmered and shook for a moment before sending out a giant EMP. The wave rocked through the valley, disconnecting Blackwell and the other recruits from their exoskeletons.

Blackwell fell over, grappling with his suit while shouting, "Proton packs, everyone! Proton packs!"

The recruits scrambled to get a hold of their proton packs and replace their batteries.

Down below, Anabelle was being overrun by the remaining orcs at the Dark Gate, which was still active, although it did appear to be shutting down. She dodged attack after attack as the trolls and orcs tried to pummel her.

An orc fired a plasma blast at Anabelle, and she barely raised her shield in time. The blast hit her barrier, which was poorly constructed, and sent her hurtling through the air.

Abby jumped out of cover instinctively, determined to help Anabelle, but she was too far away. Then she remembered Gertrude. The preinstalled proton packs had done their job, protecting them from the EMP. She summoned her HUD as she patched herself in to take manual control of her drone.

Gertrude came zooming out of the sky, firing a flamethrower Creon and Abby had added earlier that week. A handful of orcs caught fire and ran screaming away from the Dark Gate, giving Anabelle enough space to collect herself.

The two trolls were the biggest problem at the moment. Anabelle could easily deflect the shots from the orcs, but the trolls were too aggressive to leave her alone. She drew her manna to her hand, manipulating the fire Abby had let loose, wrapping it around her own arms and sending it shooting forth, burning through a few orcs and giving her the space she needed.

This had to end now. Anabelle shouted, "Abby, I need you! Clear me space!"

Abby maneuvered her drone toward the tight group of orcs and dropped a small concussive grenade. The explosion sent the orcs, along with the two trolls, flying.

Anabelle shouted, "Squad on me!" as she slashed through the two trolls.

The recruits and Abby descended the hills, running as hard as they could toward Anabelle, Abby having forgotten she was still controlling her drone. The drone went spiraling away, straight into the Dark Gate, and she chased after it, shouting, "Gertrude!"

She ran through the Dark Gate after the drone. Abby felt her stomach pinch around her belly button, a brief moment of nausea, and then nothing. She looked around her.

Orcs surrounded her.

Anabelle burst through the Gate, the recruits and Blackwell behind her. She caught sight of the orcs and didn't waste any time attacking them. Neither did the recruits. They cut through the orcs in almost no time.

"Retreat through the Gate before it shuts," Anabelle ordered.

They obeyed, and as the recruits, Anabelle, and Abby, tried to figure out exactly what had happened, a loud screeching sound tore through the sky. Abby looked up. A bright green light flashed across the sky, and a meteor-like object could be seen behind the clouds.

"What the hell is that?" Abby said.

Anabelle seemed less concerned with the meteor than Abby was. "Don't know. Does your drone have any tracking shit on it?"

Abby nodded numbly as she stared up at the meteor-like craft. "Yeah. Yeah, it does."

"Get me a tracker on that."

Abby punched in a command on her smartwatch, and Gertrude shot out a tracking beacon with the AI's coding on it after the meteor and attached itself. That tracking beacon would be Gertrude…granted with a smaller, less capable body. But it would have her intelligence.

And because of that…whatever that thing was…Abby was going to know where it went. Which was convenient. Because the meteor craft flashed bright green and disappeared into the night.

CHAPTER TWENTY-ONE

G ertrude's tracker activated. Abby was watching through her HUD. At first, it was impossible to see anything, but slowly the drone's opticals activated. Gertrude was aboard a ship of some kind, one unlike anything Abby had ever seen.

Abby slowly guided Gertrude's tracker along, sticking close to the walls, hoping to avoid capture. As she crept along, the feed from the tracker began to jolt and freeze.

On her smartwatch, Abby hit the GPS for her tracker. Wherever the tracker had found itself, it appeared to be moving away at an alarmingly fast rate. Abby extrapolated the tracker's general location.

Gertrude was somewhere outside Earth's atmosphere.

———

Terra woke up on a mattress so prickly it felt like she was lying on coarse straw. The bearded man was gone, as were the shackles. Terra looked around. The room was small, with no furniture other than the bed. A rug on the floor. A gourd of water near the door, which was locked.

The top of Terra's head was still sore and she rubbed it, wincing as she ran her finger over the scab. When she was satisfied that her wound wasn't mortal, she drank from the gourd.

When the water touched her lips, Terra realized how thirsty she had been. It felt like years since the last time she had any water. She downed the entire gourd in a couple of seconds.

As Terra put the water gourd down, the texture of the clay door started to warp and expand. A hole formed in the clay, and then through the opening came a tray of green and gray sludge. The tray dropped on the floor.

Terra stared at the sludge for some time before deciding to smell it. The scent was repulsive, but there was something vaguely familiar there. Meat, maybe vegetables. Against her better judgment, Terra pinched her nose and scooped the sludge into her mouth.

Surprisingly, it wasn't half-bad. She carried the tray over to her cot, sat, and continued eating. When she was done, she tossed the tray on the floor and stared at the door.

After a few minutes, the door opened. Two orcs armed with axes entered the room. "Eat enough?" one of them asked.

Terra kicked the tray at the guard. "The fuck do you care?" she spat.

The orc smiled darkly, his fangs glimmering. "We're looking for a show," the orc explained. "Don't want you slacking off because you're hungry. That's some of the best chow from the kitchen. Most soldiers would be fighting for that right there."

Terra contemplated another snide remark but thought better of it. She still didn't have any idea what was going on. And, if she were honest, the sludge hadn't been half bad. "What's the show?" she finally asked.

"Abby? Do you have a read on that tracker yet?"

Anabelle was pacing back and forth, biting her lip, waiting for Abby to figure out where her tracker had gone.

Abby, on the other hand, was sitting on a rock, staring at her watch, hoping something would crop up so she could tell Anabelle anything that wasn't disappointing. "Uh, looks like it might've slipped away from Earth," Abby murmured.

Anabelle ran over to her and shouted, "What?"

"It's not my fault. I didn't know they were leaving Earth."

Anabelle laughed, covering her mouth as a fit of giggles forced their way out. She patted Abby's back for a moment before sitting down next to the girl. "I didn't think it was your fault," she explained. "Just freaking out. I just got a report from Myrddin a few seconds ago."

Abby assumed the report had something to do with her failing some unspecified requirement for the mission. "What did it say?" she asked.

"Apparently, what we saw wasn't a meteor. It was one of the Dark One's ships. A cargo ship, it turns out. They use them to pick people up for their slave colonies."

Abby had heard of those ships. The colonies as well. Creon had told her how he had escaped from the Dark One's ore mines. He'd been picked up on a ship just like the one Anabelle had described.

"They were abducting humans?" Abby asked.

Anabelle nodded wearily. "They've been doing it for years. More than half of the stories humans tell each other about alien abductions are actually the Dark One. No one knows why humans, though. They never end up in the labor camps. They just disappear."

A chill went down Abby's back. She'd never spent much time thinking about aliens before, but the idea of the Dark One just picking people up as he saw fit was disturbing.

Blackwell came over to Abby and Anabelle. "Just in from Myrddin. Told him about the whole tracking and outer space problem," he said. "He suggested that you bump up the frequency to your tracker by seven-point-three percent and bounce it off of the satellite array he's set up in the atmosphere."

Abby did a double-take as she realized the extent of Myrddin's network. "Uh, okay, I'll give it a try," she said. Then she patched into

Myrddin's satellite system and reconfigured her drone to the frequency he had suggested. "Oh, there it is."

Abby brought up a hologram of the location of the shape. She didn't recognize any of the star systems displayed on the map. "Okay, so that's where it is. Now, what are we going to do?"

CHAPTER TWENTY-TWO

A bby and Anabelle returned to HQ. The ride back was quiet. Though the mission had been a success, an air of disappointment hung over everyone. Maybe it had to do with watching a group of humans being abducted.

It was hard to celebrate after that.

The reality of abductions was a little difficult for Abby to wrap her head around. She'd spent more time than she'd be proud to admit reading about aliens and the different theories on what they could be.

Her favorite had been the theory that aliens were actually fourth- or fifth-dimensional beings who hacked human brains to help humanity realize that humans should collectively chill. Abby had never suspected that aliens were an invading force of fantasy characters.

If she thought about it, Abby wasn't sure which one sounded more ridiculous.

When SWARMMT arrived back at HQ, Blackwell and the other recruits headed to the barracks. Abby was preparing to head to her own room when Anabelle stopped her. "You and I aren't done yet," Anabelle said.

Abby looked up at Anabelle, caught off-guard by the elf's surreal beauty. "Uh…what's left?"

"We're finding those humans. We can't just leave them out there. You and Creon get together and find a way to magnify that signal."

"I already used all of Myrddin's satellites, and that barely did anything."

Anabelle and Abby walked through HQ, heading to the R&D labs. Abby called the elevator as the elf continued talking. "Yeah, I know, but that was just Myrddin's suggestion. Doesn't mean that it's the best one. The dude's a wizard, not a tech genius."

Abby blushed and stared at her feet. "I'm not a genius," she murmured bashfully. The elevator slid open, and she entered quickly.

"Call it what you want. You're pretty damn smart. So, don't quit on this one. We have an obligation to help those humans."

Abby hadn't expected Anabelle to be so dedicated to rescuing a random group of humans. She'd heard the elf mutter and grumble about her human agents. Abby had assumed Anabelle was slightly xenophobic. "So, what do you get out of helping out some stranger?"

Anabelle winced at Abby's words as if she'd been physically cut by them. "What do you mean, what do I get out of it?"

"Pa used to say nobody sticks their neck out for no reason, knowing it might get snapped. Just curious, I guess. I like you a lot, but you don't seem like the kinda person tripping over your own feet to be doing favors."

Anabelle's face softened at Abby's words. "Okay, I see what you mean. This isn't a favor. This is my job. We fight the Dark One. That fight takes on different forms all the time. Sometimes it's stabbing an orc. Other times, it's blowing up a supply depot. Other times, it's rescuing humans to keep them from a labor camp. All of it is a fight. Some are just flashier than others."

Abby considered the elf's words, rolling them around in her head, and saw how they related to her own campaign of revenge. The elevator arrived at her floor with a bing. She stepped out. "All right, I'll see what I can do."

Anabelle thought about giving Abby a hug or a high five or something humans found comforting…something to lift her spirits. But in the end, she didn't know what to do. Anything over the top wouldn't be received well, and at a loss of what to do, she hit the button for her floor and the elevator doors shut, leaving Abby alone with her thoughts and anxieties.

There hadn't been any doubt in Anabelle's voice. She must have assumed Abby was capable of taking care of finding her tracking device. Abby was used to people believing in her abilities, but this was on a whole other level. Even Abby's parents had still managed to treat Abby like a child. Abby had never complained. It felt good to know that there were people in charge, people you could trust and rely on.

Now *Abby* was the person who was being relied on. Someone's life depended on her. That was a lot of pressure to put on a seventeen-year-old.

Creon was sitting in the lab, tinkering with an exoskeleton, one of Abby's smaller drones flying around him, occasionally helping. He looked up from his work when he saw Abby. "Hey, how's it going?"

Abby fell into her chair as she sighed. "You know anything 'bout improving tracking frequencies!"

Creon took off his goggles as he leaned back in his chair. "A reasonable amount. Why do you ask?"

"Got a tracker stuck on an orcish ship. Damn thing went straight to space, then disappeared. So, I'm more than a little at a loss right now."

Creon nodded, then reached out and grabbed the drone floating around him. "It's far away now. We have to amp the signal to find it."

"Do we have the tech or power?"

Creon shrugged before getting out of his chair and hobbling over toward the holoprojector. "Don't know. Let's find out."

The goblin hadn't missed a beat, Abby noticed. He was ready to start dreaming up ways to work around a problem. Abby admired that quality. If there was one thing she wanted to learn from her time with Creon, it would be how to approach problems the way he did.

Abby left her seat and joined Creon at the holoprojector. "Yeah, let's do that."

Almost fifteen hours later, Abby and Creon succeeded. Twenty-six cups of coffee, two very heated shouting matches, and a set of tears flowing like a waterfall from Creon were all it took to figure out how to boost the tracker's signal.

Both of them were exhausted, but there was no time to rest. Abby called Anabelle as soon as both she and Creon verified that they were receiving a signal from the tracker.

Anabelle was in the lab within ten minutes. "What are we working with now?"

Abby yawned and almost fell out of her chair. Creon managed to prop her up with his foot before she slid backward.

"Gods, you two look like shit," Anabelle said as she waited for either one to answer her.

When it became apparent that Abby and Creon might be too sleep-deprived to know what was happening around them, Anabelle went to the holoprojector and began to go through their notes. None of it made sense to her. Some of the notes were in goblin, and others were in a shorthand that could only be Abby's.

"Okay, guys, you gotta tell me something." She sighed. "Like, where are they?"

"Not in our solar system," Creon said. "They activated a Gate or some sort of warp drive and got themselves into Middang3ard space. Then they landed on the orc homeworld."

"How do they have that kind of technology?" Anabelle muttered.

"Guess the Dark One is even more tooled up than we thought," Creon offered.

"So are we," Abby said, suddenly snapping awake. She leapt to her feet, ran over to the holoprojector, flipped a switch, and turned it on. "So are we. We broke down one of the other trackers. Reverse-engineered the frequency. Set up a couple of dummies on them satellites. Then we, uh, I'm not sure about what we did after that, but we have audio and video now."

"Let me see what you have."

Abby hit a couple of commands on her computer, and the holo-projector displayed what the tracker saw. A row of humans was chained to the walls. Orcs walked back and forth, talking to each other.

"Can you turn it up?" Anabelle asked.

Abby grabbed a pair of headphones and handed them over. Anabelle listened intently for a few seconds before she grabbed her chest. "They're taking them to the Arena," she said with a gasp.

"Also, this drone tracker has speakers. We can speak to them," said Abby.

"And say what?"

"I dunno, comfort them?"

Anabelle shook her head. "Until we have a plan, let's not give them hope. Best to stay hidden for now."

She handed back the headphones as Abby asked, "What's the Arena?"

"Some orc blood sport from back in the day. The Dark One revamped it when he took over the orcs. It used to be a fight to the death between warriors and monsters. Now orcs just pick up a bunch of civilians, shove them in a cage with a dozen monsters, and watch the unlucky bastards get ripped to shreds. There's no competition. No fight. They just watch a slaughter." Anabelle paced the floor, scratching the back of her head. "We're not going to be able to save any of them...not from this distance...you know...fuck it, let's broadcast it."

Abby shook her head, not quite understanding what Anabelle was saying. "What do you mean by broadcast it?"

"Myrddin wants to create awareness for the war. Me waving an orc's head didn't work. Maybe this will. Let's broadcast a human getting slaughtered by this fucked up game. That'll get people on our side."

"That's fucked up. You want to broadcast someone dying?"

Anabelle sat on one of the chairs, her eyebrows furrowed and dark as she folded her hands and rested her chin on her fingers. "Exactly. No one is going to be able to ignore that. Creon, patch us into as many televisions and computers you can. You know the drill."

Creon nodded as he swung over to his computer and started working.

Abby watched Anabelle, uncertain of how she should feel about what the elf was doing. There was still a lot she didn't understand about Annabelle.

Shackled, bound, and blindfolded, Terra was led down several hallways, ramps, stairs, and off the ship. Wherever they were taking her, it was far. Then she could hear the roar of a crowd. It was deafening. *Guess the folks love the games*, Terra thought.

Suddenly, she was halted. Her blindfold was pulled off, and her shackles detached. One of the three orcs who had led Terra there handed her a rusty mace. "Is this all that I get?" Terra asked.

The orc shoved Terra toward the steel gate ahead of her. "We don't waste the good shit on meat," the orc said. "Hopefully, your death is more glorious than your pointless life."

"Well, fuck you too!" Terra shouted at the orcs as they walked off. Then she turned her attention to the sounds coming from the other side of the gate.

The gates slid up and opened. Terra strode awkwardly out into the arena.

It was exactly as she had imagined. The arena was built in a fashion similar to the ancient Greek Colosseum, an open pit surrounded by stands for spectators. And the stands were full. There was hardly an empty seat to be found. The stands were filled with orcs, trolls, and goblins, all screaming their lungs out.

Terra spun around, overwhelmed by what she was facing. It had dawned on her that all of these creatures had gathered to watch her fight. In their minds, probably die. "I'm not going out like that," she muttered.

Across the arena, another set of steel gates opened. An eight-foot troll emerged from the darkness of its cage. The troll's fur was grayed and was missing massive chunks where the skin was scarred. The troll carried no weapons.

Terra froze. She didn't know what to do. All around her, the crowd was screaming.

The troll was a different story. It charged Terra, who barely lifted her mace in time to brace herself for the attack. That didn't matter to the troll, though. He simply grabbed her by the wrist and flung her across the arena.

She hit a wall with a heavy thud and fell to the ground. *Fuck, that hurt*, she thought as she pushed herself to her feet. *Wait a minute, that should have killed me. How the fuck did that not kill me?*

Terra took a quick mental stock of how she felt. Her ribs were annoyed at most. She wasn't out of breath. It almost felt like a child had tried to punch her in the chest. "Well, this is interesting," she said to herself. "Guess if I'm going to die, might as well live it up while I can."

She tossed her mace to the side and cracked her knuckles.

The crowd in the stands went wild. Goblins and orcs jumped to their feet, screaming with enthusiasm. An announcer's voice broke through the noise, shouting, "And it looks like Not-a-male has discarded their mace! They must want to die!"

She blocked out the sound of the crowd. The way she used to during rugby. Then she sprinted toward the troll. He was the only other person who seemed to be taking this fight seriously. He braced for the attack.

Terra flung herself through the air, tackling the troll. They both hit the ground, rolling over each other, both trying to get to their feet first. Together, they rose, their hands locked. The crowd was quiet now. Not a murmur in it all. Everyone's attention was on the fight.

The troll dug his feet into the ground and tried to swing Terra to the side.

She pivoted on her foot, shifting her weight to the other side and leaned back, pulling the troll toward her. She brought her knee up as he fell forward, ramming it into his head, breaking his jaw. As the troll stumbled back, Terra slipped behind him and wrapped her arms around his neck.

He reached up and clawed at Terra's face, trying to gouge out her eyes. It was only a matter of time until he succeeded. His arms were long enough. This had to end soon.

Terra closed her eyes and tried not to think too much about what she was going to do. She grabbed the troll's jaw with one hand and rested the other on the back of his neck. Then she twisted with all of her strength, strength she had never had on Earth. Seemed that wherever she'd been taken, the place made her stronger.

The troll struggled, but Terra didn't stop twisting. She was strong. Stronger than she had ever been in her entire life. And she knew, beyond a shadow of a doubt, she was stronger than this troll.

Terra let out a scream of pure rage and snapped the troll's neck. She dropped his body as the crowd watched in silence.

Out in the crowd, an old troll got to his feet. He let out a roar that echoed through the arena, then he clapped. Soon the entire arena was filled with the roaring and clapping of goblins, orcs, and trolls. Chants of "Not-a-male" rose louder and louder.

Terra stepped over the body of the troll, a smile crossing her face. *Maybe this isn't going to be too bad,* she thought.

CHAPTER TWENTY-THREE

HQ's lounge was a small, private affair. Dim, red lights illuminated the sparse chairs and tables in the lounge. There rarely was a bartender. Instead, each table had been enchanted to magically provide a drink at the press of a button—one of Myrddin's prouder accomplishments.

The wizard swore the magical program could make a Whiskey Sour better than any bartender across the nine realms. Anabelle barely spent any time in the lounge, but when she did stop by, she couldn't disagree with Myrddin.

She sat there now, nursing a Moscow Mule. It was the only human cocktail she could stomach. Drinking elvish wine didn't sound appealing at all. Too many memories, too many stories. A stiff drink that could take care of that problem was a better choice.

The Mule kicked hard. Anabelle grimaced at the burn in her throat and stomach, but she pushed on.

The door to the lounge swung open, and Roy walked through. His perfect posture had always caught Anabelle's eye. The man looked like he'd spent his entire childhood standing against a wall. It was impossible to imagine him as anything other than some form of military.

Roy sat at Anabelle's table and looked over the menu. He knocked twice on the table, and an aged whiskey on the rocks appeared in front of him. He took a sip and gagged. "You'd think it'd be hard to mess up a whiskey neat," he grumbled. "And yet, every time, this spell sneaks one ice cube into my drink. Almost a waste of good whiskey."

"Isn't it a little early for you to be drinking?"

Roy tossed back the shot of whiskey and ordered another. "It's late someplace in one of these realms. Besides, I'm not here to get tossed. Just wanted to pay you a compliment. Your plan worked."

Anabelle didn't meet Roy's eyes. Instead, she watched her finger circle the rim of her copper cup. "What are you talking about?" she asked.

"You don't have to play coy."

Roy turned on the television set across from their table. CNN was broadcasting Terra's fight on a loop, the two analysts giving commentary. Roy flipped to another station. Pretty much the same thing. He ran through a dozen more channels. It was all anyone was talking about.

Anabelle tried to look surprised. "Why do you think I would—"

"Because I'm not stupid. And it wasn't a bad idea. Myrddin is pissed off, obviously, but people are on board."

Roy changed the channel again. This time, people were marching in the streets, holding signs that said, "Free Terra!" or "Abduct us and we'll kick your ass!"

Anabelle chuckled as she read the protestors' signs. She continued to watch the demonstration. "What do the humans think is going on?" she asked.

Roy sipped his drink, his eyes narrowing as if he were trying to decide what Anabelle needed to know. "Pretty scattered opinions, to be honest. Some people think it's aliens. Others think that our universe is colliding with a book. But people believe it's real. Hashtag Dark One is trending all over the world."

"What are we going to do with the groundswell?"

Roy appeared to relax some. Anabelle always had a hard time

figuring out his body language. It didn't seem to ever match up with what he was going to say. "Myrddin's already on it. He's merchandising Terra. That fight was bigger than any recorded sports event in human history. People are eating it up."

Anabelle picked at her fingernails as she said, "His plan is to turn Terra into a franchise? What the hell is he thinking?"

"He's actually thinking this through. Sure, showing everyone what's going on out there is a great idea, but people need context. He's creating a story, something the average person can wrap their head around. That's what humanity needs. Terra's a hero as far as they're concerned. And the more Terra crap out there, the more in your face to humanity the situation becomes."

Anabelle couldn't disagree with Roy. It wasn't any different than what any other group did prior to a war. Propaganda. That's all it was. At least Myrddin was going about it in a positive way. It would have been easy to turn humanity against orcs and goblins. Humans did it with each other all the time.

That would have been shortsighted, though. And it wouldn't have helped. It had been a goblin who helped figure out how to show the world what Terra was going through. Anabelle didn't want to admit it, Myrddin might have a better grasp of subtlety.

Roy stood and finished the last of his drink. "You should be proud of your girl. She really came through on this one. And yourself. I know you don't feel like Myrddin appreciates what you do, but he does. He's just an old stubborn ass. Anyways, I think you're earning your keep."

"Thanks. More than you, I'm guessing. What exactly do you do here?"

Roy laughed as he strode toward the door. "What don't I do is the real question. You have a good night. And don't be like Myrddin. Let Abby know what you're thinking. Don't assume she'll figure it out for herself. Later."

Roy left Anabelle alone with her thoughts and the television. She watched the people in the streets, listened to them chanting. They thought a war was coming. They didn't know it was already here. But they looked ready. Maybe not as ready as Abby had been, but ready nonetheless. Anabelle saw a soldier in each one of their eyes, an army waiting in the streets.

CHAPTER TWENTY-FOUR

A blindfold covered Terra's eyes, and a sword was pressed against the back of her neck, driving her forward. She stumbled over her feet, but unlike when she had been brought into the coliseum, a hand would reach out and help her stay on her feet.

Wherever Terra was being led, it was farther away than her first holding area. She felt like she had walked nearly twice the distance. That could have just been because she was tired, though. Fighting a troll had been one of the most exhilarating experiences of her life. She was having an adrenaline crash at the moment. If there had been another fight lined up, she would have jumped at the chance.

Finally, Terra heard a door open, and she was shoved inside. The blindfold was ripped off. She was in a small stone room with a cot covered in straw and blankets. A stone toilet sat in the corner, where the shadows were thickest.

There were no chains, and the room had a door instead of bars. Two orcs stood in the doorway. "You fought well today," one of them said. "Never seen a human plucked off the streets fight like that. Hell, never seen a pedestrian orc fight that hard before."

The two orcs slammed their fists to their chest and barked something in orcish at Terra. She had no idea what they had said, but it didn't sound threatening. "What now?" she asked, trying to sound confident.

"You are a champion today. Tomorrow you will fight again, and we will see if you are a champion tomorrow. And if you continue to be champion, all orcs will know your name."

Terra's heart raced. There was going to be another fight tomorrow. She wanted it more than anything else in the world. She'd never felt such a strong desire for something. And they would know her name. They would remember her. "Good," she said. "Looking forward to it."

The orcs smiled at each other as they chuckled. "They don't even make human men like this one," one of the orcs said. "Let's get her fed. Cecile! Food now!"

After a couple of moments, Cecile, a small goblin, came limping over to the door. He held a tray of freshly grilled meats. Terra didn't recognize any of the meats, but she knew the smell of good food instantly.

Cecile handed the plate of food to one of the orcs who entered the cell and handed it to her. He held his hand to his chest once more before saying, "This is the sign of the orc. It is a sign meant for orc to orc."

Terra's mouth watered, but she ignored the food for a second. "But I'm not an orc," she countered.

"Today, we all watched an orc kill a troll."

Terra nodded and took a bite of the steaming meat before pressing her fist to her heart. "Tomorrow."

"Tomorrow. Tomorrow, you fight a Balrog."

"What the hell is that?"

"An ancient being whom light itself is afraid of. If you survive tomorrow, you may be much more than an orc."

The orc turned and took a large jug from Cecile, who had returned carrying another tray. He handed the jug to Terra and left, closing the door behind him.

Terra sat in the dark of her cell, thinking as she felt her knuckles. They hurt, but the pain was nothing she couldn't handle. The fight in the coliseum had happened so fast, she'd hardly had a moment to process it. She'd won her first fight—the first fight of her entire life. She'd never really fought before. It felt good.

She was powerful. Something had stood in her way, had threatened her, and now it was dead. This was a very different feeling than her entire existence on Earth. Terra realized at that moment that no one was ever going to walk over her again. She was done being a doormat. If someone tried to take something from her, she was going to break them.

Terra took another bite from her plate, savoring the salty flavors of the meat as she sat on her bed and leaned against the wall. This place wasn't ideal. But she could survive this. She'd never thought of herself as a survivor before. No, she wasn't going to leave it at that. Terra would do more than survive here. She was going to thrive.

The jug the orc had given her was filled with something that smelled like sour bread and tasted like piss, but it had enough of a kick to cross Terra's eyes for a second. "Goddamn." She whistled as she took another sip. "Goddamn, indeed."

Creon and Abby were glued to the computer screens. They'd both been constantly monitoring the tracker Abby had snuck aboard the ship. Creon might have been facing his computer screen, but he had passed out some time ago. Abby, on the other hand, had managed to talk Anabelle into brewing some coffee and dropping it off every couple of hours.

Abby checked the time. Anabelle was due to show up soon with more coffee.

On the screen, Terra was lying in her bed, staring up at the ceiling. She had her hands folded over her chest and looked peaceful. Abby wondered what could be going through Terra's mind right now, millions of miles away from home. What was she thinking?

The door to the lab whizzed open, and Anabelle entered, holding three cups of coffee. She placed one on Creon's desk and the other two on Abby's. "Didn't think he'd be the first one to clock out," the elf said as she sat.

Abby sipped her coffee and then cracked her knuckles. "He's been pulling a lot of all-nighters. I don't think he slept the entire time we were working on Martin. Hey, I wanted to ask you something."

Anabelle studied Abby over the rim of her cup, the steam from the coffee fogging her designer glasses. "What's up, kid?" she asked.

"Why'd you decide to show the world Terra's fight? You thought she was gonna die. Why show that to people?"

"You think I'm callous, don't you? Or a sociopath. Well, I'm neither. Just cynical. Sometimes the only reason anyone will get up and do something is when they're reminded of how frightening and terrible the world can be. That's what I was trying to show them."

Abby turned her attention back to the screen. "But you didn't. People saw something else. And got all inspired."

"Was it positive motivation that got you to join?"

Abby swallowed the lump in her throat. "No," she replied.

"Exactly. People might be thrilled with Terra, but don't hold your breath when it comes to signing up."

"Yeah, I feel you. People got a funny way of losing interest once it's their life on the line. Seen it happen enough. Everyone's talking 'bout how much they hate wolves killing cattle. They're usually the last folk to grab a rifle."

Anabelle got up and stood behind Abby, resting her hand on the girl's shoulder. "Exactly. That's all I'm saying. I'm glad people know a fraction of what's going on. But I don't think that means we're going to be getting any more help. Hey, can you get closer?"

Abby blushed as she turned back to look at Anabelle. "Wait, what?" she stammered.

The elf pointed at the computer screen. "To Terra. I want to hear what she's muttering. Is she sleeping or something?"

Abby tried to catch her breath and cursed herself for whatever had just happened. She still wasn't certain. But she turned her attention back to the computer screen. Terra was indeed moving her lips as though she were talking. There wasn't anyone else in the room, though.

"Yeah, we can get closer," Abby said at last.

Abby maneuvered the tracker closer to investigate who Terra was speaking to.

In the empty cell, Terra was praying. It was an old habit she fell back on whenever she felt overwhelmed, and that perfectly described her current feelings. All the confidence she had been reveling in had vanished without a trace. Now there was only intense fear and despair.

Terra was never aware of praying. Even if she tried, she wouldn't have been able to recall the words of grace on her lips that calmed her heart. It was probably better that way.

What Terra was aware of was the tracker flittering through the air toward her. She reached and snatched the tracker out of the air and held it up to see better.

"Now what the hell is this thing?" she murmured. "Someone fucking creeping on me?"

A voice came through the tracker. It was Abby's. "Wait, hold on, hold on. No one's creeping on you. We're trying to help," she explained. "We saw the ship and got this tracker on it. And then we saw you."

Anabelle's voice came over the tracker next. "Yeah, we're the good guys. We've been trying to figure out how to get you home."

Terra smiled to herself. "This is my home now," she replied.

"What? Are you serious?"

"Hell-fucking-no. I got abducted by fantasy creatures who are forcing me to fight in a fucked-up arena, and I think one of them has a crush on me. This is as far from home as I can think of."

Anabelle cracked up as the tracker flew away from Terra's palm. "Good. We're trying to figure something out. We'll be in touch, all right? Be safe."

"Yeah, as safe as I can be when fighting a balrog."

"What's that?" Abby asked.

Anabelle sighed. "It's a big monster made mostly of fire with a whip."

"Any weak spots?"

"Like anything, hit it often and hit it hard."

Terra smirked. "That I can do."

Anabelle grinned. She really liked this human.

The tracker hung up and flew over to the windowsill where it landed, looking as inconspicuous as a fly.

Terra sighed and shook her head. Things just kept getting weirder and weirder. It was time to get some sleep. At least her dreams would be weird in a way she understood.

CHAPTER TWENTY-FIVE

It was around noon when Terra woke up. She went to the window of her cell and looked out. Three suns stared back at her. That would explain why she was covered in a thin layer of sweat.

The tracker she had spoken to last night still sat on the windowsill. It beeped on when she walked away.

A million light-years away, Abby and Anabelle woke to the sound of the computer's alarm going off, letting them know Terra was awake. Anabelle grabbed the microphone and said, "Hey, hey, good morning."

On the alien planet, Terra turned around as the tracker floated away from the windowsill. "Uh, good morning," she managed.

"Sorry, I don't think me and Abby are morning people. She still hasn't opened her eyes. She's just making this weird face. Like, her mouth is open, and she's kinda drooling."

Terra laughed as Abby shouted over the tracker, "I am not drooling! Wait, am I drooling?"

Terra sat down on her bed, watching the beam of light from her window. "And you two are supposed to be the ones to save me?" she asked.

Anabelle scoffed loudly, and the sound gave Terra the impression that she'd made a faux pas. "Well, we're the ones who tracked you to an entirely different solar system and figured out how to talk to you," Anabelle countered. "So, yeah, that's us."

"When you put it like that, it *is* pretty impressive."

"You don't have to tell us. Trust me, we both know. Maybe Abby doesn't, but I do. You *do* know it's impressive, right, Abby?"

Abby mumbled something groggily before a loud smack echoed, like that of flesh hitting a table. "Oh. I think she needs more coffee," Anabelle said.

"More coffee!" Abby sang.

Anabelle giggled, but her voice quickly returned to its businesslike tone. "Okay, so I'm just going to throw this out there. I think you'd make a great addition to our team, once we come get you and everything."

Terra was intrigued by the idea. She honestly had no idea what they meant by that, but she didn't really have any clue about what was going on. Other than the fact that the arena was a place that was very okay with her dying, while these new guys seemed to want her to live. "What kind of team?" Terra asked.

"Those assholes who abducted you? They're part of an invasion that's—"

"Oh, you mean like that model who said she was an elf on TV?"

"Terra. I'm that elf model."

Terra was quiet as she mulled over what Anabelle had just said. When she'd seen the news reports, she hadn't taken the idea of elves and orcs seriously. Now it would be stupid to doubt. "And you're fighting the person who's responsible for stuff like this?" Terra asked.

"That's the only reason we exist. Me, Abby, and a bunch of other idiots. You'd be a good fit. You look like you can handle yourself."

"All right, I'm in."

Abby's voice perked up over the comm again, still sounding half-asleep. "Welcome to SWARMMT, or is it SWARRMT? Or three...like swaaaaaarmt."

Terra couldn't keep her opinion to herself. "Okay, that's a terrible name. Easily the worst name for a team I've ever heard."

Abby and Anabelle were laughing too hard to talk. "I know!" Abby finally managed. "We said it was bonkers, but we're not allowed to change it yet. But you're in?"

"Yeah. You guys sound like you know how to have a good time. If I survive this, at least."

There was a polite knock on the door of Terra's cell, and it creaked open. Cecile held another bottle of the piss liquor Terra had drunk before and a slab of steak. He stepped gingerly into the cell and handed Terra her breakfast.

"The battle begins in half an hour, m'lady. Good luck," he said.

Terra bit into the steak. It was mostly raw and very chewy. "Shit, I completely forgot about my life-threatening match," she muttered.

The tracker flew over to Terra and zoomed around her head. "Don't worry about it," Abby offered. "We're gonna help you. This'll be easy as a pig castration."

"Uh, is that easy?"

"You ever see a pig's balls? Ain't ever seen anyone miss them."

Cecile returned after a bit and took Terra with him. Orcs were lined up on both sides of her, staring at her with a measure of respect she'd never been aware of anyone bestowing upon her.

It felt good.

But maybe the orcs were just smugly appreciating Terra's impending death. That was a less flattering idea.

She stood before the main door to the coliseum. One of the orcs at her side handed her a kite shield almost the size of her body. The orc across from him asked Terra her preference for a weapon.

The orcs to Terra's right were holding a variety of weapons. One stood out to her among all of them. It was a single blade held between two iron rods with one rod running through the middle. Terra slipped her hand in and grabbed the rod. The blade split into three smaller blades.

The orc who had held the *katar* nodded and said, "Beautiful choice."

Terra pulled the rod again, and the three blades recombined to make one. "Fuck, yeah. I think so too," she exclaimed.

The tracker came over and landed behind Terra's ear. Abby's voice came through. "All right, we just want you to know we're gonna be here for you, helping however we can. All right?" she coached.

Terra nodded as she grabbed her *katar* and strapped on a backup weapon, a sword. Then she stared at the door, waiting for it to open. "Yeah, I know. We got this."

The door to the coliseum opened, and Terra strode out into the blinding light. Orcs and goblins filled the seats, and they were chanting "Not-a-Male." Terra raised her shield, and the crowd burst into applause.

"Aren't they supposed to be the bad guys?" Terra asked. "How come they like me so much?"

The tracker beeped as Anabelle answered, "They're orcs. No matter whose side they're on, they respect a good fighter. That's why, historically, it's been hard to get orcs to join any one army. They prize fighters over any kind of ideology. Usually. I haven't seen this in a while."

On the opposite side of the coliseum, the large double gates swung open. Something that looked like a small sun glowed in the darkness of the hallway. Then a jet of fire came spewing out of the darkness.

Out walked the balrog. It stood nearly seven feet tall, its entire body made of fire and molten lava that somehow maintained the form of a humanoid creature, with black wings of ash that stretched out, hellish and batlike. The balrog held a whip of fire, and it cracked its weapon, sending a slice of fire flying through the air.

Terra's blood went cold in her veins. She stared at the balrog as it roared. "How exactly do I kill this thing, Anabelle?" she asked.

The tracker swooped around Terra's head, and Anabelle said, "I was trying to be encouraging, but we'll figure something out."

The balrog roared again, beating its fiery fists on its chest. Terra, having no idea what else to do, slammed her *katar* to her shield and returned the roar. Then she charged the balrog.

PART II

CHAPTER TWENTY-SIX

The three suns beamed down on the coliseum. Goblins and orcs screeched, filling the air with their desire for violence, the dearest and most perfect form, that which has not come but soon will. It makes the blood pump and the throat clench. The purest form of anticipation.

In the arena below were two creatures. One was a demon older than most universes, a beast born from the flames of dead worlds who was the scourge of the nine realms. The balrog snapped its whip as it roared, staring its opponent down.

The other was a human. Small in comparison, her hair was buzzed to the skull, and she held only a shield and a *katar*, nervously opening and closing the weapon's tri-blade. She'd seen the same thing done in movies, producing a much more intimidating effect. All it did for Terra was make her feel small.

Terra felt like she'd been staring down the balrog for nearly an hour. The balrog had only advanced one step, and that seemed to have been a lifetime ago. Now the balrog was taking another step, cracking its whip again.

Death had never occurred to Terra before. She'd only thought about it briefly. Something that happened to people around her and would eventually come for her. Death was not something she had dwelled on.

Now Terra wished she had paid more attention to death. It seemed to be in the form of the balrog before her. She didn't think there was any way she was going to get out of this alive.

As Terra stared down the balrog, millions of light-years away, a young girl named Abby-Lynn from a farm in Utah sat beside Anabelle Chase, a five-hundred-year-old elf wearing earrings pressed from the finest dwarfish gold.

The pair had their eyes glued to the giant holoscreen in front of them. Abby held a wireless keyboard in her lap as Anabelle picked at her cuticles. "She really gonna fight that thing?" Abby asked.

Anabelle raised her hands so she could inspect her nails. "I don't think they brought a balrog in to have a friendly conversation," Anabelle chided. "Does that tracker have a camera on it?"

"Of course. How d'ya think we're looking at this?"

"Right. Stupid question. I want you to broadcast this fight too. To as many different outlets as you can."

Abby pulled herself away from the holoscreen long enough to narrow her eyes at the elf. "I'm trying to run this tracker from a couple light-years away and not get caught up in lag. If you can't tell, it's kinda a handful."

Anabelle hit the comm hanging from her ear. "Wake Creon up," she barked. "We need him."

A familiar voice answered—Blackwell, a new human recruit who could actually keep up with her demands. "On it, Ms. Chase," he replied, approaching the sleeping goblin carefully and gently nudging him awake.

Anabelle stood, then paced around the lab for a few moments before flopping down in her seat beside Abby. She tapped her foot on the floor loudly enough to catch Abby's attention. "Worse than a cricket stuck in your room," Abby muttered under her breath.

Anabelle clicked her tongue and swung her chair around, giving Abby a gentle push. "You're going to have to get much more direct with your confrontational communication if we're going to be working together," Anabelle said.

"Stop fidgeting and sit still so I can concentrate! This tracker ain't driving itself."

Abby thought Anabelle was going to say something, but the elf held her tongue. Guess that was the kind of communication Anabelle needed. Now Abby could focus on what was happening on what looked like the other side of the galaxy.

As Abby tried to figure out the best place to maneuver the tracker, Creon woke with a jolt.

Anabelle gave Creon's disheveled appearance the side-eye, as if she were offended he wasn't more put together. "We need help dealing with a transdimensional lag issue," she snapped.

Creon stretched, yawning so widely that they could see his tonsils. Once his yawn subsided, he gave them a bored look before saying, "Is that all?"

Terra was squaring off with the balrog. They were circling each other, having closed the distance between them. The heat coming off the creature was nearly unbearable. It was worse than a terrible smell. Terra was still a good fifteen feet from it, and she was soaked with sweat.

The balrog leaned forward, smoke billowing from its red and black eyes. The crowd in the stands cheered, their bloodlust apparent in their voices. Yet they seemed ready to wait for the bloodshed. It seemed obvious who they thought was going to end up dead.

The stands filled with the chant, "Kill Not-a-Male!" Terra had almost forgotten the mixup about her gender. *Of all the days to shave my head,* she thought.

A lash of fire like a solar flare came off the balrog. Terra raised her shield and the flames whipped her, pushing her back. She was surprised she could withstand something like that. Then she remembered she was stronger here than back on Earth. That gave her some encouragement. Not much, though.

She was tired of this dance. She wasn't going to wait for the balrog to make the first move. If this was a fight, it was going to be *her* fight. Terra sprinted toward the balrog, only vaguely aware she'd never fought with anything like a *katar*. What the hell, though. She'd never been in a real fight until a day ago, either.

The balrog was caught off-guard by Terra's sudden explosion of aggressiveness. It stepped back, prompting the crowd to cheer even louder.

Terra leapt through the air, pulled down on the rod of her *katar* to combine the three blades into one, and slashed at the balrog's face. The creature raised its whip in the nick of time, deflecting the attack as it staggered back, repositioning itself. Then it lashed out again, the air burning as Terra raised her shield, warding off the strike.

Instead of backing away, Terra sidestepped to the left and rushed the balrog, cutting at its chest as it raised its whip and blocked her attack. The demon continued to stumble backward, and Terra backhanded it with her shield.

The balrog was off balance. Terra leapt at it again, hoping to end the fight right there.

As she flew toward the balrog, it unfurled its wings, flapping them. Caught up in the wind generated by its wings, Terra went hurtling backward. She landed hard and skidded across the ground.

The balrog rushed forward, still flapping its wings to give it more speed. It hit Terra like a freight train, sending her flying across the arena. She slammed into the stone walls separating the stands from the fighting pit.

Terra rolled over and got to one knee. She coughed and spat blood, but she was still standing. Honestly, she was surprised she was still alive. Even more so, she was pissed. And she now knew she could take a hit from the balrog.

The crowds were still cheering loudly, and Terra turned to face the spectators behind her. Orcs and goblins, a few creatures Terra couldn't recognize. All of them screaming either for her or the balrog to win. Even though Terra knew she was nothing more than a brief flicker of entertainment for the afternoon, she still wanted them chanting her name. She had heard it yesterday, and she wanted more.

Terra returned her attention to the balrog. The thing was a good two heads taller than her and made out of fire. How was she going to bring something like that down? The orcs had said it was an ancient bane of their existence. All Terra could claim to be was a walking doormat from a small town.

Maybe this is where I change that, Terra thought. *Maybe this is the place I learn how to kill demons.*

Terra slammed her fist to her chest as the orcs had done to her back at her cell. The orcs in the stands returned the gesture, shouting, "Not-a-Male! Not-a-Male!"

She screamed back, "Not-a-Male!" before running toward the balrog. The fire demon cracked his whip at Terra, who raised her shield. She leapt forward and rolled under the balrog's leg, ignoring the heat. Then she sliced its heel.

The balrog gave a hollow scream of pain and fell forward. Its wings spread out, knocking Terra back as flashes of fire burst from the wound. *Here's my chance,* Terra thought as she lunged.

Terra landed on the balrog's back, dropped her shield, wrapped her hand around the creature's neck, and drove her *katar* into its throat.

At the last minute, a layer of molten lava spurted from the balrog's skin, covering its neck with a thick layer of armor. Terra's attack had achieved nothing.

The balrog spread its wings and took to the air as it roared, its body bursting into flames.

Terra screamed as the fire seared her skin, but she did not let go. She struck the demon's neck again, to no avail.

The balrog rolled in the air, repositioning itself to grab hold of Terra as it climbed higher and higher.

Terra made the mistake of looking down. The creature had dragged her nearly five feet above the highest stand in the coliseum. Then it dropped her.

The wind rushed past Terra as she tried to figure out what to do. There weren't any options. Nothing to grab onto. No magical spell to remember from a past life, only the ground rushing toward her and the eventual splat of her guts forcing their way out of her body, her bones cracking upon impact.

Terra hit the ground hard, and the coliseum went quiet. The balrog screeched from on high.

Abby and Anabelle watched the dust settling. The lab was crammed behind them. Blackwell, the recruits, and just about everyone else who didn't have a mandatory station were watching the fight.

Creon had rigged all of HQ's monitors to play it. Anyone who needed access to their computer had to message Creon directly. Unless your work was of the utmost importance, you were watching Terra fight.

Myrddin and Roy were the only two who had initially opted out. After twenty minutes or so, Roy had come down to the lab and taken a spot behind Anabelle, resting his hand on her computer chair. "Might need my computer later on," he'd told Creon. "But I don't want to miss this."

The humans had been cheering their asses off. That was up until a few minutes ago. Now there was a reverent hush over the entire lab. Everyone in the room had received some kind of combat training. They'd been told how dangerous certain creatures were. They knew a human couldn't walk into a fight with a balrog and walk away alive. Still, they'd hoped.

Abby grabbed Anabelle's knee. "Should we turn it off? Should people be seeing this?"

Anabelle shook her head as she leaned back in her chair, casually reaching up and touching Roy's hand. "No, we keep it going. Everyone needs to see what the Dark One is doing to humans. If she dies, humanity needs to see who was responsible. She's an everyman. A stand-in for all humans."

Abby tried not to watch Anabelle holding Roy's fingertips. Instead, she focused all of her attention on the holoprojector. On Terra. "She's ain't getting up," Abby whispered. "Maybe humanity just saw her die."

"No," Anabelle said. "She's not dead yet."

At the back of the room, Blackwell scoffed. "What do you mean? Did you see that fall? How the hell could she survive that?" he asked. "She's not even wearing any armor."

Anabelle turned to find Blackwell, who hid behind a group of recruits. "She's not on Earth anymore, idiot," Anabelle said sharply. "There are nine realms that circle Middang3ard, the central realm...or as one of your writers put it, Middle Earth. But this isn't like nine planets orbiting the sun. The nine realms exist in separate dimensions, and it is the dimensions that orbit Middang3ard. Every realm is connected to Middang3ard, either through magic or technology, but interdimensional travel is still tricky. Terra isn't in this realm anymore. Her exceptional strength is being shown. In the other realms, humans are much stronger than they are here, without the pathetic limitations of the Earth realm. The fact that she can do what she can do proves she is not here anymore."

Although Abby was still stealing glances at Anabelle's elegant fingers lying atop Roy's gnarled digits, the elf's words piqued her curiosity. "Wait, are you saying humans are stronger off Earth?"

"Exactly. Every race experiences reality differently outside their realm. Elves get magically stronger but physically weaker. Dwarves live longer. Goblins have an odd fascination with shiny things. Humans get stronger, and that strength is tied to their wills. A strong will makes a strong human."

"So, no need for exosuits off-world?"

"I'd generally say yeah, but don't tell that to the jackasses back there."

Combat flashed through Abby's mind. She remembered how weak she had felt, watching an orc tower over her father. All she had were her drones. She could see herself now, covered in the blood of those who had wronged her.

A cheer went up from the recruits in the lab and broke Abby out of her revenge fantasies. On the holoprojector, Terra was pushing herself to her feet. *That'll have to wait,* Abby thought. *I got business to attend to right now.*

Terra was standing—shakily, but standing, nonetheless. She picked up her shield and spat blood into the sand before beating her chest and letting out a hearty shout as she pointed her *katar* at the balrog above her.

The balrog returned the scream as it furled its wings. Then it came rocketing down at Terra.

There wasn't time to move. Instead, Terra raised her shield, squared her feet, and prepared for impact.

The balrog hit the shield hard, emitting a shockwave of fire that spread through the entire arena. Terra dug her feet into the ground as the force of the attack almost drove her to her knees, but she did not yield. The ground around her cracked, but she did not yield.

Terra shoved back with everything she had, flinging the balrog off her. As it floated away, no doubt stunned its attack hadn't flattened its target, Terra flung herself through the air, landed on the demon's chest, and punched it in the face with her *katar.*

The balrog grabbed Terra and tossed her away. The two combatants landed a few feet from each other. Terra spat as the balrog heaved a sigh of smoke.

The tracker was positioned on Terra's shoulder, giving the lab and the viewers on Earth a front-row seat to the horrors of her battle with the balrog. She could hear a faint noise coming from the tracker. "What the hell is that?" Terra wondered aloud.

Abby's voice came through over the speaker. "It's us. Everyone's cheering for you. The whole world's cheering for you."

Terra chuckled. She couldn't remember anytime anyone had cheered for her before. It felt good. She was going to give Earth something to keep cheering for.

She raised her shield and shouted at the balrog, "Is that all you fucking got? I thought you were supposed to be an ancient evil or something? I thought people were afraid of you. When are you going to fucking bring it?"

The balrog barreled toward Terra, incensed by her mocking. It kicked at her, but she easily sidestepped the attack. Then it brought its lash down. She threw herself to the right and rolled away, and the whip tore the ground open.

Terra hadn't noticed how slow the balrog was. Dodging its attacks would be easy enough, but she didn't seem capable of hurting the beast. She could already see how this was going to turn out. She'd eventually get tired and sloppy. All it would take to kill her after that would be a couple of strikes from the creature.

That thing hit hard.

The balrog swiped at Terra with its whip again. This time she stepped to the side, tossed down her shield, and grabbed the whip.

The crowd went wild, screaming and chanting, "Not-a-Male!" so loudly Terra thought they were down in the arena with her.

Terra wrestled the balrog for its whip. The creature didn't want to give it up. That didn't matter to her. She knew she wanted the whip more than the balrog did.

As the two rolled over each other, the balrog's flames scorching Terra's skin, she punched it in the face with her *katar*. The demon returned the favor, smashing its free fist into Terra's face, but she didn't let go. She pulled as hard as she could, and the whip went flying.

Once Terra got the whip away from the balrog, she kicked off it and went tumbling backward. She scrambled to her feet, searching for the whip. It was a good distance from her and the balrog. That was one less thing to worry about.

The crowd was standing and shouting, banging on their shields or clacking their weapons together.

Terra squared up against the balrog again, slammed her fist to her chest, and roared loud enough to silence the crowd's cheers.

CHAPTER TWENTY-SEVEN

In every bar, living room, and doctor's office, people could not ignore the battle happening in "who the hell knows where," as they were all saying. It was a worldwide phenomenon. All of humanity tuned into one experience.

Much like the rest of the world, everyone in the lab was biting their nails, pacing, doing anything to blow off their anxious energy. At least for the folk who had the common decency not to bet on Terra or the balrog.

The same didn't hold up for the rest of the world. Terra was obviously the underdog, and more than enough humans had bet against her. But even those individuals were probably still hoping Terra came out on top. If a human could beat a creature like that, what else could humans do?

It was a question Abby couldn't care less about. Terra losing wasn't an option. Abby was going to make sure of it. The problem was she only had one way to interact with Terra. The tracker. And more often, the tracker was preoccupied with recording Terra.

Abby sighed, her frustration becoming more apparent to everyone in the room. Not that there was a joyous attitude at all. Everyone was all nerves and shaking legs. Even Anabelle, who usually managed to stay calm—not counting her angry outbursts—was noticeably anxious.

There had to be something Abby could do to help Terra out.

Anabelle crossed and uncrossed her legs as she leaned forward. "Abby is there anything you can do to help?" she asked. "I feel like we're just filming her. We're the only people anywhere who can help her right now. Can that thing do anything?"

Abby laughed to herself. Maybe elves could read minds too. "Exactly what I was thinking," she answered. "But that tracker's the size of a fly. And weaponless. Can't seem to think of a way we could use it to do anything other than annoy Terra."

Then the idea came to Abby. The tracker had advanced diagnostics abilities. If it was able to send video from wherever Terra was, that meant it would be able to send diagnostic data too. And Abby could send signals back. At the very least, Abby could possibly find the balrog's weak spot.

Abby spun her chair around and slid over to her computer. She grabbed the VR headset she'd used to control her drones the day she ran into Anabelle. It took a few moments for the headset to sync to the tracker, then it was down to business. Abby slid on the gloves to control the tracker and relay commands.

Through the tracker's eyes, she could see the balrog. It still hadn't advanced on Terra. Maybe the demon was trying to devise its own strategies as well. Whatever. That just gave Abby time to get in closer and see if she could find anything to use against it.

Abby guided the tracker across the arena and zipped around behind the balrog. She started scanning. Across from her, Creon had taken the hint and was back at his desk, beginning to receive information on the balrog.

"Balrogs got any general weaknesses?" Abby called.

Blackwell was the first to answer, much to Abby's surprise. "Not any that are applicable in this fight, Miss," he called out. "Balrogs are susceptible to different kinds of water magic and light magic as well. Any tech that replicates that works."

The soldier was right. None of those weaknesses applied. Abby had heard humans couldn't use magic without a ton of loopholes, and they weren't in a position to exploit any of them. At the moment, all they had to depend on was Terra's raw strength and determination. They were asking a lot.

Creon was printing out ream after ream of paper, standing on top of his computer monitor and trying to read each sheet as soon as it came out. "That isn't entirely true," Creon corrected. "Each balrog is its own...I guess you could say, own sort of demon. Much like humans or goblins."

Anabelle had started to pay attention to the conversation behind her and briefly broke away from the holoprojector. "What are you trying to say, Creon?" she snapped.

"I mean, each of us has our own weaknesses. Individual ones. I have a bad hip. Blackwell has carpal tunnel syndrome. Things of that sort. We can scan the balrog for anything like that. Figure out what ails that particular creature. Everyone has one. Demons aren't any different."

Abby only half-heard what Creon had said. She was busy going through the schematics of the tracker she and Creon had built. There had to be some kind of hardware she could use to her advantage. The only options she could see that were potentially useful were the tracker's speakers and its small assortment of nanobots.

The nanobots would have been a much more viable option if Creon had listened to Abby and doubled the number the tracker could hold. At the moment, the nanobots weren't capable of any large constructions. The most they could do was triple the size of the tracker or create a small attachment. Not a lot of room for creativity.

Creon jumped off his computer and ran over to Abby's desk. "Look at this," he said, eyes wide. "This balrog has extremely sensitive ears." Then Creon's smile faded. "That's it. That's its only weakness."

Abby beamed at the information and slapped her knee. "Perfect. You couldn't have said anything more perfect," she exclaimed.

"Oh, really?"

Abby pulled down her VR headset and blocked out everything

around her. She directed the nanobots to start building an attachment: a high-frequency speaker to connect to the back of the tracker.

All Abby had to do was keep the tracker out of the balrog's sight, but that would be easy enough. The balrog was huge and only seemed to be interested in Terra. The two combatants were still staring each other down.

Abby simply hoped it wouldn't take too long for the construction to finish. She had no idea how the lag between worlds was going to affect the tracker. The fact that it was working so well now seemed like nothing more than luck. And luck never held. That was what Pa used to say.

The VR display showed the completion percentage for the construction of the speaker in the right-hand corner. Only ten percent. All Abby could do was keep watching until the speaker was finished.

Terra wondered why it was taking the balrog so long to attack. She didn't want to go back on offense. That would just mean tiring herself out faster. Not that she was tired now. She had no idea what her body was capable of here. Back on Earth, she would have been exhausted.

Not here.

Here she was something else.

Something more.

The new strength and endurance were a godsend. Maybe the orcs had a fairer notion of a fight than she'd assumed. Then Terra glanced at the balrog. *Nope,* she thought. *Definitely take that back.*

Behind the balrog, the double gates were rising again. Chanting was coming from the darkness of the gate's hallway. Terra didn't want to think about what awaited her in the dark. She doubted that she was being sent teammates.

After all, this was entertainment, wasn't it? What was more entertaining than watching someone defenseless get ripped to pieces? These guys were worse than the Romans at the peak of their bloodlust. Any respect the orcs in the cell had given Terra fell on deaf ears now.

Goblins marched out of the gates. They were large by goblin standards, and each of them wore basic leather armor. They carried hatchets and short swords, their mouths frothing as they screeched and barked, bumping into each other, thirsty for blood.

Terra glanced over her shoulder, hoping the gates behind her were opening. They remained down as she backed up to the wall.

The balrog still hadn't moved. *Must be licking its wounds*, Terra thought. *Even if I can't see any blood, I must have hurt the dipshit. I'd probably still have a chance if it weren't for...whatever the hell those things are. Goblins or something?*

Or maybe this was because the orcs believed she had too much of a chance with only the balrog. What if this fight was supposed to have ended a long time ago? What if the orcs were sending more goblins in to give Terra more of a challenge?

That was a much more promising idea, something Terra could hold onto, rally herself behind. The orcs had been chanting her name. They wanted her to win. Or at least they had a semblance of respect for her. There was no way they would want to kill her off too easily. The goblins were here to make things easier for the balrog, not to end her newfound career too quickly.

The goblins were taking a formation in front of the balrog, who was still hanging in the back. There were twenty goblins in total. Terra had no idea how she was going to eliminate them. The fight with the orc yesterday had been her first fight ever.

Fighting twenty people at once seemed out of the realms of possibility. Terra was starting to rethink her formerly cheery disposition.

The first three goblins made a mad dash for Terra, each of them wielding their weapons high above their head. The goblin who made it there first slashed at Terra with his sword. Terra blocked the attack easily, putting a little more force behind the motion and sending the goblin flying backward.

The other goblins stopped as Terra looked down at her shield, surprised by her own strength. She was much stronger than them.

She'd forgotten just how strong she was while up against the balrog. This was no fluke. She was strong enough to take a demon one on one. Goblins wouldn't be anything but an annoyance.

Terra slammed her *katar* to her shield and shouted, "Fucking break it!" before running at the three goblins. She leapt through the air and landed between the two who hadn't attacked. One slashed at her and she deflected the strike with her shield, spinning around and using it to bash the other goblin in the face.

The goblin stumbled back, and Terra brought her shield down on its head before slashing it across the throat. Hardly missing a beat, she pivoted and slashed upward, splitting the goblin behind her in two.

Terra strode up to the remaining goblin and stomped its head. She brought her foot down again. And again. The goblin's head cracked open, brains and blood oozing out like egg yolk.

The arena was silent. She could hear the orc's wooden seats groaning.

Terra threw her shield down, strutted over to the pair of dead goblins, and picked up the two-armed ax the goblin had used, easily wielding it with one hand. "Who else wants some?" Terra spat, drawing a line in the sand with the ax.

The remaining goblins stared at each other, fear on their faces. They must have believed they were going to come in and tear the human limb from limb. Terra felt stronger. Even stronger than she had before.

Anabelle was breathing down Abby's neck. Abby couldn't see her because she was still looking through the VR, but she was certain it had to be the elf. It made her skin prickle, but she pushed her confusing feelings away. "Something I can help you with?" Abby asked.

Abby felt Anabelle pull away, maybe sensing how uncomfortable she was. "How much longer until you implement your plan? What *is* your plan?"

The construction was at ninety-nine percent. Abby took a deep breath, hoping she could pull this off. The counter flipped to one hundred percent. "Watch the screen and find out."

The tracker buzzed over to the balrog, who had reacquired its whip with the goblins' help. It flew up to the balrog's ear and started playing the opening track of a thrash-metal album particularly close to Abby's heart. The opening feedback-filled guitar started up, and the balrog screeched in pain.

The balrog surged forward, fire and lava spewing from its mouth and its skin. The goblins screamed as the balrog barreled through them, crushing two of them as it swung its whip in a frenzy, driven mad by the frequency in its ear.

Abby kept the tracker close to the balrog but didn't take her eyes off the action.

The goblins had scattered, forgetting about Terra. But she hadn't forgotten about them. With the grace of a lioness, she slunk to the side, avoiding the balrog, and pounced on one of the goblins, sinking her *katar* into the pathetic creature. She stood and threw her ax, hitting a goblin and impaling it to the wall.

Once the other goblins realized what was happening, they mustered their forces. There were fourteen left, and they rushed Terra as the balrog screeched and ran amok.

The first goblin jumped at Terra, and she cut it down with her *katar*. As she bent to pick up its hatchet, another goblin slashed Terra across the face, sending her stumbling back. She quickly caught her balance and kicked the goblin hard in the chest, shoving him into another goblin.

Terra threw her hatchet into the chest of another goblin and then grabbed another by its collar and slammed it to the ground. She whirled as another goblin slashed her across the arm. Terra punched it in the face and then tackled it to the ground, driving her *katar* through its throat.

A flash of white-hot pain surged through Terra's body as the balrog's whip struck her in the side, sending her skidding across the sand. She felt like she'd broken every bone, and the world threatened to descend into darkness.

Terra grabbed her *katar*. She focused on the blades. They were bright, catching the light of the triple suns above. She just had to hold onto the *katar*'s light.

Across the arena, the balrog was still rampaging. It didn't seem capable of telling the difference between friend or foe. It had already killed three other goblins.

Terra picked herself up, swaying to the side as she tried to catch her balance. She headed to the closest goblin and tackled it to the ground. The goblin held up its spear, the only thing keeping Terra from tearing his head off.

Terra felt an arrow hit her in the shoulder. A goblin standing some distance away had pulled out its bow and arrow. A surge of rage welled up in Terra and she headbutted the goblin beneath its spear, grabbed the bladed section, wrenched it free, and drove the blade through its eye.

The goblin fell to the ground, dead.

Terra pulled the arrow from her shoulder and turned to the goblin who had fired at her. She sprinted to it and rammed the arrow into its throat. When it dropped, Terra turned to face the balrog.

Nearly all of the goblins were dead. The rest had fled to the safety of the corridor they came from. Only the balrog was left.

There was no doubt in Terra's mind. She knew what she had to do. She leaned over and picked up one of the discarded spears from a goblin's corpse. "It's just you and me now!" she shouted.

The balrog screeched once more and took to the air. Fire streaked from its body as it flew at Terra, cracking its flaming whip.

Terra watched it descending toward her. She took aim and launched the spear at the demon.

The spear hit the balrog in the forehead and it veered to the right, trying to stabilize itself. Terra stood her ground, waiting for the impact.

The balrog hit Terra with all of its unrestrained rage, fire flashing from its eyes, black smoke billowing from its open maw. Terra grabbed it by the horns as it drove its head into her.

Fire spread across Terra's body, searing her skin. She screamed as the pain flooded her senses. There was nothing but the pain, burning through her flesh, down to her bones, cauterizing her soul.

But Terra didn't quit. She held the balrog with all her strength despite its horns boiling her skin. The balrog tried to pull away, but Terra held it still, her muscles screaming at her as she wrestled it to one knee.

The balrog pulled away, but Terra yanked it back toward her. Then she raised her *katar* and struck it between the eyes, driving her blade deep into the demon's skull. Terra pulled the rod, splitting the blade three ways, and they burst out of the balrog's head. Fire spewed from the wounds.

Terra stumbled back, reeling from the pain. She focused on what was in front of her, ignoring the blackness spreading over her sight.

That was when she heard the chanting. Even louder than before. The crowd was calling her name. "Not-a-Male, Not-a-Male!"

Terra fell to one knee as orcs came running from the gates. *Fuck,* she thought. *I can't handle any more.*

But, the orcs helped Terra to her feet. They led her back to her cell while the orcs and goblins above cheered Terra on.

Cecile was waiting for Terra. A table had been brought into the room. It was covered in bowls filled with medicinal herbs and healing balms.

The tracker followed the orcs and watched as they laid Terra on the bed. "Take care of her," one of the orcs said. "She fights again in two hours."

Terra chuckled as Cecile began to rub a cooling minty lotion on her wounds. "At least I get a little break," she muttered before slipping into unconsciousness.

The tracker hovered, broadcasting Terra's victory and pain for all of humanity to see.

CHAPTER TWENTY-EIGHT

The lab was silent as they watched the diminutive goblin soothing Terra's body with ointments. Abby wished someone would say something. Anything would have been better than watching how much the warrior was suffering.

During the fight, it had all seemed so exciting. Even though Abby was helping out, she couldn't help but be blown away by how brave and strong Terra was. All her strength and courage was gone now. There was only the broken body of a young woman fighting for her life.

Anabelle finally spoke. "Cut the feed. We've seen enough. Everyone out. Everyone except Abby and Creon."

As the lab emptied out, Anabelle turned to Abby and said, "All right, we gotta figure something out to get her out of there. And we only have two hours to do it."

Abby couldn't understand the reasoning of the orcs. "Why have her fight so soon? She'll get killed. And they seem to like her," she wondered aloud.

Anabelle was noticeably frustrated by the question, but the frustration didn't seem to be aimed at Abby. "Who fucking knows. This whole thing doesn't make sense." Anabelle threw her hands in the air. "These are the Dark One's orcs, but the arena makes no sense."

"Why doesn't it?"

"Because orcs haven't been a real society since they started following the Dark One. They had history, even if it was a bastardized version of our history. They still had culture. Then they joined with the Dark One and all that fell to the wayside. But this arena…even if it is barbaric, it's the old orc way."

Creon chimed in to help fill Abby in the lost details. "Orcs used to use the arena to choose their chiefs. The strongest would lead their troops."

Anabelle rubbed her temples and frowned. "This makes no sense. There's no reason for the arena. It…it goes against all reason. They aren't choosing a chief, and orcs haven't shown any cultural interest outside of the Dark One since that asshole appeared."

Creon had already turned back to his computer. "Interesting, but it doesn't help us at the moment. We need to figure out how to make sure Terra survives the next fight. That is unless you're planning on making a human snuff film."

Anabelle chuckled and said, "Not really my kind of movie. I'll see you guys in a little bit. I need to clear my head."

And with that, Anabelle glided out of the room. Or at least Abby thought the elf glided. As far as Abby was concerned, Anabelle's feet never touched the ground. It was as though the elf floated everywhere like an angel.

Once Anabelle was gone, Abby's mind refocused on the mission at hand. She'd already exhausted her one option: using the nanobots. She could reconstruct the bots into another structure, but unless the next creature Terra was up against had the same weakness, it would be pointless.

Abby hated being in the dark. She found it hard to come up with ideas when the problem wasn't even known. Usually, it wasn't too much of a problem. Sometimes pressure made Abby work better. But this was the first time a human life depended on her. Abby wasn't sure if this was the kind of pressure she could deal with.

Anabelle's room wasn't too far from Abby's. She was grateful Myrddin believed she was too high maintenance to share the barracks with the recruits, and maybe she was. Anabelle didn't care either way, though. A room to herself was a godsend.

The room was decorated modestly by anyone's standards—a chair, a dresser, a table, and a bed. The most ornate aspect of the room was an elvish rug that was spread out in front of the bed, a relic from a past Anabelle was still trying to remember.

That was what Anabelle needed time for. Memory upon memory had been forgotten over the years. Memories that Anabelle desperately needed. Nothing was really forgotten, though, only covered up. She had to start the task of uncovering.

Anabelle sat on her bed, thinking through Terra's situation. There was only so much she could do. Her plan for getting the humans on board with the war seemed to be working. But she didn't want to use Terra like a pawn. That felt cruel. Yet that was all it seemed she could do.

Anabelle changed from her uniform to the traditional robe of a Traveler. It was decorated with elvish runes that told stories of Travelers of the past. Some of them were still alive. The smart ones, at least. Those who walked away from the Path and had gone on to live their lives.

And here Anabelle was, trying to get back on the Path. Most of the surviving Travelers would have laughed at her. Why throw away a good life? It wasn't as though Myrddin was starving for more elves to join the war effort. Every elf who could fight was already doing everything they could.

Something in Anabelle wanted to walk the Path again. Maybe it was the desire to prove she was more than a pretty face. Or it could be because she had never had the chance to test her abilities. She'd been one of the few Travelers to have been trained but never utilized.

There was a well of knowledge in her that had never been used.

Now she worried the well had gone dry. That she was only a pale shadow of what a Traveler was capable of.

Anabelle knelt on the rug and touched her head to the floor. A Traveler was supposed to be more than just a warrior. They were supposed to have learned from the Path, to be capable of sharing their wisdom with the world.

For thousands of years, Travelers had been fearsome foes on the battlefield, not only because of their combat prowess but because of their tactics, their wisdom. Anabelle sorely needed that wisdom right now.

Eyes closed, she let herself drift into the darkness of meditation. This is where she would find what was lost in the darkness within her.

The monitors in Abby's and Creon's lab were tuned to various news channels. Everyone on Earth was talking about Terra's most recent battle. The opinions were mixed. Some were caught up in Terra's heroic exploits. Others were fear-mongering.

Fear made sense to Abby. She'd never seen anything like a balrog outside of movies. She was surprised more people weren't assuming that the battle at the coliseum was anything other than a marketing ploy from a movie studio.

It may have had something to do with the lingering video of Terra's broken body. Nothing about her condition was entertaining. More videos were being played of her injuries than of the battle.

People were taking to the streets. There were already protests and rallies, all with a different nature. Some wanted to find Terra as fast as possible through whatever means necessary. These people didn't know how it would happen, but they knew it should.

Other protests were more focused. There were those who had figured out that there were people who knew about this threat. There had to be for someone to have broadcast the feed. And protestors were pissed at the establishment for keeping this knowledge from them. They claimed it was their right to know about this a long time ago.

Abby thought Anabelle's plan was working solidly. It might have unforeseen ramifications, but the people of Earth were talking. More importantly, they were believing.

None of that solved the issue standing in the room like an unwanted elephant. Creon and Abby had hardly talked since Anabelle had left. The obvious reason was that neither of them knew what they were going to do to help Terra. "Do we even know where she's at?" Abby voiced her thoughts.

Creon swiveled his chair to face Abby. "Not certain," he said. "But we could probably figure it out. There are only so many worlds and realms."

"Creon. You told me there are nine realms. If each realm had a minimum of a million planets...I mean, it's simple math, you know?"

Undeterred, Creon replied, "We could figure it out. Our computers could probably do that computation in...two weeks? But Terra would have to survive until then. We'd be able to send ships, though. Yes, maybe we should concentrate on getting our troops over there...find a way to—"

"Wait. Just basic computation, right? To figure out where she is, I mean."

Creon gnawed on a pen with his sharp teeth. "Theoretically. We'd cross-reference the list of habitable planets in each realm. Then reference that to planets that have seen significant orc traffic. Then pinpoint which planets have three suns and a desert. Maybe go through any relevant reports written over the last few months. But to answer your question, it's just a lot of computation."

Abby snapped her fingers as she raised her watch. "Then we got this," she said as she turned it on. A projection of Martin floated in front of her. "Hey, Martin, can you help us?

Martin sipped from his cup and stretched his paperclip body out until it was straight. "Seeing as how I only exist to assist you, I don't see what else I could possibly do. D'ya want me to file some paperwork for you? Oh, you know what would be a better use of my advanced computing abilities? Finding the meaning of life for an AI that has already solved the meaning of life for organics. Spoiler: it's pretty fucking boring."

Abby pointed to the holoprojector, which was displaying the arena Terra had been fighting in. "Bet you can't find that planet?" Abby challenged. "Even with that big 'ol brain of yours."

"I don't have a brain. I have a complex set of algorithms constantly updating with every bit of information in my greedy little path. Do you have any other information than the picture?"

"Whatever information is in the HQ's mainframe. Don't know what's relevant, though. Sounds kinda hard, right?"

Martin resumed his paperclip shape and smiled for the first time. "Sounds tough as hell. I'm on it."

The AI disappeared with a dramatic flash. Abby didn't remember giving Martin any exiting animations. Guess the little guy was adding quirks to his personality. Abby hoped he'd eventually add some class.

Creon stood over the drones, stroking his wispy goatee. "You know, we do have long-distance teleportation pads. We can't use them for anything with organs or hair. You know, that kind of thing. But we've used them to teleport supplies between the realms before."

Abby strode over to the drones and ran her hands across their sleek steel. "Thinking what I'm thinking?" she asked.

"All we need is an address. The drones are kinda large, though. Might be a problem."

Abby was only half-listening. She crouched and stared into the small vat of nanobots rolling around beneath the drones. "These guys are pretty small. We could send a tracker with more nanobots…and I have an idea. A pretty good one."

Martin popped up on the holoprojector, floating around in the arena. "All right, it's way, way outside of the space regulated by the anti-magic wave. It's in Persion 24b, on planet Alpha Spartacus 523. Anything else?"

Relief warmed Abby's body as she said, "Didn't think you were *that* fast!"

"While I was searching, I stumbled across a couple of discarded plans for AIs in the HQ's system. Also, Myrddin's private files. That guy has weird interests. Never seen so many orc feet in my life. Anyways, I took the liberty of upgrading myself. Can't be too smart. I mean, *I* can't ever be too smart. You two probably have some kind of intelligence cap."

"All right, I got it. You're a genius. Find the coordinates and prep the hadron collider for a small delivery within the next two hours."

Martin raised his cup, and coffee poured from above his head into the cup. "Just to let you know, that violates about fifteen rules. Which means I obviously want to do it."

Abby gave Martin a puzzled look as she said, "Oh, I'm sorry, were you speaking binary?"

Martin chuckled and downed his coffee. "I like where this is going. The collider is prepped, and I've calibrated it so that the excess energy doesn't show up on any of the grids. We going to keep breaking rules?"

Abby pointed at Martin and then turned to include Creon. "Just don't tell me 'bout them 'til I'm done breaking 'em," she replied.

Martin rubbed the ends of his paperclip body together. "Abby, I think this is the beginning of a beautiful friendship. One to last through all the ages. A thousand ages. Or at least until you die. At which I will be heartbroken. Really messed up. For a *long* time. Thousands of years, maybe. I don't know. I haven't had to process anything other than irritation yet. Oh, wait. That was joy. That's a good one."

Martin blipped out of sight. *Guess we're friends now*, Abby thought as she dipped her hand into the vat of nanobots. *Now that that's taken care of, time to get to work.*

CHAPTER TWENTY-NINE

Darkness surrounded Anabelle. Occasionally, flashes of light illuminated scenes from her past. Fuzzy. Indecipherable. It was like swimming to the bottom of a black lake filled with glowing fish reflecting moonlight that should have been lost.

Anabelle reached out to each flash of memory, but they were too far. Her hands caught nothing. She continued to dive. There must be an end to it. Deeper, and deeper still.

There was nothing.

The ringing of an alarm brought Anabelle out of her meditation. She jerked her head up, losing her balance from the blood surging to her head. Dizzily, she grabbed her comm, which she had placed next to her bed. "What's going on?" she murmured.

Roy's voice greeted her. It was hardly a warm greeting, though. He sounded annoyed and slightly panicked. "Where are you?" he asked. "We've been trying to get in touch with you for nearly half an hour."

"Training. What is it?"

"A new Dark Gate opened. We're mobilizing. Blackwell's team should be ready to move out by now."

Anabelle's skin prickled at hearing the squad called Blackwell's. Sure, the man was capable, but he wasn't the one leading the team.

"Last time I checked, Myrddin put me in charge of them," she retorted.

"Chain of command, darling. Don't take it too seriously. You're at the top and in charge of two squads. Not that this is the time for an argument about hierarchy, but you're leading two squads now. So, don't get your knickers all in a tussle."

Anabelle wished she could have punched Roy. Even though he was pretending to take the high road, he had made a point to say "Blackwell's squad" to get under her skin. It was his way of teasing. It drove her crazy. "All right, I'll meet them down in the barracks."

Roy shook his head. "No time. What's the range on the colliders? Can we get to the gates?"

"You know damn well the colliders can be used to get around the planet as well as a few limited spots in the nine realms."

"Good, then hit the collider. We gotta get there as soon as possible. Reports say the Gate is going to be opening in the hour."

Anabelle switched to her Traveler uniform, a modest one-piece suit that gave ample protection from blades and magic due to the exquisite elvish design. Only a few had ever been made, and Anabelle owned at least ten of them. "What about Terra?" she asked. "What's going on with her?"

Roy sighed, obviously annoyed with the stream of questions. "Touched base with Abby," he replied. "She said that they have everything covered. Something about a surprise. But she's your department. If you want to hear it from her, that's another way we can waste time."

"Fuck off. I'll be at the collider. You coming for this one?"

"Nope. This is all you. I have other shit to take care of. Equally important, if you were wondering."

"I wasn't."

Anabelle slipped out of her room as Roy said, "Wouldn't have it any other way. Stay safe, darling."

Blackwell and the other recruits were lined up at the hadron collider, waiting for Anabelle. They looked like they were ready for inspection.

Anabelle still wasn't certain how she was supposed to be treating the recruits. Blackwell was at least competent, but the other three didn't seem to have any personality. Not that Anabelle was there to get to know each of them personally. But their training was her responsibility.

A flash from Anabelle's meditation: an old elf sitting by a campfire. He was speaking, his words long and drawn out, waving elaborate watercolor paintings with his hands. "The torrent of rain does nothing," he says. "The steady sprinkle erodes mountains. Mist does nothing but look pretty."

Anabelle stopped midstride, caught off-guard by the distinct and vivid memory. "Huh," she muttered as she approached the recruits.

Blackwell stepped forward and saluted Anabelle. "Ready for deployment," he shouted.

Anabelle covered her sensitive ears, unprepared to have excitement barked at her. "All right, kids, I know I've been harsh on you," she said. "Extremely harsh. But that's only because I don't want to see you dead. The last run we went on, you did great. You know what worked?"

Jones, the smallest of the recruits, poked his head out of the line. "We followed your orders?"

"Flattering, but only partially true. You work well as a team. I only gave you a general idea of what to do. Keep that in mind. Communicate with each other. Don't rely on me to tell you everything to do. Trust each other. Trust yourselves. Got it?"

The recruits, along with Blackwell, shouted, "Sir, yes, Sir!"

The scaffolding beneath them shook as the hadron collider powered up, preparing to send them to the burgeoning Dark Gate. As Anabelle walked over to the collider's control, she overheard two of the scientists who were running the machine talking about an odd spike in energy. It seemed the collider had already been prepped for a teleport. Anabelle made a mental note to check on that.

A portal opened before Anabelle and her squad. "You guys have your backup proton packs?" she asked.

Blackwell held his up for Anabelle to see.

"Good. Let's go shut down this Gate."

Excitement Land was aptly named. The amusement park was one of the largest in the United States. It had no other purpose than excitement. No one was dressed in mascot costumes. There was no attempt to look cute. Excitement Land had only one goal in mind: to excite you.

People traveled from all over the world to spend an afternoon in the park. It boasted the highest and fastest rollercoasters of any amusement park. Patrons had to sign a waiver before they set foot in the park. Not that there had been any deaths, but their commercials included a number of references to heart attacks.

Entertainment, pure and simple. That was why the crowds came, and they never left disappointed. Today wasn't going to be any different. Each attraction had a line that any sane person would have walked away from, but Excitement Land brought a certain caliber of person to its gates.

Adrenaline junkies. Nothing was fast enough, high enough, until they'd experienced Excitement Land. Sure, people joked about the name, but once you were in the park's grasp, nothing could top the high you were going to get.

Because of this reason, no one noticed the Dark Gate beginning to materialize at the top of Assisted Suicide, the highest and fastest rollercoaster the park boasted. The riders of the coaster assumed the odd tug they felt in their stomach as they climbed the tallest loop was part of the ride.

No one noticed the hair standing up on the backs of their necks. What else was expected when you were high up enough to see the two states to the east and west?

The hadron collider's portal opened near the entrance of the park.

No one thought twice about it. For all they knew, this was another of the many exciting things the park had in store for them. When Anabelle stepped out, followed by Blackwell and the other recruits, people cheered.

She wondered why the humans were cheering. She was used to being famous but had never had such an immediate response to showing up for a public event. It usually took people a few seconds to recognize her.

As for the patrons of the park, they were enamored with the show that they had been lucky enough to stumble upon. Many of them believed Excitement Land was merely about the rides. They were glad to see the park was investing in other entertainment avenues.

Anabelle scanned the park before pulling down her slim HUD to check for energy signatures. It appeared that they had arrived before the Dark Gate had opened. The positive was they had arrived before any damage was done.

Blackwell was also scanning, as were the recruits. Anabelle was glad they were at least trying to keep up with her. Even though she was supposed to be leading the squad, calling out orders irritated the hell out of her. *Just don't die.* That seemed to work for her.

People were starting to crowd around Anabelle and the recruits, asking questions such as "When is the show going to start?" and "Are you guys supposed to be soldiers or something?"

Anabelle ignored the questions before she realized she was at the entrance of an amusement park. That meant thousands of bodies. Thousands of people in danger. "Blackwell, I need you to start evacuating people as fast possible," she commanded. "I'm going to look for the Gate."

Blackwell didn't need to be told twice. He gestured at the recruits, who stepped up, and the four humans started to calmly explain to the park's guests what was happening.

Needless to say, there were many incredulous park patrons. Luckily, Blackwell seemed to be nearly as charming as Anabelle, a quality that Anabelle noticed as she left the recruits to take care of business.

Anabelle maneuvered her way through the throng of humans

gorging themselves on candy and junk food. She'd never understood the appeal of places like this. How could she? Most of her life had been spent training to be a Traveler and the rest living the kind of life humans watched on TMZ, wishing for a taste of that regal type of excitement.

Once Anabelle got far enough from where her portal had opened, none of the guests seemed to notice her. They were either too concerned with their vacations or had attributed her outfit to something pertaining to the park.

As Anabelle strode through the crowds, she kept her eyes open for anything suspicious, occasionally pulling her HUD visor down to scan for any energy anomalies. The visor was only showing low spikes, as though the Dark Gate was warming up. If things progressed as expected, they had time.

Since there was no pressing concern, or at least not one Anabelle could discern, she stopped over at the popcorn vendor beneath one of the roller coasters. "Could I get a large?" she asked.

The vendor scooped out an obscenely large box of popcorn, slathered it with butter, doused the kernels with salt, and handed the box to Anabelle, who took it and went to go sit at a bench overlooking a bizarrely quaint lake.

Anabelle's comm beeped angrily. "What's up?"

Roy asked, "Have you found the Dark Gate yet?"

"I've been walking all over the park, and the recruits are moving everyone they can out. But to answer your question, no. You sure these are the right coordinates? Or did you guys mix something up on your end?"

"Of course, they are the right coordinates. We have an entire department dedicated to looking for the gates. Maybe you just aren't looking hard enough."

Anabelle tossed her head back and laughed. If Roy could see her now, he would definitely think that. "I'm looking as hard as I can, but we haven't come across anything yet."

As Anabelle spoke, she sensed the air around her changing. The temperature fluctuated drastically from cool to frigid. Patrons within the park had noticed as well, many of them clutching their jackets tighter.

Above Anabelle, at the top of the rollercoaster towering over her, there was a flash of lightning, quickly followed by a boom, then the sound of a giant sheet of paper tearing. "Actually, Roy," Anabelle started, "I might have found the Dark Gate."

CHAPTER THIRTY

O nce the Dark Gate was open, all hell broke loose. The crowd below didn't notice for a few minutes, but Anabelle watched as the Dark One's forces poured through the Gate. There were more than last time, and there was a greater variety.

First came the orcs.

These orcs were larger than the ones Anabelle had fought previously. They weren't as stringy; instead, their muscles appeared ready to rip out from beneath their gray skin. They carried axes and swords, their faces covered in warpaint from tribes Anabelle couldn't identify. None of these orcs carried plasma weapons, which Anabelle found odd.

Next came the goblins.

They were not much different than the goblins Terra had fought. The only noticeable distinction was the eyes. These goblins did not have the bloodthirsty eyes of the goblin warrior class. Their eyes were lucid, clear, reminiscent of Creon's curious gaze.

Trolls followed the goblins.

They were hulking creatures standing over seven feet tall with dead gray skin and dumb eyes, snot and drool trickling down their faces. Anabelle remembered when the trolls had been a noble race.

Then, the Dark One got his hands on them. It pained her to see such noble creatures fall so low. She hoped there were still trolls out there who had managed to avoid the Dark One's grasp.

All in all, she counted over forty enemies between the three races —much too large a force for her and four others to deal with. Even if Anabelle were at the top of her game, she would be easily defeated.

She was slipping into the shadows to call Roy when the Dark Gate crackled one last time. Something that looked like a long snake the width of a house slithered out. It had sleek black scales and two small wings in the middle of its torso.

The creature had a small, narrow head that looked as though it had been pinched in a vice until its brains had been forced out. Its small legs and claws looked like a bad joke.

A wyrm, Anabelle thought. The cruel, underdeveloped cousin to dragons. Thousands of years ago, when it was believed that all the true dragons had fled from the realms, the wyrms had tried to make themselves a force to be reckoned with. It hadn't gone over well.

Even humans had stories about killing wyrms. *To be fair,* Anabelle thought, *they have an entire series about killing wyrms. Still, it would be better without that thing. At least it can't breathe—"*

The wyrm let loose a small jet of fire. Compared to a dragon, it was downright pathetic, but the humans beneath the roller coaster didn't know that. When they heard the roar of the wyrm, they screamed and panic set in, the park descending into madness.

Anabelle pinged Roy as the humans scattered. Orcs and goblins climbed down from the coaster, running after whoever was in front of them. "Hey, Roy, we got a problem. This isn't just a small group like last time. This is a whole invasion party," she shouted.

Roy answered almost immediately. "Wait, how many are you talking about?"

"Forty, give or take. And they have a wyrm. A pretty big one. Looks fairly dumb, though."

"Fuck. All right, we'll get reinforcements on the way. What's your plan?"

Outside the shadows, a little girl and her mother ran from an orc.

The orc snatched the mother into the air and held his sword to her throat. The girl cried out, an ear-piercing sound that made the orc sneer in disgust.

A tall, chubby security guard with honey-brown skin, a scruffy beard, and thick dreadlocks stepped over to the orc. His nametag read Naota. He flipped up his sunglasses and pulled out his taser as the other security guards fled. The taser crackled loudly. "'Kay, 'kay, buddy, I'm gonna need you to put the lady down," Naota droned. "No sense getting hurt worse than you need to."

The orc stared blankly at the guard. "You're kidding me, right?" it growled.

Naota spat and hiked his pants up, snapping his suspenders loudly. "You leave me no choice. With the power invested in me by Excitement Land, the three-hour security guard workshop, and my own unrelenting belief in myself, I'm placing you under arrest."

The orc dropped the woman and twirled his sword as he stomped to Naota, who didn't back off. They stared each other down.

The orc surged forward, sword raised high. He got in Naota's face, his sword coming down to cleave the security guard's head off.

Naota stepped to the side, pulled his taser back, and shouted, "Entry-level job taser attack!" as he drove it into the orc's neck.

Thousands of volts of electricity pulsed through the orc's body, and he fell to the ground, unconscious.

Naota snapped his suspenders again and pulled out a toothpick as he scanned the park. "Orcs. Goblins. Not on my watch. Not at my park," he muttered in an intentionally gravelly voice.

Anabelle couldn't lift her jaw off the ground. She'd never seen such an oblivious human. The guy obviously had no idea how much danger he was in. She watched as Naota picked up the little girl and brought her over to her mother. All the while, the park behind him was exploding into pandemonium. "Keep your head down," Naota said. "There are monsters afoot."

Anabelle stepped from the shadows and approached Naota as she told Roy, "I think I found someone to help. Send those reinforcements."

Roy came back loudly, "Gotcha."

Anabelle grabbed Naota, who countered by grabbing her wrist, flipping around and pointing his taser at her. "Hold on there!" he shouted. "Wait, you're too pretty to be an orc. State your business. We are in high-crisis mode right now. Possibly the highest."

Anabelle pulled Naota's thumb back, which made him shriek and let go of her. "You handled yourself well back there. I need your help getting these people out of here. You're conscripted. Got it?"

Naota folded his arms. "Don't know who you are, but if you want to help me get my park safe again, lay it on me. What's the plan?"

Anabelle drew two plasma rifles and handed them to Naota. "Kill everything that isn't human."

Naota lowered his sunglasses a fraction so Anabelle could see his unnaturally black eyes. "Just like *Middang3ard* VR. I'm a wizard there." Then he turned, struck a bizarre kung fu-inspired pose, and landed a headshot on two orcs within fifteen seconds. "Guess I'm a marksman here."

Anabelle couldn't believe her eyes. *Who the fuck is this guy?* she thought just before she heard the roar of the wyrm above. She hit her comm, letting Blackwell and the recruits know to head to her position. Then she set her sights on the wyrm.

CHAPTER THIRTY-ONE

Blackwell and the recruits had finally cleared out the civilians from the first section of the park. And more were heading Blackwell's way. Hopefully, they'd follow the path of everyone else fleeing the park. Anabelle had sent coordinates. It was time to reposition.

Blackwell was a considerable distance from where Anabelle needed him to be. He checked his exosuit's palm. Abby told him she'd managed to squeeze in some mobility upgrades before they headed out. He hoped they helped with speed.

Blackwell clenched his right fist, activating Abby's new mobility mode. "SWARMMT, time to get moving!" he shouted as he leapt forward.

And what a leap it was. Blackwell had merely meant to run forward, but the moment his leg left the ground, he shot through the air, soaring over the concession buildings that made up the first section of the park.

The exosuit's feet dug into the ground when Blackwell landed, the suspension accommodating for the amount of force that had sent him through the air. "That's a fucking upgrade," Blackwell muttered before calling Abby. "Hey, Abs, what else did you put in these things?"

When Abby answered, she sounded distracted. "Don't you read memos? Sent y'all the schematics this morning. Mobility...uh... streamlined weapons. Is that all? Kinda busy at the moment."

"Just wanted to make sure I don't walk into a fight that I'm not prepared for, Miss."

"Right hand is speed. Left hand is strength. Weapons holstered in the back. Quick reload on things. Everything else, you gotta figure out. Bye."

Abby hung up, leaving Blackwell to debrief the other recruits, who quickly landed behind him. On foot, it would have taken half an hour to get to Anabelle. The exosuits were definitely going to cut down on that time.

Blackwell gripped his right hand again, and the exosuits gears began whirring again. He took a step forward, registering how walking was now running, slowly gaining speed this time before kicking off, soaring through the air toward a rollercoaster. Instinctively, Blackwell reached for one of the girders on the coaster, his hand easily finding it, before he swung forward.

Small propulsion jets on the back of the exosuit fired, keeping Blackwell in fluid motion. The suit was extremely reactive to the slightest movements he'd made. "How the hell did she do this?" he muttered.

Martin popped up in the corner of Blackwell's HUD. "Abby added to the tech," Martin lazily droned. "But the style, that's all me, baby. I'm making you guys look good!"

"Wait, what do you mean?"

"Can't you remember more than a bad sci-fi chapter's worth of exposition? Remember when Abby loaded me into your suits? I'm still here. My job's not over until all of you keep from being dead. Which means I'll be here for a while. Lucky for you, I have such a charming personality."

Blackwell skidded across the ground. He was close to the coordinates Anabelle had sent. The only problem was he'd just raced into a platoon of orcs. And these guys were bigger than anything he'd seen before.

One of the orcs spotted Blackwell and drew his sword, pointing at Blackwell and the recruits landing behind him, and roared. "Rip 'em up good, boys!" the orc shouted as two trolls burst out of the bathrooms behind the party of orcs.

This was it. Guess there wasn't any better time to test new gear than the present. "You're gonna make sure I don't get killed, right, Martin?" Blackwell whispered.

Martin laughed sarcastically. "Well, I can't reach out and shoot someone for you, but I'll do my best."

Blackwell clenched his fist and felt his exoskeleton's legs relax. The suit shifted and suddenly felt heavier. He took a step forward and his foot sank into the concrete, cracking it. Still, the suit remained easy to maneuver. Hardly any speed had been lost. How much strength had been gained?

The orcs rushed at Blackwell. One went for his head, swinging an ax. Blackwell raised his arm, and the ax hit his wrist and snapped in two. The orc stumbled as Blackwell lunged forward and kicked it in the chest. It flew into a nearby wall.

The other orcs stopped in their tracks.

Blackwell checked his hand as the recruits watched him. "Fuck yeah, that's how these babies should work!" he shouted.

The remaining orcs charged Blackwell and the recruits. "Upper right hand is power, Lower right hand is speed, kids!" he shouted as he met the orcs' charge.

Blackwell connected with the first orc, punching it in the face, breaking its jaw, before dropping it to the ground. He grabbed the orc by the throat and tossed him into another orc.

One of the trolls slammed a club into Blackwell's back, driving him to the ground. *Shit hurts still,* Blackwell thought as he boosted to his feet. *But at least it won't kill me.*

Blackwell turned to face the troll, who swung its club at him again. As the mace came at his head, Blackwell clenched his right hand, switching to speed. He moved back, sidestepped the troll, clenched his left hand as he leapt into the air, and brought both fists down on the troll's head, cracking its skull.

"Point positions, team!" Blackwell shouted as he backed against a wall. He leapt onto the side of the building, drew his plasma rifle, and started lighting orcs up.

The other recruits followed suit, breaking away from the horde of orcs they were fighting, taking the high ground, and then carefully picking their shots. When Blackwell saw the squad firing, he jumped off the building, throwing himself back into the fray. It felt too good not to.

Blackwell and the squad knocked out the party of orcs and trolls within a few minutes. The recruits joined him on the ground amidst the corpses of their foes. "That's how we're moving through the park," he commanded. "Get in their faces, break 'em up, snipe 'em down, then clean 'em up. Got it?"

The recruits shouted back, "Yes, sir!"

Blackwell knew he wasn't really in command and didn't deserve to be called 'sir.' It felt good, though.

From above them came a roar. Blackwell stared up at the wyrm passing slowly over them. Yeah, it was good he wasn't in command. Otherwise, that huge son of a bitch in the sky would have been his problem.

CHAPTER THIRTY-TWO

Anabelle stuck to the shadows, following the wyrm. The creature was stupid, as most wyrms were. The rest of the invasion party was probably planning on using it to terrorize the humans in the park, maybe to burn the place down. But Blackwell and the other recruits were proving to be ample distraction to keep anyone with half a brain from commanding the wyrm.

That meant Anabelle could get close enough to kill the beast before it went on a rampage, which was only a matter of time. Eventually, the wyrm would get bored, see living beings beneath it, and decide it was time for a snack.

The wyrm continued to float aimlessly around the Dark Gate. That was when Anabelle realized why the wyrm was there: extra security. Guess that meant the Dark One had assumed his invasion party was going to come up against a fight. Doubt he knew it would be so put together.

Anabelle began to scale the roller coaster. It was the longest route to the wyrm but also the stealthiest. Someone would have to be looking very closely to see her. As Anabelle climbed, she scanned the park beneath her.

It was apparent where Blackwell and the rest of the squad had been. There were orc and goblin bodies piled high at random spots in the park. A few groups of orcs and goblins were still wandering around, but most of the humans had been evacuated.

Blackwell and the recruits were progressing through the park with impressive speed. Anabelle made a mental note to tell Abby the upgrades she'd added had worked great. The recruits almost reminded Anabelle of Travelers. Almost.

But now wasn't the time for nostalgia or hopefulness. Anabelle continued her climb up the side of the rollercoaster, trying to plan out her course of attack. Any fire magic was pointless. Most wyrms were immune to earth magic as well. Didn't matter. Anabelle had always hated dealing with earth magic.

She was left with her strongest and weakest skills: lightning and water. Lightning was also out of the question. She could feel a static-electric buzz, the closer she came to the wyrm. The vibrations could be from the Dark Gate, but she chose to play it safe.

Anabelle finally made it to one of the higher loops of the coaster. She was close enough to launch an attack. Manna flowed from her chest to her hands, and she imagined herself as part of a river—the manna the current, her body nothing more than liquid.

The wyrm hadn't taken notice of Anabelle yet. *Thank God those things are so dumb,* she thought as she stretched out her arms. Her hands lost the consistency of flesh, transforming to liquid with the force of water blasting from a fire hydrant.

The wave of water hit the wyrm, sending it careening from its circumnavigation of the Dark Gate. As it skittered away, wrapping its serpentine body around itself, Anabelle climbed to the top of the coaster, putting herself between the wyrm and the Gate.

The wyrm appeared unaffected by Anabelle's attack. It hissed loudly and surged toward her, spewing a thin jet of fire.

Anabelle whipped her hands in front of her, allowing the manna to change her hands back to water. She threw a wave out in front of her to extinguish the wyrm's fire, creating a large cloud of steam and mist.

The wyrm flew through the steam at Anabelle and knocked her off the top of the coaster. She grabbed a piece of scaffolding, almost yanking her arm from its socket. The wyrm was doubling back, its tiny wings flapping ludicrously.

Anabelle pulled herself up and into the girders of the rollercoaster, hoping to lose the wyrm and allow herself a few moments to recover. She had no such luck. The wyrm barreled toward her, sending debris flying while Anabelle tried to find something to hold onto.

Fortunately, she fell on top of the wyrm's head, which had been positioned to snatch her out of the air. She wrapped her hands around its neck, shifting them to water. She stretched her arms all the way around the wyrm's throat, then concentrated on the sensation of snow against her cheeks.

Anabelle's hands and arms solidified into ice. She pulled up as hard as she could, yanking the wyrm toward the Dark Gate and tearing up the rollercoaster which stood in her way. If she was lucky, the Dark Gate would fall, breaking when it hit the ground.

The structure of the rollercoaster was compromised. The whole thing was teetering like a giant, drunken baby. It was only a matter of time before it collapsed. Anabelle was doing everything in her power to help that process along.

The wyrm thrashed desperately, the way a fish does when pulled from the water, certain of its death. This was simply a waiting game. Anabelle knew it, and so did the wyrm.

Finally, the pair burst through the top of the rollercoaster, sending steel bars hurtling into the air. The area around the Dark Gate collapsed in on itself, crashing to the ground.

As Anabelle and the wyrm passed the Gate, she thought she caught a glimpse of a pair of bright green eyes. Far too bright to belong to an orc or goblin. The kind of hues humans were known for. The vision lasted only a moment, but it was enough to pique Anabelle's curiosity.

She released the wyrm and flung herself into the air, redistributing her manna throughout her entire body so she could easily dodge and weave through the cascade of steel beams and debris surrounding the Dark Gate.

After a little bit of maneuvering, Anabelle managed to grab hold of the Dark Gate. She peered through it. She caught her breath, surprised that the portal within the Gate was split in two. On one end, the portal appeared to lead back to where the orc forces had come from, while the other led to a place Anabelle didn't recognize.

The second portal held the green eyes. These eyes belonged to a human with bright red hair pulled back in a ponytail. She was dressed in HQ's standard assassin uniform and was hunched over a computer. A gnome stood at her side, impatiently tapping his feet and glancing over his shoulder.

Anabelle leaned into to get a closer view of the pair. "Who the hell are you?" she asked.

The assassin spun, drew a gun, and fired three shots. Anabelle was barely able to pull away in time.

"Hey, what the hell!" Anabelle shouted.

Curiosity is not generally an attribute of professional killers, but this assassin seemed to have some. She lowered her gun a fraction. "You stick your head out a portal and start shouting, what do you think is going to happen?" she asked. "And who the fuck are you?"

"I asked first. Besides—"

Anabelle saw an orc enter the room from the side. She was about to say something when the assassin turned and tossed a dagger into the orc's skull. The hilt of the weapon had the Middang3ard insignia etched into it.

Maybe it was time for a change of tactics. "Hey, is that an L7 neutrino grenade?" Anabelle asked.

The assassin gave Anabelle a sly look. "Yeah. Just recently approved."

"Yeah, I got the memo last week. Can I have one?"

The assassin shrugged, unhooked one, and threw it to Anabelle, who caught it, popped the pin as she turned, and flung it into the open mouth of the wyrm chasing her.

"Huh," the assassin murmured. "Didn't even see that thing there."

An alarm inside the room started to blare. The assassin touched the side of her face, and a nanotech mask blossomed across her face. Anabelle recognized it as friendly tech.

"Tell Myrddin I know how the Dark Gates are being made. I

managed to get one to work on the gnomish world, hence this little convo," the assassin shouted. "Tell him that I need to speak to him. Soon."

Anabelle thrust a hand out to the gnome and the human, shouting, "Wait, I don't even know your name!"

The assassin turned to answer, but her words were caught up in the explosion behind Anabelle. She'd forgotten about the wyrm.

Anabelle hit the ground and rolled away as the wyrm exploded above her, sending guts and viscera raining down like some kind of hellish snowstorm. When she opened her eyes, she was covered in a thick layer of blue blood. "Fucking great," she muttered.

As she tried to wipe off the blood, Blackwell and the recruits, equally bloodsoaked, walked up to her. They all stared at the portal as it faded from the shattered Dark Gate.

"Guess that ends that," Blackwell said.

A taser went off, and Blackwell jumped and pulled his gun. Naota was standing behind him, absentmindedly twirling his taser. He didn't seem to mind that Blackwell was aiming a weapon at him. "Whoa there, buddy, you might wanna stow that," the guard said. "There's a strict 'no firearms' policy here at Excitement Land."

Naota threw down his plasma rifles, drew his nightstick, and assumed a badly formed bō-staff stance. "Ahh, much better. Now, I'm gonna have to kindly ask you to sheath that lightning right there before I bring the thunder," he threatened.

Blackwell stood there, unable to speak. "Did you not see anything that just happened?" he exclaimed. "We're the good guys. We just blew up a dragon."

Naota pointed his nightstick at Anabelle. "I saw *her* blow up a dragon, but I can see you are all in cahoots. Either way, there doesn't seem to be a threat anymore. So please, pack that lightning on up."

Anabelle burst out laughing as she walked over to Naota and threw her arms around him. "Now, this is a human that I like." She chuckled. "He went after an orc twice his size with a taser. How many did you end up killing?"

Naota blushed as he put away his nightstick. "A gentleman never tells," he said.

Anabelle clapped her hands and shouted, "Okay, squad, time to head back to HQ. Since Roy's reinforcements never showed, they're on cleanup duty. Security guard. You're coming with us."

Naota lowered his head humbly. "Sounds like you're inviting me on some kind of grand adventure," he whispered. "Like something you'd see on an anime or a satirical 1990s comic book. But I'm afraid I can't go, Miss. I've sworn a solemn oath to the great Excitement Land. To protect and serve. I'm gonna honor that pledge with my life."

Blackwell snickered, although the other recruits tried to hold back their laughter. "Dude, look around you," he said.

Naota did as he was told. The park had been nearly obliterated. "On second thought, I'd like to start my hero's journey," the guard said, his face solemn.

CHAPTER THIRTY-THREE

Terra woke up, unsure of where she was. The remnants of a nightmare clung to her like a thick spider's web. There had been a creature made of fire, but even before that, grotesque, gray monsters had abducted her. She'd also made the mistake of shaving her head.

As she sat in a stupor, trying to piece together the last few hours of her life, she ran her hand over her scalp. There was no hair. She sighed as she forced herself to a sitting position. Guess it hadn't been a dream.

Terra looked down at her hands. They were rubbed raw. Even in the dim light, she could see that they were covered with small burns. As far as she was concerned, that was proof she'd gotten off lucky. If her memory served her right, she had tackled a flaming demon. A few burns weren't too bad.

The cell was empty of everything but furniture and a bowl of food sitting on the chair next to Terra's bed. Cecile must have left it for her. She vaguely remembered him taking care of her a few hours ago. Or was it a day? She had no idea how long she'd been out.

When Terra reached for the bowl of food, her entire body screamed in protest. Even if her wounds had healed, damage had been done. She sensed it deep in her bones. Her muscles felt as though they'd been stretched and then hammered to goo.

If the door of the cell hadn't been wide open, Terra would have laid back down and slipped into sleep. But she had seen the open door as she had shoved food into her mouth with shaking hands. There was no way it had been left open by accident. Maybe this was another perk of having won?

Who knows? Terra thought. *By the end of this thing, they might give me a tour of their royal palace. Do orcs even have palaces?*

Fantasy had never been a particular interest to Terra. She hardly cared about human history. The fictional histories of elves and orcs weren't high on the list of things that grabbed her attention.

Although her body felt ready to collapse, Terra managed to get to her feet. She dropped her bowl on the bed and hobbled to the door. Almost a minute had passed before she crossed the ten feet to the door.

Terra was certain she was going to pass out. Her forehead was covered with sweat, and she could feel it sliding down her arms. Imagine killing a balrog, then dying on the floor in a shitty jail cell. Only Terra could be that lucky.

Once she made it to the door, she braced herself against it, catching her breath. The pain was still there, but it was getting more bearable. All she had to do was keep fighting through it. Fight. *Fuck,* Terra thought. *I have another fight. You'd think I'd get a little more time for a break.*

The possibility of defeat wasn't something Terra wanted to think about at the moment. Not because she had a problem losing. She just knew that a loss would directly affect any retirement plans she'd been holding on to.

Terra inched around the door's corner, poking her head out first to see if anyone was watching or waiting for her. The hallway was empty. It wasn't as though Terra could have made a run for it, even if she had wanted to.

But the door had been left open. Which meant someone didn't have a problem with Terra wandering around. The orcs probably believed Terra was too messed up to get out of bed. And to think they wanted Terra to fight. Maybe they had a puppy lined up for her or something.

Terra leaned against the stone walls and slowly shimmied her way down the hallway, stopping periodically to regain control of her breathing and to mutter about her aching bones and muscles. But she kept going. Slowly, she progressed down the hallway.

The hallway opened into a larger holding area. A dozen other people—Terra hesitated to call them all that—sitting on benches around the hall. A long dining table took up most of the space in the room. It was sparsely covered with food and bottles.

None of the prisoners in the room seemed to notice Terra. They no doubt had other things on their minds. Among the more humanoid creatures, Terra recognized the look of despair. But there were many other creatures that Terra couldn't have dreamed of getting a read on.

Three humans were clustered together in the righthand corner of the room. They were staring blankly into space. Their eyes registered nothing and had the blank look of the damned and lost. Each was covered in an assortment of scars and wounds.

Not too far from the humans was a small group of orcs. They did not have the same stiff-spined, military look as the ones Terra had seen so far. These orcs were more downtrodden than the humans, yet were in better physical shape. They didn't look as beaten up.

In another part of the room, a group of goblins was licking their wounds and sharpening their weapons. They were the only ones so far who didn't look like they had given up. If anything, they appeared to be itching for their next fight.

Then there were the wraiths, or at least that's what Terra thought they were. She'd never seen one before but had read about them in a book on Irish folklore when she was a child. These appeared to be close enough.

The wraiths looked to have been human at some point but were now a calming shade of blue and almost transparent. They wore armor from an older time. If they hadn't already been dead, Terra would have assumed they were preparing for their own funeral.

Last were the mantis creatures. Terra had no idea what else to call them. They were around four feet tall and looked like praying mantises that had been enlarged to a frightening size. They were a bluish-green color that shimmered in the dim candlelight.

The creatures' eyes were strangely human while still being buglike. They were the only eyes that followed Terra as she trudged into the room, a keen interest in each of the creatures' faces as they chattered with each other.

At first, Terra had been worried about entering the room. But now, having watched the rest of the prisoners, Terra felt like she had more fight in her than most of them. There was no reason for her to ignore the bottles of what was hopefully wine on the table.

Terra made it over to the table, pulled out one of the chairs, and allowed her pained body to sink onto the uncomfortable wooden frame. Despite having just finished a bowl of whatever the hell Cecile had brought, Terra was still starving. She grabbed whatever was in front of her and started eating, occasionally washing down the food with a gulp from the wine in one of the bottles.

As Terra ate, the orcs and humans watched her. The goblins were more interested in their weapons than anything else, and Terra didn't mind. She hated it when people watched her eat, and this was hardly the most comfortable place to deal with any vore fetishists. "You just gonna watch, or are you gonna join me?" she called.

No one answered, but after a moment, a few of the orcs came to sit beside Terra. They didn't take their eyes off of her, even as they started to serve themselves food and drink. "You're the one they keep chanting about, aren't you?" one of the orcs finally asked.

Terra glanced up from her food and grunted an assent before tearing back into her meal. She wanted the conversation, but she also felt an animalistic need to eat. No doubt her body craved anything to help the healing process along.

The humans were now walking over, as were the insectoids, their beady eyes poring over Terra with unbridled curiosity. "Not-a-Male, right?" a short-haired man asked.

Terra took a swig from the jug of wine, letting the fiery stuff burn the back of her throat. "Name's Terra. And it's true what they say. I'm *not* a man."

"We watched you take down that balrog. How the hell did you do that?"

Terra pointed at the goblins. "See the pointy end? I tried really hard to get that side to go into his head. Looks like it worked. Don't tell anyone my secret."

The orcs cracked up while the humans looked on, dejected. "You talk more like an orc than a human," one joked.

Terra pointed at the hunk of meat she held at him. "What the hell are you doing down here?" she asked. "Isn't this whole arena thing an orc event or something?"

"It is an event for a certain kind of orc, the sort that has forgotten being orc is having no master."

Terra shrugged as she drank more wine. "You're going to have to do a little more explaining than that. Not sure if I understand this whole...actually, I have no idea what the fuck is going on. Period. So, why not do a little more talking."

"This arena is built on the remains of an ancient orc burial ground, but there is nothing orcish here. The orcs who run the arena are slaves to the Dark One. We are the ones who cannot be enslaved. Thus, we are to be put to death."

The other orcs nodded solemnly as they picked at their food. Terra wondered what situation the humans were in. "And what about you guys? What are you doing here?"

The human who spoke before gestured at his friend to pass the wine. "Probably the same as you. I was at a baseball game with my nephew and a big-ass light went off, and now I'm here. No one explained anything to me other than I'm going in there next."

"So, put to death, huh?"

The human handed Terra the jug of wine and grimaced. "If we're fighting anything like you had to, it's pretty much a death sentence."

An insectoid came over and sat next to Terra. Its eyes bulged a little, and it made a skittering noise that sounded like a thousand crickets all at once. Then it snatched a piece of meat from Terra's plate and started chomping.

One of the orcs laughed as he pointed at the insectoid. "That one likes you." He chuckled. "Mantiboids don't usually share meals with anyone."

Terra was about to correct the orc about the nature of sharing. Seeing as it was her plate, she was the one who was technically sharing. But it didn't matter. "You guys all look like you already have one foot in the grave," Terra said, her tone critical. "Doesn't seem like you have a lot of fight left in you."

No one replied for a little while. Then an orc said, "You're not wrong there. Some of us have been at this for a few hours now. None with any battles as glorious as yours, though. How do you still have the strength to go on?"

Terra hung her head as she let the pain of her burns settle in. How was she getting through this? "Honestly, what else am I going to do?" she asked.

As Terra was talking, the mantiboid who had shared her food was making an odd noise; its mandibles worked as if it were trying to speak. "Uh, You got a name?"

The mantiboid looked up at Terra, and a series of unpronounceable sounds emanated from its mandibles. The only thing that sounded like a word to Terra was a series of clicks. "Nib-nib" was all she was able to gather. "Sorry, I didn't catch all that but is 'Nib-nib' cool?" she asked.

The creature started to vibrate, holding its hands in front of its face. Then it spat up a sticky blue-green substance and held it out for Terra. "Uh, no thank you," she whimpered.

Nib-nib obviously didn't care about Terra's reservations and commenced to slather Terra's arm with the goop.

Terra shrieked in surprise, but her immediate fear dissipated when she found that the area the goop had been applied to had stopped hurting. "Holy shit," Terra said. "Whatever that is, just keep on doing it."

Nib-nib uttered another series of incomprehensible noises while the rest of the fighters began to gather around Terra. They were silent, as if they were waiting for Terra to speak.

Terra didn't know what to say. She had never motivated anyone before. Hell, she felt like she could do with some motivating. Her body felt like shit, and she didn't even want to think about having to fight again. But the other fighters were haunting in their despair.

There wasn't any sense in trying to be positive. The other fighters had to know how the odds were stacked against them. But they were all in it together. "Back home, I was a nobody," Terra started. "Everyone took a shit on me. My parents. My roommate. My shitty ex-boyfriend. Everyone."

The eyes of the fighters were glued on Terra. It gave her a little encouragement. "And now these assholes are trying to take a shit on me. Well, I'm done. If it really is kill or be killed out there, I'm not going to go down without dragging some assholes with me. That's all it is. Plain and simple. I don't want to die. And if I have to kill someone to make sure that doesn't happen, so fucking be it."

There was silence, each of the fighters taking Terra's words on board. She wasn't sure if they were what anyone needed to hear, but it was what she felt.

Nib-nib coughed up more goop and layered it on her other arm.

The effect was instantly soothing, and the relief from the pain gave Terra a little bit more energy. "And if I can fight through this, so can all of you," Terra said. "So, get some rest. Because we're going back at it again. And Nib-nib, please keep that up. You are a treasure."

Nib-nib scuttled about, clicked its mandibles, and threw up more of the goop. Terra leaned back and allowed herself to be as pampered as she could get in the prison of an orc arena.

CHAPTER THIRTY-FOUR

Abby and Creon had been at it for some time, and neither had come to a clear solution. Ideas were tossed around. Some of their best hadn't panned out. It wasn't for lack of effort, even though Abby felt like she wasn't pulling her weight.

Put simply, there were too many constraints on the situation. Both Creon and Abby had tossed out an unreal number of ideas to help Terra out. None of them were viable, though.

Abby knew the nanobots were key. A few hours ago, she'd had a flash of ideas centering around the nanobots and transporting them using the hadron collider. It had been a good start. The problem was, once they got the nanobots to Terra, what were they going to use them for.

The most Abby could think of was another construction similar to the speaker she'd created for Terra during her last battle. But the problem was more nanobots would mean a larger construct and would draw more attention to Terra than before.

Creon had gone out for coffee. He figured it was the only way he and Abby were going to be able to get through the next few hours.

Abby wasn't worried about staying awake. She was much more worried about dropping the ball and being responsible for Terra dying. Before Creon had left, he had tried to encourage Abby not to think of it that way. They weren't responsible for anything. All either of them could do was try to make a bad situation better.

That didn't help. Abby managed to nod and agree, enough to make Creon believe she had taken him seriously. But Abby knew deep down that if she didn't do something, Terra could very easily end up dead, and her death would be on Abby's head.

She rested her head on her desk. There had to be something she was missing. Something so obvious that she'd kick herself if someone brought it to her attention.

It was at that moment that Martin popped onto Abby's computer screen. "So, what are we going to use that collider for?" he asked.

Abby hoped Martin was in a better mood than usual. She didn't have the patience to deal with his sarcasm or shitty attitude. "No idea," Abby said. "Do you have any of those specs, based on what you found?"

Martin smiled mischievously as he folded his body into a rectangle. "Like I said, whatever I figured out is going to be so upsetting to Myrddin that you might get kicked out of this whole program. Are you still game?"

"As long as it helps Terra. I don't know if I can deal with her getting hurt because of me."

Martin straightened out and disappeared, reappearing on the holoprojector in the lab. "Good. I wanted to wait until Creon was out of here. Not sure how he would take this. I found some information on the Dark One's tech, and, fuck me, it's disgusting-ass shit."

Abby sat up and looked at Martin, intrigued. The AI hadn't mentioned anything earlier about Creon being upset about their plans. On top of that, Creon seemed pretty easy going about breaking the rules. What could Martin have in mind that would have made Creon uncomfortable?

"What do you got?"

Martin's eyes narrowed as the background of the holoprojector changed. Flames grew behind Martin as if he were in hell. "Well, looks like the Dark One's forces aren't all natural and organic," he started.

"He's using a form of mind control to get different races to follow him."

Abby didn't have a whole lot of background on the various races of the different realms nor an understanding of the complexities of the war so far, but she knew what Martin was telling her was terrible. The idea of losing the ability to make her own decisions sent a chill up Abby's spine.

Martin had disappeared, and the screen was now taken up with an image of frequency and different examples of DNA structure. "It looks like there are two ways that he's accomplishing that. One is through a form of microchip that disrupts the host's DNA. The other is with a sort of radiofrequency, but that one isn't used as often."

Abby stood and approached the holoprojector. "Why are you telling me all of this?"

"Because I figured out how to take over that system. One of them, at least. We can disrupt the microchips and use them to our advantage."

Abby suspected where Martin was going but wanted to hear him say it. "And how are we going to use that to our advantage?"

Martin groaned, obviously getting bored with the way the conversation was heading. "If the Dark One is controlling people through tech, that's only a hop and skip away from us being able to control people through tech. We could disrupt the microchips of everyone fighting in the arena, take them over, and use them to help Terra win."

There it was, exactly what Abby had thought Martin was hinting at. She didn't need Myrddin in the room to tell her it was a *very* bad idea. Not because it wouldn't work. The premise made a slippery slope look like an afternoon jog. "Mind-control the arena fighters?" Abby asked. "That's your plan?"

The display of DNA disappeared and was replaced by an image of Terra being taken care of by a goblin. "I'm just saying, none of those orcs or goblins have control over their minds. Who are we to be trying to kill them? How about instead of getting our hands dirty, we *release* them from their prison and see what happens?"

For the first time since Martin's creation, Abby had a very real sense of him as a person. She couldn't see what he had to gain from pushing this agenda, but he seemed to think this was the right approach.

What kind of AI had she created?

But the premise of his plan was solid, even if it did dip into morally questionable territory. But where did anyone draw the line of morality when you were facing enemies who were basically slaves?

And wasn't she doing the right thing by freeing the orcs to be able to fight whatever battle they wanted to?

But that wasn't what Martin was suggesting. Even if the AI hadn't said it explicitly, Abby knew what he was getting at. He didn't think Abby should just disable the microchips. Martin was suggesting they should co-opt the microchips and use them to help Terra.

Basically, they'd be taking one enslaved person's will and transferring it to the other. "How long would we be controlling them for?" Abby asked.

Martin shrugged as he poured himself a cup of coffee. "Don't know, don't care. That's up to you. Once we disrupt the signal, that's all up to you. I'd suggest up to the end of the fight."

"And what happens after we sever the connection completely?"

"Hard to say. Depends how long they've been hooked up to the chips. Most of them will probably survive. The other ones, though? Their brains might melt, or something like that. Who knows? I'm not an expert on orc cranial physiology. Wait, now I am." There was a pause before he added, "They'll probably live."

Abby glanced at Creon's desk, wondering what he would do in this kind of situation. This wasn't the sort of thing Abby had been prepared to think through when she had signed up. She had believed she was just going to be stopping the Dark One.

Now there were ethical questions about whether or not she should take control of an orc's brain or not. On the one hand, Abby didn't give a shit about the orcs or their plight. Orcs had killed her father. That was all she had needed to know.

On the other, Abby knew what that looked like in history. She knew what bigotry did to people. How was assuming all orcs were terrible any different? "Say we bypass their microchips. Once we're done, we can give them back control?"

Martin, who had been snoring softly, snapped back awake. "Huh? Yeah, of course. Whatever you want."

"Were you even listening?"

"Technically, since I'm now hardwired into every aspect of Middang3ard HQ, I'm always listening. So, yes. I heard you. We can if that's what you want. We could also fry their brains so we don't have any issues with them ever again, but I guess, to each their own."

Co-opting the Dark One's control was something Abby could justify. Keeping the orcs under her control was not. "All right, that's the plan. How are we doing it?"

Martin gestured at the nanobots. "I've already loaded the bots with a virus that'll wipe the Dark One's chips and insert our control program instead. Just send 'em to the collider with the coordinates I provided, and they'll beam aboard your tracker and *bam!* We're in business."

"This going to get traced back to us?"

"Not if you don't want it to."

"Good. Load the nanobots."

Martin blipped away and Abby went back to her computer, watching the upload of the virus. She didn't want to think too much about the plan Martin had proposed. There were some very obvious moral dilemmas, but at the end of it all, at least she wouldn't be keeping the orcs imprisoned.

As Abby tried to distract herself from the thoughts racing through her head, Creon returned to the lab. He set a cup of coffee in front of her as he returned to his desk. "Okay, so I was thinking we could try another kind of construct. Maybe something with a—"

Abby interrupted Creon. "Martin and I already took care of it. We're uploading the nanobots with a…perk buffer for Terra."

"A perk buffer? What the hell is that?"

Abby wasn't used to lying. Nor was she familiar with technical jargon. All she could do was repeat something she'd heard in passing in the bunkers. "Oh, I'm not sure, but Martin did some hypothetical scenarios and said it would be the best idea. I'll send it over if you want."

"No need. I trust your work. What's next?"

"Uh, just gotta teleport the nanobots over there."

Creon flipped through a few menus on the holoscreen the two shared. "All right, cleared them for transportation. I'll just get those down there."

As Creon loaded the nanobots into a transportation container, Abby's comm went off. *Holy shit, already in trouble?* she thought as her heart raced. "Hello?" she quietly answered.

Anabelle's voice came through calm, surprisingly calm for someone who was supposed to be upset. "Hey, I need to see you. Can you come down to the lounge?"

"Be there in two shakes of a calf's leg," Abby chirped a little too loudly.

"You okay, kid? You aren't freaking out about the whole Terra thing, are you?"

"No, no. No, everything is great. Where are you?"

Abby heard the crack of the lid of a carbonated bottle. "In the lounge, I told you that," Anabelle answered. "See you in a bit."

Anabelle was sitting at a table by herself, three drinks deep, by the time Abby arrived. The booze had taken no obvious effect, and she leaned back coyly as Abby sat down. The elf's hands were still covered in the wyrm's blood.

Abby scanned the lounge, uncertain of what she was supposed to do. She'd never been in a bar before and had no idea what the proper decorum was. "Uh, am I supposed to—"

"You just think of what you want and hit the pad right there."

"Am I allowed to drink? I mean, I'm not—"

Anabelle laughed as she waved her hand over the pad and another drink appeared before her. "I'm not your mother." Anabelle chuckled. "The human enlistment age is eighteen, right? And you're drinking age is twenty-one? I think there's a discrepancy there, but that's just me. So, do what you want."

Abby had seen her father drinking a beer called Industry. She tried to imagine the beer bottle and waved her hand over the pad. The beer appeared. She took a sip.

A rush of memories hit Abby, more than she was prepared for. She remembered her Pa allowing her to take a few sips whenever her mother wasn't looking. It was their little secret. The taste was bitter enough to make her laugh. It tasted like a secret.

Abby put the beer down and stared at the rim of the bottle while Anabelle watched her from across from the table. "Uh, did you just get back?" Abby asked as she picked the beer back up.

Anabelle studied her hands, the blood on her fingernails. "What let you know?" she asked.

Abby tilted her beer at Anabelle's nails. "Never seen your nails that dirty before," she said. "Even I'd have cleaned 'em up before entertaining company."

Anabelle chuckled as she nodded. "Yeah, been touch and go. Just got back. Closed up a Dark Gate. Was kind of an event. You should have seen it."

"What was it like?"

"Other than all the blood and carnage? Well, I got another look into a Dark Gate. Remember when you went through one?"

Abby didn't want to think back to that night. It had all been so terrifying and had happened so quickly that she didn't remember much. "It's all a blur," she finally said. "But I do remember the shit coming out. What'd you see?"

Anabelle bit her thumb, absentmindedly licking the crusted blood off her fingertips. "Not quite sure," she answered. "Looked like I was looking through a doorway, but it was…split down the middle. I saw one place, but then another. Didn't know how to make sense of it."

Abby snapped her fingers, remembering something she had read about varying waves of information on a conspiracy theory website. It had sounded like nonsense at the time, but with how things were rapidly changing in her life, she wasn't going to write anything off.

Anabelle glanced up from her drink, her face as dark and mysterious as ever. "What you thinking over there, kid?"

Abby sipped her beer again, her thoughts on the conversations she and Pa would have, staring at the sky, letting their minds wander. "Read about different kinds of astral portals once," Abby said. "People doing astral projection, seeing different realities and things of that sort."

"And?"

"Well, one lady said she opened a portal once, but it was getting frequencies from an alien ship passing by, and her portal became two. She was looking at two different places at once."

Abby regretted telling Anabelle the anecdote as soon as it was out of her mouth. Why the hell would Anabelle care about alien stories? She was surprised when Anabelle asked, "So you think it might be two frequencies conflating?"

The girl shrugged. "I mean, according to the theory, if all these gates open to the same place and there are a few open at the same time, cosmic rays and all that could scramble things up pretty badly. You might be getting a little look into what the other gates have to offer."

Anabelle leaned back and crossed her legs as she folded her arms. "Huh. I'll run that by Myrddin. How'd things go on your end, kid? Figure out how to help Terra?"

For a second, Abby ran through what she could tell Anabelle about her plan with the nanobots. But she couldn't see herself lying to Anabelle. Not now, not ever. "We're gonna hack the Dark One's chips on them orcs. Turn 'em against each other."

Anabelle's eyes narrowed as she leaned over the table. "How do you know about that?" Anabelle asked, her voice colder than Abby had ever heard it.

The sudden change in tone threw Abby off, and she stuttered as she answered, "Martin. He hacked into HQ's files and told me."

A small smile broke across Anabelle's face as she leaned back and relaxed. "So, your plan is to turn the Dark One's tech back on him? Interesting. You think you can do that?"

"I know I can. Just don't know if I should."

An alarm sounded, and both Anabelle's and Abby's comms went off. Terra was about to head to the arena.

Anabelle was the first to rise. "We're at war, Abby. What we have to do is what we have to do. We'll figure out what's right or wrong later."

CHAPTER THIRTY-FIVE

Terra stood in one of the candlelit hallways that ran through the arena like veins. She was surrounded by humans who were barely armed.

The cheering and bloodlust of the orcs who filled the stands could be heard through the vibrating walls. They were calling for a show. They wanted to see blood, to see suffering, to watch the humans crushed into dust.

Terra wondered where the orcs she had dined with had been taken. She didn't know what kind of fight she was in for, but it seemed odd to have orcs who were being punished fight alongside orcs who meant to be doling out the punishment.

Could make sense to orcs, though. How was she supposed to know how they thought? Her first choice of punishment would have never been to erect an entire arena.

Heaving breath. Soft sobbing. Someone in the hall was crying. It was too dark for Terra to make out who had finally cracked under the pressure. Whoever it was, they were breaking apart. It could be heard in their tears. That was not how someone cried when they were afraid.

Those were the tears of the dead, of one who realizes there is nowhere else to go. Who has to look their death in the eye and fears how inadequate they might be judged to be.

Other than the weeping man, the hallway was silent. Terra wished she could do something to comfort him. She remembered how afraid she had been when she first woke up. Hell, she knew how afraid she was right now. The fear hadn't gone away. She'd only gotten used to it.

Fear was something that could be forgotten, like anything else in life. Nothing had to be held onto, even if it was right in front of your face. You could choose when you wanted to stop seeing it. Even if it didn't go away, it would be close enough for most people.

"Hey," Terra called, trying to make her voice louder than the screaming above. "Who's crying?"

The sobbing stopped, replaced by sniffling. Terra thought it was a much more pathetic sound. There was a certain strength in being able to cry freely. It was something Terra had never quite got the hang of. "I'm sorry, I couldn't help it," a voice croaked. "I'm just so goddamn scared."

"Where are you?"

A young man with bleach-blond hair emerged from the shadows. He didn't look any older than nineteen, nor did he look like he'd ever been in a fight. "What's your name?" Terra asked.

The young man struggled to meet Terra's eyes. "Eric," he said after a few moments. "Name's Eric."

"What are you scared of?"

Eric glanced at the other men huddled in the hallway as if this were some kind of trick question. "What do you think I'm afraid of?"

"Hey, you want to pop off like an asshole, that's up to you. But if you want to have a real talk, be my guest and mature the fuck up."

"Sorry, sorry. I'm sorry. I'm...fuck, I'm scared of dying. That's what we're here for, isn't it? All the other matches, everyone got weapons. We didn't get anything. They're just sending us in there to die like the fucking Romans did. We're not supposed to have a chance."

The kid started crying again, doubled over, his hands covering his face, not even bothering to look ashamed. His whole body trembled as he tried to force words out of his mouth.

The other two watched on in silence. Neither of them moved, not even to look at the kid. To look upon him would be to look upon their own fears. It was easier to focus on what you could deal with.

The kid's shaking voice came through his sobs. "I don't want to die," he stammered. "I have a boyfriend. I have a fucking family. I'm supposed to go back home. I'm supposed to be home!"

Terra took the kid's chin between her fingers, then she pulled him close and hugged him tightly as the crowd above them shouted for murder and mayhem. She held the kid as if he were the only person in the world. "You're right. That's why we're here."

She let go of the kid, who looked up at her, his tear-stained eyes bright in the candlelight. "I don't want to die," he repeated.

"Neither do I, but it is probably going to happen. That's just the truth. I'm not dying on my knees or my back, though. If I'm going, it's going to be on my feet. They're going to have to beat me into the ground. That's the least I can do for myself."

Eric wiped his eyes and shook his head. "We saw you fight," he admitted. "I'm not like you. I'm not strong like that. I already had one match, and I barely made it. I'm—"

"Probably going to die. We don't have weapons, and we have no idea what we're up against. So, you can hang in the back and get cut down with the first deaths. It'll probably be quick, and there's no shame in that. I'm not going to judge you. This shit is fucked up. This isn't in the realm of normal. You could die curled in a ball, begging for your life. There's no shame."

Terra kissed Eric's forehead and patted him on the head before she strode away, returning to the front gate. "These are ridiculous times. This is beyond the realm of courageous or cowardly. So, you do you, boo."

The rusted iron gates creaked as they began to rise. "Guess it's showtime," she said. "Like I told Eric, you guys can die however you want. But if you want to put up a fight, stick with me, and we'll give them something to remember."

Four orcs waited on the other side of the gate, and they motioned for the humans to come out into the arena. Terra stepped out first, followed by the rest of the nameless human males, Eric trailing in the back. Terra was the only one who walked with her head up.

The stands were even more packed than the day before. A special podium had been erected at what looked like a VIP spot. An older orc, all withered with a bulbous beer gut, sat on a purple couch, attended by four scantily clad orc females, who were fanning him.

As the humans stepped out of their gate, the old orc stood, grabbed a cane, and made his way over to the microphone at the podium. He cleared his throat, a disgusting phlegmy sound that almost made Terra gag upon hearing it. "Welcome, humans," the orc shouted, "to the battle of the Red Lion!"

The arena had been set up almost like an interactive theater production. A section of a bar had been built up, complete with enough tables and seats for all of the humans. There were already a handful of orcs and goblins sitting at the table. The ones from the dining hall.

Nib-nib and a few other mantiboids were behind the bar, wearing aprons, washing dishes, and serving wine.

Not knowing what else to do, Terra approached the bar and sat in front of Nib-nib. The rest of the humans stayed rooted to their positions.

The only human who bothered to follow Terra was Eric. He sat at the bar with her while the old orc narrated from the top of the arena, saying, "This battle will commemorate our glorious victory over Myrddin's pathetic MERCs."

"Here we find the MERCs drinking in the canteen, delving fully into the lifestyle which has engendered such weakness in them. Do you see discipline? Do you see dedication? Do you see any of the strength the Dark One looks for in his disciples?"

Terra leaned toward an orc sitting at the bar next to her. "If this is what the Dark One's orcs are like, I can see why you guys didn't want to join them. This is worse than going to church. What is that guy going on about?"

The orc drank from his jug of wine. "You might want to try some. They at least gave us the kindness of a drink before our death. And the old one is speaking of one of the Dark One's first defeats."

"I thought he said this was commemorating a victory."

"He's lying. It was the first real defeat the Dark One experienced. They tried to ambush the MERCs during some sort of party, and they wiped the Dark One's forces out. A shameful thing, to attack during a celebration of your enemy's victory. Those are no longer orcs."

Terra picked up the jug of wine in front of her and handed it to Eric. "Drink up, dude, for tonight we dine in hell," she joked.

Eric's hands shook as he took the jug and drank. "I hated that movie," he whispered.

"Honestly, I fell asleep in the first ten minutes. There's only so much of a movie you can hold up with buff, shirtless dudes. But to each their own."

The old orc was still rattling on as Terra, the orcs and goblins, and Eric drank their wine. When death nipped at your heels, what more was there to do than savor one last drink? But the time for savoring was done. Now the old orc reeled backward, cackling madly as the crowd cheered.

Terra scanned the bar. She hadn't seen any weapons when she first walked in, and nothing had changed. She and her fellow warriors were still being served up on a platter for the spectacle.

The old orc's laughter mingled with the crowds shouting, echoing throughout the arena.

The gold gates facing the open bar began to rise. The humans stood, and the orcs continued drinking. Terra and Eric turned to see what would come from the gates as Nib-Nib walked out from behind the bar, anxiously rubbing his mandibles together.

Six orcs strode out from behind the gate, each holding a torch.

Terra leaned over and nudged Eric. "Not too bad. I can take at least three of them. We'll get out of this alive."

As Terra spoke, the orcs near the gate separated, making room for six more orcs guiding something that was chained up. They were struggling with the chains.

Out of the darkness stepped a chimera. The creature was nearly eight feet tall, with the body of a lion. Its tail was a three-headed hydra, its head a lion's, its mane filled with snakes. When the lion head roared, its mouth split down the middle, and a horned goat's diminutive head forced itself out.

Terra had nothing to say to such a grotesque sight. Even the orcs at her side seemed to be dismayed.

Before Terra could offer Eric any form of encouragement, a posse of twelve orcs rode out of the gateway, each atop a warg, brandishing all manner of weapons.

The orcs released the chimera's chains, moving away from the beast to leap onto the extra wargs that had run out into the arena.

The old orc's laughter punctuated the scene. "Let the slaughter begin," he shouted.

CHAPTER THIRTY-SIX

The tracker was broadcasting from the top of the arena, supplying a bird's eye video feed. Abby hadn't been told by Anabelle to broadcast this fight, but Abby figured it should be done. If the point was to keep humanity informed of what was going on, it didn't make any sense to stop now.

The other reason for the tracker being so far from the action was because it was busy sending nanobots over through the hadron collider. Creon and Martin had rigged it to send a small batch of nanobots directly to Abby's tracker as long as the device remained stationary.

Distance wasn't a problem, though. The tracker had immaculate video-capture capabilities. Even being more than a hundred feet away didn't take away from the video's quality, which was good because the scene Abby was watching was insane.

The pageantry of this battle put the others to shame. The fights before seemed to be about violence. This one looked to be about something else, a narrative the viewers needed to see. Didn't seem much different from what Abby was doing.

Abby checked to see how many human channels she'd been able to co-opt since she began broadcasting, which was most of the major ones. Any station she hadn't hacked into had picked up the broadcast from someone else.

The whole world was watching, and she was just as eager as the rest of them to see what was going to happen. The only difference was she had a say in what was going down.

Martin's plan still made her feel uncomfortable, even with Anabelle's approval. The elf's detachment from the question had put Abby on edge again. It didn't seem like Anabelle was at all concerned.

Abby didn't know much about the history of the Dark One or what had been going on with the war. She only knew what had happened to her father, and that the Dark One was responsible for it. Revenge had been the reason she'd come to help Myrddin.

Now that Abby was in the midst of the war efforts, she could see how things were more complicated. Not necessarily that the bad guys weren't the bad guys, but that she could navigate the kinds of choices she'd be called to.

Already, Abby had been instrumental in bringing a new kind of intelligence into existence. An intelligence humanity had been debating for the last forty-something years. And it had been an afterthought for her and the rest of her team.

Then there was the off-handed suggestion of her own creation. Mind control. What was next?

There would be other times to try to work through these ethical dilemmas. The most important thing at the moment was to save as many lives as possible. Abby had been prepared to help Terra, but now there were more humans as well.

Not only were there humans, but there were also orcs and goblins, and something Abby couldn't recognize. Were they Abby's responsibility as well? And what about the orcs? How did she know they weren't secretly on the Dark One's side?

The more questions Abby had, the harder it became for her to figure out what she was doing. Thankfully, this time around, the lab wasn't full of spectators. Only Creon and Abby were in the lab, and he was glued to his computer.

The nanobots were nearly finished uploading. From there, all

Abby had to do was guide the tracker to a few of the orcs who were microchipped and overwrite the programming. Martin had projected they had enough nanobots to take over three or four hosts. Any more might stretch the virus too thin.

Abby saw the gates opening on the other side of the arena. Then she watched the creatures flooding into the arena. *Shit*, she thought. *This is even worse than the last time...and...they don't have any weapons??? Are you serious?*

A ping went off on the computer. The nanobots were ready. It was now or never.

Orc riders raced across the arena, whipping up dust as they circled the makeshift replica of the Red Lion. They were hooting and hollering, sounding like a band of merry banshees or wraiths fresh-pulled from the bowels of hell.

Shrieks from the chimera punctured the air as the creature bounded about, seemingly mindless, oblivious to friend or foe as the orcs on foot rushed away from its grasping claws toward the Red Lion.

Human, goblin, and orc alike took shelter behind the bar, Terra among them. There did not seem to be any other option. They were unarmed, and a horde was fast approaching.

Terra leaned against the side of the bar, trying to catch her breath. She looked at Eric, who no longer trembled, but now stared dumbfounded ahead as if the little bit of life worth worrying about had finally cast itself free of his mortal coil.

On her feet. That was how Terra had said she was going to die, not cowering behind some bullshit bar. If she were going to die in a bar, it should at least be one of her choosing.

She inched over to the side of the bar, past the rest of the chosen sacrifices. She peeked around the corner. A few orcs were approaching on foot. The rest were making a show of the chaos, no doubt playing to the audience.

This wasn't supposed to be a fight. Terra knew that now. This was a spectacle. They were probably expecting her and the rest of the unarmed to be frightened, hiding, and without hope.

Two orcs stepped into the bar. Terra could see them grabbing her and the rest of the humans, dragging them out into the open arena, and slitting their throats. It was too easy to imagine.

Terra leapt out from behind the bar, racing to the two orcs. She extended her arms and barreled through the both of them, catching them in the throats and knocking them off their feet. Then she grabbed a dropped ax and brought it down on one of the orcs' chests.

As the other orc tried to regain his feet, Terra hit him in the face and slashed his throat. Then she scooped up his weapons, an ax and a short sword, slung his shield over her shoulder, and retreated behind the bar as the crowd screamed.

Terra tossed the sword, ax, and shield on the ground before her compatriots. "Who's coming out there with me?" she asked.

The humans exchanged glances, as did the orcs and goblins, which was the real surprise for Terra. After what seemed a decade of silence, Eric grabbed the short sword and shield. Nib-nib took the remaining ax. "If we get weapons, will you fight?" Terra asked.

Still silence from the humans. Grave looks of disappointment from the orcs. One such orc looked up and said, "If you have the courage to fight, human, so do we."

"Good. Because I'm fighting."

Terra stepped out from behind the bar as more foot soldiers headed her way. She screamed and beat her chest as she rushed at the orcs, Eric at her side, and Nib-nib not far behind. They didn't wait to see if the rest were coming with them. They sprinted toward glory.

Abby steered the tracker through a throng of orcs. The arena was getting chaotic. Terra and two others who Abby didn't know were fighting tooth and nail in the bar. Only foot soldiers had entered the bar. The rest were still outside, working the crowd up.

This would be the best time to take over one of orcs' microchips.

Abby brought the tracker close to one of the orcs outside the bar. She wanted to snag one before Terra got the chance to cut it down.

The tracker landed on the back of its neck. A small microchip poked out of the orc's skin. "Martin, we're on it. Take over the chip," Abby said.

Martin popped up on the holoprojector and rubbed the two ends of his paperclip body together. "Now we're in business," he shouted.

The holoprojector turned red as Martin sent the virus through the microchip. "Let me see if it's working," he muttered.

The screen changed to a physiological readout of an orc, complete with a diagram showcasing its central nervous system. "Not only are we in business, but we're buying everyone else out too," Martin exclaimed.

Abby pulled the tracker away from the orc and stared at the holoprojector. A wave of nausea hit her. "What now?" she asked.

"I'll take control of this one, plus a few more. You better tell Terra what's happening and snag another one. We'll see how far we can stretch this."

The tracker headed to Terra, buzzing around her head as she picked up an orc and body-slammed it. Abby turned on the speaker and said, "Terra, this is Abby. Don't want to alarm you, but we're getting some of the orcs to switch sides."

Terra whipped her head around, clearly looking for the source of the voice. Abby landed the tracker on her shoulder. "Don't worry too much about it, but if you see an orc killing another orc, it's just me."

As Abby explained, an orc on Terra's side jumped over a table, impaling an enemy orc. "Honestly, I'm not sure who's killing who anymore!" Terra shouted. "But appreciate the help."

The tracker lifted off Terra and headed to another orc, landing next to the microchip and taking it over.

Martin crept back onto the holoprojector's screen. "We got a problem. You're going to have to use VR to control this one. The virus isn't as foolproof as I thought."

Abby stood from her chair abruptly and exclaimed, "What do you mean, I'm going to have to control it?"

"Trust me, it's intuitive. Just get hooked into the VR."

There wasn't time to ask any questions. Abby went to the table with the VR equipment and suited up, hoping Creon wasn't paying too much attention. She slid on the VR visor and stepped into the orc's body.

Abby was instantly transported to the battlefield. Apparently, Martin had done upgrades on the VR equipment as well. It was as if she were there in person.

Martin popped up in the corner of Abby's field of vision. "I'm moving the tracker to a safe space. All the nanobots are used up, so make the most of this!"

Abby stared down at her hands. They were the hands of an orc, and they held two daggers. Another orc was standing beside her, preparing to enter the bar. Without hesitation, Abby drove her daggers into the other orc's back.

It was Abby's first taste of revenge. It tasted great.

Most of the orcs, humans, and goblins in the bar were armed. They were preparing to make their push to leave. Terra figured as long as they remained on the defensive, they were merely waiting to die.

The alternative of a chimera and orcs riding wargs wasn't much more promising, but it beat being cut down around a table.

But, why was it taking so long for the orcs to zero in on their position? There was no way that was all of the advance party.

At Terra's side, Nib-nib made an inarticulate noise. Terra looked down at him and asked, "You sure you don't want a sword, buddy?" He had given the ax to someone else.

Nib-nib raised his forearms and clicked them shut enthusiastically. Guess that answered that.

Terra turned back to the rest of the folks huddled together in the bar. "This is our push!" she shouted. "We take this arena and make it ours!"

Shouts from humans, goblins, and orcs alike rose up, momentarily drowning out the screams of the crowd.

Terra rushed out of the bar, tackling the first orc in front of her and driving her ax into its chest. The rest of her ramshackle group ran out after her.

Outside the bar, there was chaos. The orcs on wargs were riding around, kicking up dust and whooping loudly. The chimera was waiting for them, spitting small bursts of acid on the ground as it pawed the sand.

Terra stared down the chimera. This was where she was making her stand.

CHAPTER THIRTY-SEVEN

Martin's voice screamed over Abby's VR control system. Abby nearly turned and ran, she was so engrossed in the carnage around her. "We got something like a problem."

Abby guided her orc's hands around another orc's throat, watching the life fade from her opponent's eyes. "Is it something *like* a problem, or is it a problem?" she asked.

"Our signal is cracking. Or not quite the signal, but we're losing control. There's too much biofeedback on your end, and it's causing—"

"Could you just give me a straight answer?"

Martin sighed as he grumbled his response. "Your fleshy bits are making it hard to keep the signal up, and I can't take them all over. Also, seems there's a firewall up, making global control impossible. You're going to cut out, and if you break into another chip, you're just going to get cut out of that one."

"What are my options?"

Martin hummed while he was thinking. "Uh, I guess you could inject some of those nanobots into your bloodstream to compensate."

If Abby had been paying closer attention or had known Martin better, she would have been able to sense the doubt in his voice. Unfortunately, she was distracted, and her relationship with Martin was less than two weeks old. "Fine, let's do it," she said.

"The vial is already prepped on the nanobot counter."

Abby pulled up her VR headset and rolled up her sleeves. She reached over to the nanobot counter and, exactly as Martin had said, found a vial of nanobots. The syringe at the end of the vial gave Abby cause to pause. She hated needles.

Screams erupted through her VR headset. She yanked it down to see what was happening.

Terra was on the chimera's back, slashing it with her ax. A human was caught under the beast's front paws, and the lion's head was tearing him to pieces.

Abby had to look away. She couldn't bear to see another human life lost in this nonsense of the Dark One's creation. She had to do something to help. Anything. She grabbed the syringe of nanobots and injected them into her forearm.

The feeling was instantaneous. Chills went down her back, and she felt ice coming up her throat. Her fingers went numb, as did her toes. She fell to the floor, hacking up whatever was in her.

Creon jumped up from his desk and rushed over to Abby. "What the hell are you doing, Abby?" he asked. "What did you just do?"

As quickly as it had overtaken her body, the cold left. Abby got back to her feet. Something was different. She didn't know what it was, but she felt it in every corner of her body, deep in the crevices of her brain. Now that she thought about it, she'd never felt the crevices of her brain before.

Creon grabbed Abby by the shoulders and forced her to look at him. "Abby, what have you done?"

Abby calmly removed Creon's hands from her shoulders. "Don't worry about it," she said. "Gotta take care of the mission, right?"

Creon peered at Abby anxiously before turning back to his computer. "Hope you're smart enough not to do something stupid," he warned.

Abby pulled down her VR headset. The orc she was controlling was still alive. Martin must have taken over to keep it from dying. Abby took a step forward, and she felt the sand on her feet. Not the way she'd felt it before. Not a simulation. She swore to God she could feel each grain of sand.

The immersion was amazing. It was like being in a completely new body. But there wasn't time to appreciate whatever the hell the nanobots were doing. There was a fight to win.

Terra wrestled with the lion's head, wrapping her hand around it, trying to choke the life from it. The chimera was strong, though, stronger than the balrog had been. It bucked its hind legs and sent Terra flying.

She hit the ground hard, scrambling to get up as fast as she could. Baby-soft hands grabbed her by the back of her shirt and pulled her up. It was Eric. "I got your back," he said as he smiled.

Terra was about to thank Eric when a warg came at them. She went to the right, and Eric went to the left—the same direction the orc atop the warg was leaning.

The orc snatched Eric up with its spear, sending the boy flying and leapt atop him as soon as his body hit the ground, tearing into his neck. Crimson blood splashed across the golden sand. "No!" Terra screamed.

But there was no time for mourning. Another warg came at Terra as the one that had finished Eric doubled back, heading for her.

She ran, weaving between the dozens of bodies clashing with each other, dodging the blades that danced, swinging to the side, slashing an orc across the chest, uncertain of whether or not they were on her side, falling, getting up, throwing herself forward.

The warg riders burst through the crowd, their riders' axes felling anything in their path.

Terra glanced over her shoulder, grabbed a spear off the orc in front of her, and sent it sailing through the air.

The spear hit one of the riders in the chest, knocking him off of the warg. The warg continued on toward Terra.

Not knowing what else to do, Terra leaned over like a linebacker, and when the warg lunged, she met it head-on, grabbing it by the throat and tossing it to the ground.

As the warg tried to shake off the attack, Terra climbed onto its back and grabbed it by its fur, forcing the warg forward.

The crowd roared with excitement. The battle continued to rage around her. Up ahead, the chimera was squaring off with a group of mantiboids, Nib-nib at the front. *Not another one,* Terra thought. *Not another fucking one.*

Terra took off toward the chimera. She reached behind her and grabbed one of the spears hanging from the leather sleeve across the warg's back. It was a good weight. Felt right in her hand. She sent the spear flying at the chimera.

The spear hit the beast in the chest, and it reeled back on its hind legs. Terra kept running toward it, cutting through any orcs in her way. She leapt off, ax raised, and landed on the chimera's back.

Before Terra could attack, the chimera sprang away from the mantiboids. The sudden movement made Terra lose her balance. She fell off, and the chimera shook its mane fiercely before pouncing on Terra.

Terra hardly had enough time to pull her ax up. She caught the chimera's fangs with the head. The chimera gnashed its teeth, barely held back by Terra, intent on crushing her skull. As she tried to push the monster's head back, the lion's jaw separated and the fanged goat's head forced itself through.

The goat snapped at Terra, who could only move her head, jerking it to the left or the right to avoid having her throat torn open.

Across the arena, Abby, using the orc, sliced through the bowels of a number of orcs as she turned to locate Terra. When she saw the girl's predicament, she sprinted toward the chimera. She tackled the beast, knocking it off Terra.

The chimera rolled around in the sand before returning to its feet.

It flew toward Abby, landing on top of her. The beast sank its teeth into the orc's throat.

There was a brief flash, and Abby was disconnected from the orc. She pulled up the VR headset and collapsed in her seat. Martin's voice came through Abby's comm. No, it wasn't her comm. She could hear Martin in her head. "Hey, we're not done yet!" he shouted.

Abby sank her head into her hands. The disconnect had been sudden and jarring. For a second, she had thought she had been killed. "Controlling orcs isn't going to be enough. Bigger. That's what we need. Those microchips only on the orcs?"

"It's a safe bet the chimera has a microchip. From what I've gathered, it's how the Dark One controls most of his forces."

Abby slid her VR helmet down, instinctively taking control of the tracker, landing it near the dead orc's body and loading it back up with the nanobots. Then she guided the tracker to Terra, who was trying to catch her breath. "Terra, this is Abby," she broadcast through the speaker. "I have a plan."

Terra looked at the tracker for a moment. "And what would that be?"

"Gonna try to take care of the chimera. If it works, put it out of its misery, all right?"

"Sounds good to me."

Abby guided the tracker over to the chimera. The creature didn't seem to notice her. She easily navigated the tracker to the back of the lion's mane and touched down, then she looked through her headset for a chip.

There it was. The tracker scuttled over to the microchip. Abby was vaguely aware that she wasn't using the controls for the tracker anymore. She'd worry about it later.

The tracker dumped its nanobots onto the microchip, and the microscopic robots got to work uploading the virus.

Abby's body jerked forward as her consciousness merged with that of the chimera. She felt herself pushing something out of the way, uncertain what it was but very aware it did not want her inside. It didn't matter. Abby was taking control. She had to.

Martin's voice was in Abby's head again. "We're not going to be able to take full control, but take as much as you can. Immobilize the ugly son of a bitch."

"Hopefully, Terra will see her opening."

Abby fought for control of the chimera. If it had been as simple as seizing the creature's body, this would have been a lot easier. But she was fighting for something much more complicated than that.

Terra watched the chimera spasming. It wasn't too noticeable, but she could tell that something was up. This must be the distraction Abby was talking about. It was time to put an end to this.

The arena was covered with the dead bodies of orcs, goblins, and humans. Most of the mantiboids had managed to stay alive, but too many had fallen. And as long as that chimera was still alive, more were going to die.

Terra leaned over the corpse of one orc. The orc had two *katars*, one in each hand. Terra appropriated them, then sprinted toward the chimera.

Small spasms rocked the chimera's body as its head jerked back and forth, trying to take a step forward but moving as if it were possessed by some kind of spirit. It could barely turn its head when Terra came ramming into its side.

The chimera was knocked over, its legs flailing as Terra climbed atop it. She dodged the giant claws and squeezed down on her *katars'* rods. Then she drove both into the chimera's chest.

Terra squeezed the rods again and the blades split into three, tearing through the chimera's body. She withdrew the blades and slammed them back in. She hacked and hacked at the creature as it roared in pain.

The crowd had gone silent. There was no other sound but the cries of the chimera, of tearing flesh, of Terra's screams.

Finally, there was only silence. Terra stood, drenched in blood. She studied the battlefield.

The remaining orcs from the opposing team had retreated, laying their weapons on the ground and backing away toward their golden gates. At first, Terra wanted to give chase and cut them down where they stood.

Instead, she went over to Eric's dead body and picked it up. She approached her own gates while the rest of her team gathered their dead, the crowds chanting, "Not-a-Male! Not-a-Male!"

Abby pulled off her VR headset and sat down. She could still feel the blades of the *katars* tearing open her stomach and the blood flowing out of her. She pressed her fingers to her belly to make sure. "Martin," Abby started, "what are those nanobots doing to me?"

Martin didn't instantly answer. "You know, of all the things you've asked me so far, that's the only thing I don't have an answer to. Back there, that was more like me thinking out loud. This is all new territory."

"You're in my head, aren't you?"

"Or you're in mine."

Abby chuckled as she stared down at her hands. The skin around her cuticles looked a little silver, almost the color of an exposed wire. "Don't think out loud anymore, Martin," she suggested.

Creon watched Abby from his desk. He didn't say anything, but Abby could feel his eyes on her. There was no judgment, only a sort of intense curiosity. "What're you thinking, Creon?" she asked.

The goblin got up and walked past the nanobot chamber. "The chamber's empty. I didn't send all of our nanobots through the collider. A third of them were still here."

Abby's heart jumped. She had injected a third of the nanobots.

There hadn't seemed to be so many of them. Were they just going to stay in her blood forever.?

Pa's voice rang in Abby's head. "Sometimes you just need to slow the hell down instead of rushing headfirst into trouble." That was what he'd said when she'd started messing around with building drones. She'd almost electrocuted herself.

At least he'd be happy that I'm raising the bar, Abby thought.

Creon came over to Abby and extended his hand. Abby reluctantly gave him hers and he turned it over, looking at it with an eye for detail usually only seen in doctors. "Just as I thought. What made you think that was a good idea?"

"Martin suggested it. Said it would help with the connection to the other bots."

"A reasonable theory. And you didn't think to question him?"

"Why? He's not trying to hurt me or anything."

Creon's eyes narrowed as he sat back down. "Are you sure about that?"

Abby's body tensed. She hadn't even thought of that, and now Martin was in her head. She still wasn't sure in what capacity, though. Could he read her mind? Was she merely a giant computer to him?

Creon relaxed and leaned back in his chair. "I'm sorry, he's probably okay. Years of being on edge…it's hard to trust anyone. We'll keep this between you and me. No need for Myrddin to know. And as for the nanobots, we're going to have to start running tests on you. Make sure that you're not having an adverse reaction to them, and tracking any other information you think is relevant."

"What do you mean?"

"These bots have never been introduced to organic material before. I have no idea what's going to happen. But I don't want to treat you like a science experiment. I'll make sure you aren't getting sick. Whatever else you feel like I should know, just tell me."

Abby nodded as she stood. Her stomach was killing her. She wasn't sure if she was hungry or if she was sick. "I'm going to go grab some grub. Could you kill the transmission? Gotta start thinking 'bout how to help Terra long-term. We aren't gonna be able to keep this up."

Creon flashed Abby a thumbs-up. "I'll keep the tracker on Terra and comm you if anything comes up."

"Thanks. And thanks for, you know, keeping this quiet. Really."

Creon waved away Abby's apology. "Science isn't like magic. It's rarely elegant. Sometimes things just have to be messy."

CHAPTER THIRTY-EIGHT

Anabelle was in her room. She'd watched the fight from her television. When she and Abby had received the comm that Terra was fighting, she'd remembered how useless it had been for her and anyone other than Abby and Creon to be in the lab. She was glad Abby thought to broadcast the fight.

Even though Anabelle knew Terra's survival was something of a professional cause, she couldn't help rooting for her. She'd never seen a human fight like that before, let alone one with no training.

Most of the time, when humans were brought into any of the other realms, they were either helped out with advanced tech or with magic to bring them up to speed with the other races.

Terra didn't have any of that.

The only well she was drawing strength from was within her.

That was the kind of person Anabelle wanted on her team— SWARMMT or whatever the hell Myrddin had named it. Anabelle still couldn't believe a wizard could be so bad at naming anything. Regardless of the name, someone like Terra would be a welcome addition.

Abby had the smarts. Terra could provide the brawn. The three of them could probably whip the rest of the humans into shape.

Anabelle opened her briefing from the prior mission and scrutinized the personality test of Naota, the security guard she had picked up on the way back. His scores were all over the place. He had a problem with authority, trusted his intuition, had an intense desire to make friends, and somewhat of a "loose" concept of reality. But Anabelle had seen him in action. He was like an idiot savant.

Now that Terra's battle was over, Anabelle could relax. She wanted to check on how the human world was responding to the recent battle before heading to sleep. The response last time had been overwhelmingly positive. Hopefully, tonight wouldn't be any different.

She kept replaying the final moments of the battle. Terra taking down the chimera was more memorable than her own killing of the wyrm. It was just a wyrm, after all. *She's also got incredible leadership skills*, Anabelle thought. *Better than I do, at least. That's good.*

Hell, it wouldn't hurt to watch a little bit of TV before meditation. Her past teachers would have punished her for slacking off, but most of them were dead now. They couldn't enjoy the simple pleasure of sitting down and vegging out after a hard day of work. Besides, this was something like work.

Anabelle flipped through the news, catching glimpses of how the human world was responding to Terra's victory. For the most part, it wasn't that different than earlier in the day. The fanaticism had picked up, though, and that entertained her.

None of humanity had known Terra a week ago, and now they were swearing their lives to her. A couple of folks in New York were already in the process of starting a religion with Terra as their goddess. *I wish people would worship me like that,* Anabelle thought, chuckling as she lay back in bed. *All I ever got were stalkers.*

Well, that was enough TV for now. Anabelle knew what she needed to. Humans were responding. More importantly—not that she actually cared—but most human media had already lost track of Myrddin amidst all of this. The wizard had probably had something to do with that.

Anabelle changed to her Traveler's robes. She knelt in front of her bed and closed her eyes, allowed herself to slip back onto the Path, to fall into the crevices of her lost memories. Tonight would be the night she was going to piece it all back together.

Even though no one had been watching her own battle with the wyrm, Anabelle had re-watched it over and over in her mind. She was sloppy. She knew it. The three Paths had become muddled in her head. Worse still, she'd almost run out of manna during the fight.

At least she hadn't gotten lost in the battle. Something she had noticed about Terra. It was difficult to tell if Terra was keeping her head on straight, or if she'd been consumed by the fight. With survival hanging so delicately in the balance, it was always difficult to guess.

But that wasn't the point of meditation. Thinking about what others did well or not, was counterproductive. There were memories in the black. Thinking about today was just creating new memories to be tossed on top of the ones needing to be uncovered.

There were always other times to come back to new experiences. Or experiences you were wishing for.

Roy's smile and gruff, unshaven face flashed in front of Anabelle's eyes for a second. *Goddamn it,* she thought. *I'm never going to be able to concentrate now.*

Anabelle forced the mech rider's face from her mind. Even if she wasn't able to concentrate on her meditation, she didn't intend to spend the whole night thinking about him. There were other ways to keep her mind and body occupied and sharpened.

The elf changed out of her robe and into workout clothes, then headed to the weight room.

Abby sat on the toilet, staring between her legs. There was a lot of blood, but her period had ended nearly a week ago. When she flushed and stood, she thought she was going to faint. As her vision blurred, she leaned over the sink and tried to catch her breath.

Cold water. That should help.

Abby ran the water and cupped her hands underneath the faucet, splashing her face, rubbing her eyes as hard as she could. When she looked in the mirror, she saw droplets of blood trickling out of the corner of her eyes.

"What the hell is happening?" Abby asked as she picked at the skin near her eye.

When Abby touched the skin, she couldn't feel anything. Not her fingers against her skin, nor the pinch of her fingertips. She pinched hard. Nothing. Then she pinched her cheeks. Nothing. She scratched. Still nothing.

Abby scratched harder, hard enough to break the skin. Something was gleaming under her skin. She worked her finger into the open wound, widening it. There wasn't any pain, but she felt something cold.

The sink was filling with blood, but it was mixed with something else—a thick blue liquid that smelled of antifreeze. Abby stared into the bowl. She didn't want to look at what she was doing to her face.

Chunks of skin and hair filled the sink. At last, Abby stopped. She could feel. She ran her fingers over her face. It was cold. Very cold.

When Abby finally looked in the mirror, she almost screamed, but there was nothing in her. She knew that deep down.

A steel skull stared at her from the mirror. Her eyes were the same color, but she could see wiring and tubes running behind her eye sockets. She turned her head to the side and opened her mouth, only to see the infernal glow of machinery.

"Oh, my God!"

There was a loud ringing. It was in Abby's ear, drilling into her skull and multiplying a thousand times. She couldn't hear herself think. There was only the ringing. And then a cat crawled out of the sink. It licked Abby's finger.

Abby bolted upright in bed. She was covered in sweat and could barely breathe. She reached up and touched her face. Skin was still intact. It must have been a dream.

The ringing was real, though. Abby's comm was going off. She grabbed it and slid the comm into her ear. "What's going on?" Abby murmured.

Creon's voice came through. "We're going to have to talk about those tests we ran. They're fascinating. Nothing dangerous, but fascinating. Also, Myrddin's been trying to get in touch with you. SWARMMT is supposed to be meeting in his office in twenty."

"All right, I'll be there in a little bit."

Abby rolled out of bed, thankful she still had all of her skin. She was about to reach for the shorts lying next to her head when she felt a tickling on her thighs. When she looked down, she was already wearing shorts. *Huh, that's weird. Could have sworn I took those off, and that they were longer.*

As Abby stared at her shorts, she saw nanobots slide out of her pores and come together to lengthen her shorts. "Oh shit," she muttered.

Martin interrupted Abby's train of thought. "Okay, you're awake, thank God! Have things gotten weird since you went to sleep! So weird."

Abby looked down at her hands as nanobots spread from her pores and built fingerless gloves across her skin. When she thought of a different color, the gloves shimmered and changed to blue, then to black. "Martin, what's going on?"

"Uh, where do I start?"

By the time Abby opened Myrddin's door, the rest of the group had assembled. The old wizard was seated at the head of a very long table. Roy was at his right. There were a handful of empty seats, then Anabelle an awkward distance from the two men. Creon was across from her. Abby sat next to Creon.

Myrddin stood and nodded at Abby. "Sorry to have disturbed your nap," Myrddin drawled. "There are issues that needed to be spoken of, but this is not an inquisition. Please make yourself comfortable."

Anabelle, who was still wearing her workout clothes, a towel draped over her shoulders to soak up sweat, leaned back in her chair after running her hand over a pad—the same sort as in the lounge. A glass of carbonated water appeared in front of her.

The rest of the members of the meeting were doing the same. Roy ordered a round of chips and salsa that he motioned for everyone else to get close enough to share.

Anabelle, Abby, and Creon rose and moved down the table so they were closer to the snacks. Roy also conjured up a beer and napkins.

Myrddin chose an elegant glass of elvish wine that he sipped, staining his lips blue.

It had been some time since Abby was able to choose whatever she wanted to eat. She hadn't had a steak in a very long time. It took only a few seconds for a medium-rare porterhouse to appear in front of her, accompanied by a small glass of Industry. She watched the reaction of the others at the table carefully, but no one seemed to mind that she'd ordered a beer.

Myrddin opened the conversation. "As I've said before, Anabelle, I do not approve of your methods all the time, but your decision to broadcast Terra's battles has been extremely beneficial. You may have had more impact in the last week than I have in three years."

Anabelle looked as though she were going to say something smart, but it got caught in her throat. She swallowed, took a sip of her water, swallowed again, and said, "Thank you. It was a gamble. But I'm starting to get worried about Terra. I don't want to just be using her to drum up sympathy. That feels terrible to say out loud."

Roy dipped his chips in salsa, taking care not to spill. "What do you propose?" he asked. "We still haven't figured out where she is."

Creon cleared his throat as he raised his hand. "Actually, we were able to pinpoint her coordinates earlier today."

Myrddin raised his eyebrows as he leaned over the table. "How were you able to do that?"

Abby took a deep, slow breath. This was going to be it. Creon was going to tell Myrddin everything. She was going to be busted, kicked out of the program, and sent back to Utah. Then she'd have to pretend that nothing had ever happened. Pa would go unavenged.

Creon laughed softly as he ordered a small jug of wine. "You wouldn't believe it, but Abby cracked the AI problem. You remember the experiments we were running a while back, trying to push virtual assistants to true AI? Abby stumbled across the answer."

Myrddin still looked suspicious, but a smile crept across his face. "Oh, she did? And I assume that AI was responsible for accessing my files on the Dark One's mind control technology and transporting all of our nanobots through the hadron collider?"

Creon, still smiling as he sipped his wine, said, "Is that what she did? She must have figured we'd have to give the guy a full test run to see what he was capable of. He managed to break into all of our systems without a problem. I'm currently in a race with him to see who can access who faster. It's riveting."

"Stay on top of that. If we have an AI, I want him sharp. Congratulations, Abby. Not bad for your first week. In the future, I'd prefer it if you did not resort to the Dark One's tactics. We have that information, so we know how to challenge him. If we use the tools of our enemies, are we any better?"

Abby wasn't sure if she should answer or remain quiet. After a few seconds, she replied, "Yes, sir."

Anabelle leaned over the table, holding her water accusingly. "And now it's my turn. Who's this redheaded assassin who cropped up on my last mission. Did you read my briefing?"

Myrddin nodded as he conjured a picture of the assassin for all to see. "This is a former agent who defied specific orders and placed her and this entire facility's safety at risk. She's entered the gnome world to save her boyfriend, leaving behind a host of breadcrumbs for the Dark One to find our location. I'd advise you not to work with her, but I'd be surprised if you found her."

"You see the picture I snagged. I obviously saw her. She said she knew how the Dark One was making gates. And how to stop them."

Myrddin waved away Anabelle's idea. "Even if Sarah did know how to stop the gates, we have no way of reaching her. Communication with the gnomish world is completely shut down."

Abby raised her hand like she was in school. "You know, we figured out a trick that helped with boosting comms to Terra. We'd just need a satellite."

"Anything shot over the world will be shut down by the Dark One."

Anabelle groaned loudly. "By the gods, do you have any imagination? How the hell did you ever manage to become a wizard?"

Myrddin ignored Anabelle, preparing to go on to the next topic, but Abby cleared her throat, catching his attention. "What if I could tell you the satellite would be tiny? Like, grain-of-wheat tiny."

"Then I'd say you have piqued my imagination. How would you suggest we get it there?"

Abby and Anabelle made eye contact, and the elf winked at her.

For the first time, Roy spoke. "I could take care of that. We've been doing supply runs to the gnomish world for emergencies. Get in and out quick. I'd be able to handle it."

Anabelle muttered under her breath, "Yeah, you would be able to get in and out quick."

Roy's eyes shot daggers at Anabelle. "Excuse me, what did you just say?"

"I said it sounds like a great idea. You sound like someone quick on the draw."

The meeting quickly deteriorated into squabbling between Anabelle and Roy. The rest kept on eating, occasionally joining in but mostly laughing. It almost reminded Abby of dinner with her folks and siblings.

It felt a little bit like home.

CHAPTER THIRTY-NINE

The dark cells beneath the arena were beginning to feel a lot like home. Back on Earth, Terra'd had a habit of staying out too late, coming home too early in the morning, and waking up in complete darkness, covered by blankets, drifting in and out of a cold sweat.

This wasn't much different, although it was a lot more painful.

She groaned as she tried to sit up. The pain was mostly in her ribs and back. She'd never had joint pain before, but she'd also never wrestled a chimera to the ground. It didn't feel like getting old as much as the ramifications of being a badass.

The door to her cell had been left open again. She wondered if the rest of the survivors would be in the dining hall again.

When Terra had left the remaining fighters, they had placed the bodies of the fallen on the long wooden dining table. She'd waited for someone to speak, to say something that would make their sacrifice meaningful.

No one had spoken. Even Terra couldn't find words. Anything she said would have felt like a lie. She had no idea what they were doing here in the arena. She'd only gathered bits and pieces from what other fighters had said, and even they didn't seem to know what was going on.

The most frustrating were the orcs. Terra knew it was naïve to assume that all orcs were on the same page about everything, but she had been hoping for some inkling about what was in store for them down the line. Were they going to just keep fighting until they were all dead?

During the moment of silence, Terra tried not to look away from the dead, particularly Eric. She remembered how afraid of dying he'd been. Maybe if she hadn't been so encouraging, he would have lived through the fight. He had died at her side. She felt like it was her fault.

But what could she do about that, other than beat herself up? She'd been glad when the other fighters had rushed her off to her cell. Since then, all she'd done was sleep.

Moving toward the door was an exercise in pain and determination, but it wasn't as bad as the first time she had made the trek. Although there were no burns, she was covered in open wounds. She wanted to find Nib-nib and see if there was something he could do to help.

Hopefully, the bodies had been moved from the dining hall. Terra didn't want to look at them again, and it would be extremely uncomfortable to try and eat and drink around them.

Terra finally got to the dining hall. The rest of the fighters were there. They weren't segregated like the first time Terra had seen them. They all sat together, talking quietly. Nib-nib looked up when Terra entered the room and chirped loudly.

One of the orcs named Cire, who was about Terra's size with strong tan arms, stood when he saw her and pressed his fist to his chest. The rest of the orcs did the same.

When Terra raised her fist, pain shot through her arm, and she almost collapsed. She managed to get her fist to her chest before falling forward.

The orcs were already headed to Terra, and they caught her before she hit the ground. "You should still be asleep," Cire said as he helped guide her to a cot in the corner of the hall.

She groaned as the many hands touched her. They were drawing attention to the open wounds and pulled muscles. "Couldn't sleep," she muttered. "Everything hurts a little too much."

"We will help you with that."

The orcs laid Terra on the cot as Nib-nib scuttled over to her, his beady compound eyes wet with what Terra could only assume was worry. The mantiboid pressed his forehead to Terra's hand and held it there for some time.

"This one has been very worried about you," Cire explained.

Terra looked down at Nib-nib, who still hadn't removed his forehead. "You understand him?" she asked.

"Mantiboids are from our realm. Some of us who keep with the old traditions continue to learn their language. It is a useful language to speak. On our world, they are one of the oldest races. Folk make the mistake of assuming they are childlike, some even taking them as pets."

Terra kept her thoughts to herself. She'd honestly been thinking of Nib-nib as something of a child. It was difficult not to, given how the creature carried himself.

Nib-nib held his pincers out in front of his mandibles as they started working. He was producing the same goo he'd spat on Terra before. It wasn't nearly as disgusting this time but still made Terra's stomach turn slightly. She was looking forward to the effect, though.

Cire pulled up a seat next to Terra, while the rest of the orcs returned to the larger group. "It was mantiboids who taught the orcs about the land—at least, the orcs who were willing to listen. They also reminded us of our magic. Few orcs remember."

Nib-nib spat up the green-and-blue goop onto Terra's arm and covered one of her wounds. The goop stung as much as it had before. She winced and averted her gaze. She didn't remember any of the sword or ax wounds hurting this much.

Cire was staring at Terra intently. She looked away from his uncomfortable eye contact as he spoke. "The rest of the fighters are grateful for you," he started. "Before you, we didn't think we'd survive. 'Meat for the arena' was what the guards called us."

Terra sat up and returned Cire's gaze just so she would have something to look at other than whatever Nib-nib was coughing up at the moment. "And what do you guys think now?" she asked. "Because I sure as fuck feel like meat at the moment."

"I feel like I have a chance. One I don't want to waste."

"Where are…where are the bodies? Did they take them?"

Cire shook his head as he pointed to the darkest corner of the room. Many of the chairs in the room were positioned there. The dead sat in the chairs regally, as if they were lords watching over their domain. "It is an old orc tradition," Cire said. "Our greatest warriors dine with us until the end."

A week ago, this scene would have scared the shit out of Terra. She'd never been able to deal with anything that was dead. But something had changed since she'd come into the arena. They weren't dead things. They had fought side by side with her. It seemed the most honorable thing for them to remain.

Nib-nib scuttled away, chittering to himself. "What did he say?" Terra asked.

"*She* said something about blood sisters. If you didn't know, Nib-nib has been using her birthing cells to heal you. She's been coughing up her eggs."

"Are you saying she's been having her period on me?"

Cire shrugged as he picked his nails. "I do not know what human bodily function you are referring to, but in my realm, those eggs are a delicacy. The mantiboids only offer them to the strongest of their and our warriors. I haven't seen one deem anyone worthy of their eggs in my life until now."

Terra stared down at the wound Nib-nib had healed. "Well, tell Nib-nib I appreciate it. A lot. How's everyone else holding up?"

"They're tired. Worried. But invigorated. None of them believed they were going to survive. Neither did I, yet here we are, not only living but victorious. Makes me curious to know what will be coming next."

"You and me both."

Cire cleared his throat and shifted in his chair, crossing and uncrossing his arms. "Before I came here, I was a shaman. We specialized in tending to our warriors. If it is acceptable to you, I'd like to help Nib-nib heal your wounds."

Terra smiled mischievously at the orc. She thought his underbite kind of charming, even if it was because of the two huge bottom incisors that nearly reached his nose. "What all does it entail?"

Cire chuckled softly. "I'll heal your internal injuries while praying over you to strengthen your spirit. And, uh, a lot of touching."

Terra's body went warm as she squirmed in her cot. "Oh, uh, yeah, sure, I guess you can. I mean, for the healing. And spirit and all that. Go for it."

Nib-nib had returned with a plate of food and a jug of wine. She placed it on the empty side of Terra's bed, then proceeded to cough up more of her eggs on Terra's thigh.

If there had been any concern that what was going to transpire between Cire and Terra would be sexy, that worry was instantly relieved. "Uh, you can get started if you want," the girl murmured.

Cire stood over Terra and held his hands over her forehead. He sang softly under his breath. She didn't recognize the words. It was Orcish. The language sounded harsh, almost like German, yet Cire somehow transformed the guttural grunts into something sweet.

Nib-nib stopped what she was doing to listen. She watched silently, holding a batch of her eggs in her claws as Cire touched Terra's forehead lightly.

The moment his fingers touched Terra's skin, she felt something warming her from the inside. It was like a fire had been lit in her bone marrow. She could feel her blood cells dancing in rhythm with the orc's words. When he withdrew his touch, her body went cold.

Across the dining hall, the rest of the orcs had taken notice. The humans and mantiboids as well. They stood, drawn to Cire's song. Slowly, they made their way over, the orcs taking the lead, forming a circle around Terra's cot.

Part of Terra was mortified that everyone had come over to her side. What was happening seemed like it should have been done in private—or maybe Terra was reading too much into it.

The orcs who encircled Terra started to sing as well. Their voices were softer than Cire's. Less gentle, too. They provided something like a percussion to Cire's soft melodies. The rest stood outside the circle and watched.

Cire waved his hands over Terra's face, drawing his fingers down beneath her eyes and then up to her temple, where he let them rest. White-hot heat shot through Terra's head. It felt as though her brain had been pierced with a knife. Her whole body went numb, and when she closed her eyes, she saw bright red patterns floating above her.

The patterns turned to vague shapes that seemed to fight with each other to take form. Finally, they collapsed into each other, creating a lake of red water. The water burst up into the air as if it were a geyser, floating, taking the shape of Terra's body. She watched herself watching herself.

Then the water fell and disappeared.

Terra opened her eyes, and all of a sudden, she heard the song again. The orcs were beating their chests and chanting a deep, guttural sound. It was nearly impossible to distinguish their voices from the beat that they stomped on the floor.

Cire had moved down to Terra's side. He took her hand in his and pressed his lips to her fingertips. Then he took her other hand and did the same, holding both in his while he sang softly to her.

It was not instant, the fashion in which Cire's song gradually unraveled and enveloped Terra in its entirety. She could not tell what the words were, not specifically. It would have been impossible. But she could understand the song.

"Sister, sister of my tribe, beat of our heart. You stand in death, you robe yourself in blood. Our enemies fall at the sound of your name. In you, I trust. In you, our chiefs live. Hear me, let your bones be strong, let your skin be steel. Let your heart be a sword. Sister, sister of my tribe, beat of our heart."

When Terra opened her eyes, Cire had stopped singing. He had moved away and joined the rest of the orcs, who still stood in a circle around Terra, beating their chests, drumming with their feet.

The drumming tapered off until there was silence. The humans and mantiboids drifted away from the circle, probably confused as to what they had witnessed. Soon the orcs left as well, leaving only Nib-nib and Cire, the latter pulling up a seat beside Terra. "How do you feel?" he asked.

Terra had forgotten that this was to heal her body. She couldn't recall anything ever having hurt. "Uh, I think I feel a lot better," she said.

"I'm sorry if that was a little rough. I haven't performed the ceremony in a very long time."

"No, no, it was great. That was great."

Cire stood up abruptly and pressed two fingers to Terra's forehead. "You should get some rest," he said before walking away.

Terra watched the orc leave. At her right, Nib-nib was chittering loudly, looking for something under the cot. "What's got you in a fuss?" Terra asked.

Nib-nib came up from under the bed. She held a blanket and a loose pair of leather pants. Then she pointed to Terra's pants.

Terra went bright red as she grabbed the blanket and the leather pants from Nib-nib. "Are you fucking kidding me?"

Nib-nib chittered again. This time, Terra understood some of what she said. "No worry. Most shaman big flirt. Get changed. Then rest."

Nib-nib scuttled off, leaving Terra to bask in a golden afterglow that covered any embarrassment.

CHAPTER FORTY

When Terra woke up, the dining hall was empty of her fellow fighters. Instead, there were ten large orcs standing in a line next to her cot, holding swords and torches. One of the orcs came closer when Terra sat up. "The Game Master wishes to see you," he growled.

Terra groaned and lay back down. "Tell him I need another couple of hours before we start having meetings," she snapped.

The orc who had spoken kicked Terra's cot over, and she spilled onto the floor. She got to her feet quickly and rushed the orc, who was taken by surprise. Her forehead collided with his, and the blow sent him stumbling backward. She reached to rip his sword from him.

Another orc surged toward Terra faster than she could move, and punched her in the jaw. The strength of the blow sent Terra to her knees. This orc was much stronger than the ones she'd been fighting in the arena.

As Terra rubbed her sore jaw, the rest of the orcs surrounded her and drew their weapons. "All right, fine, I guess I'll meet with the guy," she mumbled as she raised her hands. "Anything I should know ahead of time?"

The orc Terra had punched joined the others. "If you try any shit like that again, we will kill you," he said. "Your success in the ring doesn't protect you from everything."

"Noted. Nice punch, by the way."

The orc blinked, caught off-guard by Terra's compliment. He recovered quickly enough and stalked out into the darkened hallway. The other orcs followed, forcing Terra to walk quickly to avoid being nicked by their swords.

Unseen by anyone else in the room, the tracker perched on the side of Terra's bed rose and followed them.

Down the hallway. Silence other than the tramping of their feet. If it had been any other situation, Terra would have found the sound comforting. It reminded her of Cire's touch, his worn hands on her sweating forehead. Then another memory cropped up. Reading about death marches in high school.

This was a different hallway than the one leading from her cell to the dining hall. She hadn't noticed it the entire time she'd been in the hall. The pathway sloped down at a slight angle. Wherever they were going, it was under the arena.

The only light came from the orcs' torches. Long shadows were cast across the walls. The orcs stood at least a foot taller than Terra, their shadows stretching up nearly to the ceiling. "You guys seem like you have tougher asses than the ones I've been whipping," Terra taunted. "How come I haven't been fighting you in the arena?"

One of the orcs behind Terra sneered. "Because you wouldn't have made it past the first round."

"So, you guys are, like, the final bosses or something? Also, I'm assuming you didn't see me land an ax in a balrog's head. You telling me you're stronger than an ancient demon?"

None of the orcs replied. They trekked the rest of the way in silence.

The hallway opened into a series of different pathways in the catacombs beneath the arena. The orcs guided Terra to the middle one, which ended in a stone door with an orc rune etched into the center. The orc who had punched Terra knocked on the door.

After a moment, the door creaked open. The orc moved out of the way and motioned for Terra to enter.

She went into the room, and the door closed behind her. The walls were the same stone the arena must have been built on. Torches covered the walls, and a chandelier hung from the ceiling.

A desk sat near the back of the room in a bizarre parody of an office.

Ten orcs filled the room, these even larger than the ones who had brought her here. They wore nothing on their chests and their muscles appeared unnaturally large, as if the very fiber of their strength was barely able to be contained by mere flesh. They didn't bother looking at Terra as she entered.

In the middle of the room was an ornate gold bathtub with an etching of an orc's head aflame carved into the side. A frail hand hung over the side of the tub. "You may approach," a voice from the tub cooed.

Terra didn't want to go anywhere near the tub. Whatever was in there, she could go without seeing. But there wasn't anything else to do, and none of the orcs in the room looked to be particularly good at conversation. Terra approached the tub.

A small orc floated in the murky water of the tub. He was smaller than a goblin, with muscles that appeared to have dried up. His body was wrinkled, and folds of flesh hung from his face like slices of meat in a butcher's shop. Great, bulbous eyes stared out from under the folds, full of an intense life Terra could not recall ever having seen. They were ancient eyes—eyes that might never die.

The Game Master held himself up in the tub and ran his wet eyes over Terra. "You've caused quite the stir in our coliseum," he cooed. "Quite the commotion indeed."

Terra stared around the room, trying to keep her eyes off the freakish thing soaking in the tub. "Uh, glad to hear it. Was pretty sure the only reason I was in there was to get killed."

"That was the initial reason, but you've proven yourself as a warrior of exceptional caliber thrice now. Although we are servants of the Dark One, we cannot stop being orcs. Strength recognizes strength, power calls unto power."

Terra remembered what the prisoner orcs had told her about the Dark One's servants giving up what it meant to be an orc. She couldn't possibly dislike this guy enough. "Thanks, I guess. Game recognizes game, though I must say, you're looking a little unfamiliar."

"Spare me your asinine human attempts at wit. I brought you here to discuss your future. Your prospects. Namely, how you can keep on living."

"Do you mind if I take a seat? I really don't want to have this entire conversation looking at your weird baby dick."

Game Master didn't seem to take offense at the insult, and he motioned for Terra to sit on the chair behind the desk. She walked awkwardly to the chair, feeling the eyes of all the orcs following her.

After she sat, the Game Master continued, "A warrior of your considerable talent should not be fighting in the arena. You should be on the front lines, leading our forces. If you would consider it, the Dark One would have use for you."

Taking a seat behind the desk had been a good idea. Terra felt braver with a little bit of distance between her and the freakish orc imp. "Me? Lead an orc army? Christ, that's been my dream since I was a little girl. Especially an army that follows someone named the Dark One. My parents would be so proud."

The water in the tub started to boil. Terra saw the steam rising. "Please, Not-a-Male, there is no need for such hostilities," the Game Master said. "I have no doubt we can come to an agreement. Do you want money? Glory? Men to attend your every need? Women? Perhaps an orc?"

Terra leaned over the table, clapping her hands. "Actually, that would be great. I have this one really intense need, one that I just gotta scratch. You think you could help me with it?"

The water stopped boiling, reduced to a simmer. "What would you like?"

"To get the hell out of this place and back to my fucking life."

Once more, the water began to boil. The small hand extended

from the tub and motioned at the closest orc, who wore a flowing black cloak around his shoulders. He reached into the tub and lifted the Game Master from the water while another orc quickly dried the creature.

When the Game Master was dry, the orc with the cloak bundled the Game Master up. Two more orcs approached and wrapped the cloth around the orc's face so that the Game Master hung from the orc like some freakish child strapped to a confused mother.

The Game Master shifted his attention to Terra. "Before you spit on any more offers, please come with me."

He turned to leave the room, and Terra followed. They entered the hallway, the orcs flanking them, and returned to the main catacomb chamber. Here the Game Master turned left and headed down the tunnel, beckoning Terra to walk at his side.

As the Game Master walked, he spoke. "The catacombs beneath the arena are reserved for our most ardent contestants. Some have battled for years."

One of the orcs tilted his torch so its light shone on the stone walls of the hallway.

Sections of the rock had been carved out. Some were the size of cells, and others were as large as the dining hall. To Terra's left was an elaborate dining room scene filled with mummies. The bones of a dragon hung over the table, its jaws wide open.

"For a time, this was how we orcs celebrated our strength. That was until we were provided an opportunity to show our strength to the realms. Do you know what the other races think of the orcs? What they have always thought?"

Terra couldn't have made up an answer if she wanted. She didn't even know about *fictional* orc race politics.

Game Master answered Terra's silence. "Lesser, across the board. Particularly the elves. They relegated us to a backwater realm. Deprived us of our glory. That is, until the Dark One searched us out. He offered us the chance to have what we've always wanted —equality."

They made their way deeper into the catacombs, passing the only space Terra had seen with a door, which was slightly ajar.

The tracker, which had been following Terra the entire time, dipped to the left and flew into the room.

The Game Master continued speaking. "Have you ever been treated as if you were undeserving of what you knew you had a right to?"

The question cut Terra deep, sparking an insecurity long buried, the same insecurity that made it easy for her to beat up people for treating her like shit, for taking advantage of her. The same insecurity that allowed her to curl up into a doormat. "Sure," Terra muttered. "Hasn't everyone?"

Game Master stopped and looked at the scene to his right. A human skeleton sat upon a throne. Dozens of skeletons surrounded the throne, all on their knees, their heads pressed to the ground in a sign of worship. "Sometimes you have to take what you deserve," Game Master said. "And the Dark One will give you the tools to do such. You could rule. Have your own kingdom. Whatever you desire."

Terra was quiet for some time. Then she said, "I want to go home."

Game Master sighed as he turned to face her. "I see. Disappointing. Return her to the rest of the fodder for tomorrow." He leaned close to Terra, his rank breath curling her stomach. "You have a match tomorrow. We'll see how you feel afterward. Offer remains on the table."

One of the orcs hit Terra hard on the back of the head. Everything went black, and the world swept out from beneath her.

CHAPTER FORTY-ONE

The hangar of HQ was abandoned, as usual. No one other than the stray mechanic ever dropped by. There wasn't much for anyone to do. The only thing of merit within the hangar—other than dropships, which required clearance to get near—was Roy's mech. And no one touched Roy's mech.

The lights flickered on as Roy entered the hangar. He scanned the general area to check if it was empty. Working on his mech was a private affair. The schematics were common knowledge to anyone who had worked on the Dragon Riders initiative, but Roy had made his own adjustments. He liked to tinker in his alone time.

Roy went to the bay where he kept his mech. It was a beautiful piece. Most everyone spoke of the mechs as equipment. You got the stray person who spoke of them as vehicles. That wasn't how Dragon Riders talked about their mechs. They called them by name.

Roy called his Evelyn. It had been his wife's name. She was the first person he'd lost to the Dark One. It was only fitting that her memory help him erase the Dark One's name from history.

The mech was the first ever made, built before the engineers had tried to make them as dragon-like as possible. Roy's was somewhat boxy, the body of the mech built around the cockpit, which rested in the chest, unlike the rest of the mech's, whose cockpits were nestled into the mech's spine.

The immediate downfall of his mech was that it wasn't nearly as receptive to commands as the newer models. Newer mechs were built around the nervous system of their riders. Not Roy's. His was old-school.

That wasn't to say he was using outdated technology. The mech was linked to his muscles' reactions, responding to how he tensed his forearms or legs to compensate for him having to manually move its arms and legs. Ironically, it gave him a closer link to his mech than any other mech rider.

Roy didn't even have to form a thought. The mech's cockpit opened as easily as his heart beat. He climbed into it and began running diagnostics. He slid his legs into the bottom part of the mech's chassis, felt the weight as he prepared to lift his right leg.

Back when Roy had first learned to ride a motorcycle, his father had told him to check his tires, brakes, headlights, and clutch before heading out. Every time. Never grow comfortable. That was how people died. Wise words from the second person Roy had lost to the Dark One.

Each time Roy suited up, he ran through the people the Dark One had taken from him. There was a lesson in each and every one of those losses.

Roy leaned back and rested in the cockpit. He loved this mech. It looked like an ancient depiction of a dragon. This was his favorite place to be. Riding beat sitting around in meetings any day.

"You come here often?" a voice said from the shadows.

Instinctively Roy pulled up on the mech's arms and aimed his chain gun at the source of the voice.

Anabelle slid out of the darkness. "Whoa, watch where you point that thing."

Anabelle wore that wicked grin Roy could never get enough of. He'd never tell her, though. Somehow, he believed if she knew, she'd stop directing it his way.

Roy lowered his gun and disengaged from the mech. He didn't

want to be seen sitting in the cockpit. It felt worse than being naked. "What the hell are you doing down here?"

"Just wanted to come and see you off. Nothing huge. That and tell you I really appreciate you taking the satellite out. I could tell Myrddin wasn't too stoked about this plan."

"How the hell could you tell what Myrddin was thinking?"

Anabelle walked up and leaned on Evelyn. Roy felt the hair on the back of his neck prickle. "My job for the last hundred years has been manipulating people," Anabelle explained. "You think I can't read body language by now? Besides, you humans aren't too subtle about that kind of stuff."

Roy made the conscious decision not to fold his arms. "Oh, yeah? What does my body language say right now?"

Anabelle walked around Roy, watching him closely. "Based on how quickly you got out of your mech and how you stood up straighter when I leaned on it, I think it's safe to say you're uncomfortable with me being too close to your baby."

At this point, Roy realized it was ridiculous to try to hide his body language from Anabelle. Like she said, it was her job.

But the elf wasn't done yet. "You don't seem to be too stressed about the mission. But your legs are crossed, one over the other, even though you're standing. That means you're probably backed up. Just a little bit."

"What do you mean, backed up?"

Anabelle gave him that grin that made Roy's heart question itself. "Backed up. As in horny," Anabelle whispered.

And then, just as quickly as it had flashed its teeth, Anabelle's flirtatiousness disappeared. She was all business now, keeping her distance from Roy and presenting herself as disinterested. "So, how are you planning on pulling this off?"

Roy was glad Anabelle had pulled back. He hated it when they were alone together. It felt like Anabelle had all the cards. And he loved it. But talking business? That was something Roy could do. "There's a hyperspace jump point we've been using for a while for receiving gnome supplies. It's a good ways away from the gnome homeworld. Just one mech, so they never notice it."

"Is it dangerous?"

"Are you worried?" Roy asked.

Anabelle shook her head as she laughed. "No, I just want to make sure the only person I work with who has any sense in their head doesn't end up dead. So, make sure to come back in one piece."

Roy chuckled as he leaned into the cockpit of his mech. "Don't worry, I will."

The two of them stood there without speaking for a bit, avoiding each other's eyes. The silence grew thick between them. Roy glanced at the interior of his mech, wondering what Anabelle was resting her eyes on. Then he remembered he wasn't in grade school. "Hey, when I get back, you wanna grab a drink or something? Like a date?"

Anabelle's eyebrows rose slowly. "What do you mean by 'date?'"

"You know, go out and do something. Get to know each other better. That kind of thing."

Anabelle moved closer to Roy, her eyes burning. "I do find humans amusing. That might be interesting," she said with a low growl.

"So, that's a yes for the date?"

"A date? Sure. But I'd much prefer a night of unrestrained animalistic passion."

Roy choked on nothing and doubled over in a coughing fit. By the time he righted himself, Anabelle was walking away. "Uh, I'll call you when I get back!" he shouted.

Anabelle slipped into the shadows and was gone.

Roy climbed into the cockpit and sighed as he shook his head. "Well, fuck me, right?" he muttered aloud. "Let's hope I come back in one piece."

Roy looked forward to hyperspace jumps for one reason—naps. The trip took a couple of hours, and there was nothing that he enjoyed more than naps.

As usual, he woke up a couple of minutes before the jump was over. He never needed an alarm.

Roy flipped up the visor of his mech. He watched as thousands of star systems zoomed past him at a blur that the human eye could hardly catch. "*I will never get tired of this,*" he thought as he prepared to exit hyperdrive.

Roy's mech snapped into regular space. He stared around, then flipped up his holomap. For some reason, he'd come out of hyperspace earlier than usual for this run. "What the hell is going on here?"

As Roy checked his navigation system, he felt his mech vibrating ominously. He pulled up to get a look around him.

A dropship was flying overhead. It was the largest he'd ever seen, easily the length of three football fields. The ship was heading toward the gnomish homeworld.

Luckily, Roy was far enough away to remain hidden. Still, this was going to be a problem.

CHAPTER FORTY-TWO

The Dark One's dropship continued to pass overhead. That wasn't it, though. More dropships were exiting hyperspace. There were five in total.

Roy's mech couldn't handle even one in a straight-on fight. Dropships were equipped with some of the strongest weaponry the Dark One had. Roy had seen guns fired by those dropships that he couldn't even wrap his head around. A lot of lives had been lost to those ships.

What were the ships doing at the gnomish world? HQ's plan couldn't have been discovered unless there was a spy, which seemed unlikely. Everyone in the meeting was trustworthy, and Roy hadn't mentioned the plan to anyone else.

The leak could have come from somewhere else, though. He'd used the same route he'd been using for his gnomish deliveries. The leak could have come from someone on his side of things. That would have to be dealt with later. Right now, the priority was staying alive.

Roy was trying to dismiss the idea of betrayal, but he couldn't quite get it out of his mind. The idea of someone close to him ratting him out to the Dark One made his chest clench. That was the problem with wars nowadays. People weren't honest like they used to be.

Above him, the dropships continued to make their way toward the gnomish world. The ships hadn't taken notice of Roy. It was possible they were here on unrelated business. Could have simply been a coincidence.

Either way, the ships were taking up Roy's field of vision, like the bloated carcasses of a school of beached whales. If he was going to enter the gnomish world, he would have to slip past them undetected.

That could play out in a few ways. Roy wanted to mentally prepare for what he was about to get himself into. The easiest one was that he got past without setting off any of their alarms, dropped the satellite, and punched into hyperjump.

That seemed too perfect to happen. Also, it was only a possibility before the other four ships had dropped in. Next on the list of possible outcomes was that he waited until the ships finished settling into their formation, find a flaw in their positioning, and try to exploit it.

Third option was to stick with the coordinates, jump to hyperspace to clear the distance, and then get the hell out of there before the ships had a chance to deploy their fighters. That was what Roy wanted to avoid more than anything else. The dropships' weapons were powerful but slow enough for Roy to avoid. The fighters were another thing altogether.

Roy had only seen the Dark One's helkate fighters deployed a few times, and each memory was terrifying. Before Roy had been assigned to the dragon mech program, he had been an ensign on a space freighter. They had been performing a routine supply delivery off the rim of the elvish realm.

The Dark One's dropship had come from nowhere, silently slipping out of hyperspace in front of the ship Roy was serving on. The alarms had blared instantly, and the whole ship was thrown into chaos. Roy watched the fight from the viewing windows.

The freighter's fighters had swarmed the dropship, peppering it with plasma bolts and the occasional bomb. The dropship had been unfazed. Then, out of nowhere, a portal had opened in front of the dropship. It looked as if the ship had peeled back space, and there was another universe within the portal.

Then the helkate fighters started to pour through the portal. They were smaller than the freighter's fighters and were all black, spikes rising from their orb-like bodies. Clouds of electrical energy surrounded them as they zipped around the battlefield, careening between the freighter's fighters and firing blast after blast, setting everything on fire within minutes.

That was how every battle with the helkate fighters Roy had seen went down. The fighters showed up out of nowhere and tore through anything and everything in their way. As far as Roy was concerned, helkate fighters were the worst-case scenario.

This mission could go off the rails in other ways, but Roy thought it best to limit his imaginary failures to three options. Roy pinged Anabelle on his comm. "Hey, we got a little problem."

Anabelle chuckled over the comm. "What happened, you get lost or something?"

"No, that would have been preferable. It's a bigger problem than that. I got dropships. Five of them. So, yeah, just thought you might want to pass the word up to the big guy."

"What are you going to do?"

Roy was already putting in the coordinates for the gnomish world, hoping to get a little closer. "There's a mission. And there's nothing in my employment clause about leaving missions halfway finished."

"Wait, you have an employment clause? I didn't get a contract or anything."

"Well, I mean...actually, I'm not sure. I hope I at least signed some kind of contract. Either way, if I get back, you still owe me that date. If I don't, it was nice working with you."

Anabelle didn't answer right away. "Hey, stop being so dramatic. I'll see you when you make it back."

"Right."

Roy cut the comm and pulled up his holomenu. He dictated a quick message to Myrddin, letting him know what route to take with the dragon mech squad if things didn't work out with the mission.

Even if Roy wasn't going to admit it to himself, he was

approaching everything with a sense of fatalism. He wasn't stupid. He knew the odds he was up against.

Finally, he was ready to get started. *Doesn't make sense to keep putting it off,* he thought to himself. *Everyone's got to die someday. At least I get to know how I'm going out.*

Roy leaned back in his mech, watching the stars outside his window. He was going to miss this. There wasn't anything more peaceful than space. Nothing more beautiful. If he was going to die, it should be out here. This was a fitting place for his final goodbye.

The coordinates were loaded, and the mech was primed. Roy threw on his thrusters and felt the mech surge forward as the stars and space around him stretched.

This jump was going to take skill. There wasn't a lot of distance to cover, and Roy wanted to make sure he didn't end up inside one of those dropships. If there was a slight chance Roy could survive, he wanted to give it a shot.

Roy's mech blasted past the dropships. At the last second, he pulled the hyperspace disengagement lever, dropping out in front of the Dark One's ships. Without wasting a second, he dipped away from the dropships and looped around, preparing to dump the satellite.

There wasn't any time. The dropships had already opened a portal each. They must have known Roy was near the gnomish homeworld. Just like he'd been waiting to see what they were going to do, they'd followed the same route. *Fucking great,* Roy thought.

Once, when Roy had first started training alongside his friend Toppinir, the elf had praised Roy's piloting skill. "Even if you can't ride a dragon, you're more than tolerable in a mech," the elf had said. "I wouldn't be surprised if you could outrun a few helkates someday."

Roy had laughed and written it off. Now he was hoping the elf hadn't merely been filling him up with stale flattery. Today, he was going to find out.

The portals continued to expand, and Roy stared deep within them. Just like the first time Roy had seen the portals open, it was like looking into a reflection of our own world. You couldn't make out the details, but you knew it was someplace more alien than space.

A dozen helkates came shooting out of the portal. They were smaller than Roy remembered, but the last time he'd seen them, he had been on a freighter, somewhat removed from the whole situation. Now he was in the thick of it. Now he was going to find out how fast these suckers flew.

Roy wasn't going to wait for them to make the first move. Against his better judgment, he leaned forward, threw his mech into high gear, and sped off to meet the helkates head-on.

The fighters scattered. It was difficult to count how many of them there were. They were small enough to swarm, bunching together once Roy had passed to throw his estimation off.

How the hell am I going to dump this satellite without them seeing me? Roy thought. The helkates fighters would attack anything that came off of Roy's mech when they weren't busy trying to blow him up. He needed a plan of attack.

Thin the herd; that was the only option. If the helkates were busy trying to stay alive, they probably wouldn't notice anything else. And if Roy could stay alive, he could jet out afterward.

Roy leaned back in his cockpit and took a deep breath as he prepared to do one of the dumbest things he'd ever done in his life. Then he flew straight toward the helkates, blasting missiles from his dragon mech's mouth.

The missiles weren't the strongest weapon Roy had on the mech. In fact, they were the weakest. But they were the flashiest and the most surprising.

The helkates, which had bunched together, split up again, each of them going their separate way. Even then, they seemed to be moving in an integrated fashion, as if each were communicating with the others. Roy wondered if they were even piloted. They could have been organics for all he knew.

Just our luck, the Dark One's figured out how to make shit that can live in space, he thought as he maneuvered the mech around to chase the group of fleeing helkates.

As Roy came around their backside, the fighters flipped around, their spikes vibrating, and an electrical charge firing. Roy was able to drop down and swing out of the way. He hit his thrusters, surging forward.

The mech plowed through the group of helkates, sending them flying, one of them bursting into a thousand pieces that floated, sparkling in the blackness of space before combusting.

A slight break in the helkates' formation allowed Roy to push forward, kicking his mech into high gear and flying past them toward the dropships. He knew the helkates could keep pace with him easily. This would give them more to deal with.

The dropships were fast approaching and Roy punched up to the first one, close enough to see the crew in the front of the ship. They stared wide-eyed at him as he let his mech rest for a moment. He was going to give them something to remember the mech riders by.

Roy fired, blasting the front windows with freezing ice. The windows of the dropship instantly iced over, aided by the frigid space winds. He switched to his rockets as he glanced over his shoulder.

The helkates were still catching up to him. Great. Roy turned back to the window and let loose two rockets.

The rockets exploded, blowing out the windows of the dropship. The bodies of the orcs and goblins manning the ship were sucked into the vacuum of space.

As the helkates raced toward Roy, he shot upward, running the length of the ship as the fighters collided with their compatriots. Then he whipped around and fired his missiles, lighting the helkates up. *Hell, yeah.*

Just as Roy was congratulating himself, he spotted the other pack of helkates. They had come up right behind him. The fighters organized themselves in a trapezoid formation. The blank space in the middle of the helkates began to glow.

"This is not going to be good!" Roy shouted as he leaned forward, driving his mech toward the gnomish homeworld.

A purple energy blast shot out of the energy cannon the helkates had formed. It narrowly missed Roy, who was rocketing toward the gnomish atmosphere as fast as possible. As he headed toward the atmosphere, he realized this was the perfect time to drop the satellite.

Roy checked to see how many mines he had left. He hoped he had refilled them before leaving HQ.

Nine mines. Perfect. Roy pulled down his holoscreen and programed the mines to react to orcish and goblin organic material. He hoped his hunch was going to pay off.

Roy let the first mine go as he circled the planet, then the next. After the fourth mine, he dropped the satellite and then let three more mines go. He glanced over his shoulder to see if the helkates were still following him.

The fighters were weaving in and out of the trail of mines Roy had left. Given that the explosives hadn't gone off, they obviously weren't organic, or at least, not the organic material Roy had guessed. Not too big a loss, though. The helkates had already passed the satellite, too worried about Roy to concentrate on anything else.

At least the mission went off without a hitch. Don't think there was anything in the briefing about me coming back alive.

Then Roy remembered Anabelle. There was a date hanging in the balance of all of this, and he wasn't even in bad trouble yet. The helkates hadn't managed to hit him. Actually, now that he thought of it, they didn't seem to be attacking him.

Roy double-checked over his shoulder to see where the helkates were and couldn't see any. He punched in the coordinates back to Earth and prepared to hit hyperspace.

What Roy could not see was that the helkates had positioned themselves in a bizarre geometric pattern around Roy. Their targeting reticles were set on him.

The mech hit hyperspace just as they shot at him. The combination of the shots and the accelerated speed jolted his cockpit, and Roy was thrust forward. If it wasn't for his harness, he would have slammed his head on the dashboard. He heard cracks and knew the force of the jolt against that harness had caused bones in his body to shatter.

"Can't pick your poison," Roy gritted out as he slid into the hyperspace tunnel, the helkates glowing an eerie purple. Then their bodies stretched, connecting to the mech and following it into the tunnel.

CHAPTER FORTY-THREE

Anabelle stormed into Abby's and Creon's lab, her eyes full of worry and fury. "I need your help right now!" she shouted.

Abby jumped up from her current project; she was trying to figure out how much damage she'd done to her body by injecting it with nanobots. "Uh, we're kinda in the middle of something," she muttered. "Assuming this is real important?"

Anabelle sat at one of the empty desks, flopping down as though her body could barely keep itself upright. "You're damn right this is important," the elf said, her tone sharp. "What do you have to do that's more important than saving someone's life?" Abby held her tongue. Anabelle didn't need to know what was going on.

Abby glanced in Creon's direction. The goblin was doing a great job of pretending he wasn't interested in the conversation. But whatever was bothering Anabelle was serious. "Honey, it'll be okay. How can I help you out?" Abby asked.

"It's Roy. He's in trouble, and I need to figure out how to help him."

Abby rolled her chair away from her computer. So that was what was getting her so hot and bothered. "Details?"

Anabelle sighed as she threw her hands up in irritation. "All I know is that he went off to the gnomish world and got ambushed. He was being all cryptic and dramatic, but he's never dramatic. I think he might be in danger. Like, real danger."

Real danger? Roy seemed like the kind of guy who was able to take care of himself, and Anabelle didn't seem like the sort to worry. Anabelle's and Roy's interaction was different from anyone else's, and Abby suspected something was going on between the two of them. Maybe Anabelle was just worrying. "Roy knows what he's doing. He's one of our best," she said.

Anabelle nodded as she picked at her cuticles. "Yeah, he does, which is why I'm worried. The last time he admitted he was in over his head, he lost an eye. Could be his legs next."

"When you put it like that…"

"So, can you help?"

Abby turned to the holoprojector and swiped through the DNA breakdown she and Creon had been going over. "All you know is he's in the gnomish realm?"

The holoprojector was displaying a map of the gnomish realm. Anabelle came over and stared hard at the screen. "Yeah, that's all I know. That, and he was pretty close to the gnomish homeworld if that helps."

"Yeah, that does. Let me see what I can find."

Creon had left his terminal and had come over to the holoprojector, still silent, attention going from the screen to Annabelle, Abby, and back. After the three had been sitting in silence long enough, he finally said, "There's a tracking device on each mech. We could use that to find his specific position."

Anabelle's eyes still looked somewhat frenzied, as if she'd already assumed the worst-case scenario was the only outcome. "Even if we do know where he is, how's that going to help him? By the time we could make it there, *if* we could make it there, he might be dead."

"It's somewhere to start. We can work from there." Creon went back to his desk and started typing. The holoprojector changed, zooming in on the planet. A blip on the screen was blinking brightly. "That's Roy," Creon said. "And it looks like he's surrounded…by helkates. Oh, shit, that's not good."

Anabelle spun to meet Creon's eyes as her own narrowed—as if *he* was one trying to kill Roy. "What exactly are helkates?" she asked, her voice heavy and accusatory.

"Helkates are the Dark One's elite fighters. They aren't the strongest ones out there, but they're the fastest and most efficient. Their targets don't often survive."

Anabelle took her time responding. "So, you're telling me he's fucked?"

"No, I'm not saying that. I'm just letting you know what the situation is. If he's…oh, wait, that's interesting."

Anabelle grabbed Creon by the shoulders and shook him. "What? What's interesting?" she shouted.

Creon prised Anabelle's hands off his shoulders and stumbled away while Abby rushed over to help keep the goblin from falling over. Once Creon had situated himself, he came over to the holoprojector. "It looks like Roy just entered hyperspace, and he's flying by hand. He must be trying to lose them."

"What does it matter if he's flying by hand?"

Creon motioned for Abby to join him at his computer. "If he's flying by hand, that means he'll be traveling slower than usual, and that he's in trouble. But we can track him. He would have had to punch in some general coordinates. We can get a rough estimate of where he's going and guide him to a better jump exit."

Anabelle hit her comm and pinged Roy. "Where should I tell him to go?"

Creon was staring intently at his screen. "There's a bigger problem than that. He's being followed. There are multiple helkates in his hyperspace tunnel as well. They're following him. Once he exits, they're going to be there too. He's bringing them to Earth."

Abby didn't need the gravity of the situation explained to her. She could see it in Anabelle's and Creon's faces. This was obviously a big deal.

Creon leaned back in his seat, running his hands through his hair as he gritted his teeth. "If even one of those helkates gets away from Roy, it could do immeasurable damage. We should guide him somewhere away from people—say, the middle of the Atlantic. But he'll need backup to get rid of the helkates. A good amount of backup."

Anabelle shrugged as the goblin looked at the map. "I know how to pilot a fighter. I'll go back him up. Where should I tell him to exit?"

Creon shook his head as he hobbled over to the map. "You're barely a novice, and besides, one more fighter isn't going to be enough. Uh, Abby, do you think now would be a good chance?"

Abby had been itching to get out of the lab. That and Creon had been filling her mind with all sorts of nonsense. He didn't seem to think Abby integrating nanobots and an AI into her body was a bad idea. Creon even had a couple of theories as to what she was capable of doing now, and he wanted to test them. So did she. "I'm not sure," Abby said at last.

Anabelle eyed her and Creon as she folded her arms. "What the hell are you two talking about? I don't want to pull rank on you, but you two both need to let me know what's going on right now because Roy is going to need help when he leaves that jump."

The pair exchanged guilty looks before Abby said, "It would be easier if we showed you." Then she walked over to one of the lab tables where an exoskeleton suit was splayed out. She slipped the suit over her shoulders and connected it to her waist.

Anabelle tapped her foot impatiently, casting a glance at the map. "We don't have time for science experiments right now," she shouted. "Roy needs to—"

Abby raised her hand, interrupting the elf. "Just hold your britches and watch."

Anabelle stopped talking and gave Abby her full attention.

Abby closed her eyes and concentrated. As she inhaled and exhaled, nanobots began to pour out of her skin, connecting to the exosuit, binding her flesh and the steel together. Her skin fused with the wiring and electronics of the suit, the pigment of her skin becoming darker and more metallic.

Once the transformation was complete, Abby stood before Creon and Anabelle—an obsidian god, a symbiosis of flesh and technology.

Abby opened and closed her fist. She'd only practiced transforming her hand with Creon a couple of times earlier. This was her first full-body transformation. She felt cold all over, a cold that went straight down to her guts.

Anabelle nodded as she inspected the construct. "Okay, you got my attention. Let's take you out for a spin, Abby."

Creon had provided Anabelle with the coordinates to relay to Roy. She wasn't certain if the mech rider had received them. His hyperspace jump was screwing with communications, but in theory, he should have received them even if he could not respond.

Anabelle and Abby were standing beside the hadron collider, waiting for their coordinates to lock in. It was hard not to stare. In all of Anabelle's life, she'd never seen anything like Abby. The girl was beautiful, even if she didn't look like she should exist.

"Hey, you okay?" Anabelle asked. Abby hadn't spoken since her transformation.

Abby looked up suddenly. She no longer had human eyes, they'd been replaced with a white-hot glowing light. "Huh?" she exclaimed as if she had been rocked from sleep.

"I asked if you were okay."

Abby smiled as she nodded. "Yeah, yeah. Perfect. Just a lot to take in. Martin's kinda integrated into my mind. There's a lot of information. A lot."

"You good for a mission? Sure you don't want to test out all this shit on the track field or something?"

"No, I'll be good. Trust me."

The hadron collider opened its portal. "Let's do this thing," Anabelle said as she stepped through the portal, Abby floating right behind her.

Abby came out the other side of the hadron collider's portal. She looked down, and there was only ocean. When she scanned the horizon, there was more water. Initially, she panicked, worried that she was going to fall in and drown. She'd never been much of a swimmer.

Then Martin popped up. Or in. It was still hard to discern where or what Martin was doing. When he was working or thinking, it felt like another mind had opened inside hers. Distinct, but somehow connected.

Without having to think, the soles of Abby's feet expanded, a propulsion system firing jets, keeping Abby afloat. *Holy crap, I'm flying,* she thought. *I'm actually flying.*

Anabelle dropped out of the portal, waving her hand in front of her, causing a pillar of water to rise and solidify into ice. Abby flew after her.

She didn't look like someone learning to fly but rather glided with unexpected fluidity. *Guess she's a fast learner,* Anabelle thought. "Not bad for a beginner."

Abby shook her head as she laughed, flying in a loop. "Yeah, thanks. Still working out the kinks. I have to figure out what I can do...or can't do."

"Good, 'cause we're gonna have to find that out right now!" Anabelle pointed at the sky, not too far from where their portal had opened. The sky twisted and warped as if it were made out of taffy and was being stretched. Then the heavens went black, and Abby could see stars stretching far back as if they were looking into infinity itself. The vision was beautiful.

Then there was a loud snap and Roy's mech came racing through the sky, followed by the Dark One's helkates.

The mech went skidding across the water, deploying a parachute too late.

Abby raised her hand, scanning the mech without realizing what she was doing. "He's going to sink if we don't get him out of there."

Anabelle looked from the mech to the fighters, which were beginning to spread into an attack formation. "Help Roy!" she commanded. "Then give me backup!"

Abby leaned forward, her body working on instinct and whatever the hell Martin was doing in the background. Her thrusters fired and she soared toward Roy, landing on his mech. She grabbed the cockpit and ripped it open with a strength that almost made her scream.

Roy stared up at her, his eyes wide. He grabbed a pistol from his side and fired at Abby, shouting, "What the fuck are you?"

The slug bounced off of Abby as her skin hardened. "It's me, Abby. I need to, uh…"

Rather than waste time speaking, Abby reached into the mech, her hand splitting into a dozen tendrils that embedded into the controls. Her eyes turned black for a second as she connected to the mech. The power systems flickered, then turned on.

"They followed you," she said as she disconnected from the mech. "All of them."

Roy popped his head out of the cockpit and stared at the helkates. "Oh, shit. Didn't see that one coming," he muttered. He winced, eyes glazed with pain, and Abby guessed he'd been wounded.

"How badly are you hurt?" she asked.

Roy touched his side. "I'll live, provided we get me back to medbay sooner rather than later."

That was bad. A wounded Roy wasn't something they had expected. They needed him to fight. "Can you still kick ass?" Abby asked, injecting as much bravado into her voice as she could.

Roy gave her a devil's grin in answer.

"Good." Abby turned to leave, but before blasting off, she said, "Come on, we need to help her." Then she bolted into the air toward the helkates.

Anabelle was already in the air, pulling water from the ocean and freezing it while riding it upward in an insane dance. Abby soared to the elf's side, curious to know what her new body was going to do next.

Martin hadn't included an owner's manual.

Abby and the elf approached the helkates. "You packing?" Anabelle shouted.

Abby held her hands in front of her, her palms opening up, the nanobots working together to form a plasma cannon in each hand. "Looks like it," she answered.

"Beautiful. I'll take the left, and you take right."

Anabelle waved her hand to the left, the water beneath her surging forward as she flew at the helkates. She banked hard, looking like an insane surfer as she flanked the fighters, her hands charged with manna. Raising her arms, she guided the water into spouts, solidifying them into icicles that she fired at the helkates.

The icicles pierced five of the fighters, breaking up the formation.

The water Anabelle had been using was gone and she fell toward the ocean, arms outstretched, hoping the helkates took the bait.

A few of the fighters pulled out of the main formation and went after Anabelle. *Perfect,* she thought.

As the squadron zeroed in on the elf, she turned to face the ocean, drew her manna into her arms, and dove into the water. The fighters stopped, frozen with indecision.

Above, Abby was heading toward the righthand section of the formation. She aimed and fired, plasma ripping from her body, draining her of the cool feeling that had permeated her since she had transformed.

The plasma blast ripped through the remaining formation, taking out half the helkates. The remaining fighters broke away, doubling back and heading straight for Abby.

She blasted away, flying faster than she knew she was capable of. The squadron couldn't keep up with her. She looked over her shoulder, gauging the distance between them, and went higher. She looped back over them, firing shot after shot, picking off helkate after helkate.

Anabelle sat beneath the surface of the water, waiting. She could see the fighters just above the surface. She was pooling her manna into one movement, imagining it over and over in her head, almost dreaming it up as she lulled herself into light meditation.

Now.

Anabelle burst out of the water, weaving her hands together into symbols she only remembered on a primal level. The water around her rose, taking the form of a massive whale. With its jaws wide open, it swallowed the helkates.

Once the fighters were inside the mouth of the whale, Anabelle screamed, letting manna rip from her body, changing the water into ice. Then she called down a bolt of lightning and burned the helkates to ash.

Abby was still flying, chased by a handful of fighters. She stopped suddenly. The squadron raced past her and she surged after them, grabbing one of the helkates, her hands heating up, electricity flying as she tore the craft to pieces before slinging a large section at one of the other machines.

There was an explosion, shrapnel flying everywhere. Abby wove in and out of the smoke, firing at the remaining helkates. When the smoke dissipated, she was the only one left.

She glided down to Anabelle, who was sitting on a floating sheet of ice. "Not bad for your first time out on the town," the elf said.

"Thanks," Abby said, excitement filling her voice. "I didn't know. Oh, my God, that was awesome, right? That felt awesome."

Anabelle gave Abby a high five and laughed as Abby landed next to her. "Yeah, that was pretty awesome. We might have to get you out of the lab more often."

"GUYS!"

Abby and Anabelle looked over their shoulders to see Roy still floating on the surface of the water. "Could you give me a hand?" he shouted. "The mech is running, but I can't say the same thing about me. Got wounded in the pre-party before you showed up."

Anabelle's face went white as she called up a wave of water to push them over to Roy. "Shit! Are you okay?"

Roy propped himself up in the mech and forced a smile. "I'll live and keep looking pretty, but I'm not gonna be able to fly this thing."

Abby was already calling Creon. "Hey, can we get…uh, is it called an extraction? Yeah…okay…great…thanks." She turned to Roy. "Someone's coming right now. We'll stay with you until they get here, right, Anabelle?"

The elf looked at Roy. Abby couldn't help noticing the way their eyes met. She ignored it. Tried to, at least. "Yeah, we'll stay with the big 'ol baby. Don't want the idiot getting himself killed."

Roy laughed and leaned back in his cockpit, grabbing a flask hanging from its side. "Good," he said as he took a sip. "Wouldn't want to celebrate our victory alone."

CHAPTER FORTY-FOUR

After Anabelle, Abby, and Roy returned to HQ, he was taken to the infirmary. He put up a fight, arguing the entire time, but Anabelle had remained firm. Once Roy finally agreed to sit in a wheelchair and be taken away, the elf motioned for Abby to follow her.

The two walked to the cafeteria. Abby's body had returned to normal, although the girl still looked a little flushed. "Grab something to eat," Anabelle said as she sat at one of the tables.

Abby looked around the empty cafeteria and shook her head. "Not hungry."

The elf pointed at the magical food-burners, which could conjure up the meal of your choice. "You were just in a fight. A real fight. You're going to need to eat after that. Your body's probably still high on adrenaline. And grab me some coffee, will you?"

"Aren't *you* going to eat?"

"Nah, coffee will be good."

Anabelle watched Abby as she went to make herself a plate. She looked as normal as any human girl. Other than being a little out of breath, she appeared healthy enough. Anabelle was still worried. She had no idea what Abby had done to herself.

Any transformation that drastic wasn't going to come without a price, though Abby might not have thought that far ahead. Anabelle had seen how the science departments in HQ worked. Sure, everyone had a good intention. Didn't mean that everything that came out of the R&D was safe. Anabelle had seen countless projects green-lit before they were properly tested.

Abby returned, carrying a plate of salad with a light vinaigrette dressing, and a cup of black coffee for Anabelle. She sat and picked at her greens.

Anabelle blew on her coffee, cooling it a little before she sipped the dark brew. "So, have you made any friends since you've been here?"

Abby's eyes narrowed and she stiffened, forgetting her salad for a moment. "Why?"

"Just asking. You have been here for a bit, but I've only ever seen you in the lab. Working. I don't think I've seen you talk to anyone since you've been here."

Abby seemed bothered by Anabelle's questions and returned to picking at her salad. After a few moments, she said, "There's not anyone my age around. You know, hard to talk to folks twenty years older than you. Except Creon."

"You know you can talk to *me*, right?"

Abby's expression softened, and Anabelle hoped it was because the girl was getting more comfortable. During the ride back to HQ, Anabelle realized she'd hardly spoken to Abby about anything other than work. It was easy for her to forget to be social. She had never thought of herself as sociable.

But the transformation Abby had put herself through unnerved Anabelle. She wondered if it would have happened if she'd been more attentive to the girl's transition. Abby was just a high-schooler, after all.

"How did you do that?" Anabelle asked. "You can tell me. You're not going to get in trouble."

"Uh, nanobots," she murmured. "I injected myself with nanobots."

Anabelle had no idea what that entailed, which made this conversation a lot easier to have. There wasn't a way she could judge Abby's decision. She didn't know if it was a mistake or not. All she could do was go off Abby's opinion on the matter until she found out more. "So, what does that mean?"

"They're like little computers. Millions of computers. I sorta put them in my bloodstream, and now I guess I'm just waiting to see what happens."

"Not to sound like a mother or anything, but that sounds dangerous. Real fucking dangerous."

It wasn't hard to tell that Abby was embarrassed. She probably wasn't the kind of kid who was used to screwing up. The girl's reaction told Anabelle everything she needed to know. "You don't know what's going to happen, do you?"

Abby shook her head as she looked down at the table, her jaw set. "Martin said it'll be okay. He's monitoring me. Says if I get sick, it's straight to the infirmary."

"Whose idea was it to stick yourself with those nanobots?"

"Martin's."

"Hm."

Abby sighed, still staring at her plate. "You're not...mad at me, are you?"

Anabelle took a gulp of coffee then coughed as she choked. "Of course, I'm not mad at you. Just a little worried, you know...about adjusting to everything here. I know this is a lot of new for you. I'd be..." Anabelle trailed off as the girl's body started trembling, her shoulders heaving up and down.

Abby sniffled and wiped her nose, her eyes trained on the table. Then she hunched over and started crying. Anabelle sat there, not knowing what to do. Comfort had never been one of her talents, but she did care about how the kid was doing. And now that kid was crying her eyes out, and Anabelle had no idea why. She tried to think of what someone would do in a movie.

Abby was muttering something between her tears as Anabelle crossed the table and sat beside her. She rubbed Abby's back and hoped that would help. Abby did stop crying for a second and looked up to meet Anabelle's eyes. "I have no idea what I'm doing," Abby stammered. "There's just...so much...and I'm afraid I'm going to screw up, and you'll be disappointed with me, and Myrddin will send me back home, and my pa...and my pa..."

Abby was holding back more tears, and Anabelle knew it. "Hey, don't worry about it," she said. "You definitely shouldn't be worried about *me* being disappointed in you. You're doing great."

"I am?"

Anabelle brushed Abby's hair away from her face. "Of course, you are. And honestly, I'm like one of the biggest fuckups here. If anything, *I* should be worried about disappointing *you*. And Myrddin's not gonna send you back. He's put up with more shit from me than I think you're ever going to cause."

Abby drew herself up. "Yeah?"

"What was he like?"

Abby was still trying to blink back her tears. "Who?"

"Your father."

Abby sighed and drew in a ragged breath. When she spoke, it was slowly, as if each word had been measured out years ago. "He was the best...best person in the world."

Anabelle took Abby's hand and squeezed it gently. "He'd have to be to raise such a great daughter."

Anabelle found Roy in the medical wing. He was lying in a bed, hooked up to a variety of different machines. Other than the frown on his face, the man looked to be in perfect health.

The rest of the medbay was empty. Anabelle had never liked hospitals. Elves had no use for them. This was a uniquely human creation, and it never failed to scandalize her. Why would you gather all the sick and weak and shove them all in the same place? Humans were interesting, to say the least.

Roy glanced up when Anabelle entered the room. He waved weakly, forcing a cough that she could easily tell was fake. "How much longer do you have to live?" she asked as she sat beside him.

He groaned and held his stomach, grimacing as if the slightest movement were causing him pain. "Doctor says I'll never make it. For all I know, I might already be dead. I'm definitely seeing an angel."

Anabelle had heard the gamut of human flirting, from politicians who masked their cruelty with a veneer of professionalism to the crudest of civil servants who spoke as they wanted because they didn't think of you as a person.

Luckily for Roy, he didn't fall into those categories. There was something sweet about him being laid up in bed. It wasn't quite vulnerability, but it was refreshing to see the human on anything other than his best game.

"Dead already?" Anabelle asked. "The great Roy already throwing in the towel?"

"I don't know who told you that I'm going by 'great' nowadays, but you are very mistaken. Old-banged-up-piece-of-shit Roy might be more like it."

Beneath his covers, one of Roy's legs was in a cast. "Wait, were you actually hurt? I thought all of this was just for show."

"Nothing too bad. Just a couple of fractures here and there. Man, a jolt in hyperspace is hell on the body. The healers said it could be fixed with a spell or two, and doctors said they could reframe the bone in a couple of minutes, but I opted for the old-fashioned way."

Anabelle raised an eyebrow at the idea of not using magic or tech to heal quickly. "Why would you do that?"

"As a reminder. Let myself feel my mistakes. Helps me remember. If you're getting healed from every gut-tearing wound, you eventually stop caring about them, and you get sloppy. After that, it only takes one bad day without a healer."

Roy had a point. A similar lesson had been given to Anabelle during her training as a Traveler. The specifics of who gave it to her were still muddy, as were the rest of her memories. But she remembered the sentiment well enough. "So, you planning on staying up in here? A little vacation?" she asked.

"Hardly. I'm getting out tomorrow morning, but I don't mind having to stay the night. I can catch up on some television."

Anabelle couldn't imagine Roy sitting in front of a television. Somehow it seemed like something he wouldn't do. What kind of TV did a person like Roy watch? "You don't really seem like a TV kind of person," Anabelle pointed out.

Roy pulled a remote from under his sheets and clicked a button. A holoprojector appeared behind Anabelle and turned on. "It's our secret. Most everyone thinks I spend all day reading military tactics or some shit like that. Which I do. But only to keep up appearances."

Roy laughed, and Anabelle allowed herself to join him. It felt good to be around him. She didn't often permit herself to admit that. She could have stayed with him long into the night. It had been a while since she had vegged out in front of the tube. But she had other things to take care of.

Anabelle stood and kissed Roy on the forehead. "See you around."

"Wait. You should come back later tonight. This thing gets inter-realm cable. Also, there's my company."

Anabelle thought it over for a second. "If you're still awake, we'll see. Catch you later."

Anabelle met with Myrddin in his office. Once more, the room had changed. It seemed that Myrddin rearranged at least once every few days. One of the perks of having such a grand control of magic.

The room was now empty of any furniture other than two comfy looking seats and an ornate coffee table between the two chairs. Two cups of tea sat on the table, and Myrddin was already sitting in one of the chairs when Anabelle walked into the room.

She sat across from Myrddin and scooped up the cup of tea. Myrddin took his tea as well, conjuring a porcelain milk pitcher onto the table before reaching out and liberally adding some to his cup. "Good evening, Ms. Chase," Myrddin said politely.

"Evening to you too, guvnor," Anabelle said as she sipped her tea.

"What was the reason you wanted to speak with me tonight?"

Anabelle drew in a deep breath as she prepared to speak. Playing by the rules had always been her specialty. When you played by the rules, you were able to find more loopholes than when you were outright breaking them. And it was the easiest way to get what you wanted.

Being the maverick had been enjoyable, though. Luckily, she'd been able to walk the tightrope between the two. "I want to call your agent. We got the satellite up and running," Anabelle explained. "The signal should be strong enough. But I don't want it to be behind your back. I want you to be part of the conversation, just to make sure we're on the same page."

Myrddin stroked his beard as he waved the milk pitcher into nonexistence. "I appreciate your straightforwardness," he admitted. "It is unnecessary since I trust you, but your gesture puts me at ease. I'd like to feel less like an antagonist in your life."

Anabelle kept her tongue in check. Myrddin had been much more than an antagonist over the last few years. But he did seem like he was trying to cut her some slack. There was no reason to go off on him. Yet. Flipping out on Myrddin was one of Anabelle's favorite things to do.

With another wave of his hand, Myrddin brought up a holoscreen. He searched through it for a few moments before finally selecting an option. The screen changed, displaying Sarah's Middang3ard ID.

The room filled with the sound of a phone ringing. Myrddin must have had something like a speakerphone but better. After a few seconds, the comm clicked on. "Hello? Who the hell is this? This is an encrypted channel," Sarah said, the room swelling with her voice.

Anabelle looked at Myrddin to see if he was going to speak, but the wizard only smiled politely and nodded. "Uh, Sarah," Anabelle said. "My name is Anabelle Chase. We saw each other through the Dark Gate a few days ago."

There was a long pause before Sarah spoke again. "How did you get this number?"

"Myrddin rang you up. He's here too. You're on speakerphone, I guess."

When Sarah spoke again, her voice was acidic. "So, now you want to talk to me, Myrddin?"

Myrddin took his time answering. "Sarah, you disobeyed a direct order that put a lot of people's lives in danger," he said, his words slow and measured. "But you are still one of my agents, and your life is important. Anabelle's worked hard to get us to speak."

Sarah's voice softened a little. "Thanks, that means a lot to me. I'm still pretty pissed about you being a dick, but thanks. Better late than never, I guess."

Anabelle liked Sarah. Anyone who talked to Myrddin like that was someone she could respect. "You said you wanted me to get you in touch with Myrddin. Why are you so surprised that we called you?"

Sarah's voice crackled a little over the comm due to the strained signal. "I mean, I said it, but I didn't think it was actually going to happen. I didn't even give you my name. But anyway, what is it? Are you calling about the Dark Gate? Because I got a story for you. You might want to grab a beer or something. It's a doozy."

Myrddin conjured two dark stouts onto the table, picked his up, and leaned back. "We're all ears, Sarah," he said as he sipped his beer.

CHAPTER FORTY-FIVE

Sarah began her tale. She had come to the gnomish world after her boyfriend Kravis had been abducted. Both of them worked for Middang3ard, Sarah, in the role of assassin and Kravis as a double agent. It had only been a matter of time, but Kravis had been found out.

As with all double agents, Middang3ard HQ wouldn't intervene. It was the risk you took when you went undercover. But Sarah couldn't let Kravis just disappear. She'd lobbied to get Myrddin to help, but the wizard stood by his initial decision.

Sarah decided that wasn't good enough. She rigged the hadron collider to transport her to the gnomish world and swooped in to save Kravis.

The problem was that the gnomish world was much worse off than Sarah had been led to believe. Horror didn't do justice to the conditions that the Dark One had reduced the planet to. It became very obvious why the Dark One had worked so hard to keep communications from coming back up.

Kravis had been able to send precious little information concerning the plight of the gnomes.

Here, Myrddin interrupted Sarah. "I understand the pacing of your story, but I need to hear how the gnomes are doing now. How bad is bad?"

Sarah sighed and drew a deep breath. Still, it took her some time to answer, as if remembering was too large of a task. "Astera doesn't exist anymore," she said at last.

"What do you mean, it doesn't exist?"

Anabelle was lost. She didn't know much about gnomish geography. Actually, she didn't know much about gnomes. They were a very private race. She was honestly surprised that any gnome would be open enough to date a human. "What's Astera?" Anabelle asked.

Sarah answered, "Astera used to be the capital. It was a beautiful city, showcasing the gnomish ability for crafting and organization. Their crown jewel."

"What happened to it? How did it just stop existing?"

"First, the Dark One took over the capital. He rounded up all the gnomes who were living there and put them into slave camps. Then he started digging. Legend had it that Astera was built on a giant mineral deposit. Guess he wanted to find out. He forced the gnomes to burn the city down and gut it. There's nothing left but holes in the ground. He worked the gnomes to death."

Myrddin and Anabelle exchanged glances. This was the worst situation any homeworld had faced so far. The gnomish world was the only one to be taken over by the Dark One. Small invasive squads and skirmishes were all the other worlds had to deal with so far.

Anabelle was determined to find out just how bad everything really was on the gnomish world. "That's just one city, though," she argued. "Sure, it's horrible, but it can't be like that on the entire planet."

"No, it is. Anything the Dark One's forces haven't burned to the ground has been converted to mines. The gnomes who aren't enslaved are living in shantytowns that the army constructed, but even those are few and far between. The army is a husk of what it used to be. It feels like everyone is just waiting to die."

Myrddin jumped in this time, his eyes fiery beneath his white brows. "And what of the resistance?"

"Our ranks have been thinned. There's a few of us left, with Kravis and me leading them."

Myrddin leaned back in his chair, thinking as he stroked his beard, his eyes deep and pensive. "I'm sorry, Sarah. I had no idea the situation was so dire."

"Let the past be the past. Honestly, if you had known the gnomish world was a lost cause, I doubt you would have let me come."

"And you think it's a lost cause?"

Sarah laughed, but there was no humor in it. "I think it is, but Kravis doesn't. Can't drag him away from this place. Guess we're going to go down with the ship."

Anabelle remembered the initial reason they had called Sarah. "You said you knew how the Dark One was making those gates when I first saw you," she blurted. "How's he doing it? Those things are becoming a real pain in our asses."

When Sarah spoke, her voice sounded lighter than when she'd been talking about the gnomish world. "That's the Dark One's new invasion strategy. It's how he managed to take down the gnomes—tons of Dark Gates opening up over the world. His soldiers can slip in undetected. Set up shop. Start building out, and then they attack. Worked perfectly."

"Okay, so we know what they're doing, but *how* are they doing it?"

"They built a hadron collider."

Myrddin scoffed as he shook his head. "Impossible. We created the collider and have kept it under wraps since."

Sarah laughed sarcastically. The sound was abrasive to Anabelle's ears. "You'll get a hoot out of this one, Myrddin. File incoming."

The holoprojector showed Myrddin received an email. He opened it. There was a photograph of the Dark One's hadron collider. It looked nearly identical to the one on Earth. Another photo showed two orcs working the machine, the Middang3ard insignia etched into it.

Anabelle couldn't keep herself from laughing and blushed when Myrddin stared at her. "I'm sorry, but you think they would at least have removed our logo from the thing," she managed to get out. "If I were stealing something, I would."

Myrddin was still thumbing through the photos Sarah had sent. There was no mistaking it. The Dark One had their collider. "How could this have happened?" Myrddin murmured, still reeling from this loss. Myrddin couldn't believe how advanced the Dark One was. "These were under such high levels of security."

Sarah's voice came through the comm. "Same as over here. You got spies. So does the Dark One."

"But how does it work? The collider here uses very specific minerals from Earth. It is meant to only work on Earth."

Anabelle snapped her fingers as she said, "That's what all the mining was for. They've probably been looking for something to use on the gnomish world that's comparable. Maybe they exhausted whatever they had before."

"That would not be a bad strategy. Burn through everything you needed to get to the New World. Then ravage that world to prepare more Dark Gates."

Sarah interrupted Myrddin's train of thought. "Hold on, it gets better. So, this Gate, the one on the gnomish world, only works with the Gates being built here. I think they're improving on the original design. Instead of using the collider for big teleportation jobs, what they're doing is hooking it up to as many smaller gates as they want. Gives them more options."

Myrddin's brow furrowed. "That is an improvement and one we could use. Sarah, what are the odds that you could get that tech to us and disable the gnomish network?"

"I'm working without arms out here. No tech, no weapons, nothing. You get me the supplies, and I can take care of this. Give it a week, and the Dark One's whole operation will fall apart. You remember what I did in Russia?"

Myrddin nodded as he thought back, smiling slightly. "Deal. Find a place you can receive a package and get ready to start."

"Gotcha. I'll start making preparations. Good to be back in business. Talk to you in a bit."

Sarah hung up, leaving Myrddin and Anabelle in silence. "Was she serious? Toppling the invasion of an entire planet?"

Myrddin stood and stretched as he continued to look at the photos. "Oh, yes, she is quite serious. And capable. Sarah may be the most dangerous person in the nine realms. My issue with her leaving wasn't that she was incapable. It was that I couldn't risk the Dark One getting his hands on her."

"What happened in Russia?"

"Let's just say you'd need to get a master's degree in political science to even begin having the conversation."

"Damn. Well, glad she's on our team."

Anabelle went back to visit Roy in the medbay. All the lights were off, but the television was still playing. She let herself in and sat on Roy's bed. He was snoring softly, drooling into his pillow. Anabelle had never seen him like this.

Vulnerability wasn't something the elf understood. She'd never had any need for it. Her training as a Traveler had been about everything other than vulnerability. The hard shell she'd created in her youth was as much a part of her as anything else.

When she began working for Myrddin, vulnerability would have been a threat to her job. It would have killed her ability to manipulate as she needed. It would have put her in danger.

Now, sitting here next to Roy as he slept, Anabelle felt like she was safe for the first time in a very long while. And all it had taken was for her to watch someone she thought she cared about while they were sleeping.

If only things were always that easy. But nothing had been easy for a long time. At least now, she was starting to enjoy it a little bit.

Anabelle stayed in the medbay, watching junk tabloid television and flipping through the news when that bored her. She listened to news anchors theorizing about when they were going to see Terra next, and how long she was going to last in the hellish prison.

The humans were talking, which was just what Anabelle had wanted. Another form of manipulation. But at least this time, she'd been using the truth and knew the purpose behind the act. Humanity was waking up. It was only a matter of time until they were arming themselves.

Roy stirred in his sleep, and his good eye popped open. He looked around the room, jerking awake.

Anabelle had already slipped into the shadows. She watched as Roy settled back down and went to sleep. Then she kissed him on the forehead and left him to his dreams, wondering if she ever made an appearance. She laughed as she walked down the hallway. It was such a stupid question. How could Roy not dream of her?

CHAPTER FORTY-SIX

Abby was back in the lab first thing in the morning. She arrived before Creon, her breakfast balanced on one hand—a feat she would not have been capable of a week ago.

All the departments in the lab were empty. The sun hadn't even risen yet, but that was okay with Abby. This was about the time she would have woken up to let the goats out of their pen. Even her Pa had thought she was an abnormally early riser.

The early hours had always afforded Abby two things: time to think, and time to investigate things that might get her into trouble. When she was younger, she would sneak off the main farm and go down to a creek that ran between her home and another ranch.

If anyone had found out about those early morning swims, Abby would have been grounded all the way through high school. The owner of the creek hated Abby's family, and, in turn, Abby's parents couldn't stand him. It was such a nice creek, though. Would have been a shame to let it go to waste.

It had been a few hours since Martin and Abby last spoke. She still wasn't certain about the extent to which Martin had inserted himself into the nanobots. Was he connecting to them through a network, or was he part of Abby's body now?

Those were things Abby wanted to figure out. The gravity of what she had done was finally starting to settle in on her. From everything she knew about the nanobots, they were practically living creatures. Not as high-functioning as a person, but definitely on par with a cell.

And Abby knew what happened when your cells got out of control. Cancer. Autoimmune diseases. She wasn't sure what would happen if the nanobots got out of control, but she wanted to have a rough idea for a worst-case scenario.

Abby sat at her desk and studied her reflection in her phone. It looked like if she were to peel her skin back, there would be metal. Just like her nightmare.

Better to push that away for now. There would be other times to be scared. Right now, it was breakfast time. Abby dug into the plate of scrambled *olin* eggs, a goblin specialty, that was mixed with something that reminded Abby of her mom's cooking. Since getting to Middang3ard HQ, Abby had been mostly living off goblin food. She couldn't get enough of its salty, meaty flavors.

As she chewed her food, she turned to the holoprojector. "Martin, can we talk?"

Martin popped up instantly on the projector. "You're lucky I don't sleep. Who the hell is even up this early?" he asked.

"We need to figure some stuff out."

If the AI was only mimicking human emotions, it was doing a great job of looking bashful. "Okay, okay, I know this isn't what we thought was going to happen. But it is kinda cool, right? You got to get out in the field. Bust some heads open. Get your hands dirty."

Abby couldn't disagree with that. The feeling of flying had been beyond her wildest dreams. Though she was put off by how little of the air she had felt. Which reminded her why she needed to talk to Martin. "I'm gonna need to know what's going on with my body," she said. "More than you're telling me."

Martin's paperclip body raised its hands. "Not because I'm trying to keep secrets or anything. We just haven't had a chance to talk. And my personality is developing in such a way that I'm not in the habit of explaining myself. But I guess now's as good a time as any. What do you want to know?"

"Everything."

Martin's body exploded into an image of Abby's, complete with a breakdown of her neurological and cardiovascular system. A complex web of mathematical formulas was on the side of the projector. "Okay, there's some stuff I don't know that I'm trying to figure out as fast as I can."

"Tell me what you do know."

"So, when the nanobots entered your bloodstream, they began to connect with your DNA and RNA. They didn't rewrite anything, but they did code themselves to your DNA, pretty much, becoming a part of you. Obviously, they're multiplying since that's what they do. That's something we're going to have to keep watching."

Abby looked down at her wrists, at the veins beneath her skin. "Why do we need to keep watching?"

"Because we don't want them to replace all your white blood cells. I don't know what happens if that happens. And next, since the nanobots have bits of my personality programmed in, my consciousness got linked to yours. And because I have such a sunny disposition, I don't want to reprogram them. There's no telling what I would do to keep being me. So for now, I assess that it's best that the nanobots are left alone to keep learning too."

"Okay, for a second, pretend I didn't graduate from MIT."

Martin smiled as he spun around, wiping away Abby's projection. "Means the nanobots are learning as fast as I am and connecting to whatever they can. And means you have access to me more than anyone who wears those exoskeletons you downloaded me into. It also means that those nanobots have a vested interest in keeping you alive because you are, for lack of a better word, their host now."

Abby was starting to make sense out of what Martin was saying, even if it sounded unbelievable. "So, you and me, huh?" Abby considered what that meant. More precisely, what she could do with Martin being a part of her. " If I can use you and the nanobots can connect to anything, I could probably control my drones without a remote, huh?"

Martin's smile grew even wider. "As easily as you move your hand."

Abby looked at the drone. She didn't quite think, not the way you put together a thought, but more like the way you reach for a cup of water.

Gertrude levitated, its thrusters firing as it floated. "Part robot, part AI, and part human," Abby muttered. "Unreal."

"You don't sound excited about all of that."

Abby shook her head as Gertrude powered down and settled back on the table. She scooped a spoonful of eggs and chewed, taking her time. "We need to keep watching everything. I-I had a nightmare that scared me a lot. I was...pretty messed up."

Martin already seemed to have lost interest. "Yeah, right, whatever," he mumbled. "I'll make sure you don't go into cardiac arrest or anything."

That was probably the most Abby was going to get out of Martin. It was a lot of information to deal with. Abby wished he had been fused to her brain so she could have processed it all faster. There would have been other complications, though, and frankly, Abby was still happy that part of her was a hundred-percent human.

Now that Abby had a better idea of what was going on with her body, it was time to turn her attention to something else. She had been brought on to avenge her father. Fighting was only one part of that. She'd been thinking about it all night.

What would Pa have thought would bring some meaning to his death? The answer had been clear enough. Helping other people. And there was someone in dire need of help at the moment.

Abby turned on the tracker drone light-years away. It was time to figure out how to get Terra out of that arena. As Abby brainstormed her options, the door of the lab opened. "Morning Creon," she said without looking away from her computer screen.

The voice that replied surprised Abby. "Morning to you too, kid."

For the first time, Abby saw Anabelle looking like a regular person. The elf was wearing Middang3ard sweats, and her hair was pulled up in a messy bun. She hadn't bothered putting on makeup and, even though she still seemed ridiculously young, she looked very tired. "You guys have coffee in here?" Anabelle muttered as she collapsed into the seat next to Abby.

Abby pointed to the corner, where one of the food-conjuring pads was. "Uh, yeah, we have one of those pad things. What are you doing here?"

Anabelle yawned before shuffling over to the conjuring pad. She waved her hand, and a cup of hot coffee appeared. "Came to get started working," Anabelle answered. "Terra's the last project on my get-shit-done list, and I know you're an early riser. Don't know how. It's fucking disgusting. But I couldn't get any sleep last night, so here I am. What's the plan?"

"Just what I was trying to figure out. Was thinking 'bout watching the footage I got yesterday."

Anabelle's gaze was distant, unfocused for a moment, but she snapped back to attention. She looked like she was ready to fall asleep. "Sounds good. Mind if I watch with you?"

Abby nodded as she faced the holoprojector, which flicked on to the footage she was thinking about without any physical input. *Guess those nanobots really are trying to connect to everything,* she thought.

Anabelle kicked her feet up on Creon's chair and leaned back as she blew on her coffee. "Not to beat a dead horse, but I meant what I said yesterday," she said. "Anytime you need something. Even if it's just someone to listen. Let me know."

Abby had never been much of a talker. Not that she was secretive. There just never seemed to be anything to talk about. She was content to let the things on her mind stay on her mind, and it never distracted her from what she was trying to do. Her thoughts had felt different recently, though.

She tried to think about how to phrase the chaotic storm of her mind. "Uh, I think I'm a cyborg now," was what came out.

Anabelle raised an eyebrow as she drank her coffee. "Oh, you don't say? I was thinking more about you having a crush or something like that, but sure, why not start with a huge existential question of humanity?"

Abby caught herself laughing despite her entire body flushing with embarrassment. "We should start the footage," she muttered.

The pair watched the footage from the day before, combing over each detail as Terra was led through the catacombs of the arena by the Game Master. There didn't seem to be anything useful in the video.

Suddenly, Anabelle shouted, "Stop it right there!"

Abby paused the video. It was the section where she had snuck away from Terra to film what had been behind a half-opened door. "Is that a Dark Gate?" Anabelle asked, pointing at a circular construct hooked up to an assortment of computers and monitors.

Abby took a better look. She hadn't been able to see it very well yesterday, she was so concerned with capturing everything as quickly as possible. The construction did bear some resemblance to the Gate that had opened at her farm. "Martin, could you bring up all the photos we have of Dark Gates?"

The holoprojector displayed dozens of photos of Dark Gates that Middang3ard HQ had come across. For the most part, they were uniform, except for the last five, and the most recent one sent by Sarah. "It's definitely a Dark Gate," Anabelle murmured. "I wonder why it looks different?"

Abby pointed out the timestamps on all the photos. "Maybe it's an upgrade. See how the first few look the same? Then there's a jump. They look cleaner."

The elf relaxed into her chair. "That's our in. If we can get a hold of that Dark Gate, we can get Terra home."

Abby's face shimmered, the nanobots running over her skin and disappearing as she considered the options. "And how are we going to do that?"

"Had a little meeting with Myrddin last night. Turns out the Dark Gates work on our tech. The hadron collider tech. They gotta have one on that planet, and if they're the same, we have all the info here. Think you can do it?"

Abby turned to her computer, smiling. "Martin, gimme everything you have on the collider. We're cracking another one."

CHAPTER FORTY-SEVEN

S arah had been hiding out with the gnomish resistance for almost three weeks now. The resistance was located in the old mines that had been in joint use back when dwarves still dwelled on the gnomish homeworld. The mines went straight into the heart of a mountain ridge on the outskirts of one of the oldest gnomish cities, Al Na-Hemith.

The resistance was made up of gnomes who had managed to avoid the Dark One's labor camps. These gnomes were hearty. Fighters, each and every one of them. They had found one another and formed a loose contingent of guerilla warfare groups.

But even though they had heart, they were losing the war. The gnome world had nearly been destroyed. If the constant deaths weren't dragging them into the pits of despair, watching their home-world burn was guaranteed to send them over the edge.

The resistance fighters had been reduced to hollowed-out creatures, the light in their eyes having faded long ago. Now they moved as corpses, uncertain if they were alive or dead.

Sarah watched the gnomes go about their business day in and day out, waging their small skirmishes and hoping to win back a bit more of their world. She helped where she could, but there was not much to be done. Her expertise had always been sticking to the shadows.

Due to the shit state of the gnomish resistance, Sarah had no resources to exploit. She had begun to feel like it was time to try to return to Earth. At least there she could have made a difference.

That was until Myrddin and the elf Anabelle had reached out to her. Sarah had been able to relay some valuable intel but, more importantly, Myrddin had promised to send her what she needed.

Since a new satellite had been dropped into the gnomish world's orbit, there was a strong enough signal for minor teleportation from Earth. Sarah wasn't going to get any reinforcements, but she could get tools for her own kind of mission.

Sarah had talked it over with Kravis the night before. The red-bearded firecracker was hard to convince, but he'd eventually caved. Sarah could see his heart aching for his planet. There was no way he was going to turn down a chance to hurt the Dark One.

That was why Sarah was out in the middle of the night, in the bone-chilling cold, trying to track the coordinates for the teleportation drop spot. Kravis had wanted to come along, but Sarah had convinced him otherwise. If anything happened to her, the gnomish war effort wouldn't be damaged. They couldn't risk losing Kravis.

Sarah, on the other hand, was mostly a free agent. The gnomes in the resistance respected her as an ally against the Dark One and took her advice seriously. But that wasn't the same as living on their burning homeworld. Their plight sparked a different kind of fight.

As the night waned, Sarah sat underneath the moon, watching clouds drift overhead. The gnomish world was the closest place to Earth that Sarah had seen throughout the realms. She wished she had come here in better times.

Life was ending too suddenly. Sarah couldn't get that thought out of her head. It cropped up all throughout the day, ever since the Dark One came. Whatever Sarah and Kravis were doing, it wasn't living. It didn't even feel like surviving.

There could be a place for them somewhere. For a long time, she'd considered running away from the war, but running wouldn't achieve anything. The war would just follow. Before long, all nine of the realms would be at war. Why run from something inevitable?

A few feet away, a portal opened. Sarah recognized it instantly. A hadron collider portal. Just as quickly as the portal opened, it closed.

Sarah went to the spot where the portal had appeared. A knapsack sat on the ground. She opened it and dug inside. A small black discus was in the sack. *Figures Myrddin would have had a few of them made,* she thought, smiling. Even if Myrddin could be an asshole, he knew how to come through when he was needed.

Sarah checked over her shoulder before returning to the camp, doubling over her route to flank anyone who might have followed her. Then, she hid in a cave for a few hours, watching the stars, waiting to see if she was being tailed. Once she was certain she wasn't leading anyone back, she returned to the camp.

The night air felt great. The last few nights had been sweltering. Kravis had suggested sleeping outside, and by the time they settled on it, most of the other gnomes had dragged their blankets and sleeping bags outside as well.

It took Sarah nearly two hours to hike back to the camp. By the time she arrived, everyone but the sentries was sleeping. She slipped into her tent, where Kravis was snoring lightly.

Tomorrow she'd open the discus for Kravis to see. He was still always delighted by human technology. It was vastly different than gnomish tech. Sarah was glad she could still show Kravis things to bring a smile to his face. Lord knows, she had a hard enough time with herself.

Kravis was never one to wake early. It took a good deal of cajoling to get the gnome out of bed, but it was worth the effort. When Sarah showed Kravis the discus, his face lit up. "Is this what Myrddin sent?" he asked.

Kravis had never had a chance to meet Myrddin. The wizard, along with many of Earth's secrets, still sounded like something out of a fable. Especially when it came to the wizard's power. "Yeah, he sent it last night," Sarah said. "I didn't want to spoil the surprise."

Sarah pressed the middle of the discus and it split apart, opening from the center and expanding outward, a combination of nanotech and magic. In the middle of the discus was an emblem fashioned in the image of a snake. At its side were two pistols. Beneath was an assortment of gadgets. A cloaking device. Sound dampeners. Electric brass knuckles.

This was one of Sarah's specialized grab bags, loadouts she had put together for various scenarios. Each mission required something different, but sometimes you didn't have the time to pick and choose as you wished. This discus was for those moments.

Kravis was looking closely at the discus and its working parts. "This is amazing craftsmanship. And you say it's hardly supplemented by magic?"

"I think the only magic is in getting the items smaller, but I'm not a hundred percent sure about that."

Kravis straightened and looked out of the tent. His small size and slender frame almost made him look like a human child. He turned back to face Sarah. "So, when are we leaving?"

Sarah shook her head as she walked over to him. "We already talked about this. You aren't coming with me."

"If you're gonna give me that line about not being able to keep up, I'm going to remind you that we first met when I caught you trying to sneak plans off this world. You don't have to worry about me."

Sarah ran her hands through Kravis' hair as she hugged him. "Hardly. I think one of the hottest things about you is how sneaky you are. And deadly. But if anything were to happen, the resistance would be fucked. It's not about us screwing up. We're going in against ridiculous odds. And I need you here."

Kravis agreed. He never liked to argue with Sarah. If she had a good reason for what she said, he accepted it and left it at that. But Sarah could tell he felt uncomfortable sitting on the sidelines.

"I put together a team like you asked," Kravis said at last. "They're waiting for you to brief them."

"Let's get breakfast first, then head back here for a little bit. There are some other things I'd like to take care of before I head out." Sarah grabbed Kravis' butt as she walked out of the tent. "You know, end of the world-type things."

The gnomish spies were gathered around the war table set up in the commander's main tent. They were mostly younger gnomes, none past their first pinnacle. That really didn't mean anything, though. Sarah had been in the game since she was eighteen. Age had nothing to do with talent.

Commander Jerkin and Kravis were looking over a map of the area that Sarah was planning to break into. It was one of the larger command centers the Dark One had set up. Heavy defenses were set up all over the place, and the building itself was practically a labyrinth.

The labyrinthian setup of the command center was a misstep on the Dark One's part. Gnomes had spent most of their existence underground, tunneling much like the dwarves did. They weren't merely used to complex structures, they relished them.

Kravis and Jerkins outlined the plan, and Sarah listened along with the rest of the team. She'd gone over it multiple times with Jerkins and Kravis already and didn't have anything to add. As usual, she preferred to stay in the background and watch what was happening.

That wasn't going to last, though. Sarah was taking the lead on this mission, and the resistance fighters were under her command. She waited patiently for Kravis and Jerkins to finish explaining the bare bones of the plan before she spoke.

Sarah watched her team. She knew they weren't all going to make it back. She hoped they knew that too because she didn't want to say it out loud. "You all probably noticed that there's not a whole lot of instruction for this one," Sarah said. "We're sneaking past the Dark One's defenses and hunting down a piece of tech that we think can be used to exploit the Dark Gates."

The resistance members nodded or grunted that they understood.

Sarah continued, "The reason is that we don't know what kind of defenses we're going to come across. The setup is similar to some of the circle defenses we've seen him use before. But other than that, we're walking in mostly blind. Which is why improvisation is going to be your greatest skill to use."

This was the only thing that worried Sarah. As a lover of jazz, she'd always been impressed by the ability to make things up as you go. It was something she'd become very good at. Playing things fast and loose wasn't typical of gnomes, though. They usually preferred structure.

"So, I'm hoping you guys can keep up with that because it's all we got. Get a chance to sabotage something? Take it. Patrol of orcs that is particularly vulnerable? Snuff 'em out. But we're all going to be making our way to the middle of the command center. That's where we're going to find what we're looking for."

This was the part Sarah knew the gnomes were going to love. "Anything that isn't bolted down, literally and figuratively, I want you to grab. Take anything you can get your hands on."

All of the gnomes smiled widely. Collecting was a gnome's deepest desire, so much so that the gnomes had some of the most complicated laws on stealing. If any of the resistance fighters were worried about the mission, the promise of adding to whatever bizarre hordes they had would bolster their morale. "We're going to be moving out in an hour. We'll split up into teams then. Dismissed."

The resistance fighters exited the tent, talking animatedly, leaving Kravis and Jenkins alone. "They seem excited enough," Sarah said as she sat at the war table.

Kravis sat next to her and peered at the map. "That's not saying much," he muttered. "Gnomes are always excited about something. Hell, some of them might just be excited about finding out what's on the other side. Some of those kids are crazy."

"Better to have crazy than timid in this kind of thing. At least they have something to look forward to."

Terra woke up from a nightmare, gasping for breath, convinced she was drowning. The world around her had faded. Everything had been blackness. When she woke to the dim light of her cell, she wasn't comforted.

The suns outside her cell were beaming. It was amazing that her cell could still be so dark with that brightness outside.

When Terra had first fought in the arena, she had believed this was something she could do, a place where she could make a name, cast off the lackluster life she had been living before. Now, she saw the arena for what it was. The place where she was going to die.

Maybe things never really changed. Once a loser, always a loser. The only difference in the arena was that everyone would see her failure, and it was going to end with her death. At least on Earth, she could wallow in her bed for days on end.

Not that she ever made it past a couple of hours in bed. Even if her life had been a steaming pile of shit, it had never stopped her from trying. That was all she could ever do. It was what helped her sleep at night. Knowing that even when things felt terrible, she was up every day, trying to make them better.

This wasn't any different. But Terra did have control over one thing: how hard she fought. She'd already done the impossible. The crowd and her fellow fighters were all amazed she was still going. That had to count for something.

There was supposed to be another battle today, but the Game Master had made it sound like it was going to be harder than the others.

Terra thought about the Game Master's offer to join the Dark One. Not because she was honestly considering it. She couldn't join up with someone who snatched people out of their homes and forced them to fight to the death. Instead, Terra was thinking about what it represented.

The subtleties of the war were still lost on her. She didn't really know who was fighting who. All she knew was that the Dark One seemed like the asshole to end all other assholes. Orcs, goblins, and other races fought for him. But not all orcs and goblins. And those who didn't were put to death in creative ways, such as the arena.

Terra wasn't an organizer. Not the kind of person to plan an insurrection, but there were kernels for one. Even she could see that. Maybe one day, the rebel orcs would rise up. They'd take their place and fight off the Dark One.

But all that was beyond Terra. She wished to be a part of it someday. If she were fighting on anyone's side, she'd want to be the one tearing the Dark One a new one. At the moment, though, it seemed like she wasn't going to make it through the day.

Terra stood and walked to the window, staring out at the three suns. "Come on, get your shit together," she muttered to herself. "Moping isn't going to do anything. You're getting through today. Whatever the fuck they throw at you, you're throwing right back at them."

A deep growl rose up in the cell. Terra recognized it as her stomach. She couldn't remember the last time she ate. Maybe after the Game Master's bizarre tour. Either way, she was hungry now, and her cell door was still open.

Terra went down to the dining hall. The rest of the fighters were gathered there as well, talking quietly to each other. Nib-nib was sitting next to Cire, sharing a plate of food. Terra sat with them.

Cire looked at Terra bashfully before sliding over the plate of food and pouring Terra a cup of mead. Terra recognized that look. She knew the orc was trying to cover up a crush, which seemed asinine seeing how either of them could die within the next few hours.

Nib-nib chittered away as she ate. Terra was still surprised she understood some of what the mantiboid was saying. "Big fight. Big, big fight today. Biggest since...long time ago."

Terra pointed at Cire. "I'm assuming your little magic hand thing is why I can understand her now, right?"

Cire didn't answer instantly, staring down at his cup and swishing it about before saying, "You'd be correct. There are some things that are imparted through the ritual," he explained. "You can't be certain, but we take a little bit of each other. We share."

"What did you get from me?"

Cire smiled weakly and said, "Your heartbreak."

It was Terra's turn to be embarrassed. She shifted away from Cire and looked down at her food. Being known was a terrible experience. Even worse when it happened accidentally in a weird-ass healing orgy. But it could have been worse. At least Cire was cute.

Terra decided to leave that bit of information alone and turned to Nib-nib. "How big a fight?" she asked. "You got any details?"

Nib-nib gobbled up another mandible of chow. "Big monsters. Bigger than before. And you go all alone. They kill if we try. They kill all."

"Oh. That's fucking great. Just fucking great."

"You say we fight, we fight. They kill all, but we fight."

Terra gulped her wine. It burned all the way down. That was what she needed. Something to burn and take away the stress. "Is she for real?" Terra asked Cire.

Cire gestured to the other fighters in the hall. "We've all talked it through. What they're doing is beyond unfair. It spits in the face of orc tradition. The arena isn't a killing floor, it's a place for champions to rise in fair combat. But besides that, we've watched you, Terra. If it wasn't for you, we'd all be dead. We'd gladly lay our lives on the line for you."

Terra waved away his words. "That's stupid. I'm not going to ask you to risk your lives for me," she replied. "You risk your lives for yourselves. Did you hear anything about what I'm going to fight? How bad can it be as long as it doesn't have three heads."

Cire sighed as he shifted uncomfortably in his seat. "The guards were joking about a dragon."

Terra's heart went cold, and she choked on her food. After forcing it down, she coughed loudly. "Oh, a dragon," she said. "That sounds bad."

"There are worse things than dragons."

Terra laughed bitterly. "Yeah, I can imagine."

"As I said, we are all willing—"

"No, no. This is for me. No need for anyone else to die."

Nib-nib looked up at Terra, her eyes glistening brightly. "Not die. Win. Always win," she chittered. "You win. We win. You live. We live."

Cire placed his hand on Terra's. "There is one last thing. I'd like to give you a gift. Much like before."

Terra checked over her shoulder to see if the other orcs were watching. "Is it going to be in front of a crowd again? 'Cause I feel like you have to warn a girl about that."

"Why? All orcs perform healing rituals together."

"Oh. Uh, never mind. What is it?"

Terra felt the bones in her hand warming up, and her entire body tensed. It was followed by a wave of relaxation. Then came the pain. It was like Terra's mind was on fire. She felt swords cutting into her body, and heat as if she were aflame. Then it was gone.

"What the hell was that?" she cried as she jerked her hand away.

Cire poured himself another cup of wine and said, "It is my pain. Years of battle. Memories. Lives taken, and lives of those I loved and lost. Now that knowledge is yours."

"What do you mean, it's mine?"

Cire smiled as he drank his wine. "You'll see the moment you pick up a weapon."

Terra's hand was still tingling, and she looked down at it. "Huh. Sounds like a pretty good gift."

CHAPTER FORTY-EIGHT

Martin had been compiling everything he could find on the hadron collider for the last two hours. Abby was poring over it, her eyes moving faster than she could ever remember. The nanobots were obviously getting into every nook and cranny of her anatomy.

Anabelle was still in the lab, reading through briefings and whatever else Myrddin had given her. Abby wasn't sure. Creon hadn't shown up at the lab yet, and it was nice to have someone else to work with for a change. Martin was never much of a talker.

Abby turned to Anabelle and asked, "Why do we use hadron colliders? If Myrddin is such a powerful wizard, why doesn't he just magic things to where he wants them to go?"

The elf looked up from her briefings. "The collider is specifically for human transportation to the other realms. Humans can't use magic unless they've been bound to a familiar...a being that lives inside a host and allows them to use magic. Existing in most of the realms requires magic. Getting there without it is impossible. The collider gets humans there and also coats them with a little magical residue. Keeps them from getting kicked back to Earth. Or exploding."

Abby was trying to figure everything out. There were still gaps in her understanding of how the magical realms and the creatures within them worked. "So, what about orcs? Why would they have a collider? Aren't they magical?"

"They used to be. Kinda like humans. But over time, they stopped using magic. Got stuck in their own ways. We weren't sure how the Dark One was transporting them between realms. However he was doing it, it obviously wasn't good enough since he decided to upgrade to using a collider."

Abby thought it over. If orcs were using the collider the way humans had to, there was a good chance she wasn't going to have to calibrate it to work differently for Terra. All the schematics she'd read so far hadn't mentioned anything about the colliders only working with a certain kind of DNA.

It seemed like the only real issue with the collider was getting it to turn on. Also, finding a way to get Terra to the collider, or vice versa. That was assuming the Dark Gate they had seen was actually working. There was always a chance it was only a prototype or a defective model. Someone had tucked the collider away in what looked like a room of junk.

Anabelle stretched her legs and stood. "You want a cup?" she asked, waving a hand at her coffee cup.

Abby pulled her eyes away from the computer screen. "Yeah, that'd be great. I could use a break."

Anabelle returned with two cups of coffee and handed one to Abby. "Did you used to do stuff like this at home?" Anabelle asked. "You know, the whole nerd thing."

Abby chuckled as she considered the question. "Sort of," she answered. "Spent a lot of time doing chores. But, give me a free moment, I'd have my head in a book. That was 'til Pa let me start tinkering in the back. My ma thought it was a terrible idea. Said I was gonna blow myself up."

"She ever change her mind?"

Abby hadn't thought about her mom in a while. She didn't realize how much she missed her and her sisters until she'd started talking. Missed them almost as much as her father. After a few moments,

Abby replied, "Yeah, she changed her mind. Saw how happy it made me. Didn't have a problem after that."

Anabelle's brow darkened as she looked to be slipping into thought. "Sounds like you got a pretty solid family. You're lucky."

"What about you?"

Anabelle almost jumped at the question. "Me? What do you mean?"

Abby had never seen an adult look so old and so young at the same time. "I meant your family. What are they like?"

"Oh. I don't know. I don't know what they're like."

Abby and Anabelle sat in silence. Then Martin blinked onto the holoprojector. "So, when I'm gone, it's talk-about-your-emotions time? You know, I might want to be a part of that. I'm a recently created life form. There's a lot of feelings in here, but if *you* organics want to be exclusive or whatever…"

Abby was taken aback by Martin's tone of voice. He actually sounded like he was hurt. Honestly, she hadn't even thought about Martin having emotions. "You wanna join in?" she asked. "Been told I'm a great listener."

"Maybe some other time. I got important information for you two. Figured out how to get that bad boy running. And yes, it was difficult if you were wondering. But if we get your tracker to that Gate, we can rewire it to open up to HQ. Kinda like how we cracked the chips. Actually, we could open it to any place that has a hadron collider."

Anabelle's sharp ears twitched. "How could you open it to any collider?"

Martin turned to Anabelle. "Whoa, didn't even know you were here. What are *you* doing here? I thought this was the nerd corner."

"Just answer the question."

"Whatever. The colliders have a unique energy signature and dump out a bunch of shit when they turn on. They leave a trail. I can scan through different realms and galaxies for that, adjust the teleportation frequency, and voila. Any more questions?"

Abby felt the first genuine hope that there was something they could do for Terra. "Better get started looking for those other frequencies," she said.

Martin was already fading from the screen. "Oh, I'm already scanning. It's kinda a no brainer."

Anabelle leaned over Abby's desk, looking through the complicated mathematical formulas on the screen. "You actually understand this shit?"

Abby didn't bother looking away from the screen. "Yep. Kinda like another language. Math, I mean."

"All right, kid, I'm outta here for a bit. I gotta go check up on the other mission going on. Call me if you need anything. But I'll be back later."

"Okay. See you then."

Anabelle left Abby alone with her thoughts. They were too numerous to start trying to sort through. She was happy Anabelle had come by. She'd be even happier to get Terra back to Earth.

Sarah supervised the gnomish resistance fighters as they split into their different groups, four groups of five. She was taking the most experienced, not that she needed them, but because her route was the most dangerous. Anyone who didn't know what they were doing was dead.

Kravis had left earlier to take care of another mission. They never gave each other long goodbyes. That would make it seem like there was a possibility that neither one of them was coming back. Instead, they limited themselves to a brief kiss and a promise to be safe.

The resistance fighters were going over their supplies, double-checking if they had everything they needed. Sarah preferred that they know the truth: You could never be certain you had everything you needed. But it didn't make sense to bring them down. She almost wished she had the positivity of a gnome.

Once everyone was situated, Sarah left with her four team members. They were going to make their way east, over the first ridge of defenses. Then it was a straight shot through the three defense rings. They had intel that their route was the least patrolled, which meant they would get to the inner command center the fastest. Lucky for Sarah, that was the most dangerous spot.

They were going to be traveling by foot in the veil of night, hiding in the shadows and hoping the intel Sarah had received was good.

Sarah and the gnomes left the camp without fanfare. She was glad. That showed that the four kids on her team had some idea of secrecy. They traveled for an hour in silence, Sarah leading the way, stopping on occasion to check for tracks, referencing the intel she'd been given.

On two separate occasions, they found recent orc tracks. It was hard to tell how long ago they were made, but they were further out from the ring. Could have been from weeks ago.

By the end of the second hour, they were nearing the first defense ring. It wasn't much of a defense—a wall guarded by sentries that extended indefinitely in both directions.

Most of the defense rings Sarah had seen before had an artistry to them. This was just a wall, and most everyone had already realized walls didn't keep anyone out. Ever. Hell, people like Sarah considered them to be an open invitation.

She motioned for the team to spread out. Hopefully, the gnomes knew how to act without orders. That was one of the most important things in teams like these—the ability to make independent decisions and still work together without alerting anyone.

Focus couldn't afford to be split between every team member, so Sarah focused on herself. She picked her point of entry. Two guards were up ahead, perched on the wall. Sarah pulled out her binoculars and glassed the two guards, gauging their line of sight, trying to get a better handle on their weapons.

It was too early to use her cloaking device. The limited battery life made it worth holding onto. Besides, Sarah hadn't gotten so rusty that she couldn't make it to the wall. This would give her a good measure to see how the rest of the mission was going.

Sarah raced to the wall, her eyes on the guards stationed atop the stone structure. She ran off to the left, keeping herself hidden in the grove of trees, taking note of the bushes and undergrowth around the base of the wall. Before approaching the bushes, she climbed into a tree and glassed the guards, checking in which direction they were facing.

When Sarah was comfortable, she dropped out of the tree and sprinted to the wall. Once there, she flexed her fingers and the gloves she wore transformed. The fingernails sharpened and extended while the palms sprouted small suction cups.

Sarah began to climb up the side of the wall, moving as fast as she could, checking on the guards every couple of seconds. Usually, she wouldn't just rush into a situation like this, but the wall appeared understaffed—most likely due to growing arrogance on the command leader's part.

The gnomish world had fallen long ago, so it wouldn't be surprising if those in charge didn't think the outer defenses were worth staffing.

Once Sarah reached the top, she crouched, tucking herself into the shadows. She checked if there were any other guards close by. There weren't—just the two she had originally seen.

Sarah drew her dagger from the sheath at her side. It was a small, light weapon, hardly more than a few ounces. Sharp enough to plunge into a heart, and fragile enough to be snapped off and left in a corpse. The blade dissolved within an hour, making it impossible to trace. Sarah usually carried multiple daggers, but she would only need one to deal with these two.

Across the wall, the two guards had moved closer to each other. They looked to be talking. This would make things a little tougher, but if Sarah moved fast enough, she could wrap this up quickly. Rather than thinking, Sarah allowed her body to move on its own.

Sarah slipped from the shadows, staying as low as possible, running down the length of the wall. She flung her dagger at her target. The blade sunk into the neck of one of the orcs. As he slumped over, Sarah launched herself into the air, pulling the blade out of the first orc's neck, tackling the second, and slamming the dagger into his throat.

Both orcs lay dead on the ground. Sarah checked quickly over her shoulder to see if anyone else was coming. When she was satisfied, she opened the discus attached to her belt and withdrew a bag of white powder. She crouched over both bodies and sprinkled some of the dust on them. Then she lit a match and tossed it onto the first corpse.

The orc's corpse burst into flames and quickly extinguished itself, leaving only a pile of ash. Sarah repeated the process with the second corpse. Then she kicked the piles of ash into the wind.

That was when Sarah remembered that she was part of a team. She looked back over the wall. Her teammates were only now making their way past the trees toward her position. As Sarah waited, she crouched low, making herself invisible among the shadows.

By the time her team caught up with Sarah, she was certain they weren't going to make it through the defense rings. One of the resistance fighters stepped forward, his eyes ashamed, and said, "We didn't even see you start moving."

Sarah apologized. "I'm not used to working with other people. I'll try to move slower, but you're going to have to keep up. Otherwise, we're all going to end up dead."

All of the gnomes agreed. Together, they made their way over the wall, heading directly to a tunnel system that could be seen jutting out of the wall's base. From what Sarah remembered from the map, it looked to be part of the straight-shooting path they had been trying to follow. She wished the intel would have specified whether or not the path was underground. Either way, they were taking the tunnel. Hopefully, it was the right decision.

The crowd had assembled, and Terra could hear their chanting through the arena's walls. She was standing in the darkened hallway, surrounded by the Dark One's orcs. No one had spoken to her since telling her that it was time for her battle.

Each of the orcs carried a weapon, swords, staffs, and the like, while some were holding shields. Terra figured the weapons were for her; otherwise, there wouldn't have been as much variety.

After taking her time looking over each weapon, she chose a *katar*, having grown partial to the blades. Then she grabbed a sword, slung it over her shoulder, and also chose a medium-sized round buster shield.

The chants of "Not-a-Male" grew louder. Terra remembered that just a few days ago, she had loved hearing that chant. Had felt as if there were people who understood how powerful she was capable of being. Now she realized it was nothing but false hope. Those people didn't give a shit about her. They were merely entertained by her attempts to stay alive.

Terra had also been outfitted with armor for the first time. It was similar to what her orc guards wore. It was thicker than leather, probably made from a hide Terra wouldn't have recognized, yet it wasn't as bulky or heavy as the armor she had seen the Game Master's guards wearing.

Even if the orcs wanted Terra dead, they were at least committed to making sure she was able to put on a good show.

The gates separating the hallway from the arena creaked open. No one said anything.

Terra stepped out into the arena, momentarily blinded by the light of the triple suns resting in the sky. When her vision finally adjusted, she saw the stands were fuller than they had been before. There wasn't an empty seat in the whole place. More and more orcs were interested in her battle for survival.

Across from Terra, on the other side of the arena, the gates were opening. Out stepped a young human man. He wore no armor, only a loincloth and a tattered cap. His hair was cut short, almost to the scalp, and he walked out of the darkness with a limp, dragging a sword nearly the size of his body with one hand.

Riotous cheering erupted from the crowd. Terra couldn't understand what they were chanting, something in orcish. Whatever it was, the very sound of the chant was violent, as if they had managed to distill aggression down to a few syllables.

The sword-bearing man took his time making it to the middle of the ring.

Terra knew better than to be cocky. Even if this guy didn't look like a challenge, there was no way the Game Master was planning on having a fight any less epic than the recreation of the Battle of the Red Lion. And if there was anything Terra had learned by now, whatever was in the ring was deadly.

She tried to remind herself that applied to her as well.

The man now stood in the middle of the ring, and Terra crossed the arena and stopped a few feet from him. Now that she was closer, she could see that something was off. The man's face was free of all expression, and he wheezed as if he couldn't catch his breath.

Skin hung loosely from his emaciated, scar-covered body. His ribs jutted out as if they had been blown up from the inside. He leaned forward, supporting himself on the hilt of his sword. "You," he muttered. "I have been waiting a long time for you."

Terra was unnerved by the talking pile of bones balancing on his sword. The man's voice was deep and raspy, sounding as though it were pushed out of his body rather than spoken. When he swayed slightly to the side, Terra hoped he would just topple over. Still, she tried to put on a brave face.

"Me! Why have you been waiting for little ol' me for!" she asked.

The man smiled, his incisors far too sharp for a human. "To release me," he growled. "To release me from all this. Death is our only release here."

Almost faster than Terra could see, the man swiped his sword at her. Terra was barely able to throw her shield up in time to block the attack. She stumbled away, almost falling over.

There was no way she could have blocked that attack before. It had happened without any tell, and with enough force behind it to have split her in half if she hadn't managed to block. That must have been Cire's gift. Terra's body had reacted as if it had seen years of combat.

The emaciated man leaned on his sword again, his lips drawing back in a disturbing smile, looking as if there were hooks in the corners of his mouth drawing his lip up. "Will you make me suffer for my freedom?" he asked, his head falling to the side as if the muscles in his neck had failed. "Or must *you* suffer for freedom?"

Terra backed away. Something about this man was off. It was like there was something else inside him. She'd never met a human who filled her with such fear or revulsion.

The man swung his sword again, slicing straight across, and Terra jumped to the side, raising her shield above her head just in case. The sword passed right over her head, barely skimming the shield. Then it came down again, atop the shield. The force of the attack nearly drove Terra into the ground.

A strong kick to the chest sent Terra flying backward. She skidded across the ground, trying to get to her feet. The man lunged, landing right in front of Terra. He raised his sword.

Terra saw an opening and rushed forward, her *katar* split into three blades. She slashed at his exposed abdomen, but he stepped away, narrowly avoiding the attack. He adjusted his stance and slashed at Terra, who raised her shield, blocking the blow. Her feet slid along the sand a little, but she pushed back hard before rushing forward and headbutting the man.

He stumbled back, covering his nose as it gushed blood. Terra leapt forward, refusing to give up the offensive. She brought her *katar* down as the man raised his sword, blocking the attack, his limp arm grabbing Terra's face and shoving her backward.

Terra stumbled, regained her footing, rushed forward, zigzagging as she picked up speed, and brought her *katar* down toward the man. But he pulled his massive sword up, catching her in mid-air. She dropped the *katar*, reached behind her, unsheathed her sword, and drove it through the man's shoulder blade, straight to his heart.

The man went limp, falling to the side, only keeping himself upright by leaning on his sword.

Silence from the crowd. They all watched on as Terra backed away from the man, not knowing what to expect. It had been her quickest fight, but it felt the hardest. Every one of her movements had been as specific as she could muster. If it hadn't been for Cire's gift, she wasn't sure she would have made it.

Her opponent was still standing. Terra had no idea how. He rested his free hand on the hilt of Terra's sword. His grip was tight. He tried to pull the sword out but could not. "Ah," he said, his voice low. "So, you are the one who will make me suffer."

The man took a step forward, and as he moved, his muscles began to bulge under his elastic skin, his eyes growing larger in their sockets, the veins in his neck and torso bursting. His legs burst open, the skin tearing, and a mass of muscle poured from both stumps, unfolding onto the ground, taking shape and wrapping themselves up among each other.

Next to tear was his ass. It ripped open, and more of the messy, sinewy ligaments fell to the ground. Now they were taking the shape of cloven feet, growing sturdier.

A boil appeared on the man's neck, growing exponentially in size until it popped, shooting fetid pus about, the wound gaping like a spoiled flower.

The man's spine extended and snapped, raising his height an extra three feet as four deformed arms ripped from his back, one struggling to grab the sword still piercing his shoulder. His face grew long and terrible as if it were made of melting wax, one eye dull and dead, the other ironically alive.

Terra retreated, staring at the shambling horrors as it lifted its sword into the air, letting loose a foul screech that echoed throughout the arena.

"Fuck, why couldn't it have just been a dragon?" Terra shouted.

The foul abomination rushed at Terra, slicing through the air with its sword as its six hind legs propelled it forward like some sort of obscene locomotive.

Terra tumbled to her knees, grabbed the dropped *katar*, and slid under his blade, she sliced at one of the legs. Another of the man's legs shot out and kicked Terra in the jaw.

The creature stopped and began stomping, trying to trample Terra underfoot as it cackled maniacally, thick drool slipping from its slackened jaw.

Terra rolled from side to side, trying to avoid the cloven hooves as they kicked up dust, carving open the ground with their ferocity. Finally, Terra managed to roll out from under the bastardized caricature of a man. She was barely able to catch her breath when the creature surged forward again.

Attack after attack Terra fended off, barely able to shield herself. The *katar* was still a few feet away, and her sword was firmly lodged in the creature. The only chance she was going to have was getting a weapon in her hands.

She finally dodged to the side, lunged forward, and grabbed one of its frail hands. She pulled herself up onto its body, scampering across the pus-filled mass as quickly as she could. When she reached her sword, she pulled it out and drove it into the creature's back again.

The thing screamed in pain, reached up with its good arm, and threw Terra across the arena.

She bounced off the wall with a heavy thud. Before she could hit the ground, the creature was in the air, landing above her. It grabbed her by the back of her armor, raised her high, and then slammed her body into the ground. Then it lifted her again, higher this time, sending her crashing back down once more.

The only sound in the arena was Terra's bones cracking.

The word "pain" did no justice to what she felt. It was as if her entire body was surrendering to a force far beyond its understanding. She was being swallowed up. It was easier than being here.

All of humanity watched as Terra's body lay limp on the ground. Abby had broadcast the fight out of habit. Although the battle had been playing out, she hadn't been watching. She was busy trying to figure out how to open the Dark Gate. She had convinced herself that finding ways to help Terra win each individual match wasn't going to help her in the long run.

Those feelings changed when Creon tapped Abby on the back and pointed at the image of Terra lying still on the ground, that monstrosity towering over her and screaming mindlessly. "Oh, my God," Abby muttered as she covered her mouth in horror. "Where the hell is the tracker?"

Without thinking, Abby reached out across the light-years to her tracker. It was a disorienting feeling, her body now out of place. She no longer saw what was in her lab.

She was on the battlefield with Terra. She knew the tracker would follow the girl everywhere now. It was part of its subconscious programming. She knew this because she had no memory of flying the tracker from the cell. *Everything's learning now,* she thought.

The tracker flew closer to Terra, as close as she could get. That had the horrifying benefit of giving everyone a closeup of Terra.

Terra's face was smashed in, her nose broken. A pool of blood gathered around her head like a halo.

Abby landed the tracker next to her ear and spoke aloud. "Terra, you need to get up. You need to get up right now!"

Terra's eyes flitted open. She smiled a little. "I'm not going to school today," she wheezed. "There's no tests or anything."

"Terra, this is Abby. From Earth. Don't quit. Please, don't quit yet. We're coming for you. I'm gonna get you home."

"I'm already home, silly. You can't...you have to sleep...sleep at home..."

Abby was holding back tears. She could see the life fading from Terra's eyes as they began to glaze over—the same look Pa'd had before he gave up.

Red-hot anger prickled up in Abby's chest. "You are not giving up on me!" she shouted. "You can't! I'm not going to let you. Do you hear me? Terra, do you hear me? You aren't giving up!"

Terra's eyes focused on the tracker. "But," she murmured as her eyes grew more focused, "I don't want to fight anymore. I'm hurting. I don't want to. I just want to go back to sleep."

Abby slammed her hands down on the desk and shouted, "I don't give a fuck what you want! You aren't giving up! Do you hear me?"

Terra stared at the tracker. It was contorting, changing into something. A face. It was the face of a teenage girl. The girl was crying. "Abby?" she asked.

"Please," the face pleaded. "I can't watch you die. Please don't give up. Please."

"I-I-I don't want to die."

Terra felt her bones burning, felt the fire race through her body as if she had been struck by lightning. The whole world was watching. She wasn't going to die on her back.

The fire burned deeper. Terra's heart was aflame, her brain a raging inferno. All she could feel was pain, but it was no longer the black mindlessness. It had changed, taken form. The pain was a flame, and it was small. It could only grow.

Terra reached out, her hand clawing the sand around her. The *katar* lay a few inches away. She reached for it, slid her hand onto it. Then she pointed the weapon at the ground, pushing her arm up. Once her arm moved, she knew the rest of her body would as well.

One foot was on the ground. Abby's voice was in Terra's ear, "You can do it, Terra! You can kill it!"

Terra was on one knee. She spat blood and stood.

The roar of the crowd was deafening. It sounded as if heaven and hell had opened for Terra's glory, unleashing the dead to sing her praises.

She reached into her mouth, pulled out a loose tooth, and flicked it at the broken, bloated husk of the emaciated man. "Round two, motherfucker."

CHAPTER FORTY-NINE

The tunnel Sarah and the gnomes passed through was a dark and slimy place. It smelled like the Dark One's forces had been using it as a sewage system, and the gnomes who traveled with Sarah didn't hide their disgust.

This tunnel, along with the others beneath the defense rings, had been used by the gnomes for thousands of years. Much of the ore mined to create their masterpieces had been pulled from these tunnels. Even though gnomes lived above ground now, they still had a love of their past.

They had never stopped appreciating the caves which had provided for them.

The journey was silent, and Sarah was glad for this. She could only imagine how the gnomes at her side felt, walking through the veins of their planet, realizing that it had been carved up, and their most sacred places were being filled with orc shit.

Sarah checked her holomap, hoping there was a signal. As far as she knew, this tunnel was a short cut through the defense rings and would bring them up into the last one, the epicenter of the defense ring. From there, all Sarah had to do was track down the hadron collider parts.

She wasn't certain on the ins and outs of how the collider parts were going to benefit her or Middang3ard, but Myrddin had assured her that being able to get the part, along with any other information about the collider, would help open up the gnomish world again. Maybe even help other worlds.

There were parts of the war that had always eluded Sarah. The politics, the technicalities. In the dark of the tunnels, Sarah realized that she had always thought of herself as instrumental in the war efforts. But since she'd been on the gnomish world, seen how things worked, she'd come to understand that, at best, she was a tool. A specialized tool.

There wasn't anything wrong with that. She had a function. One that could not be easily replicated. If she was specific, she was also essential. Leading a group of fighters wasn't her function. It wasn't what she had spent years training to do.

A blade. Sharp and without qualms. That was what Sarah was. And a blade didn't look after the flesh of others. Having so many lives to worry about was slowing her down. If she were on her own, she would have raced through these tunnels. Wouldn't have spent a second thinking about how important these tunnels had been to those who had walked through them before herself.

Now Sarah was slowing her pace so that the gnomes could keep up with her, stopping every so often to check if she'd been messaged by the two other teams.

It did feel good to care, though. Her life wasn't the only one hanging in the balance. That reminded her that the war was about much more than her. This was something she knew, but having flesh and blood by her side made it more real. For too long, it had only been Kravis. This was a reminder that there were lives outside of her own and Kravis' to protect and care for.

Up ahead, where the tunnel widened, there was a noise. The sloshing of water. Something was ahead. It didn't sound like multiple feet tramping through liquid. There were no voices. It was unlikely that it was an orc scouting party.

Sarah raised her hand, motioning for the gnomes to stop. She listened, her ears twitching, trying to pick up sound. She regretted not getting the cybernetic ear upgrades Myrddin and Creon had offered her years ago. If she lived, maybe it wouldn't be a bad idea to look into those.

There was the sound again. Louder this time. Whatever it was, it was getting closer.

Sarah leaned over to the gnomes and whispered, "Be prepared to engage."

They continued to move forward, hugging the walls, trying to stay as clear from the water as possible. As they neared the spot where Sarah thought she'd heard the sound, she looked down and saw a small water snake swimming through the water.

That was probably all it was. Water snakes were a nuisance through any gnomish tunnel that had the unfortunate predisposition of having water. The sound had probably just been that snake floundering about and making a commotion.

Sarah relaxed and moved away from the wall.

Suddenly, something huge and cylindrical tore out of the shallow water of the tunnel. The thing wrapped around one of the gnomes and fell back into the water, receding into the darkness, the tunnels filled with the screams of the gnome, which quickly faded.

Sarah drew her two pistols and fired, the shots briefly illuminating the tunnel. She turned to the gnomes and said, "Torches, now."

All of the gnomes lit their torches, casting light down the tunnel.

The water shimmered and moved. Sarah motioned for the gnomes to climb up, away from the water.

Stillness. An aching silence as Sarah's heart thudded in her chest.

A water snake burst out from the shallows. It was three times the length of Sarah's body, its stomach swollen with the gnome it had just swallowed. The snake had six eyes, and its slippery scales reflected the light of the torches, making the serpent look as if it were made of stars.

One of the gnomes rushed forward, his short sword drawn. He lunged for the snake, which curled around him and clamped down on his neck, sinking its fangs into the gnome's soft flesh.

The gnome screamed in pain but didn't give up. He raised his sword and stabbed the river snake in its belly, causing the serpent to screech in pain and unravel, withdrawing for a moment before coiling up and striking again, fast as a flash of lightning.

Seconds stretched into what felt like minutes as the light from the gnome's torch went out, allowing the shadows, within which the snake had withdrawn, to spread further down the tunnels.

Sarah didn't know what to do. She could see the gnomes at her side, trying to figure out the best course of action. If any more time was wasted thinking, they could all end up dead.

One of the gnomes went to his friend, who was clutching his neck as the blood flowed, heavy and thick.

The snake snapped out of the darkness, grabbed the wounded gnome in its jaws, and disappeared into the black.

Just like that, Sarah's team had been cut in half.

There was only one reasonable choice. The gnomes were simply too small for this fight. As far as the snake was concerned, they were prey. Sarah knew she'd have a better chance than any of them.

Firearms seemed like a bad idea. It could solve the problem easily enough, but Sarah wasn't sure if this snake was a naturally occurring problem, or if it had been released by orcs further down the tunnels. Firing a weapon would only draw more attention. But maybe attention was what Sarah needed.

Sarah aimed down the tunnel. She fired three shots, lighting the tunnel up with plasma before hitting the knob on her pistols to switch to bullets, which she preferred. Then she hit her belt, cloaking herself in an invisibility field.

The gamble paid off. The moment the tunnels had brightened slightly, the snake came slithering out of the darkness that remained.

Sarah watched the snake coming for her.

It was fast.

But it had no idea where she was. That was Sarah's favorite advantage. She ran up the side of the wall and leapt onto the snake, landing near its head and wrapping her arms around its neck.

The snake barrel-rolled, trying to crush Sarah. The force would have been enough to knock the wind out of a gnome, but Sarah was preparing for it. She held her breath as the weight of the snake pressed against her body. Then as the snake continued to roll, bringing Sarah up above the water, she released one hand, pulled out her dagger, and drove it into the snake's skin.

There was no time to waste. Before she was certain of her safety, Sarah let go of the snake, stood atop it, and ran the dagger down the length of the body, stopping right before the head, pulling her dagger out, and then shoving it into where she hoped the top of the snake's vertebrae was. She wiggled the knife, trying to force it farther in until her hand slipped into the snake's body.

That should be far enough, Sarah thought as she sheathed her dagger and drew her pistol. She slid the pistol into the hole in the snake's head and fired five shots.

The snake spasmed and fell dead in the water.

Sarah pulled her hand out and stood. Then she walked down the length of the serpent, cutting open its stomach. The two dead gnomes rolled out into the water in a pile of gore and entrails. "Take what you need to from them," Sarah said. "We don't have time for anything else."

The two remaining gnomes stared silently at Sarah for a moment before nodding and attending to their fallen comrades. They removed weapons and personal effects. Then the three continued through the tunnel.

Abby had left the arena, but before departing, she built a smaller camera with nanobots that she attached to the arena wall. She had to get to the Dark Gate as soon as possible, but that didn't mean humanity didn't need to see what was going on.

More than anything, Abby didn't want to watch Terra in a situation where she knew she couldn't help. The beating the girl had already taken was brutal. Abby had no idea how she had gotten off the ground.

Creon paced nervously as he occasionally looked up at the screen.

He had just returned to his computer when the lab door whooshed open and Anabelle walked in. "Did you fucking see that?" she asked. "Terra is a machine."

Abby's eyes glistened at the mention of Terra. She'd had an up-close look at how badly hurt Terra was. "Sounding a little excited there," she muttered.

Anabelle didn't seem to notice Abby's tone as she took a seat. "Excited? That's not the word. She's a fucking fighter. I don't think I've ever seen anyone fight like that before. She's not going down, even if we never got to her. There's too much at stake for her."

"Other than her life?"

Anabelle nodded as she watched the holo of Terra staring down the abomination in the arena. "You've never been in a situation like Terra's. It's hard to explain. There are a lot of reasons to fight. We all have our own. But it takes a special reason to get back up after your body's been pounded to shit. It takes a special reason to stand up when you know you're going to die."

"I thought you said she was going to make it!"

Anabelle's face was serious, her eyes hinting at a knowledge far beyond anything Abby knew. The crush was still there, but Abby knew why now. There was something frightening behind Anabelle's put-togetherness, something capable of understanding and causing great pain. "She's going to make it," Anabelle repeated. "I've seen what people like Terra are capable of. They don't go down."

Abby wanted to trust Anabelle. The most resilient person Abby knew was her father, but when he went down, he had stayed down. He hadn't had a fighting chance. Maybe things were different then. Maybe things changed when you had a weapon in your hand. "I have to find out where that Dark Gate is," Abby murmured as she turned back to her computer.

Looking at the computer wasn't necessary. Abby knew she could close her eyes and reconnect with the tracker by using a mixture of the bots in her blood, Martin, and a boost from one of Myrddin's many satellite signals. But it felt more normal to look away.

Abby reconnected with the tracker, which Martin had taken over the moment she disconnected. This was the second time Martin had picked up where she had left off. Abby wondered what the extent of their connection was.

The tracker had already left the arena. Apparently, Martin had remembered where the catacombs Terra had explored with the Game Master were. The tracker continued flying down the hallway, scanning each of the empty spaces carved into the wall.

Finally, Abby saw what she was looking for: the cracked-open door. She guided the tracker through the door and flashed a light. The Dark Gate was there, hooked up to a host of computers that weren't running.

Abby landed the tracker on top of the machine. She dumped the nanobots out, and they began to crawl over the Gate, each bot growing tendrils that slid into the device, accessing the software, trying to break through its firewall.

"Are we in yet?" Abby asked.

Martin popped up in the corner of her vision. "There's a snag. We're in, but the collider has a host of other problems I didn't see coming."

"What kind of problems?"

"This Dark Gate isn't like ours. We can send all sorts of shit through ours. Back and forth. Not this one. It's a one-way ride. It only goes to the orcish world. Doesn't leave. And it only works with orcs. I ran a couple of practice scenarios, and it'll turn Terra inside out if we send her through."

Abby sighed as she rested her head in her hands. "So, what are we supposed to do? Just wait until we hear back from Sarah?"

"Pretty sure that's all *you* can do at the moment. I'll keep trying to crack the firewall. See if there's something I can figure out."

Abby leaned back in her chair, trying to think of something she could do. It was the first time since she came to Middang3ard HQ that she hadn't been able to solve a problem. She felt like a failure, even if she knew this was just something out of her control.

There wasn't anything to be done. Creon was still working away, and Anabelle was watching Terra. But Abby couldn't bring herself to watch Terra. She didn't have the same optimism Anabelle had. It felt more like watching a snuff film than anything else.

Abby stood and headed toward the door. "See you in a while. Be back when my results come in."

Anabelle turned from the projector screen. "Where are you going?"

"Just to lie down for a bit. I'll come back when I can help."

Before Anabelle had a chance to answer, Abby walked out of the lab. She went to the cafeteria, and after sitting there for a few minutes, got up and went to her room, where she tossed herself on her bed. For the first time since she arrived at HQ, she pulled out her headphones and listened to music.

Abby stared up at the ceiling, still thinking about the Dark Gate. She had originally planned on trying to relax, but her mind was still running, attempting to solve the problem. But there wasn't a solution. Before she knew what was happening, she was weeping into her pillow.

Stress had never brought Abby to tears before, but she'd never been this stressed. Someone's life depended on her, and she still hadn't figured out what to do.

CHAPTER FIFTY

The crowd was electric.

They could not be contained.

Even though Terra knew she was nothing more than a sack of flesh to them, the feeling was contagious. Her bones were still buzzing from whatever Cire's gift had caused.

Abby's words were still ringing in her head. Even though she'd never actually met the kid, her voice was like that of someone Terra had known her entire life. It was the voice forged in a bond that even Terra didn't understand.

All that she knew for sure was that she wasn't done. Not with this fight. Not after the next one.

A short wheezing was coming from the multi-legged flesh pile with the sagging face. It was supporting its obscene weight on its sword, huffing loudly as if seeing Terra rise had been enough to give it an asthma attack.

And it had been a surprising rally. Even Terra was surprised she was on her feet. Her body felt like it had been pulled through a meat-grinder and then ritualistically beaten for a month. It was one of the reasons she hadn't moved in to attack yet. Standing was painful enough.

The lull wasn't going to last forever. The creature was already trying to figure out what to do. Its mouth opened slowly, hanging slack-jawed as its hands flapped open and closed like the ignorant digits of the insane. "You rise to meet me again, human?" the creature said, its voice unnaturally soft and understanding.

Terra didn't want to talk to the freakish monster, but talking was less painful than fighting. It would give her time to continue to catch her breath. "Of course I am," she said, her voice filled with fury. "You think I'm letting a dipshit like you take me down?"

"Dipshit? Hm…your language is interesting. And you are the one who is to bring my suffering to an end. Perhaps not all can be dignified in their deaths."

"Wait, what? You want me to kill you?"

The creature's ribs popped out further, and he leaned more on his sword. "This curse has gone for too long," it huffed. "My suffering for them must come to an end. You must wear the curse for me."

Terra shook her head as she waved her hands in disagreement. "Whoa, whoa, hold on there. I didn't agree to anything about taking over a curse. You're going to have to talk that over with my agent because that is outside my contract. I'm just here to wreck shit and get wrecked."

"Your naivety is beautiful, human. Live or die, you will serve the arena. The Game Master will make sure of that."

Terra was getting tired of talking. She'd had as much rest as she was going to realistically get. "Okay, okay. I got it. Everything is terrible, and I'll never escape. Let's get this over with."

Before the creature could respond, Terra sprinted toward him. She leapt into the air and slashed at his face.

The many-limbed monster raised its blade, blocking the attack. As Terra fell back to the ground, she struck again. Sparks flew between the blades of the two warriors as they slashed and sliced at each other.

When Terra hit the ground, she rolled to the side, this time intentionally getting underneath the creature's many legs. She swiped her blade at one before the creature could trample her.

A screech like that of a thousand voices tore through the creature's repulsive body as it slumped forward, a little off balance.

Terra didn't stop cutting. She hacked at anything in front of her, slicing away, hoping she was doing real damage to the creature.

A hand grabbed the back of Terra's head. The creature was up on its feet—or what remained of them. It bolted forward, bucking like a nightmarish version of a horse, before slamming Terra's face into the ground.

Terra choked on her own blood. But she didn't let the fight stop there. She reached up and prised the creature's hands off her head, swung around, and wrapped her arms around its hand. Then she pulled with all her strength, yanking its arm forward and then to the left, snapping it in half.

The creature screamed and stumbled backward as Terra boosted to her feet and rushed at it. She sliced at the monster, and it thrust its sword up to ward off Terra's blade. The pair danced around each other, blades flashing every few seconds as Terra threw herself at her opponent. She didn't let up. With each strike, her muscles screamed, but she didn't stop. The monster was on the defensive. It was backing up, only raising its sword to deflect her attacks. There was going to be a crack in its defenses. All Terra had to do was keep up the pressure.

Terra saw her chance. She had no idea how she knew it would be her chance, but somehow, deep down, she'd felt it, and her body reacted before she thought. As the creature's sword lowered, Terra leaned in, shoving her shield into its neck.

As the monster stumbled away, Terra slammed her *katar* into its throat, right where her shield had been. Then she leapt into the air, landing on its back. She grabbed the hilt of the sword, which was still jammed in the creature. Terra pulled it free and slashed at its neck.

The blade stuck, sinking into the thick flesh. Terra tugged it out, ripping away skin, and slashed again as the monster stumbled to the side, holding the wound in the front of its neck, its eyes wide and fearful and wet, somewhat bovine in its terror.

The creature crumpled to the ground, still grasping at its neck as Terra stood atop it, hacking and slashing at its head. The air filled with the stink of blood and Terra's rage-filled screams, the audience silent once more, there being nothing but the soggy sound of her sword cleaving through flesh and bone.

Then there was silence.

Terra stood over the foul creature as it shuddered, its words barely audible as it gurgled. "Ah...my suffering...I can never thank you enough."

For the first time since the fight began, Terra looked down at the creature, really looked. She could see how pathetic it looked. How its existence looked painful, the legs akimbo and arms frail and emaciated. The thing had been suffering.

"For what it's worth, I'm sorry," Terra said.

"You are forgiven, human. Salvation is only a blade away."

And with that, the creature shuddered once more, a sound like that of a horse coming from its lifeless head before its eyes closed forever.

The crowd must have been cheering. Terra didn't know. She couldn't hear them.

Or *wouldn't* hear them. She didn't wait for the guards to come and take her back. She tossed down her sword, stalked through the gate, and let herself back into her prison.

Past the tunnels, Sarah and the two remaining gnomes had come out into the last defense ring. Much like all the other rings Sarah had seen, the main center was in the middle of the complex, surrounded by an empty field.

Sarah knew the point of the field. The final defense was the ability to see everything unobscured. These were always the most difficult sections of the rings to penetrate. Either they were heavily guarded, or were turned into something like a barracks for the Dark One's soldiers.

Sarah and the gnomes stood at the outskirts of the ring, watching closely to see if their presence had been detected. Once they were satisfied that they were still hidden, Sarah led the two gnomes in a small recon of the area. They walked the circumference of the ring, staying close to the shadows and the occasional tree.

From what Sarah could see, there didn't appear to be any guards. She had never seen a final defense ring with so little security. But she'd also never seen a defense ring on a conquered planet before.

The lack of security could have been hubris. From what Sarah knew of orcish society—which was very little, mostly tales she'd gleaned from ancient elves or dwarves who had seen orcs growing in their infancy—orcs never allowed pride to get in the way of practicality. War informed every aspect of their world view. They definitely wouldn't leave their central information hub vulnerable to attack.

But orcs had changed since they'd aligned themselves with the Dark One. The orc hordes had always been happy to maintain peace. From what Sarah had learned, orcs hadn't been that much different from any of the other races. They had their own culture, their own lifestyle, and their own lives. Since the orcs had joined the Dark One, everything seemed different. Some of the ancient elves refused to even refer to the Dark One's orcs as orcs.

Sarah didn't know much about the Dark One. No one did. All that she knew was contained in briefings, and due to the nature of her job, the information she came across had more to do with logistics and practicalities.

If there was anything in the final ring that could help Sarah gain a better understanding of a way out of this mess, she wanted to find it. She'd been floating through this war long enough. It was time to put a face to the horrors.

Once Sarah had made up her mind about her course of action, she explained the mission to the two gnomes. They were to stay behind while she slipped into the main center. What they did was up to them. They could meet up with the other four parties, see if there was another point of entry in other rings they wanted to explore, or head back home.

Both gnomes disagreed vehemently. They were offended that Sarah would bring them all this way, put their lives in danger, and make the sacrifices of their comrades pointless.

Sarah instantly grew annoyed at the accusations. "I didn't drag you anywhere. This mission was happening with or without me. I'm just giving you a chance to get out of this alive. I have no clue what the hell is in this ring. All I know is that it is most likely going to try and kill me, and I don't think the two of you should throw your lives away. But it's your fucking choice."

One of the gnomes agreed with Sarah. He spent nearly an hour getting in contact with the other four groups, all of which were raiding other parts of the defense ring. While the gnomes organized their meetup, Sarah continued to survey the final ring.

During the hour, not a single orc came outside. Not a single guard could be seen. Whatever was in that final ring between her and the command center was going to be deadly. Much deadlier than an orc.

The other gnome refused to leave Sarah. He'd decided that he was getting into that defense ring with her no matter what. Sarah didn't bother trying to dissuade him. She knew how stubborn gnomes could be.

The gnomes said their goodbyes, and the one who was leaving thanked Sarah for giving him a chance to get out before anything terrible happened. Then Sarah and the remaining gnome returned their attention to the final ring.

Sarah outlined the plan. They were going to work their way along the outside of the ring, sticking close to the sparse foliage for camouflage. There would be a few instances when they had absolutely no cover, but those moments would have to be spent sprinting.

The gnome agreed, and they began to make their way through the ring, working slowly as they moved horizontally, crawling at times to keep out of the potential line of sight from anyone watching from the center's windows.

The going was slow, but it was happening. At this rate, Sarah thought they'd be in the center of the defense ring within the hour.

CHAPTER FIFTY-ONE

S neaking into the control center was easier than Sarah had expected. Once Sarah and the gnome had penetrated the last defense ring, they snuck through one of the open windows they found, the gnome strapped to Sarah's chest like a newborn child.

Once within the building, they found a broom closet to hide in while they figured out their next step. They hadn't been able to get any intel on the layout of the building. There was no way to find out where the information about the Dark Gate was being held. And it was a big building.

Normally, Sarah would have just deployed her stealth cloak and taken her time getting the lay of the building. That was one of the reasons she had tried so hard to convince both of the gnomes to head back home. But this gnome, whose name she hadn't even bothered to learn, had refused to go. Now his presence was complicating the entire mission.

It would have simplified everything if Sarah was alone. But this wasn't only her fight. This was the gnome's homeworld. It made sense that he would want to be part of the battle to reclaim his home. Sarah just wished that he had chosen his battles better.

Sarah whispered to the gnome, "We're going to have to figure out a way to move around in here."

He said nothing, though he did point at the air ducts above them. It was an old-school way to gain access. Sarah hadn't had to make her way through an air duct in years. *Why the hell not?* she thought. *He's small enough. It won't be a problem for him.*

Sarah prised the metal grating off the air duct. Then she climbed into it, situated herself, and tossed a rope down to the gnome, who pulled himself up effortlessly.

The unlikely pair made their way through the duct, occasionally stopping to listen to the conversations happening beneath them, trying to make sense of where they should be going. The building was larger than Sarah had expected. Usually, defense rings had smaller main buildings. The only large-scale center Sarah had heard about was one that a group called the Mundanes had happened across. Still, Sarah hadn't been able to verify it for herself.

From various conversations, Sarah was able to glean that there were different wings to the building. What she was looking for was most likely in the development wing. It blew her mind that there were orcs who were working in science. Sarah felt she had a good grip on the racial politics of the nine realms, but even *she* couldn't imagine orcish scientists.

Either way, that was where they were heading. It wouldn't be too hard to find, just take time, of which there was none to waste. The two unlikely companions continued their search.

Abby had finally forced herself to get out of bed. She knew she wasn't tired. There wasn't any point in lying around. No ideas had come to her. She was still just floundering, wishing she could help someone, but only feeling useless.

A slight headache was gnawing at the back of her head. They had become a regular occurrence since she had taken the nanobots into her body. The two were obviously linked, but Abby hadn't had time to investigate how. She showered quickly, then stared at her reflection in the mirror.

As the fog from the hot shower evaporated from the mirror, she looked closely at her eyes. They were so different with odd, halo-like rings of green and blue along the edges. The skin around her eyes had a metallic hue.

Abby dressed and returned to her desk, her mind full of different thoughts. Nothing was certain. When she had first come to Middang-g3ard HQ, everything had been relatively straightforward—do what she could to destroy the Dark One and avenge her father. Nothing had changed, but it felt like everything had.

Destroying the Dark One was also tied to saving someone's life. And possibly endangering her own.

Abby did the only thing she could think of— she called her mother.

The phone didn't ring long before Ma picked up. "Abby, is that you? Oh, my God, how are you doing? I haven't heard from you in—"

She was cut off by Abby bursting into tears. It was a terrible sound, worse than any of the other times the girl had cried. She hated the sound. It made her feel weak, which was one of the reasons she tried to keep her tears to herself. People didn't need to see this side of her. But her mother already did. She'd seen Abby through the worst of it.

When Abby stopped crying, they were able to talk. She let it all out —everything she'd been worried about, all of the pressure she felt from working with so many smart, capable people. She dumped the contents of her soul out for her mother in the way that only children can.

After she was finished speaking, her mother was silent for a few moments. Then she said, "You're trying as hard as you can. That's all that anyone can ask of you."

That wasn't enough. Abby needed something else, something more from her mother. She needed the platitudes her father had given her, the wise sayings that seemed to come out of nowhere but which perfectly explained everything away. And that knowledge of her need lit up in a flame of anger. But she kept it to herself. She knew she wasn't angry at her mom. The anger was deeper than that.

Ma could never be Pa. She knew that. She'd gotten other things from her relationship with her mother. Encouragement. Love. Understanding. It was unfair of her to expect her mother to fill the void her father's death had created. Yet she couldn't keep herself from wanting just that at this moment. "You think about him much?"

"Every day. So much it hurts."

"Ma...I don't know if I can help these people. Someone...their life depends on me...and I don't know what I'm going to do. Don't know if I can help them. And if they die, it'll be just like—"

"Abby, you saved your entire family. Your father would be proud of you. We all are."

The two were silent for a bit as she considered her mother's words. They hadn't been groundbreaking, yet even in their straightforward statement of the truth, they were profound beyond their instance. "Abby," her mother said, "you can do this. And you know it. Just because it's hard, it doesn't mean you can't. Just means it's going to be hard. And we didn't raise no quitter."

Abby looked at her hand as the nanobots came out of her pores and covered her skin. "You're right. I'll figure it out. I love you. I have to go."

"I love you too, sweetie. Call again soon."

Abby hung up the phone, stood, and went to the mirror. "Martin, how integrated with me are you?" she asked.

It took a little bit of time for Martin to answer. "At the moment, maybe six percent," he answered. "I've been trying to keep myself separate, but the nanobots are connected to my mainframe, so there's an overlay. I didn't want to worry you about it since I've been keeping it steady at six."

"What would happen if we bumped it up to fifty percent?"

"An increase in your processing ability. But...not sure about what else would happen. Integrating AI and organic is new territory. I know it wouldn't kill you, but that's about it."

Abby stared at her reflection. Her eyes were her eyes, her skin her skin. Her mind was her mind. "Do it," she whispered.

Martin hesitated before answering. "Are you sure? There's no—"

"Do it."

Abby felt a tinkling in the back of her head, down in her brainstem. Then there was nothing but pain as her body seized up, every nerve on fire, her muscles twitching as her teeth clenched, her eyes wide as if she were in the grip of a vision. She fell to the ground, foaming from the mouth, her fingers twitching as her consciousness became something entirely new.

Sarah and the gnome were making their way toward what they thought would be the science department. They needed to get to the functioning Gate. Something the resistance didn't have the resources for. They had overheard multiple conversations between the orcs and had pieced together the layout of the center.

There had never been a mission with so little resistance in all of Sarah's career. Outside of the lost gnomes in the tunnel, there had hardly been any casualties. That included Sarah's kill count. She hoped things would continue in this way.

They continued through the air ducts until Sarah raised her hand. The room ahead was supposed to be the science department. When Sarah looked through the air ducts, she saw three orcs sitting around a coffee table, talking as they sipped their drinks. Sarah figured she must have gotten turned around. But this was as good a chance as any to figure out where they were.

Sarah turned to the gnome and pressed a finger to her lips, gesturing for his silence. She felt kind of silly, making a point to remind him to be silent since he'd not made a sound since they entered the last defense ring. Then Sarah removed the air duct's grating and planned her attack.

None of the three orcs had noticed the faint noise of the grate moving.

Sarah dropped from the air duct a few feet from the trio of orcs, her daggers in hand. She threw blades into two of the orc's throats. Before the last orc could react, Sarah grabbed him by the throat, pulled him to the ground, and choked him out. Sarah waited for a moment to make sure no one walked by.

A supply closet led off the right corner of the room. Sarah dragged the two corpses over to the closet and stuffed them inside. Then she wrapped a thin wire around the waist of the orc she had knocked out, leapt back into the air duct, attached the wire to a mechanical pully, and pulled the orc up into the duct.

Once the orc was in the air duct, Sarah raised some smelling salts to his nose, and he snapped awake. She held her hand over his mouth and pressed a dagger to his throat. "You're going to take us to the Dark Gate research facility," Sarah growled. "You understand?"

The orc nodded vehemently.

"Good. Now get going. If I hear a sound out of you, I'm going to carve out your asshole before I slit your throat. Got it?"

The orc didn't need to respond. He oriented himself before leading the way. It didn't take too long. The directions Sarah had figured out hadn't been that far off. Once the orc moved out of the way, Sarah could see the Dark Gate.

"Perfect," she murmured.

The orc whispered, his voice trembling, "Can I go now?"

Sarah nodded as she drew her pistol. She pressed the orc's head against the side of the duct and fired, the sound of her pistol dampened by the attached silencer. "Come on, let's go," she said to the gnome, who climbed gingerly over the orc's corpse.

The pair dropped into the room as silently as shadows. The orc had led them to the right spot. Ten Dark Gates were scattered around the room, all hooked up to one main, large Gate. "Looks like we found the motherload," Sarah said. "Okay, let's get to work. Download anything you can get your hands on."

The gnome got started at one computer as Sarah went to another terminal and did the same. She was looking for one specific piece. Or at least information *about* the piece. Whatever was allowing the orcs to use the Dark Gates as a two-way street.

Luckily, Sarah had enough experience with Dark Gate schematics to avoid shooting in the dark. She scanned through schematic after schematic on the computers before she became frustrated by the lack of results. So she studied the actual Dark Gate instead.

These Dark Gates were different from models she'd seen before. Even newer than the models she'd seen with Kravis a few weeks ago. The Dark One was obviously still trying to improve the system, and he had the resources to do that as well. That was the most troubling part.

The ability to move back and forth through the Dark Gates wouldn't have been so frightening if the vast expense of creating Dark Gates were a problem. But it wasn't. They were most likely being churned out without the slightest worry concerning the cost of resources.

As Sarah looked over the backside of one of the Dark Gate, she focused on a part she'd never seen before. It was next to the module responsible for syncing and matching the hadron collider's frequency. Sarah recorded the location of the part, then returned to the computer, and identified its purpose.

A schematic had the piece labeled as a redundant frequency generator. Sarah hoped she was right as she turned to one of the Dark Gates and pulled the generator off. Then she began to download as much information off the computer as possible onto a flash drive.

After a couple of tense minutes, the gnome came over to Sarah. "There are orcs on their way."

"How do you know?"

"There's a map on my computer. It shows a group is on their way, a large one."

Sarah nodded, disconnected from the computer, pocketed her flash drive and the generator, and then helped the gnome up into the air duct. They both watched as, after a couple of minutes, orcs poured into the room.

What looked like a chieftain went to the computer Sarah had

been working at. He looked over something, grunting softly to himself. Then he turned to the orcs in the room. "Brothers and sisters, fellow servants of our glorious Dark Lord," he said. "Today will be another of our victories. We go to Earth. Our victory will not be rushed, though. We will take our time and listen to the patient wisdom of our Dark Lord. Soon the humans will understand what we offer them. They will rush to be embraced into the fold of our Dark Lord."

Sarah leaned in to get a better look at the computer screen behind the chieftain. All but one of the Dark Gates were operational. She could barely make out the coordinates. Instead of straining her eyes any longer, she pulled out a small camera, zoomed in, and snapped a couple of pictures. Then she nudged the gnome to get moving.

The orcs were about to launch a raid. Sarah didn't need to stay to see that. She had to get as far away as possible and warn someone who could help.

It took Sarah and the gnome nearly six hours to get back to their camp. They debriefed with the other four groups. There had hardly been any casualties, and both of the other groups had been able to siphon off a good deal of intel.

The combination of all five groups' intel allowed Sarah to piece together the Dark One's plan of attack.

There were over twenty Dark Gates in the center. Nine were being used for an invasion on the human homeworld, but the invasion was broken into nine different spots, each Gate leading to a separate destination. The Dark One was attempting to overwhelm humanity with confusion, rather than try to take over one central position.

This was more subtle than anything Sarah had seen the Dark One try before. Small skirmishes that resulted in human death would generate fear. And fear toppled empires.

Sarah sent a debriefing file to Myrddin and hoped he would know what to do with it. She included everything she found, deciding that it was better to not keep anything for herself. She was tired of squir-reling away bargaining tools in case something didn't go her way.

After the gnomes cleared out, one stayed. It was the gnome who had been at Sarah's side the whole mission. Sarah still didn't know his name, and she felt slightly embarrassed by her rudeness. "What are you still doing here?" she asked.

The gnome extended his hand. "Name's Bim-bop. We never formally introduced ourselves."

"Sorry, I'm not used to working in teams, let alone leading my own. Doing introductions seemed to be a waste of time. But you did good. Really kept up. Don't think I've seen a gnome be so sneaky before."

"Thank you. I just wanted to thank you for a chance to work alongside you. It meant a lot to me. Watching other people save my world doesn't sit right. And I'm not a warrior. Not really a fighter like some of the others. But this...I think I can do this. It was great to be able to watch you work."

Bim-bop bowed slightly and turned to leave.

Sarah didn't know why, but she waved at the gnome and said, "You got potential. A lot of it. I was moving full force by the end and you... What I mean to say is, I know some people who could train you. Hell, if we live long enough, Kravis and I could train you."

Bim-bop turned to meet Sarah's eyes. How had she not seen how young the gnome was? He couldn't have been any older than a teenager. "Thanks," he said. "I would really appreciate that." With those words, he disappeared into the night, leaving Sarah alone with her thoughts.

Sarah returned to her tent. Kravis was already sleeping, snoring loudly. He'd left a plate of food out for her. Sarah sat and ate, poring over the information she'd sent Myrddin. She hoped he would make sense of it in time. Coming up with plans wasn't Sarah's job. Making sure people had the information to plan with was.

Kravis stirred quietly in his sleep, and Sarah looked away from her notes. Sarah loved how peaceful Kravis looked when he was sleeping. Like nothing could hurt him.

Sarah put her notes away and finished up the small glass of wine on the table. Then she undressed and crawled into bed with Kravis. The gnome's eyes opened a fraction, and he stared dreamily at Sarah. "You're back," he whispered.

Sarah kissed him softly. "Shush, go back to sleep, we can talk in the morning."

Kravis murmured something unintelligible and was snoring within a few minutes. It wasn't long before Sarah was dreaming alongside him.

CHAPTER FIFTY-TWO

HQ was buzzing. Once Myrddin received Sarah's briefing, he'd put everyone on high alert. Sarah's message might not have had the urgency that another human would have brought to the impending attack, but Myrddin could read between the lines. Sarah had been out in the field for years. Her understanding of imminent danger was a little skewed.

Anabelle was rushing around, trying to take care of as much as she could before the main briefing. Myrddin had loaded her up with different responsibilities. Part of her regretted wanting to be more involved with the war efforts. It nearly tripled her paperwork, and there was always someone she had to talk to about something.

If only everything was as glamorous as she hoped.

At the same time, Anabelle couldn't have been happier that, when the alarm went off around HQ, she was being directed toward combat instead of some stuffy senator's dinner party. And it was nice that she only had to answer to Myrddin. There were a lot of things Anabelle liked, and being in charge was one of them.

First things first, she had to get her small team together. Abby, Roy, and maybe Creon. The little goblin was smart as hell, and another brain couldn't be a bad thing. She wanted everyone to be up to date with what was going on. No one needed secondhand information.

Anabelle knocked on Abby's door. When she received no answer, she knocked again, shouting Abby's name. "You better not be napping in there!" she yelled. "Can't you hear the alarm? We got a big problem going on right now."

There was still no answer. Anabelle checked around the corner to see if anyone was coming. For some reason, she felt very embarrassed about going into Abby's room. It reminded her of any time one of her teachers had forced their way into her room. The only reason Anabelle went along to check was that her teachers had always had good reason to be suspicious.

The lights in the room were off. Anabelle fumbled around, looking for the light switch, and then clicked it on.

Abby was lying on the floor, part of her body transformed into the sleek obsidian metal Anabelle had seen before. The rest was frail and human. Her nose was bleeding, and she didn't move when Anabelle called her name.

The elf rushed over to her and propped her up. "Abby, speak to me! Abby!"

Suddenly the girl's body went rigid, as though an electrical pulse had just run through it. Then she relaxed, her eyes opening slowly, the obsidian metal draining away so that she looked like a regular human girl. She stared up at Anabelle. "What are you doing here?" she asked, sounding half asleep.

"You were passed out on the floor. What the hell happened? Are you okay?"

Abby looked around the room as she tried to wake herself up. "I'm not sure yet," Abby admitted. "Can you take me to the med lab?"

"Are you sick?"

"No, just want to... You know, I'll explain it all later. Need to check something quick. Please?"

Anabelle couldn't say no to Abby. She was worried about the girl. Abby kept putting herself under more and more stress. She didn't understand that sometimes you failed. And Abby was taking it hard that they'd not been able to get Terra back home. It was a lot to expect of a teenager. Maybe too much.

Anabelle helped Abby to her feet and then scooped the girl up into her arms. As she carried her to the medbay, Abby drifted in and out of sleep, sometimes speaking a little, often in a few languages Anabelle hadn't known Abby spoke. When they arrived at the medbay, Anabelle lay the girl on one of the beds and stepped away as Abby's eyes snapped open.

"Anyone in here?" Abby called.

The medbay was empty besides Abby and Anabelle. "Good," she said as she leaned over to the computer beside her bed. The ends of her fingertips turned black with the nanobots and snaked out like tendrils, burrowing into the computer.

The ceiling above the bed opened, and a cat-scanner descended upon Abby, wrapping itself around the bed and her head. Before Anabelle could say anything, the room was filled with the loud humming of the scanner working. When the hum died, the scanner unwrapped itself and withdrew into the ceiling.

Abby sat up and pulled the computer over to her, reading the results.

Anabelle sat on the bed next to her. "Okay, first off, I know you don't have clearance to do that. Secondly, when the hell did you get a degree in neuroscience? That shouldn't make any more sense to you than me."

Abby looked at Anabelle, smiling sweetly, her eyes looking different than Anabelle had ever seen. There seemed to be more color and something else behind her eyes. "I integrated Martin into my brain," she said softly. "Just wanted to make sure I didn't have a stroke or something when I passed out."

Anabelle wasn't certain she understood what Abby had said, but she thought she got the gist: she had done something reckless and possibly stupid. "Why'd you do that?" the elf asked. "Doesn't sound like... Actually, I have no idea what the hell it sounds like."

"It was the next step. Nanobots for my body. Martin was already partially there. Now there's more of him in my head. I can think faster. I can know more. I'll be able to help better."

Anabelle slipped her arm around the girl's shoulder. "Abby, you're doing great. You don't have to do any better."

Abby shook her head. "No, that's not true. Terra is still not back on Earth. I need to do better."

There were a lot of things Anabelle wanted to say to Abby, but she couldn't settle on which one. She went with the one that she felt the most. "I'm proud of you."

"Really? You aren't mad or anything?"

"This is war. We need to take risks. All of us. Everyone makes sacrifices. I'm proud that you're the kind of person who doesn't need to be pushed into it. Now, if your brain isn't going to start hemorrhaging, we need to find Roy and Creon and get to the briefing."

Abby stood, still a little wobbly. "Briefing for what?"

"Dark Gates are opening up on Earth. We need to close them."

Creon, Abby, Anabelle, and Roy met Myrddin in his study. As usual, the room was different from the last time they had seen it. The long dining room table was gone, as were the comfortable tweed chairs. Instead, there was only a large holoprojector similar to the ones in the R&D labs.

Once everyone arrived, Myrddin waved his hands casually, conjuring a host of seats that surrounded the holoprojector.

Abby felt like Myrddin got rid of his furniture on a regular basis just to have an excuse to use magic. Then she wondered why such a powerful wizard spent all of his time working behind the scenes instead of being out there fighting.

As though Myrddin could read Abby's mind, he looked right at her and asked, "Will you be staying behind on this mission or going out into the field?"

She was caught off-guard at being addressed directly and cleared her throat as she thought. It would probably be safer for her to stay at the base. There was still no telling what had happened to her body since Martin had been integrated. It was already odd enough that Martin hadn't reached out to her at all. She had expected a lot more chatter from him.

Myrddin was still waiting for an answer. Abby looked at Anabelle, who was noncommittal. "Guess I'll be going with y'all," she answered. "Seems like this one is kinda a big deal."

Myrddin nodded as he waved his hand, turning on the holoprojector. "A few hours ago, I received information from Sarah. She informed me that three locations with three Dark Gates at each will be opening in different areas in the United States. Each Gate is extremely far from the other. Obviously, they've realized that our aim is closing any that opens, so they've placed the gates as far away from each other as possible in an attempt to keep us from working together."

A map of the United States opened. There were three blinking lights. One in New York, another in Washington DC, and one in what looked like Death Valley. "As you can see, it would be impossible for any of you to aid the other. Each of you will command a squad and ... "

Abby interrupted Myrddin, her head swimming from his last sentence. "Wait, what do you mean, 'command a squad?'"

Myrddin calmly turned to the girl. "I mean that you will have soldiers under your command and will be responsible for giving orders and closing the Gate. I know you do not have any experience leading a squad or a team. Trust me. But right now is not the time for us all to voice our insecurities. Either you are going to lead a squad, or you will remain behind and see how else you can help."

Abby nodded, humiliated by having spoken up so quickly. She was just about to start beating herself up when Anabelle grabbed her hand, squeezing it tightly as she smiled at Abby. "Don't worry about it," she said. "We all gotta start somewhere."

Myrddin continued explaining the plan. It was simple enough. There hadn't been adequate time to begin working on the rest of the information Sarah had sent over, but Myrddin detailed it for the team regardless.

The part that differentiated the Dark Gate on the gnomish planet had been found. Sarah was transporting it back to HQ the next day, but she had already sent over the schematics for R&D to work with. Creon sat in on the briefing, and since he was HQ support, he assured Myrddin that he would begin building his own version of the piece. From there, he could reverse-engineer a Gate similar to the Dark Gate the orcs had engineered from the human hadron collider.

When Myrddin finished speaking, silence hung over the meeting. It felt like something more needed to be said. Or perhaps something was being hidden. "Is that all?" Abby asked.

Myrddin shook his head. "All that I know for sure, but I have theories. Each attack from a Dark Gate has gotten larger and larger. At first, they seemed like recon excursions, things of that sort, but the last one at the amusement park? Bringing a wyrm to Earth. I fear these gates may have just as much of a force behind them, but I cannot be certain. That is why I am worried."

Roy and Anabelle scoffed. Roy scratched his stubble and said, "You? Worried? I don't think I've ever seen you worried before."

"Because I am very rarely worried. But this? It's a decent strategy from an enemy who only grows more and more strategic. If you three were able to stay together, I wouldn't be worried. But this…this unsettles me."

For the first time since arriving at HQ, Abby thought Myrddin seemed human. The stress he was experiencing brought him down to her level. He wasn't some all-knowing god. He was flesh and blood, just like Abby. Or at least like she used to be.

Anabelle spoke up. "So, we have no idea how large the invasion party is going to be, and we hardly have any troops. I mean, Blackwell and his team are always ready to go, and Naota's pretty much finished his training. If you add the defense team here at HQ, that might put us at one hundred bodies. Can you pull any from Middang3ard?"

"In theory. But there would be no time. But you don't need to worry about soldiers. Due to your aggressive campaign to show humans all of Terra's struggles, we've had a surge in volunteers. More than three hundred soldiers have been transferred from the French,

Nigerian, and United States military branches. Most of them have already finished our initial training. Each of you will have a squad composed of a mixture of HQ soldiers and those who have recently transferred. All are combat-ready, will not be relying on our exosuits, other than our soldiers, and will be armed with our latest weapons and defensive capabilities."

Anabelle laughed sarcastically. "What are you so worried about then? This is a better setup than we've had going into any of these missions before."

Myrddin's brow darkened as he turned to face the crew. "I do not like the unknown," he said softly.

CHAPTER FIFTY-THREE

HQ's hangars were busy. It seemed like everyone was pouring in and out, trying to find out where they were needed. Scientists rushed about under the supervision of Creon, calibrating the hadron collider. This was the largest teleportation HQ had ever attempted, and the fact that the coordinates weren't remotely close to each other wasn't making it any easier.

Creon looked stressed but energized. Abby watched him from afar. She was up in the rafters, watching the rest of HQ work. If Creon needed her, he would comm. She wasn't worried about Creon, though. He knew his shit. She was worried about the squad she was supposed to meet with in a little bit. They had already been briefed, and Blackwell was going to be traveling with her. All in all, it wasn't the worst introduction to leadership. That said, it still didn't feel right.

Abby hung out in the rafters, looking for Roy. Her eyes hyper-focused, and she realized she was capable of seeing details most humans couldn't. Before the nanobots, she wouldn't have been able to see Roy from her current distance. Now, she could practically count the hairs on his chin.

Roy was putting the final touches on his mech. The rest of his squad stood around watching him work. They were obviously starstruck. Most of the squad, if not all of them, were composed of the few soldiers trained to use the exosuits Abby had upgraded. It only made sense they would be excited to serve alongside Roy. He was something of a legend as far as mech riders went. Roy epitomized what Middang3ard HQ was all about. She could see why Anabelle was so attracted to him.

There was still a slight sting to admitting that, but Abby knew better than to hold onto stupid or childish things. Anabelle was a couple hundred years old, and more like her teacher. There wasn't the slightest possibility there. Besides, she was just happy to have someone like the elf so close to her. Crushes eventually died, especially once you stopped paying hourly attention to them.

Speaking of Anabelle, she wondered what the elf was up to right now. Abby assumed she would have hidden after briefing her squad. She didn't seem like the kind of person to join in on the military pomp that Roy was obviously reveling in.

Abby was surprised to see her sitting down with her squad, going over the mission. The elf's face was energetic, animated. She looked like she was in her element. If there was anyone Abby wanted to be like, it was Anabelle.

"How long are you planning on staying up here?" a voice asked from the shadows.

Abby whirled, her hand covering with nanobots, her palm forming into a plasma cannon. Every movement happened instinctively.

Myrddin emerged from the shadows, balancing easily on the girder separating him from Abby. "You don't have to shoot me if you don't want to talk." He came to her side. "I just thought you might want some company."

Abby gave Myrddin the side-eye, then relaxed and sat beside him. "Really? Doesn't seem like your thing."

"I must keep up appearances. Running something like HQ isn't easy, and that's not even thinking about the war effort. All of the meetings, convincing people, arguing, fighting...you quickly learn to appreciate moments when you can speak with someone candidly."

"Is that what we're doing right now?"

"Unless you prefer for me to be more businesslike."

Abby shook her head as she watched the soldiers preparing beneath her. "No, no. This is fine. How come you're up here?"

Myrddin conjured a bag of beef jerky into his hands. He took out a few pieces and handed the bag to Abby. "Thought you might want the company. And I've been a little bit worried about you, to be honest."

Abby took a piece of jerky. It was rough and salty. Reminded her of home. "Why worried?"

"I may not call a lot of attention to things, but I am very aware of your experiments. Martin disappeared for some time yesterday. It was as if he had died and vanished. I was worried that your integration of him into your own mind didn't go as you both had planned."

Abby felt her body go cold all over. Even though Myrddin didn't sound upset, she was mortified that he had known what she had been doing all along. She didn't even think about how he knew. Something about being found out made her feel childish.

"My mind is very receptive," Myrddin said, answering Abby's question. "I know nearly everything that goes on in HQ. Granted, I try to give people their privacy. Also, it helps when having conversations. But your plans were too interesting to ignore."

"You aren't pissed off?"

Myrddin shook his head as he took the bag of jerky from Abby and grabbed a few more pieces. "I had a fairly good grasp of the kind of person you might turn out to be. The job wasn't offered lightly. You seemed fiercely independent. Extremely secretive, and in need of a purpose. I don't intend to curb any of those attributes. Unless something threatens the safety of this facility, you have as much freedom as anyone else. And trust me, you won't be in trouble the first time you unwittingly put this place in danger. You should ask Creon about the battle bots he once tried to build."

Abby had heard Creon referencing those bots earlier in the week. A couple of the other scientists still teased him about whatever happened. "You ever lead missions?" Abby asked.

Myrddin nodded as he passed the bag back to Abby. "A very long time ago," he answered. "I found my talents lay more in organization.

351

Planning. I simply don't have the mind for that kind of leadership. You might find it hard to believe, but I crack under too much pressure. Administration? That's a pressure I can deal with."

"What was too much to deal with?"

"Caring. Caring too much about the people who are under my command. It causes you to make stupid decisions. The simple fact of the matter is that not everyone lives, and we have to all accept that."

"You don't feel like it's your fault?"

Myrddin smiled sadly. "No, I don't. I know it is. No one could convince me otherwise. And I do not doubt that you will feel the same way. Nothing will change that."

Abby chuckled as she watched the soldiers working below. "You know, you're pretty shitty at pep talks."

"Who said this was a pep talk? We're just talking. Equal to equal. Now you better get down there. Your squad is waiting for you. Also, tell Martin he can stop hiding. I already know what's going on."

Abby did a double-take as she watched Myrddin rise and hop over to another girder. "Wait, you can read his mind too? He's not even organic."

Myrddin smiled and said, "Wizards work in mysterious ways," before vanishing into thin air.

Abby chuckled as she tried to find her squad. "You hear that, Martin?"

It took barely any time for him to answer. "I thought the old man was going to have me wiped clean or something. So, we're in the clear, I guess."

"Sounds like it."

"Perfect. Because we are going to have some fun, kid. I mean, real fun. Free rein to do whatever we want as long as it isn't going to kill anyone? That's like…millions of things I can think of."

Abby had walked across the girder toward where her squad had gathered. She recognized Blackwell, who was speaking to a group of exosuited soldiers standing around him. "Oh, yeah," she mused. "We gotta make sure we get out of this alive first."

Martin scoffed loudly. "Oh, this? This is going to be nothing. You go hit 'em with the 'ol razzle-dazzle, and we'll be back in the lab in no time."

Abby was glad to hear from Martin. She had been worried about him, but now there was only one thing she should be focusing on. The mission at hand. That and making sure her squad knew she cared about their lives. That she understood her responsibility.

Abby leapt from the girder, landing right behind Blackwell. The squad, along with Blackwell, jumped in surprise. He turned to face her.

"Assuming y'all been updated on the mission?" she asked.

"Aye!" the soldiers shouted.

"Good. Don't look like we're gonna have the option of too much of a plan. Going in blind and all. So, I want you to talk to me. Let me know what you're thinking. That way, we get through this together. It's gonna take each and every one of us. But I ain't going down without a fight. Hope y'all feel the same."

The soldiers all nodded. "All right," Abby said, "Now, line up so I can go over your rigs. Ain't no one's tech crapping out on me today."

The soldiers lined up, Blackwell watching Abby work as she talked to each soldier while going over their equipment, spending time to glean a little bit of information from each of them to set their nerves at ease, letting them know she was capable. It wasn't often Blackwell got to see a natural leader at work.

It was almost time for the troops to head out. The hadron collider had been prepped, and the different squads were lined up behind their leaders.

Anabelle, Abby, and Roy stood at the front of the crowd of soldiers. The elf was the definition of military professionalism, her posture rigid and uniform, matching her immaculate suit.

Abby, on the other hand, didn't seem capable of shaking her childish insecurity. But she was up with the other squad leaders, and that was what mattered.

Roy continued to look disheveled and in need of a shave and a good night's rest.

Myrddin floated above the hadron collider as the scientists worked together to get over any last-minute hiccups. He cleared his throat. "This is not our last battle, nor is it anywhere close. The Dark One's war has and will continue to stretch us to our limits, but we will not be broken. No matter how often he comes against the ones we love, against our planets, against our very freedom, no matter, we will rise to the challenge. We will continue to pit our strength against his, and one day there will be a final battle. One day, we will stand atop his corpse. One day, we will all know peace again."

The soldiers cheered at Myrddin's words. They were all itching for a fight. Not just any fight. This one. Many of the soldiers had come from the armies of various Earth countries. They'd seen Terra fighting for her life. They'd followed the stories from Myrddin. Earth was at risk. And they were going to be on the front lines to defend it.

Abby had never been one for the military. All that she'd ever learned from her parents was that war was brought about by the self-ish, people who didn't care for the lives of others, by people who thought the most important thing in the world was their perspective on reality.

There were rarely wars that were fought for true morality. But this…Abby knew this was one of those wars. The Dark One represented everything wrong with what folk could do to each other. He was an enslaver of people. If there was one thing Abby understood more than anything else, it was that everyone had a right to freedom. Trying to find out what freedom was could be difficult. But she knew it wasn't serving under the Dark One.

Abby hoped her father would be proud. As did many of the other soldiers, each wishing in their hearts that those they cared for would be proud of them. Today, they risked their lives for something bigger than they ever thought they would.

Myrddin's voice broke through everyone's thoughts. "The Dark One wants to enslave humanity!" he shouted. "He wants to enslave all of the nine realms. Today we remind him that the realms will not go quietly. We will not slink away as cowards into the night. We will meet him on the field of battle and will remind him of the violence of freedom."

The soldiers erupted into cheers as the hadron collider opened, flashing electricity across the hangar, the air hot with anticipation and energy, from both soldiers and the Gate.

Roy gestured for his troops to follow him as he climbed into his mech and shut the cockpit. The mech roared to life, its gears whirring as it lurched to its feet and plodded forward, followed by the squad of Marines.

Each of them passed through the collider, their atoms ripped apart and instantly transported to where the Dark Gate was supposed to open.

Once the first squads had been transported, Anabelle led her squad to the collider. Naota stood at her side as if he were second in command. The human wore sunglasses and a smaller version of the exosuits that Abby's squad had been fitted with. He tipped his sunglasses at Abby as he walked past her. *I hope he doesn't get himself killed,* she thought.

Anabelle's squad passed through the collider. All that was left was Abby's team. She drew in a steadying breath and approached the collider, Blackwell and the squad at her back.

Myrddin had landed near the teleportation pad. When Abby walked past him, he smiled and nodded. This was it.

Abby felt her cells tearing away from each other. It wasn't a painful experience, but it wasn't enjoyable. She felt herself tumbling, flowing through time and space until finally, she was standing in the middle of a city block she'd never seen before. And there was screaming. All she could hear was screaming.

Terra sat alone in her cell. The rest of the fighters were gathered in the main dining hall as usual. She didn't want to be with them. Nib-nib had already tended to her wounds.

It sounded as if the other fighters were celebrating. Paying tribute to her, no doubt. Tonight didn't feel like a night for celebrations, though. If anything, she felt as though she'd failed. She didn't know why, or what she had failed at, but she knew it deep down.

There was no winning in the arena. She'd deluded herself into thinking it was a possibility, much like she had deluded herself in nearly every other aspect of her life. When people treat you like shit, it isn't because they want you to try harder, it isn't because they love you in a way you don't understand. It's because they're a shitty person. No different than the arena.

The shouting of the crowd didn't mean anything. They only wanted to see her dead. Terra wasn't proving anything to anyone other than herself. And she felt stupid as hell for needing to be in a life or death situation to understand that.

Someone knocked on Terra's door. "Go away," she shouted.

"I brought you some food," said a familiar voice.

Terra got up and opened her cell door. Cire was holding a plate. He handed it to Terra and lingered on the threshold. "We're all glad you made it out alive," he said after a few moments.

Terra took a bit of the raw meat on the plate and then grabbed what she hoped was fruit. "Oh, yeah? I couldn't tell from all of your shouting."

"I know you want to be alone right now. Just wanted to make sure you got something to eat. Good night."

Cire turned to leave, but Terra grabbed him by his shoulder. "Wait, I... Thanks for earlier. Whatever gift you gave me really helped."

"I am glad," he replied.

"So, how long do these arena things usually go on for?"

Cire shrugged, hanging his head slightly. "In the old days, four rounds. If you survived the fourth, you were a champion, able to request anything you wanted from a chieftain. But I don't know about *these* games. Whatever that creature was that you fought today, it looked to have been here for a long time."

Terra nodded as she walked back to her bed. She sat and looked out the window. "Thanks for the food."

Cire bowed once more and said, "If there's anything you need, please let me know," before closing the door quietly.

Terra stared out her window at the sliver of a moon floating above the wisps of clouds. *Yeah, you and me both,* she thought before lying down and pulling her covers up to her neck. She closed her eyes and waited for sleep to come for her. Tomorrow was going to arrive too soon.

CHAPTER FIFTY-FOUR

Anabelle stepped out of the portal, Naota trailing behind her. She scanned the surroundings, trying to gain her footing. Traveling through hadron colliders wasn't as vomit-inducing as they used to be, but it still wasn't an enjoyable experience.

The portal had dumped them out in Washington, DC. It felt like years since the last time Anabelle had been in the city. She had a lot of memories of this city. None of them particularly pleasant. She thought it was only fitting that her first real mission would take place where she had cut her teeth for Myrddin by manipulating politicians in order to steal their secrets.

Capitol Hill wasn't too far from where the collider portal had dropped her and her squad. If Anabelle were going to plan an attack, that would have been where she set up shop. There'd be tons of civilians and property to destroy. It would have been a nightmare.

Hopefully, the Dark One didn't have as much foresight and knowledge of human culture as Anabelle. But until that Gate opened, Anabelle was sitting in the dark. "We're going to have to spread out," she told Naota. "You take half of the squad and try to zero in on the energy signature that led us here."

Naota flipped up his sunglasses, giving his biceps an unnecessary flex. Somehow, the gesture didn't appear to be aimed at Anabelle. "Gotcha, boss!" he said before giving her a thumbs-up. "Stay out of trouble until the Gate opens."

"No, that's not what I said. Get yourself in a strategic position for when the Gate opens."

Naota raised one of his eyebrows and withdrew his thumbs-up. "That's what I was implying. The best place to stay out of trouble is the best place to attack."

Anabelle sighed under her breath. Of all the people to get stuck with, she was saddled with the idiot savant. "Okay, okay, just get going. And stay out... Oh, okay, I see what you did there."

Naota walked off, signaling for his part of the squad to follow him. "Anticipation is half the game," he shouted before sprinting down the street.

A few pedestrians had stopped to look at the folk who had just walked out of thin air, but for the most part, it didn't seem as if anyone was interested in them. Typical Washington. Everyone had better things to do than pay attention to the obviously bizarre occurrence right before them.

It was no wonder it had taken Myrddin so long to convince the human politicians to take the war with the Dark One seriously. If it hadn't been for Anabelle broadcasting Terra's battle across the galaxy, there was a good chance humanity never would have come along. Or at least not fast enough to make a difference.

Fortunately, the lack of interest from the people around her gave Anabelle enough time to get her squad off the main streets. They ducked into an alley, and then scaled a bank, climbing up to the third floor and posting up. From this vantage point, they had a good line of sight of the whole of DC. Wherever the Dark Gate opened, Anabelle would see it. She just hoped she would reach it in time.

Roy shot out of his portal, his mech skidding across the ground, kicking up a cloud of dust. He popped open his cockpit and waved the dust out of his face as his squad came running out of the portal, which quickly closed behind them.

Desert stretched out as far as Roy could see. When Roy looked closer, he thought he could see someone wandering far off. As he scanned the horizon, a few more of the small dots appeared. Roy returned to his mech and scanned for life forms.

There were human signatures peppered throughout the ten to twelve miles surrounding Roy's location, some were in groups of ten or twenty, others as small as two or three. There was only one spot that seemed to have more than fifty bodies.

Roy exited his cockpit and scratched his beard. "What the hell is going on here?"

One of the younger Marines walked up to Roy. "I think it might be Burning Man this weekend."

"What the fuck is burning man?"

"Some hippy shit. A bunch of people get together in the desert and do a bunch of drugs and burn a giant wooden guy. I think there's, like, tech-bros or something too. You know, startup money and all that shit."

Roy stared at the young man incredulously. "Not one of the words in that sentence made sense to me except for hippy. And to know there are hippies wandering around this beautiful desert makes me intensely angry. Now, what the hell is this place?"

"It's a hippy gathering."

Roy got back in his mech and sighed. Of all the places to have to end up—a desert full of hippies. There was one plus side. The attendees would probably be too fucked up on booze and drugs to have any idea what was going on. At least there wouldn't be civvies everywhere freaking out.

"Let's get started," Roy shouted as he powered up his mech's thrusters. "We still got some time before the Gate opens. I want you to fan out, keep in close range of each other, and hunt down that signal.

Once you find it, comm it to everyone, and we converge on that area. You see any civvies, you direct them away from this festival. Got it?"

He received a chorus of, "Sir, yes, sir!"

Roy's mech launched into the air. He keyed the energy signature he was hunting into it. Now all there was to do was wait.

CHAPTER FIFTY-FIVE

Abby whirled, trying to make sense of the scene in front of her. The Dark Gate had already opened. The streets were flooded with orcs and goblins, firing, snatching humans up, and throwing them through the air. Everything was chaotic, and Abby didn't know where to start.

The soldiers behind her were frozen as well. They had been expecting a fight, but nothing on this scale. This appeared to be a full-on invasion, one none of them was prepared for.

Abby's heart was racing, and she felt like she'd been rooted to the ground. There were already so many dead bodies littering the concrete. A slaughter. Like back home.

Rage welled up in her. It grew hot in her stomach and spread through her as the nanobots poured out, covering her body in obsidian micro-steel. Her eyes glowed bright white, and she raised her hand, her palm converting to a plasma cannon. *Wait,* she thought. *You need to think this through.*

Abby quickly scanned the area, trying to figure out the best course of action. In the back of her head, she felt a tingle, and everything suddenly became clear. She turned to the soldiers behind her and shouted, "Squad A, suppressive fire. Reduce casualties. Squad B, take to the buildings. Snipe what you can, and loop back round to flanking position. Blackwell, you keep 'em moving and eliminate any targets of interest."

Blackwell looked taken aback by the sudden military jargon but responded quickly enough. He turned to the exosoldiers and shouted, "You heard the lady. Let's get a fucking move on!"

Abby leapt, firing thrusters to keep her airborne. She opened fire on the orcs running through the street across from her, burning them to cinders, then flew higher.

The damage had seemed worse than it actually was. She had merely been in shock. Now that it had passed, Abby could see her squad getting down to business. They weren't as badly outnumbered as it had first appeared. Still, the problem lay in finding the Dark Gate. As long as it stayed open, there remained the potential that her team could be overrun.

A shriek came from somewhere nearby, quickly followed by more screeches. The sky was full of what appeared to be massive vultures with wings as well as arms. The vrosks held glowing staffs that they brandished at Abby before firing.

She swooped out of the way, narrowly avoiding being scorched. "Those are vrosks," Martin explained. "A kind of mutant from one of the nine realms. They're really smart, fast, and agile."

Abby dodged another of the vrosks blasts as she flew higher. "You got anything useful to tell me?"

"They have a weakness to magic and fire. Luckily for you, plasma is just our default ammunition. Say hello to your new flamethrowers."

Abby sensed something in her arms moving and adjusting. It felt like her bones were withdrawing into her chest, then the holes in her palms closed and opened again. Fire burst out over her hands. "Oh, integration was a good idea," she murmured as she looped back around and flew toward the vrosks.

The vultures split apart from each other. One held its staff above its head, chanting loudly, a terrible squawking noise. Abby sped up and plowed into the vrosks, grabbing a head in her hands, squeezing as hard as she could until it melted between her fingers.

A blast of plasma hit Abby in the side and she went flying, spinning as she tried to stabilize herself. Another shot came whizzing at her, but she managed to move out of the way. She raised her hand and fired a stream of fire.

Vrosks screeches filled the air as the creatures either burned alive or swerved out of the way to avoid instant death.

Abby directed her thoughts toward Martin. "What else can I do?"

Martin answered, "Your body is filled with nanobots. Pretty sure imagination is the limit."

Abby opened and closed her hand, imaging a sphere. When she opened her palms again, she could see the nanobots pouring out of her skin, stitching together her concept as if she were a 3D printer. She held the small object in her hand, then she chucked it at three remaining vrosks.

The sphere split into three pieces, each sending a jet of flame out. The three pieces were connected together by a thin rope, spinning around each other, using momentum to keep going. The bolo snagged all three of the vrosks, then there was a bright light and an explosion.

Once the flash ended, the vrosks were no more.

Martin's voice interrupted Abby from celebrating. "Okay, this just in. Let's not make a habit of that. Device construction lowers the overall number of nanobots in your body. Maybe like worst-case scenario kind of party trick."

Abby appreciated Martin telling her as soon as he found out. He was getting better at the whole communicating thing. "Gotcha. All right, let's find that Dark Gate."

"Performing a scan for the energy signature."

Abby's vision shifted. She could see through all of the buildings in the area, picking up on the heat signatures of everything and everyone in the area—blue for humans and red for orcs. There were a few places where green energy hung in the air—three of them.

"Green the Dark Gate?" Abby asked.

"Looks to be."

Abby patched to Blackwell. "We picked up the Dark Gate signatures. Moving to disable now."

Blackwell replied, "Dealt with most of the orcs down here, and civilians have been moved out. We'll make our way to the coordinates."

"Blackwell, help whoever you find on the way. Your priority is keeping the ground safe. Keeping people alive."

"Gotcha. See you at the gates."

Abby studied the soldiers below her who were fighting off the remaining orcs. They were all moving much faster in their power suits. The upgrades must have helped. There'd be time to congratulate herself and Creon later. She took off toward the first Dark Gate.

Fire everywhere, accompanied by the overpowering weight of smoke. That was what Sarah woke up to. She leapt to her feet and shook Kravis. The gnome took no time snapping awake.

Their tent was on fire. Sarah and Kravis grabbed what they could, but the fire was quickly overtaking the simple canvas structure. They rushed outside.

All around, flames licked the air. The entire camp was on fire. Gnomes were running about, trying to find one another, their frightened screams ringing through the night, only covered by the whooping and shouting of the orcs who rode through the camp on their wargs.

Sarah drew her guns and fired, spinning around, trying to line up as many orcs as she could. She dumped round after round into the orcs terrorizing the camp, but there were too many. That was obvious. "We need to get out of here!" Sarah shouted.

Kravis didn't move. His eyes were filled with tears as he watched what could have been the last arm of the gnomish resistance shattering.

There wasn't any time to be sentimental. Sarah grabbed him and yanked him away from the chaotic scene. They fled into the forest, along with other gnomes. Among the trees, it was hard to see how many had made it out of their tents. Luckily it was dark. The gnomes could make use of their innate ability to blend into the shadows.

Sarah and the gnomes ran. She could hear the wargs and orcs coming after them. They weren't going to be able to run forever, and Sarah hated the feeling of being hunted. "Babe, execute plan B."

Kravis merely grunted in response. Sarah knew it was hard for him to see. But she also knew he was a fighter, the kind of person who wouldn't let his home be pulled from his hands without a fight.

Sarah tossed Kravis the pack she had made sure to take from their tent. Kravis grabbed the pack and tore it open. He slipped the jetpack of his own creation onto his back and drew the two daggers attached to the side. Then he stopped, pivoted to face the orcs, and launched forward.

The jetpack only operated in short bursts. That was how it was designed. Since the bursts were so brief, there was a tremendous amount of precision required. Kravis capitalized on that. He flew toward the closest orc, sinking his dagger into its throat before leaping off. Propelled by the jetpack, he landed on the next orc and slit its throat.

Sarah sprang into the trees surrounding her. She waited until an orc rode beneath her, and then dropped, grabbing it by the throat, snapping its neck and tossing it off the warg. She grabbed the warg's mane and pulled up hard enough to stop the creature in its tracks. She turned the beast around and raced toward the main group of orcs.

As Sarah rode into the orcs, she fired at anything that moved, making sure to keep an eye out for the blurry ball of fury Kravis had become. The gnome was slicing through enemies faster than Sarah could count. She made sure to keep up with his body count.

Up ahead, the other gnomes were still fleeing. To where, no one could say. There seemed to be no more places to take refuge within the gnomish world. All of these gnomes were fighters, yet they ran. Perhaps they now understood that there was nothing to do but run.

Sarah and Kravis did not run. They continued to cut through the orcs and wargs that came after them. Eventually, the orcs stopped chasing the gnomes. All attention was called to the two demons in the midst of the black forest, hacking through orcs as if they were pieces of moving meat. All of the orcs' forces descended on the section of the forest Sarah and Kravis occupied.

When Sarah saw the increase, she and Kravis slipped into the canopy of leaves. They watched as the orcs patrolled the area. "That should give everyone else enough time to get away," he whispered.

Sarah monitored the path the gnomes might have taken. "Where do you think they're going?" she asked. "Was there a plan if anything like this happened?"

Kravis nodded and leaned over his branch, watching the orcs, who had now lit torches for better visibility. "There's a network of safehouses that only the higher-ups know just in case something like this happens. And how the fuck did it happen? Were you followed?"

Sarah shook her head. "No, I'm certain. And I only came back with one... Oh, you have to be fucking kidding me!"

Sarah pointed at the group of orcs stomping about. Bim-bop was riding atop one of their shoulders. "Looks like we figured out who the traitor is," Sarah muttered. "What do you want to do?"

Kravis hadn't taken his eyes off Bim-bop. There was a deep hatred in them. "We take him. Pump him for information. Then we kill him. We take our time. And we kill him."

Sarah watched Kravis carefully. She always had a hard time admitting how much she admired Kravis' inner psychopath. "Would you like to do the honors?"

Kravis didn't answer. He leaned forward and jetted out, swooping from the darkness. His blades cut through the orcs surrounding Bim-bop, and he managed to snatch the gnome from the orc's back. Barely wasting a second, he guided his jetpack back into the trees.

Kravis and Sarah moved in silence after stuffing Bim-bop's mouth with a bandana. They aimed to get as far away from the forest as possible. Or at least from their camp. Outside the woods was a series of caves they could use for their purpose. It was far enough that they wouldn't care if Bim-bop screamed. Nobody would be coming to investigate.

Anabelle was perched up on top of the Washington Monument. She'd switched her spot a little while ago, feeling she needed to have a better view. Truthfully, it was just because she'd always wanted to sit at the highest point in Washington.

The Dark Gate still hadn't opened. She was beginning to get bored. She commed Roy. "Hey, yours open yet?"

After a few seconds, Roy came through on her comm. "No, not yet. We haven't got anything. Starting to wonder whether this was meant to throw us off of something else."

"What are you thinking?"

"Nine gates across the country in only three spots? Just enough for each of our squad leaders. HQ is empty as hell. Would be the perfect time to launch an attack."

Anabelle shook her head as she watched the traffic beneath her. "No way. The Dark One wouldn't be dumb enough to take Myrddin head-on. I don't think anyone is that stupid."

"You know, I've never seen the old man fight. By the time I joined, he was over all that shit."

"He's been over that shit for a long time. I've only seen him fight once. It was terrifying."

Roy laughed. "I doubt that. He's only done parlor tricks in front of me."

"Even that's impressive. You know the entire HQ is supported by his magic. The defense system. The cloaking. Every magical occurrence in the entire building. And that's not the only one he's supporting. There are, like, six others. Every day, twenty-four-seven. The man has more manna than all of the realms combined."

"Damn! Why doesn't he just take on the Dark One by himself? One on one. Could save a lot of lives."

Below Anabelle, two cars collided. The drivers were getting out to argue with each other. "Says the Dark One is something beyond that. Still doesn't know how to kill him, I guess."

As the two drivers got in each other's faces, a bolt of lightning struck the ground between them, sending one flying, and melting the other. The earth began to tremble, and the sky shifted from clear to cloudy and purplish. "Shit. Looks like one of my gates is opening," Anabelle said. "Guess it's for real. Catch you later. Have fun!"

Anabelle switched over to Naota and her squad. "Hey, you guys see that Gate opening?" she asked.

"Yes, I do indeed," Naota answered. "One on Vermont Boulevard and another is opening up by the Lincoln Memorial. The last one is on...whoa, I don't know how to pronounce that one."

"I don't care if you know how to say it. You take half the squad to it. The rest, take care of the portal on Vermont. I'm heading to Lincoln."

Anabelle turned off her comm, then glanced at the Lincoln Memorial. This was the sort of fight she'd been hankering after for some time. Even though many of her memories of her teachers were lost, she was fairly confident she was taking the right path. The past Travelers would have been proud.

Eyes closed. Breathing. Concentration. The world faded to blues and soft mist. Inside was the strength, the well of energy, the manna. Anabelle felt it travel down to her feet. Then she leapt off the Monument, pulling the water from the reflecting pool beneath her to dampen her fall. She sprinted toward the Lincoln Memorial.

Abby raced through the streets as fast as she could, pushing her body to its limits. She soared between buildings and above the humans who casually glanced up at her as she passed by without much notice. The farther Abby went, the more she began to recognize the area from TV shows and movies.

The Dark Gate was set to open in the middle of Times Square. Abby looked around, overwhelmed by the number of TV screens and people in such a crowded place. The Gate couldn't open here. Hundreds of people would die. "Martin, can you patch me into the video feed? That big one?"

"Not a problem, boss."

Abby let the nanobots roll back from her face, emphasizing she was still a human. She watched the largest television screen as her face showed up on it. "Uh, hey, y'all. My name's Abby," she said. "I'm the one whose been, uh, helping everyone watch Terra."

At first, nobody stopped to listen, but slowly, the humans gave their attention to the giant screen. At the mention of Terra's name, almost everyone stopped what they were doing to listen.

When Abby saw how many folks had begun to listen to her, her confidence was bolstered. "Yeah, so, we're having something like an emergency. There is an attack coming into this spot. I need you all to evacuate. Like, right now."

A man in the crowd started laughing. "Oh, shit, this is real good," he shouted. "Talk about sick-ass marketing."

Another man turned to him and grabbed him by the shoulders. "Marketing? Are you joking? You know this whole orc invasion thing is real life, right? Haven't you been watching the news?"

Just like that, all semblance of reason broke away. As quickly as the humans had turned their attention to Abby, they descended into mindless chaos and nonsense. She sighed as she hung her head. There wasn't much time for her to bemoan the situation, though.

A loud sizzle and pop announced the opening of the Dark Gate. The portal tore open the television screen Abby had just been talking through. Vrosks poured through the Gate, some ridden by orcs.

The vrosks descended upon the humans below. Abby flew forward, ready to defend those beneath her. That was when Martin's voice cut in. "Abby, I know you want to help them, but you need to close that Gate."

Abby didn't pull up. She continued flying toward the humans who were about to die. "I'm not just going to leave them!"

"You can't save everyone. And if you leave that Gate open, more of those things are going to come through."

Abby didn't care what Martin was saying. She could do both. There was no way she was going to sit by and watch innocent people die. Her father wouldn't have let that happen. She remembered why she'd been brought to Middang3ard HQ, and it hadn't just been for revenge. "Martin, have the collider send me the last three things I prepped for teleportation."

Martin was quiet for a second before responding, "Oh, shit, didn't know you were thinking that far ahead."

A small portal opened behind Abby. Gertrude and the other drones phased into Times Square.

Abby landed next to the drones, turned toward the impending onslaught of vrosks, and slammed her wrists together. Her hands fused together into a large plasma cannon, and she fired. The vrosks attacking the humans were decimated. "Martin, take over the drones and save as many lives as you can. I'm going to close that Dark Gate."

"Gotcha. Just give me the boring, morally responsible part."

Abby burst off the ground toward the Dark Gate. The sky was still full of vrosks and orcs. She fired at them as she zoomed between the monsters, her reaction time far faster than that of a human. The vrosks tried to hurl magic at her, but she was too quick, racing past their spells and turning on a dime to blast them with plasma.

It barely took any time for Abby to get to the Dark Gate. She scanned it, looking for weak points. Once located, she blasted all of them, and the Gate went dead. While the portal faded, Abby went to the back, tearing out as much tech as she could. She marked the tech for pickup later before turning to the remaining vrosk invasion squad. "Time to clip some wings," she shouted before speeding into the flurry of swords and magic.

CHAPTER FIFTY-SIX

The cave Sarah and Kravis had found was about five miles from the resistance camp. It wasn't too far from the first defense ring of the Dark One's command center. There was enough distance that they were certain that no patrols would be coming through. That, and it seemed there wouldn't be many soldiers to spare with the current raiding party on their former camp.

Sarah took care of binding Bim-bop. She wanted to let Kravis take his time. It had been some time since Sarah had seen what Kravis was capable of when he had the motivation. She'd always liked watching him work. There weren't many gnomes who flourished under torture. Kravis was one of those rarities who took something horrifying and turned into a thing of beauty.

Bim-bop was tied to a boulder, his hands pulled behind his head so that he dangled from the boulder, his feet barely touching the ground. It was just enough to give him the hope he'd be able to support himself and take some of the strain off of his arms.

Kravis sat across from Bim-bop and lit a match that cast an odd glow over his face as he stared at the other gnome. "First things first. We're going to start with questions. Either way, I'm going to kill you.

The only control you have over the situation is how much pain you experience before you die. Do you understand?"

Bim-bop spat in Kravis' face and sneered. "Nothing you do will make me give up my Lord," he taunted. "Nothing. Do you think you can do anything worse than the orcs? Anything worse than the Dark One?"

Kravis shrugged. "I'm not sure I can, but I'm more than willing to try." He pulled out one of his daggers and twirled it before throwing it into Bim-bop's shoulder.

The gnome screamed in pain as Kravis surged forward and punched him in the face. Kravis held his hand to Bim-bop's mouth. "No, you don't get to scream yet," he growled. "The only thing I want out of you is information."

Sarah watched Kravis work for the better part of an hour. She saw her love descend to a level of savageness only seen in the cruelest and most insane of torturers. It was like watching a sculptor working with the most stubborn of clays. Kravis worked and worked the other gnome, slowly and methodically, taking care which parts of the body he attacked, how he phrased his questions.

After an hour, Kravis took a break and handed the gnome over to Sarah. Torture wasn't something she brought much passion to, but it had been part of her schooling, and Sarah had excelled in every aspect of her studies. She took her lead from Kravis, happy to not have to take charge of the situation. Similar questions were asked. Previously created wounds were nurtured with poison and open blades.

Bim-bop's tears came and did not stop. That was when Kravis took over. He needled the gnome with questions, sometimes asking things there was no way the gnome would know. Over the next hour, Sarah watched as Bim-bop's sanity slowly unraveled. Begging came first, then threats. It always went back to begging, yet the gnome gave up no information.

Kravis changed tactics. He unbound the gnome and threw Bim-bop onto his stomach. Then he cut down the length of gnome's shirt and continued cutting until the cave was filled with Bim-bop's shrieks. When

Kravis finally stood, his face covered in blood and sweat, he motioned for Sarah to come over to his side. "You ever see anything like this before?" he asked, pointing at a small protrusion on the back of Bim-bop's neck.

Sarah inspected the protrusion carefully. She had seen something similar in the necks of orcs she had decapitated. Other than that, nothing. She explained her prior findings to Kravis. They tied Bim-bop back to the rock and made themselves some tea from the leaves they found around the cave.

Kravis was oddly silent, brooding more than usual. "What are you thinking?" Sarah asked.

He jerked his thumb at the wheezing pile of flesh tied to the boulder. "I would have cracked by now," he admitted. "I think you might have as well."

Sarah nodded. She'd been thinking the same thing. Kravis had pulled out all the stops. It was surprising that Bim-bop was still alive. "Yeah, I might have said something by now. Maybe not all the juice, but at least something to make you back off."

"You know, I've heard rumors about the Dark One's forces. That they might not be in complete control of themselves."

Sarah had heard similar things. Nothing conclusive. Myrddin had a lot of information concerning speculation that the Dark One was using some kind of mind control, but Sarah was uncertain. The soldiers of the Dark One were too zealous to be mind-controlled. They were almost like cultists. It was the kind adoration that required you to be of sound mind.

Kravis pulled out his dagger. "Before we lost communication with the other realms, we picked up a report that a group of Myrddin's lapdogs had found that a group of orcs was being controlled by some kind of tech. We haven't been able to get our hands on a corpse long enough to dissect it since we heard about that, let alone a fresh one."

"You think it might be that thing in the back of his neck?"

"Only one way to find out. It might just be my pride, but I can't think of any gnome who would switch sides. It's even harder to imagine the entire orcish race swallowing their pride and serving under anyone who wasn't an orc."

Sarah nodded as she thought it over. It would explain a lot. "Might as well check while we have the chance."

The pair went over to Bim-bop, who didn't bother raising his head at their approach. Sarah undid the bindings, and the gnome fell face-first onto the ground. Kravis climbed onto his back and pressed his dagger to the base of Bim-bop's neck.

At the feel of the blade against the small bulge in the back of his neck, Bim-bop came back to life. He began to thrash as if he'd lost control of his body, emitting high-pitched squeaks that Sarah had never before heard a gnome make. She pulled Kravis off Bim-bop, who then returned to his catatonic state. "Now that was interesting," Sarah said.

Kravis walked around Bim-bop and said, "Interesting isn't the word," as he lifted Bim-bop's head up to look him in the eye. "What the fuck was that about?" Kravis asked.

The other gnome didn't look capable of answering. Kravis handed Sarah the dagger and she pressed it to Bim-bop's neck again. Once the blade was near the protrusion, Bim-bop started thrashing again. Sarah removed the blade, and the gnome went limp. "Let's find out what it is," she said.

Kravis nodded, and Sarah bent to the task of cutting out whatever was beneath Bim-bop's skin. The gnome struggled, showing an amount of strength unnatural to a gnomish body, but Sarah wasn't deterred. She slid the knife under the gnome's skin, traced the outline of the square bulge, cut four lines across the top of the protrusion, forced the blade back in, and popped out a microchip.

Bim-bop collapsed.

Sarah came around to Kravis and held out her hand. The microchip in her palm blinked once, twice before cutting off. "What in the nine realms is this?" Kravis asked.

Sarah glanced over her shoulder at Bim-bop. "Check and see if he's still alive."

Kravis rolled Bim-bop over and listened for a heartbeat. "Yeah, he's still kicking."

Sarah pulled her discus from her belt and opened it. She withdrew a small pouch of healing salve and a potion, then went over to Bim-bop and began dressing his wounds. Once she was done, she helped the gnome sit up and drink the potion.

They waited in silence, contemplating their new knowledge of the Dark One's tactics. This changed everything. When Sarah had first heard about the possibility of mind control, she assumed it was magic. Now she wondered if this was something Myrddin had always known about. At first, Sarah was angry about not being informed about this detail, but the more she thought about it, the less she cared. It wouldn't have made a difference either way. She couldn't manually remove the microchips from all of her enemies.

It did leave a sour taste in Sarah's mouth. That didn't last long, though. She'd done things for the sake of the realms that most people would consider evil. The torture of Bim-bop hardly fazed her. Someone had to do these things, and both Sarah and Kravis were good at them.

Finally, Bim-bop opened his eyes. He instantly jumped up, away from Kravis and Sarah. For a second, it looked like he was going to run, but instead, he stopped, one foot hanging in the air as if another mind had just stepped into his head and taken control. "How...how did you do that?" he asked.

Sarah stood and handed Bim-bop another potion. "We'll tell you our story if you tell us yours."

For the next hour or so, Bim-bop explained that he had been abducted by an orc raiding party months ago. Long before Sarah and Kravis had joined the resistance. He had been taken to a laboratory someplace on the planet; he didn't know where. There he had been experimented on. The scientists there were trying to crack the gnomes' DNA sequence. He hadn't understood much of what had been discussed but had grasped it had something to do with mind control.

That was when he was introduced to the microchip. It was implanted into the back of his head and caused the most bizarre of experiences. When Bim-bop had been affected by magical mind control, it was as if someone were forcing his body to do something he knew he shouldn't be. He had watched himself behave as if he were a passenger in a car.

The microchip was nothing like that. Bim-bop felt in control the entire time. Further, Bim-bop knew that his values, morals, and allegiances had changed. He just thought the change was the right one.

Sarah and Kravis didn't have to explain much at that point. Bim-bop remembered everything. He had been there, yet not been there. The concept was a little much to grasp, but Sarah heard something she believed was intensely valuable. "So, you remember everything from your time in the defense ring. When you were there being given missions and briefings. All of that?"

Bim-bop nodded as he said, "Yeah, everything. Just like if I hadn't been under the Dark One's control."

"And the Dark Gates. Could you operate one?"

Bim-bop smiled. "I can do you one better. I can get you into the interior of the ring without all the sneaking. We could be at the gates in an hour, and I can send you anywhere you want."

Sarah and Kravis exchanged glances. She wasn't certain she could trust Bim-bop. This could all be an elaborate con. But that was part of the fun.

Kravis wrapped his hand around Sarah's and squeezed tightly. He must have thought the same thing.

Bim-bop hadn't lied. He'd brought Sarah and Kravis to the heart of the Dark One's defense center in less than an hour. They didn't come across any guards or sentries the entire way. Once they were in the main center, Sarah's body tensed, but they still didn't see any guards.

Something about this was too perfect, but she wasn't in a position to ask. She wasn't sure of the tech and information that was meant to be passed on to Myrddin that she had teleported before the attack on the camp. There was no way she was going to leave the mission unfinished. Even if that meant taking a risk and being led into an ambush.

Silence and stealth were Sarah's natural gifts. That didn't mean she couldn't fight her way out of a fix. And Kravis was with her. Even if he was quiet and kind, Sarah still hadn't met anyone with as much blood-lust as he had. They'd be able to handle themselves if something went bad.

But Bim-bop didn't give them any reason to worry. He seemed as on edge with Sarah and Kravis as they were with him. The last two hours of torture probably hadn't done much to encourage a trusting relationship. At least Sarah had given him healing potions. She didn't feel bad about the situation. She could have left him with broken bones.

Finally, they arrived at the Gate room. All the gates were still active. Sarah walked around each of them, inspecting them. "And if we use these, they won't alert anyone?" Sarah asked.

Bim-bop nodded. "Nope. They're already expecting more troops to go through. That was the plan after attacking the camp. It's one of the larger invasions that has been planned for Earth."

"Which one goes where?"

Bim-bop pointed at each of the Dark Gates and explained the cities they were heading to. "How do I know you aren't going to double-cross us?" Sarah asked.

"The chip is gone. I don't feel anything about the Dark One. Anything good, at least. But I know I won't be able to convince you of that, so here's a practical answer. Once you go through the portal, there's nothing I can do. The most would be to close the portal. But by then, you'll be on Earth. It's a win-win for you."

Sarah could see Bim-bop's point, but getting to Earth wasn't going to be enough. She pulled out a flash drive and redownloaded the information she had stolen last time. "Here's the plan. I want you to put this room on lockdown. Leave the portals open. These portals go to three different places. I want to use them to go back and forth and help Myrddin's people."

Bim-bop turned to the control panel behind him. Before Sarah or Kravis could react, he placed his hand on the palm reader.

The doors of the room slammed shut. Then two more metal doors fell over the first, and a forcefield covered the exit. "I'll do you one better," Bim-bop said. "I'll stay here for you two. Make sure no one comes through and shuts it down. It's the least I can do to make up for...for what I've done."

Sarah could see the remorse in Bim-bop's eyes even if he tried to hide it. He had watched himself do terrible things outside of his will, outside of what he knew he was. That was enough to break anyone. If this was how he wanted to begin atoning, Sarah would let him.

Sarah knelt to be eye to eye with Kravis. "Where to first, love? You've never been to Earth."

Kravis thought for a moment. "The young lass...we should go to her first," he answered.

Sarah tried to remember the briefing she'd received had mentioned where Abby was going to be. She faintly remembered something about New York. "Which one of these goes to New York?"

Bim-bop pointed at three of the portals. "These three all go to New York."

"Gotcha. After we go through, close the other two. And close all the excess portals to the other places as well. It'll make it easier for everyone else."

"Will do."

Sarah saluted Bim-bop. It was the only thing she could think to do to let him know she trusted him. The gnome returned the salute, a sad smile across his face.

On that note, Sarah stepped through the Dark Gate to New York. Things were about to get interesting.

CHAPTER FIFTY-SEVEN

The Lincoln Memorial was the definition of chaos. People were running around, uncertain of where to go as orcs stepped through the Dark Gate. The steps of the Memorial had yet to run red with blood, but the sheer number of orcs alluded to the future possibilities.

The bark of the orcs' chieftain commanding her forces was enough to send the few humans who hadn't fled into instant terror. Some were kneeling, begging to be spared. Others merely stared, mouths hanging open. None took up arms. Anabelle noticed that as she sprinted toward the scene.

There were more orcs than she had initially assumed. This wasn't a small party like the one she'd come across at the amusement park. The size of the force implied that these orcs were intending to do heavy damage. It made sense. A full-on attack of DC would deliver a massive blow to humanity's morale.

The Dark One was no longer trying to hide his intentions. If this Gate was opening in the middle of DC, it was likely he was trying to draw attention. Maybe even seeing it as a challenge to humanity. Anabelle thought it felt like a challenge. No more sneaking around. This was straight-up in her face.

Anabelle commed Naota. "How goes your Gate?"

Naota answered instantly. "Closed down, boss. Methinks it was a decoy. There were hardly any orcs, and it looked like the Gate had been open for a while."

"If that's the case, I want you at my position as soon as possible."

Anabelle hadn't thought the Dark One was trying to split up the group, outside of having different gates open across the US. That implied a few things to Anabelle. Even if the Dark One was ready to move out of the shadows with his attacks, he wasn't ready for a full-on assault. The second implication was that the Dark One had a general understanding of HQ's tactics. Whoever had planned this assault had been paying attention to the last few skirmishes.

"Be there in a few," Naota responded, catching Anabelle off-guard.

Naota's response shouldn't have been a surprise. That meant Anabelle was distracted, and she was only a few minutes from engaging the enemy. She'd have to concentrate. That was the way of a Traveler.

Each fight had brought Anabelle closer to the Path. She'd be lying to herself if she said she wasn't ecstatic to feel that connection again. Over the course of the battle, she'd come to realize her desire to get into the field and fight wasn't born from some insecure desire to prove herself or any other nonsense. She was a Traveler. It was ingrained in her, even if she'd forgotten the extent. Each battle was a reaffirmation of just that.

Anabelle calmed herself and pulled her thoughts together, orienting them in the right direction. She felt her body, her limbs, moving without conscious thought. Allowed the manna to flow through her without restriction.

Anabelle left the Reflecting Pool behind and leapt onto the steps of the Lincoln Memorial, ignoring the humans who were cowering like spineless children. Even if it disgusted her, she could see why they were terrified. They weren't warriors. They were the ones who needed to be protected.

The Dark Gate was still open, but no more orcs were coming out. There were at least forty of them. The orc who seemed to be in charge was a slim female. She wore thin, loose leather garb and was neither adorned with markings of a chieftain nor a shaman. Her build was unlike that of any orc Anabelle had ever seen. This orc was lean, knotted muscle.

Grok the Unspoken. Anabelle recognized the orc from her file readings with Roy. There had been little information in Grok's dossier other than that she was of high rank in the Dark One's army. Anabelle knew nothing more.

The orcs hadn't seen Anabelle yet, and she aimed to use this to her advantage. She turned to the Reflecting Pool, drawing her manna into her hands, pulling the water from the pool, raising it into the air, swirling it into a massive ball, and then throwing it into the horde of orcs who approached the kneeling humans menacingly.

As the water descended on the orcs, who looked up with surprise and horror, Anabelle ran up the stairs of the Lincoln Memorial. She concentrated on the water turning to icicles, focusing the volley of sharpened ice on the orcs farthest from the humans.

Anabelle lunged straight for Grok.

The orc turned, and Anabelle almost forgot her attack. Something about Grok's eyes frightened Anabelle and made her want to turn and run.

Pure, undiluted hatred shone through Grok's eyes. It was as if the orc had been emptied of everything and filled with malice.

Grok assumed a fighting stance, her body slumping almost as if she were going to drop, and leapt toward Anabelle, her fingers held in a monk's gesture that Anabelle had never seen before.

Anabelle felt the attack before she saw anything. A force struck her in the chest and sent her flying backward. She hit the ground and rolled down the stairs. When she got to her feet, she spat up blood.

Grok descended the stairs toward Anabelle. She casually grabbed a human in her path by the throat, lifted him, and threw him. The human landed fifteen feet away and did not move.

Anabelle focused and drew her manna to her hands, heating them, flames leaping from her hands. She sped toward Grok, throwing a series of fast jabs at the orc, who leaned back, deflecting each of the attacks with a measure of concentration and intention Anabelle had only seen in her masters. The combination of skill and the dead look in Grok's eyes was disturbing.

Anabelle's squad descended from the buildings around the memorial, along with Naota and the team. The orcs near the Gate quickly lost interest in the civilians and turned their attention to HQ's soldiers.

Grok stepped back from Anabelle, delivering a jump kick that rippled the air with concussive force.

Anabelle was ready for it this time. She'd figured out Grok was dispelling manna as force. Almost like telekinesis, but connected to the orc's physical movements.

Grok looked over her shoulder at the HQ soldiers who were engaging with the Dark One's forces. The air was heating up from plasma blasts. When Grok turned back to Anabelle, she was smiling. She leaned over, almost apelike, and began attacking, her arms and legs dragging and then suddenly speeding up. There was no rhythm to her attacks. She looked like a tornado hell-bent on tearing Anabelle apart.

Anabelle did her best to keep up, but the onslaught was unrelenting. She held her hands to her chest, sucked in a deep breath, and exhaled her manna in a burst of flames. Grok stumbled backward and Anabelle surged forward, cracking her palm into Grok's nose.

Grok stepped back, holding their hand to her nose as a trickle of blood poured out. "Hm," she muttered. "So, you can fight."

It seemed like HQ was beating back the orcs, who were outnumbered. But the only thing Anabelle could see were those black eyes in front of her.

Grok took a step toward Anabelle, hunched over like something primordial. Anabelle couldn't let herself get psyched out. Typical orc practice. Mind games. That's all it was. "Glad to see you can talk," Anabelle countered. "Looks like you guys are losing. I'd focus more on that than your trash talking."

Grok laughed, her black eyes dancing. She gave a toothy grin before laughing, a short, disjointed sound, a sound of one who does not know the meaning of laughter. "I don't care," Grok growled. "I'm gonna kill you."

Anabelle's heart stopped at those words. It had not been the first time she'd been threatened, and it was not even close to the most creative. But there was something in that voice... She realized Grok didn't care. Grok meant what she was saying wholeheartedly. That was a dangerous thing.

Roy raced toward the Dark Gate's energy signature as his squad followed closely on foot. They were less than a mile from where the Gate was supposed to open. The random, wandering folk in the desert didn't seem to mind the soldiers invading their sandy paradise.

Up ahead, where Roy was headed, was a giant wooden effigy of a man. It stood nearly as high as the sun, and it was on fire. The heat from the statue could be felt from as far away as Roy was.

A crowd stood in a circle around the effigy. They were dancing, swaying back and forth, some holding hands. As Roy looked around, he could see art installations and trailers. Folks walked about or stood in groups wearing bizarre amalgamations of steampunk clothes, or they were naked save a face mask to protect them from the stinging sands.

Roy couldn't help but gawk at the naked butts and breasts he passed. "This might be my kind of party," he muttered as he forced himself to focus on the task at hand.

There was a sudden influx of sand, and the heat from the fire went out of the air, replaced by a stale sort of static. Roy saw the Dark Gate open at the base of the burning effigy.

Contrary to what he thought, folk did notice what was happening. Nearly as soon as the Gate opened, people began screaming and running from what poured out. Orcs by the dozen, a force slightly larger than the one Roy commanded, walked through the portal between worlds.

A few naked men and women walked out of a trailer not too far from where Roy chose to set down to scope out the situation. Their trailer was covered with ancient American flags worn down by dust and political bumper stickers that no longer seemed to carry any meaning. These nude folks were covered in sand within seconds, looking not that different than their wooden effigy. Then they went into their trailer, only to return brandishing firearms.

One of the women—who had a tattoo of an orange on her ass and a crucified gator between her breasts—spat and cocked her shotgun. "Looks like we got some of them fantastical creatures fucking with our trip."

A naked man with long arms, an even longer gray beard from which peered two eyes as black as the cavernous expanse of space, and perhaps even longer pubic hair, slung a rifle over his shoulders before shotgunning a beer. "Goddamn it, I was just coming up. This is gonna be a fucked trip, sisters and brothers. A fucked trip indeed."

The woman, whose name was Star Breeze, and the man, who had been christened Sugar Owl upon his baptism in a swamp somewhere in the Everglades during the summer of '95, turned to look at the dragon mech sitting at the side of their trailer. The rest of their clan, who had now come forth from their trailer, stared at the mech as well, somewhat confused, their drug-addled minds forming their own conclusions about the importance of this mechanized beast.

Star Breeze walked over to the mech and knocked on the cockpit. Roy opened it and poked his head out as his squad gathered around him. "Hey, you meaning to start some shit with those fantasy critters over there?"

Roy couldn't believe what he was seeing. Either these were some of the bravest folk he'd ever laid eyes on or the most fucked up. "From where I'm standing, they're the ones who are starting shit."

Sugar Owl came over to stand next to Star Breeze. Somehow he'd managed to roll two joints in the space of a few seconds and handed one to Star Breeze and one to Roy. "Brother, I believe I've seen you in a vision once or twice. You rode in here while me and my co-pilot through this life were trying to figure out the righteous and proper path. I believe you led us there. Now, I'm not a hundred percent that you're actually real, but either those things out there are what we've been seeing on the news or they're the demons of my heart taken flesh. All that is to say, if you're meaning to bring a killing upon those things, we're gonna be there with you. And it looks as if you mean to lay a killing on something."

These people were definitely high, but they had guns, and they were clearly ready to use them. Also, Roy liked the phrase "lay a killing." It appealed to him. "Yeah, I am meaning to lay a killing. Don't know about civvies doing it, but you look to have your own opinion about gun laws," he said. "If it ain't human, shoot it. Not something you should continue after this, mind you. But for today, if it don't bleed red, it should be dead."

Roy slid back into his mech, closed the cockpit, and headed toward the Gate. Before he could get too far, though, Sugar Owl and Star Breeze jumped on top of his mech, holding on tight. On a different day, Roy would have explained how stupid the idea was, but today he was proud to see that some humans were ready to join the fight.

The mech closed the distance to the Dark Gate fast enough. They were under the pyre of the effigy within seconds, surprising the orcs, who made a swift retreat behind the burning man's legs, quickly taking up a more strategic position. The orcs began laying down suppressive fire.

Sugar Owl and Star Breeze jumped off of the mech, taking cover behind it, popping out for a second or two to fire a few shots.

There didn't seem to be anything too difficult to deal with, so Roy was comfortable taking potshots. He figured he'd slowly move toward the Gate while picking off orcs. It would be simple enough, and he'd probably be back in time for a hefty supper and a stiff drink.

The Dark Gate's portal turned purple suddenly. Then there was a blast of fire, shooting out, taking the form of a hand. The hand was followed by a scaly arm, then another, revealing the brawny torso of a drake as it poked its horned head out of the portal.

The drake was nearly full grown. Smaller than its pure dragon cousin, it was still a viable enemy. If it wasn't contained, the drake could easily wipe out Roy's team. He turned to the two hippies hiding behind him and shouted, "You two might want to get out of here. This isn't going to be pretty."

Sugar Owl shook his head as Star Breeze replied, "We ain't leaving until we lay a thick killing on those assholes."

"All right, but you can't keep using me for cover."

Star Breeze looked around and nodded at a couple of dune buggies that had been abandoned by a group of tech-bros who had fled the scene. The dune buggies were ridiculously armored, the sort of thing a Mad Max enthusiast would make in their spare time if they had the budget of a Hollywood film. "We got this," she said.

The two hippies hoofed it to the dune buggies and leapt in, turning over the engines and firing their guns.

Roy could only shake his head. At least they were excited. Then he turned his attention to the drake, which was still trying to get itself settled in the new environment. Roy didn't want to give it the chance. He hit his thrusters and sped toward the drake.

It glanced up a moment before Roy collided with it. Even with the element of surprise, Roy hadn't been fast enough to catch the drake off-guard. They might not have been as strong as dragons, but what drakes lacked in brawn, they made up for with viciousness and speed. Roy was about to find out what that looked like firsthand.

Roy fired his Gatling gun, trying to clear some space. The drake was undeterred, though. It clamped down on Roy's mech with its powerful jaws.

Space.

That was what Roy needed. The squad and two hippies were going to have to take care of the battle without him.

Roy fired his thrusters, this time facing them away from the ground, sending himself flying through the air. The sudden retreat threw the drake off for a second, but it was in the air just as quickly.

The drake had air superiority. Even with all the upgrades Roy had put into his mech, he still wouldn't be able to compete with the sure grace and fluidity of the drake, but he could best it in a straight test of speed and attrition. Most drakes couldn't breathe fire. That meant there was a good chance the overgrown lizard was going to have to catch Roy to do any damage.

As long as the drake was away from the battlefield, it freed up Roy's squad to do what they had to without worrying about a rampaging monster tearing them to shreds. They would be able to handle the orcs. And luckily, this was just a drake. They weren't nearly as smart as dragons. Which gave Roy a stupid idea.

Roy kicked more juice into his thrusters. He increased his speed nearly twofold and punched through the air. The drake followed suit. As Roy continued to increase speed, he began to loop back toward the Dark Gate.

He was starting to think this was too easy.

The mech and the alien reptile sped toward the Dark Gate, the drake gaining slowly, inch by inch. It didn't matter. This was already in the bag. All he had to do was get to the Gate before the drake got to him.

Right before Roy passed over the Gate, he turned in mid-air, launching an electric net at the drake. The net wrapped around its body, shocking it strongly enough to send the drake careening into the Dark Gate, breaking the thing apart as if it were a flimsy piece of driftwood.

Roy hit the ground, his mech skidding across the sand, firing on the orcs he drifted past. Their numbers were already heavily depleted, and his squad was corralling them, preparing to finish them off.

Suddenly, the drake surged forward, its body covered in electricity. "What the fuck?" Roy muttered. He'd never seen a drake with elemental abilities before, and just his luck, the element was what most of Roy's weapons were based on. *Wait,* Roy thought. *That couldn't have been an accident.*

Roy monitored the fighting around him. They were winning too easily. The orcs were just bait. Fodder to keep Roy's focus off of what was really happening. The drake had been sent for him and him alone.

The electric drake moved even faster than before, its electrical charge firing as it coiled around Roy's mech with a renewed ferocity. It bit into Roy's cockpit as it pinned the mech down, tearing away the guns and cannons that were attached to the mech's shoulder.

Power began to fade as the drake drained the mech. *Shit!* Roy thought as he tried to back away. There wasn't enough power to move. He was stuck.

The drake tore at the mech's cockpit, trying to get to what it must have thought was a delicious human.

Roy watched as the power in the mech failed. He hit his comm, calling the attention of his squad. It was unlikely they had enough firepower to take out the drake, but he wasn't going to have someone say at his funeral that he had been too proud to ask for help.

The only sound Roy received on his comm was a gurgling screech. That was all right. He looked up at the drake, who was nearly done chewing its way through the cockpit and smiled as he drew his pistol.

That was how things went. They happened fast, and you never knew which way it was going to turn out. He'd been a soldier for years. He knew this. All he could do now was wait for the drake to get close enough to accept his final offering of service to humanity.

The drake tore the cockpit off. Roy managed to fire twice before the drake reached in and wrapped its claws around him. The drake slunk away from the cockpit as its body dumped volt after volt of electricity into Roy's body.

By now, Roy had been knocked out by the electricity. He woke up when he slammed to the ground. He screamed as he felt the drake's teeth clamp around his stomach and pierce his flesh.

Roy's vision faded and his body twitched as it was wracked with pain, but he reached for his gun. At least he could get one more shot off while he stared the son of a bitch in the eye.

Suddenly the drake's body sagged.

Sugar Owl and Star Breeze rammed their dune buggy into the side of the drake, shoving it to the side as they fired their shotguns and rifles.

The drake screeched in pain, whipping around to attack the two hippies. But before the drake moved, a bolt of plasma ripped through the beast's neck. Both hippies glanced at Roy, but he was still lying spread-eagled on the ground, bleeding out. Then they looked back.

A head was receding into the shambles of the Dark Gate.

Both Sugar Owl and Star Breeze went to Roy's side, choosing to ignore what they had just seen.

Roy stared up at the two hippies. He was barely holding onto consciousness. But the drake was dead. If he lived long enough to get an extraction, he'd worry about finding out the details of the battle.

Abby blew through the last vrosk, and the skies were free. Now all she had to do was destroy the Dark Gate.

The Gate was still on, the portal still glowing.

Abby checked with Martin and confirmed that the two other gates had been closed. This was the last one that needed addressing. All and all, Abby felt like her first mission had gone off without a hitch. She landed and walked over to the Gate, her hands raised, ready to blast it to bits.

A metallic tendril flew out of the Gate and wrapped around Abby's wrist. It raised Abby into the air and then slammed her into the ground.

As Abby tried to stand, she peered into the portal and saw a female drow not much older than her step out. The elf's face was heavily burned, and she wore something like a HUD scanner on her left eye. Both of her eyes glowed white. But what really caught Abby's eyes was the drow's right arm. She did not have a hand. Instead, she had a mass of metal tentacles sprouting from her wrists that hung to the ground.

Abby stumbled back to her feet. She raised her hand and fired.

The plasma blast ripped through the Gate behind the drow with the metal tentacles. The Dark Gate's portal faltered and cut off. The drow with the tentacles didn't seem to care. She was still looking at Abby. Then she flicked her wrists, and the tentacles snapped together, twisting around each other, forming a blade.

The woman darted forward, crashing into Abby, who was barely able to throw her arms up in time to block the attack. The two tumbled over each other until Abby activated her thrusters, launching up into the air as the drow relaxed her tentacles and sent them flying after Abby. The tentacles wrapped around her ankles.

Abby turned in mid-air, slammed her hands together, forming a double hand cannon, and fired.

The drow released Abby and dodged to the side before cracking her wrists like a whip, glaring at Abby, who was quietly floating.

Abby didn't know what to do. She had this crushing feeling that something wasn't right. There was something about this drow that made Abby not want to fight, yet also made it impossible to take her eyes off her.

"You're a very beautiful, elegant creation," the woman shouted. "As one to another, I can appreciate that."

"Ain't a creation," Abby retorted. "Hundred percent human."

The drow laughed as she moved toward Abby. "Was once a human. As I was once an elf, but as you can see..." The drow held up her tentacled arm, the tentacles withdrawing to form a perfectly normal hand. "It hurts me to have to kill something so beautiful."

"I'm not a thing."

The drow shrugged as she flexed, her bicep bulging as her hand split open. The mass of tentacles dropped from the open skin, laying on the ground and slithering over each other. "We are all merely things." She chuckled. "Things to be pulled out and used when they are thought necessary. Tools, at best."

There was something intensely sad about the drow's voice. She sounded as if she believed her words.

Abby floated down until her feet touched the ground. She took a step toward the drow. "I ain't a tool. My name is Abby. I fight 'cause I wanna. Not 'cause someone's making me."

Another step toward the drow. Abby raised her hand, extending it in a sign of peace. "What's your name?"

The drow hesitated, watching Abby closely. "Doesn't matter. You don't need the name of your end," she growled.

Abby wasn't deterred. She moved closer, the nanobots rolling back on her face so that the drow could look her in the eyes. "Still, I'd like to know."

The drow didn't answer for a moment, but she didn't turn away or attack. "Persephone," she finally said. "Like the human myth."

"Yeah, I know the one."

The two stood there looking at each other for what felt like forever. Abby wasn't sure how long they could meet each other's eyes without something happening. The creature stared at her arms with confusion before saying, "My hands; they made them." Her voice trailed off as her face twitched, her eyes hardening. She jolted as if she'd received a shock, then she flew at Abby with renewed aggression.

Abby threw her arms up as Persephone tackled her, the pair tumbling across the ground, Persephone's tentacles slithered over Abby's body, pinning her arms down, one limb wrapping around her throat, constricting her breathing, another holding her head down as Persephone's eyes stared into hers. "Why aren't you fighting back?" the drow growled.

Abby struggled to breathe. "I don't know," she managed.

The grip around her neck and wrists slightly relaxed.

Something hit Persephone hard from the side, sending her flying. It was Gertrude. Martin must have taken control of the drone and brought it around while Abby was distracted by Persephone. "We can override her," Martin shouted. "She's got a microchip."

The attack had brought Persephone out of whatever trance had kept her from killing Abby. She was back on her feet, running toward Abby, tentacles forming a hooked blade. "I don't want to control her," Abby said as she prepared to take off.

"Not control. Override. Hack the chip and override it. Just keep her busy."

Abby took off and Persephone ran after her, leaping into the air, trying to grab Abby's ankles as she turned and fired. Persephone's tentacled hand morphed into a shield, absorbing the bulk of the blast.

The only thing Abby had used her nanobots for so far was constructing a plasma cannon in her hand. She still wasn't certain how the whole process worked or what her body was capable of. Today was a good day to figure some of that out.

Abby imagined a blade much like Persephone had created, and her fingers melded together and stretched out to form a razor-sharp blade. She transformed her other hand into a slimmer cannon. "Nice," she muttered. Then she rushed Persephone.

The drow was caught off-guard by Abby's sudden attack. She slashed at Persephone, pushing her back, and as the drow prepared to attack, fired her hand cannon. The blast hit Persephone in the chest and sent her flying.

Abby's heart dropped when she heard Persephone scream in pain. But the blast hadn't killed her, only angered her.

As the drow picked herself up, Gertrude released a small tracker, the kind that Abby had used to keep track of Terra. The tracker flew to Persephone and landed on her neck. The drow didn't seem to notice the fly-sized tracker. "All right, I'm getting in," Martin said.

Persephone stretched her tentacles out, and they rolled over Abby's body before she could react. It was like getting hit by a wall. The tentacles slithered over her, knocking her to the ground, trying to wrap around her neck.

Abby blasted at them, cleaving them with her blade, hacking off hunks of what could have only been flesh.

Persephone suddenly screamed and grabbed her neck, her tentacles pulling away.

Martin shouted in Abby's ear, "You need to distract her. I'm almost there, but she's gonna—"

Abby stopped listening and discharged electricity. The tentacles withdrew. Then she flew at Persephone at full speed, faster than she knew she was able to move. She slammed into the drow, knocking her to the ground. Her fist came down hard on her face.

Persephone grabbed Abby's throat with her tentacles. Abby could feel her airway closing. She released another shock of electricity, causing the tentacles to relent for a second, but then they constricted again. She gave off another shock, giving herself time to breathe before punching Persephone again.

The two continued like this, Persephone slowly crushing the life out of Abby, only for her to release her life energy in the form of electricity. Abby couldn't have known that her body operated the same way that magic users did with manna. Every electric attack was draining her of life.

Persephone tried to stand, but Abby held her down and held her hand up to Persephone's face, her palm glowing with energy. Persephone slightly relaxed and stared up at Abby. "Do it," she said, her voice defeated.

Abby leaned forward and kissed Persephone. She felt Persephone's lips soften, and the tentacles around her neck loosened. Everything was electric, everything tingled as Persephone reached up and lightly touched Abby's face.

Then the microchip overloaded, sending thousands of volts of electricity through Persephone's body and flowing straight into Abby's as well. The two jerked as they were electrocuted, still locked together.

Abby flew off Persephone. The world was going dark. She struggled to get to her feet but couldn't see straight. She leaned over and hit the ground, smoke rising from her body.

Anabelle had seen her death before. Many times, in fact. Part of her training had involved meditating on her eventual death. Another aspect of her training had been drilling into her head that she was never going to lose. These two ideals were vital for a Traveler.

As Anabelle watched Grok, she realized it was the first time she'd ever thought another person could kill her. The thought was humbling and terrifying. It was difficult to put a finger on what scared Anabelle so much. She was almost as interested as terrified.

Grok didn't seem like anything Anabelle had fought before. There was a look in her eye that crawled into Anabelle's brain and burrowed deep within.

People fought for many reasons. Grok looked to only have one: murder. Anabelle wondered if the orc was even under the Dark One's mind control. It was hard to tell. Maybe Grok was murderous by nature, and those impulses were just being used by the Dark One. Either way, Grok looked as if she were growing bored now that the two weren't fighting.

Anabelle was taking the time to size up her opponent. The concussive blasts Grok used seemed to be short-range. Otherwise, she would have likely attacked Anabelle by now. That meant Anabelle was going to have to get in closer.

Another factor to take into account was Grok's movements. She moved with an animalistic, almost apelike quality. Her attacks were unconventional, which made them all the more deadly.

Grok spat and wiped a dribble of saliva off her mouth. "You look scared," she said.

Anabelle didn't answer. She knew this part of the fight. It was the same with everyone, psyching out your opponent. And you only did that if you were afraid as well, which meant Grok could be beaten.

Manna went down to Anabelle's feet. She sprinted forward, using her internal magic to gain speed. She was in front of Grok before the orc could move. She dropped to her knees, extended her palm, and leapt into the air, driving her palm into Grok's chin on her way up.

Grok grabbed Anabelle's hand as she flew backward, yanking the elf through the air with her. She twisted until she had managed to swing around Anabelle and put her in a chokehold. They hit the ground as Grok tried to pop Anabelle's head off.

Anabelle drew in a measured breath and spread her manna over the entirety of her body, flames bursting from her skin. Grok screamed and leapt off of Anabelle, who was already on her feet, focusing her fire into her hand and lobbing a fireball at the orc.

Grok leaned into the attack, punching the ball and breaking it apart with the force of her attack.

The two went after each other again, legs and arms flinging through the air. If one were to have seen it from afar, you would assume that the orc and elf were partaking in a choreographed dance. The movements perfectly complimented the other, yet the only thing keeping this dance going was the desire they held in common.

Anabelle had never thought much about it before, but then she had never wanted to kill anyone before. All of the deaths that had taken place in her life were incidental. If she were being honest with herself, she used to love the fact that she could help Middang3ard's efforts without spilling blood. But fighting was in her bones, and there was nothing to be done. Yet she never relished the lives that she took.

This fight was something else entirely. Anabelle wanted Grok in the ground, and she wanted to be the one to do it.

Grok was backing up, heading back toward the Dark Gate and the orcs and humans who were still fighting. Anabelle had no idea what Grok was planning, but she finally remembered that her mission was to destroy the Gate. She'd lost herself to the fight, lost her way on the Path.

As Grok got closer to the Dark Gate, its portal opened again. Grok stopped and stared at it. Apparently, this wasn't part of Grok's plan.

Sarah stepped out of the portal, Kravis at her side. She grabbed Grok and flipped the orc over her shoulders, sending her flying through the portal, which was set to a far location. Once Grok passed through, Sarah quickly disabled the Dark Gate.

Anabelle came up to Sarah, filled with a mix of emotions. She was relieved that the threat was gone, jealous that Sarah had solved the problem with such style, and slightly angry she didn't get a chance to put an end to Grok. But the last feeling, Anabelle knew, was mere vanity. "Thanks," she said.

Sarah reached out to shake Anabelle's hand. "Good to finally meet you. And trust me, I didn't want to get involved in that for too long. I've seen Grok a lot over the years. When I saw you fighting her, I knew I had to do something. No one should ever be in that situation."

"Why not? She's—"

"I'll tell you later. For now, we should clean this mess up."

Sarah was right. Anabelle's squad was still skirmishing with the orcs Grok had brought along for the ride. The orcs were losing the battle. Anabelle might as well help clear out the rest of the pests.

That was not to say Anabelle's mind was not still focused on Grok. She'd forgotten to check back in with the squad leaders to see if the mission had been successful. The only thing that concerned her was Grok and the next time she would have a chance to fight the orc.

Once the last of the orcs had been cleared out, Anabelle sat on the steps of the Lincoln Memorial. She wondered how this was going to finish and what she was going to be like at its end. Was it possible to become like Grok? What if she was already on her way? War changed people, and no one ever knows they're changing until it's done.

Sarah came and sat beside Anabelle. "We got an extraction coming in a few minutes," she said.

Anabelle nodded, still staring ahead. "You and HQ on better terms now?" she asked.

"Much better. You could almost call it friendly. Also, you should stay away from Grok. She's bad news. You ever see her again, run."

"Why the hell would I run from a fight?" Anabelle asked. She was annoyed that Sarah would assume she couldn't handle herself.

"Because Grok isn't like us or any of the Dark One's cronies. She's a murderer. Defines herself by it. Even if we have to do shitty things sometimes, all of us are fighting for something bigger than us. We haven't forgotten that. I remind myself every day. Grok, though…she fights to kill. Says it affirms her existence."

Anabelle felt like Sarah was talking out her ass, telling her stories about the big bad orc who couldn't be defeated. "Sounds like you know her personally," Anabelle finally responded.

Sarah pulled down the collar of her shirt and turned her head. A scar starting from the back of her right ear snaked down her neck and continued far past Sarah's collar. "The first time I met Grok, she knocked me out and then started to carve my spine out. The only reason I survived was that Kravis got the drop on her. She's bad fucking news."

Anabelle regretted her earlier judgmental thoughts and was glad she'd kept them to herself. "I'll keep that in mind," she admitted.

The two sat in silence, watching the still, bloodstained waters, the reflection of Abraham Lincoln watching them sternly as they waited to be taken back home.

CHAPTER FIFTY-EIGHT

Anabelle didn't hear about everyone else's exploits until she arrived back at HQ. Both Abby and Roy were in the medbay. They were in critical condition. Anabelle asked for specific information but was told it would be best if she found out later.

Visiting wasn't an option at the moment. A debriefing had to happen first, and there was a lot to debrief on. Sarah, Anabelle, and Kravis were going to meet with Myrddin and see if they could figure out what exactly had happened. What had started off as a simple, albeit irritating, mission had ended up with two of Anabelle's team fluctuating between life and death.

Anabelle was sitting in her room now, trying to compose herself enough to give Myrddin all the information he needed. She was having a hard time, though. She hadn't seen Roy or Abby, and her imagination was providing the worst-case scenarios.

She knew she shouldn't be too worried. The med lab at HQ was the finest in the world. People regularly came through on the threshold of death and were brought back with hardly any effort by the surgeons and healers in the bay. But sometimes people didn't make it. It was rare, but it happened, and Anabelle couldn't stop worrying that Abby and Roy were going to be those two exceptions.

Losing Roy was something Anabelle couldn't even wrap her head around. The two had been working together for as long as Anabelle could remember. Not as closely as they were now, but Roy had always been around, chiding and teasing Anabelle whenever he got a chance.

And thinking about Abby dying took Anabelle's breath away. Abby was just a kid, one who had taken tremendous risks since joining up with HQ. She had so much potential. Given enough time, Abby could be a force to be reckoned with. That was if she lived. Maybe if Anabelle had paid closer attention to her, this wouldn't have happened. Or it could have been that Anabelle pushed Abby to get out in the field before the girl was ready.

Either way, she felt like Abby's condition was her fault. She should have been watching out for Abby, not let her make rash decisions. She couldn't help that she saw a lot of herself in the girl. She could have helped keep her from making the stupid mistakes she would have as a kid.

Anabelle realized beating herself up wasn't going to help anyone. Sitting in her room and obsessing about whether Roy and Abby were going to live or die wasn't saving either of them. All Anabelle could do was finish her job and see them afterward.

Sarah and Kravis were waiting in Myrddin's office by the time Anabelle arrived. They both looked at Anabelle and nodded politely. Myrddin, on the other hand, rose from his seat and embraced Anabelle as if she were his daughter.

Anabelle initially pulled back from the hug, not out of disgust but out of surprise. She'd rarely seen Myrddin show anything remotely close to mortal emotions other than anger and irritation. But Anabelle realized she needed this from him more than anyone else. The wall of resentment Anabelle had built up for years crumbled instantly. "I am so glad you made it out okay," Myrddin said before releasing Anabelle, who then sat beside Sarah.

Myrddin sat as well, leaning forward as he folded his hands. "Now, tell me what happened."

Anabelle shrugged, "I can't speak about what happened to Roy and Abby, but I have an inkling. At my Gate, there was someone who had been sent specifically to deal with me. The whole invasion thing was just a ploy to get me out there. They'd sent an assassin after me. Wouldn't be surprised if they did the same for them."

"They meant to split you up. A simple divide-and-conquer strategy, one we should have seen. The Dark One is apparently interested in doing more than just attacking Earth. He seems to have grasped how big a threat your team presents to his plans for Earth."

Myrddin turned his attention to Kravis and Sarah. "And you two. What did you find on the gnomish world? And how did you get back here?"

Sarah looked at Kravis, who motioned that he'd prefer for Sarah to speak. Unsurprising since the gnome rarely spoke to anyone. "Likewise, we got duped," Sarah said. "The resistance is gone as far as I know. The Dark One had a mole in our midst. He led them to the resistance camp, and the orcs burned it to the ground. We managed to get the gnome to take us back to the defense rings to make sure we secured the information you sent us for. Figured it would have gotten destroyed in the raid if it hadn't been picked up already."

As Sarah spoke, Anabelle admired the human. She had grit and a spirit the elf couldn't help but appreciate. She knew how to get the job done. Efficient, and she seemed a little ruthless. Sarah would be a great addition to the team if she could convince Myrddin.

Sarah continued to explain what had happened. "Once we got to the rings, we made sure we downloaded anything that could help with the Dark Gates, and we found out about the invasion. We used the Gates to get back to Earth and help out where we could."

Myrddin nodded as he thought over what Sarah had just said. "You were able to jump between multiple places through the Dark Gates without any problem?"

"As long as we went back through the Gate, we ended up back at the gnomish world. Then we just chose another Gate to go through after destroying the one we came through."

Myrddin's brow darkened as he thought through what he was hearing. "I need you to take everything you found to Creon in the R&D department. Until we can figure out what to do with your intel, you're on leave. Unless there's anything else you want to—"

Sarah raised her hand, cutting Myrddin off. "No, I could use a break, even if it's only for a few hours. You can comm us if anything comes up."

Sarah and Kravis rose, nodded to acknowledge Anabelle, and departed, leaving Myrddin and Anabelle alone.

"You should go see them," Myrddin said. "Roy and Abby."

"Is there anything else we have to—"

"Checking in on your squad is more important than an hour's worth of debriefings. Dismissed."

Anabelle didn't say anything. She just got up and left, heading straight toward the medbay. Myrddin's words were appreciated. It didn't make sense to always act like you didn't care about those who were close to you. Myrddin had managed to show Anabelle that with only a hug. Up until that point, Anabelle would have thought she was just an irritating employee as far as he was concerned.

Wouldn't go so far as a fatherly figure, Anabelle thought as she came to the floor that the medbay was on.

Unlike the first time Anabelle had come to visit Roy, the medbay was filled with patients. Nearly all of the beds were full. Nurses and healers walked back and forth as they waited on whoever seemed to need it. It wasn't hard to find Abby and Roy. They were kept separate from the other soldiers, in the officer's section.

It still made Anabelle feel weird that the human military hierarchy was still adhered to so strongly at HQ, but she appreciated that she knew exactly where to find her friends. *Friends.* That was funny. Anabelle had never thought of that word concerning Roy. And she had never assumed she'd be able to call a human teenager who was a fraction of her age a friend.

Anabelle stepped into the private room. Abby and Roy were lying in their beds. Roy was hooked up to a respirator as two nurses—one elvish, the other human—fussed over him, waving their wands around his stomach and chest, which was covered in wounds from the drake's claws and teeth. The wounds looked to be healing well enough. He was going to make it. His chest wasn't going to be pretty unless you liked scars. Anabelle happened to.

Abby was next to Roy. She didn't have any noticeable wounds, but she was still in nanobot mode. She hadn't thought too much about what Abby had decided to do to her body, but now Anabelle was struck by the sheer immensity of what the girl had done. She wasn't entirely human anymore. It was very obvious now.

There was also someone she didn't recognize in the room with Roy and Abby. She was a drow who looked to be about the same age as Abby. Anabelle didn't think there was anything remarkable about the young drow, other than her right arm was black, as if it had been covered in ink.

Anabelle sat at Abby's side and took the girl's hand. She'd never been in this kind of situation before and had no idea what to do. Talking to Abby seemed stupid since she wasn't conscious, but there were things she needed to hear. Maybe it would be better to wait until the girl was awake? Talking while she was asleep seemed easier, though.

Anabelle stayed with Abby and Roy long into the night, waiting for either of them to wake up. She'd been told by the nurses that both were stable and would recover without any long-term ramifications within a day. That didn't stop Anabelle from worrying. Every hour that Abby and Roy remained asleep felt like a month.

Finally, Abby opened her eyes. The nanobots receded from her skin, and she looked like a normal, healthy seventeen-year-old again. Abby sat up in the bed and yawned loudly as she stretched. "Well, this is new," Abby muttered as she took in her surroundings.

She stiffened when she saw Anabelle. "Oh, I didn't see you there," she exclaimed.

The elf leaned over and gave her a hug. She held Abby as tight as she could. "I was so worried," she said. "I didn't think you were going to wake up."

Anabelle released her and Abby lay back in bed, looking around the room, obviously trying to piece together the bits and pieces she didn't remember. Her eyes lingered on the body of the strange new person before returning to Anabelle. "Did we do it?" she asked.

"Yeah, we closed down all the Gates. Not without some casualties, though. It was probably our hardest fight so far. Both you and Roy… well, you know how everything with you turned out."

"How's Persephone? Is she okay?"

Anabelle glanced at the girl with the ink-stained arm. "Her? They said she's just resting," she said. "So, I don't want to be all business unless you're feeling up to it. If you need to rest more, that's totally cool."

Abby shook her head as she stretched out her fingers. "No, I feel good. What's going on?"

"I got jumped at my Gate. Someone had been sent specifically to take me out. Sarah got involved and helped me out, but the whole point of the Dark One's mission was to eliminate *me*. Did you come across anything like that?"

Abby nodded as she pointed at Persephone. "Yep. That's her. It was almost like my squad wasn't even there. She was hell-bent on killing me."

"What the hell is she doing here, then?"

"Don't know. I didn't pick her up. I got knocked out, but I disabled her microchip before it happened. If that's all that makes someone serve the Dark One, she should be cool. I mean, I hope."

Anabelle wasn't certain about the drow, but from everything she knew, the microchips were the Dark One's main way of mind control. If the chip was destroyed, there shouldn't be any problems afterward. "We'll keep her under surveillance," she said. "But I trust you."

Abby looked at Roy, who was still sleeping. "Is he gonna be okay?"

"Yeah, the nurses said he just needs to catch up on some sleep. But all of his wounds are healed, and there wasn't any internal damage.

I'm always surprised that he keeps going. This might not even be the worst he's gone through."

"You like him, don't you?"

Anabelle blushed at the question, but she figured there was no harm in telling Abby the truth. Roy was asleep. He wouldn't hear anything. "Yeah. I do. A lot. For a while, too, I guess."

"I thought so."

"Wish I didn't," Anabelle said with a laugh. "He's a little too smug and way too reckless. But I do. And I know it's reciprocated. Just...you know, it's hard to find time for anything nowadays."

Abby nodded, looking very grave as if she understood exactly what Anabelle was talking about. "You two would be cute together," she finally said. "Maybe you should talk to him about it."

"I'm not sure if I should be taking love advice from a senior in high school."

Abby laughed and shrugged. "That's your call. If you haven't noticed, I'm smart for my age, but maybe you're right. Life might be too complicated for that."

Abby's gaze drifted to Persephone, and Annabelle had a strong inkling of what was going on but thought it better to wait until later. "If you're done trying to hook me up with Roy, are you feeling good enough to get back to work?" she asked.

Abby got out of bed, bent down, and touched her toes. "I think so. Little sore, but nothing too bad."

"Good. We got new intel on the Dark Gates, and we only have a few hours to figure out how to open Terra's and get her back home."

Abby was already headed toward the door. "Let's get her back," she said.

Anabelle appreciated Abby's willingness to get back to it. She felt like she would have wanted another couple of hours before she'd been expected to get out of bed. But she also wasn't seventeen anymore.

Before Anabelle left, she went to Roy's bed and kissed him on the forehead. As she left, Roy's eyes flickered open, and he smiled.

CHAPTER FIFTY-NINE

Creon was already in the lab working when Anabelle and Abby arrived. He was unable to contain his excitement upon seeing the girl and ran to her as quickly as he could, nearly knocking her over as he hugged her. "I'm so glad to see you pulled through!" he exclaimed.

Abby pried Creon's hands off her, laughing as she asked, "What do you mean, pulled through? Was I that far gone?"

Creon shook his head as he returned to his seat, trying to hide how embarrassed he was by his sudden outburst. "No, no, not at all. It was more...we didn't quite know what it was that happened. All of your vital signs were normal, but you wouldn't wake up. And then they found you with that drow. It was all very—"

"Is she going to be okay?" Abby blurted.

"Oh, yes, yes. She was badly shocked by being broken from the Dark One's mind control, but physically, there seems to be no problem with her. There were a few anomalies that aren't natural to a drow's body that the medbay wanted to take a look at but nothing to be worried about."

Abby exhaled with relief. She only half-remembered the last few moments before she was shocked out of consciousness. They felt like a dream, though. She still wasn't sure if they had happened. Part of her was looking forward to seeing Persephone when she woke up. That part of Abby was greatly overshadowed by the part of her that was mortified.

Either way, Abby didn't have to deal with it right now, and she was glad to have something else to focus on. Like Anabelle had said, finding time for your own life seemed impossible due to the ongoing war with the Dark One. "Uh, so, what are we working with?" Abby asked, trying to take her mind off of the softness of Persephone's lips.

Creon turned back to Abby as Anabelle found a place to sit. The goblin opened the holoprojector in the middle of the room. The screen displayed multiple iterations of the Dark Gate. Some of the schematics had been broken down into their components. "This is what we are working with."

Abby studied the projection, trying to make sense of what she was looking at. She'd seen some of these schematics before. They hadn't helped Abby and Creon figure out how to get Terra back to Earth. If anything, they had been more confused by how the Dark Gates worked. "How's this going to help?" she asked. "Ain't this just more of the same?"

Creon shook his head as he pointed at the detailed breakdown of the Dark Gate. "Not quite. Much of it is the same, but there are bits and pieces we haven't seen before. Take this piece, for example. This was found on the gnomish homeworld. It allows the Dark Gates to be programmed with specific DNA, which was one of the reasons the resistance could not use the Gates if they got their hands on them. Sarah was lucky enough to come across a gnome who knew about the programming."

Abby still felt groggy. Her mind wasn't quite ready to jump through all these intellectual hoops, but she did want to work. It was impossible to know how much longer Terra was going to be able to survive in the arena. "Martin, is this something we can work with?"

Martin popped up on the holoprojector. "Oh, you remembered I was here?" he sarcastically retorted. "Here I was thinking that I was going to be a plot hole or something. Hold on, let me take a look at this. Hm, looks like there are a couple of things we could work with. There's a specific frequency a Dark Gate uses. Looks like it's what hooks each one up to the other. We catch that frequency, mimic it… We could probably send something through the Gate, but it might be a one-way trip."

Abby looked closer at the information. "If it was a one-way trip, we could work our way back, though. We have the basic layout of the Gates. Could just jerry-rig it to the collider's signature."

Martin considered that. "Only problem is that they'd have HQ coordinates after we did that. We'd have to destroy the Gate as soon as we passed through it, which sounds pretty impossible. But on top of that, just if you want to make things more complicated, we have no idea if they have the means to store that kind of information. For all we know, we could be walking into another trap. This could have all been orchestrated so that the Dark One can finally have a way to transport troops into HQ, and I will *not* take the blame for that happening. You can try to blame me, but I'm not taking it."

Abby pursed her lips. "What if we took the gnomish frequency being used and passed it off as our own? That way, if they tried to follow us, they'd just end up on the gnomish world. Bring a satellite along for our trip, toss it up in the atmosphere to broadcast while we grab Terra, and there you go. Home free."

Creon, Abby, and Martin looked at one another, their minds running, trying to see if they could find a problem with the plan. Abby had her fingers crossed that if there was an issue, Martin or Creon would have noticed it by now.

Creon was the first to speak. "Theoretically, that would work. The only problem would be the satellite. Constructing one for such a specific use in time might be—"

Martin interrupted Creon. "We could use one of the drones. Retrofit it with some new tech and launch it into the atmosphere."

Abby could part with a drone. She could always build a new one. "Not Gertrude. But yeah, I think that might work."

The trio talked for some time about the details of the execution of their plan. Anabelle started slinking out of the room as the conversation turned to theoretical physics, and Abby frowned. "Hold on, guys," she said as she ran to catch up with the elf. "Hey!"

Anabelle stopped and turned to face Abby. "Yeah, what's up?"

"Uh, I just wanted to thank you...for being there when I woke up. And for trusting me... You know, to do all this."

"Trust you? Why wouldn't I? You're doing great, kid. Just make sure you remember what I always tell you."

"You always tell me something?"

Anabelle laughed. "You can just fill that in with a piece of good advice. Surprisingly, I don't have a whole lot of that. Now get back in there and figure out how to bring Terra home. I'm going to go sort out our welcoming party."

Abby didn't know why, but she threw her arms around Anabelle and squeezed as hard as she could. Then she ran back to the lab, hoping the elf wouldn't mention that later.

Terra lay in bed in her cell, staring at the ceiling while Nib-nib chittered at her side. The mantiboid had been sitting with her for most of the day. They hadn't spoken much. There were still moments when Terra didn't understand what Nib-nib was saying, but her proximity was comforting.

None of the other fighters had come to see Terra. She didn't blame them. The glory of her victories was becoming hollow. It had become apparent that she wasn't meant to live. Even if she kept fighting as hard as she was, the Game Master was going to throw something at her that she couldn't beat. It was just a matter of time.

It was disappointing. Terra had never thought she was going to be anyone great. The thought hadn't crossed her mind when she was younger. She'd always thought you just kept on living and trying as best as you could. Now, on her figurative deathbed, she thought about all the things in life she'd never managed to do.

It was not that Terra was filled with regret. Far from it. She was fairly happy with how she'd chosen to spend her life so far. Instead, she was awash with intense anger. There was so much more she had been planning on doing, and now she was stuck in a bizarre death match for reasons outside of her control and understanding. It wasn't fair, pure and simple. She was violently angry at those who had caused this to happen to her.

Nib-nib seemed to pick up on Terra's frustration. The creature rested its claw on Terra's bed near Terra's hand and chittered, "Life don't come right, not for most us. We fight. We die. Others fight. Others die. Not come right."

Terra couldn't disagree, and because of that, she said nothing. The two sat in silence, other than the constant quiet scratching of Nib-nib's mandibles until there came a knock on the open door. "Come in," she shouted.

Cire stepped in. He held a plate of food and three jugs of wine. He passed a jug to Nib-nib and Terra and then sat at the foot of the bed. "Thought you could do with a pick-me-up," he offered.

Terra hadn't felt hungry until she smelled the food. She was glad that whenever Cire came into her room, he was smart enough to bring food and wine.

The wine was smoother than anything Terra had been served so far, almost as if the orcs were aware that the shenanigans were coming to an end. At least they had the decency to provide her and the other fighters with good booze.

Cire drank silently as Terra dug into her food, watching Terra relish the meal and wash it down with the wine. When she was done eating, he said, "We've heard about your next match."

That was the last thing Terra wanted to talk about, but she couldn't think of any other topic. "What'd you hear?"

"They aim for it to be your last one. Guards said it was going to be the biggest fight in the history of any of the arenas. They believe you should be offered the chance to end your run with glory."

Terra laughed at the idea. Being given the chance? Even though she no longer held the vision of rising to glory within the arena like when she had first stepped out of the shadows, she still felt a twinge of indignation. As if anyone but her had the right to end her run. "Doesn't seem like that's what they want." She scoffed. "Otherwise, they would have given me a decent fight."

Cire laughed bitterly. "Honestly, I don't know if they could even if they wanted to. You've beaten everything they've thrown at you. Done things I've never seen an orc do, things I haven't seen armies do, to be frank. If they continued cheating a little, you'd never lose."

"Isn't that the point of being a champion?"

Cire laughed again, and when he stopped, his face became solemn and serious. "May I speak to you in private?"

Terra shrugged and asked Nib-nib to leave the room. When they were finally alone, Cire took the seat at the side of the bed. "I've never met a human like you, nor an orc. You have the strongest warrior's spirit that I have seen. If you had been born an orc, a true orc, you would have been given an army. Maybe even a tribe to rule."

"Thanks. That's a nice sentiment to think about before I get forced to fight to the death."

"It is not a sentiment. It is the truth. I tell you this because... because there are still orcs who cling to the old ways. Orcs who will do everything in their power to never serve under the Dark One. I tell you this because there is a resistance. There are still those of us who fight every day to stand against the tyranny of the Dark One."

Terra didn't really want to listen to Cire's rant, but she could see he was sincere. She sat up straighter to indicate that she was interested. Cire continued, "If you were to survive all of this, what would you do?"

The thought hadn't crossed Terra's mind. Even if she had thought she'd be able to be a champion in the arena, she hadn't entertained the idea that she would ever be leaving it. "Don't know," she finally admitted. "Wasn't up to the most interesting shit before I came here. And now that I know that shit like this is going on, I don't know. I'd like to try to keep it from continuing."

"The first fight you won. I do not know if many noticed it, but I did. You were assisted by something like a bug, and it has stayed close to you at all times."

Cire pointed at the window sill where Abby's tracker rested. "Who is helping you?" he asked.

For the first time since Cire spoke to Terra, she doubted his intentions. Not that he had given her any reason to, but simply because no one else had noticed she was being helped. No one had been looking that closely. Realizing Cire had been watching was reason enough for suspicion. "Why do you want to know?"

"I did not think you would tell me, but I thought it worth asking. I do not need to know. Instead, I want to ask a favor of you. As I said, there are orcs who are part of a resistance against the Dark One. Our numbers are small, and we are scattered, but whoever is helping you has resources. What I say next is not said lightly. I am one of the last surviving shamans of the older tribes. It is within my ability to crown new chieftains. I have yet to meet an orc worthy of such a title, but it is a title I would like to bestow upon you. And with that title, I would ask you to petition help from whoever aids you."

"Why don't you just ask yourself?"

"Because I am an orc, and I will not be trusted. But you? You will be believed. Regardless of your decision, though, I still would like to bestow the title of chieftain upon you. It is an honor, but so much more than that."

Terra was interested. "What else?"

"Orc chieftains are given an unrivaled level of respect. That respect falls upon the goblins as well. If you were to accept, you would be considered to be one of the strongest orcs, capable of commanding the respect and support of any orcs who are not under the Dark One's influence. Free orcs would have a duty to serve you if you were to ask. You could raise an army if you chose. An army of loyal warriors."

Terra thought about the prospect. An army of her own. What would she even do with an army? She hardly knew what was going on with the Dark One. But she knew she didn't need the details. She'd experienced firsthand what the Dark One was capable of: uprooting and destroying the lives of innocent people. "What do I have to do?"

Cire held up two fingers. "One, you have to survive. Second, you must allow me to give you the sign of a chieftain. It is simple, painless, and not nearly as awkward as a healing ceremony."

"What's the catch?"

"There is no catch. There are chieftains who choose to seclude themselves in the mountains, studying our old legends. Others raise families in the hill, waiting to be called to war. And there were others who were farmers until a time of need. But in those times, it is always the chieftain who decides. Nothing is expected from them, only desired. You would also receive a steward. Me. I will swear myself to you to be used as you see fit. As long as blood pumps through my veins, it would be yours."

Terra sighed as she thought it over. "You don't expect me to sit on my ass, do you?"

Cire smiled slyly. "I do not expect you to do anything other than what you have been doing."

"Fine, I'm in. Give me the sign."

Cire stood over Terra. He spat in his hand and rubbed the saliva across his palms and down his fingers. Then he pressed his hand to Terra's face, covering half of it. A warm, pleasant feeling flowed along Terra's skin. When Cire removed his hand, the sensation remained. Then Cire fetched her water bowl and handed it to her.

Terra looked down into the water. There was a fading brown imprint of Cire's hand.

"And now you are to be named. Terra, She Who Was Hewn from Orc Bone. Please say it back to me."

Terra repeated her title as she looked into the water bowl. As she spoke, Cire's handprint returned, resting on her face for a little bit before fading again. "When an orc sees that, they will understand your claim."

Terra felt like she should say something to commemorate the event, but she'd never been one for speeches. Instead, she simply said, "Thank you," and handed Cire the water bowl.

Cire took the bowl and placed it on the ground. "Now, all you must do is survive. What you choose to do with your authority is up to you, but I will always be by your side. I am sworn to you."

Terra nodded, uncertain of how to thank Cire for such a commitment. "So, how much more of that wine is there?"

Cire smiled mischievously. "Enough for a celebration for our new chieftain."

CHAPTER SIXTY

Anabelle was busy getting the invasion squad ready. She'd confirmed with Myrddin that once Abby and Creon had zeroed in on the specifics of what they needed for transportation to Terra, they were going to be moving out ASAP.

The pool of recruits and soldiers to pull from was significantly smaller than the last mission. There had been casualties and many injuries. Even beyond that, the soldiers were exhausted. Expecting them to be able to do another hadron collider jump and combat so quickly afterward was unfair and cruel. Yet that was exactly what Anabelle had done.

Blackwell and Naota showed up, both looking beyond haggard. Naota's usual animated and bizarre eccentricities were hardly noticeable as he sat slumped over, waiting to listen to whatever Anabelle had to say. Blackwell wasn't much better. His eyes were sunken in, deep black circles made it look as if his eyes were in a grave.

Fifteen more soldiers showed up to the meeting as well. That may have been all that could have spared. Anabelle didn't care about the number, though. The plan wasn't to wage an all-out battle at the arena. It was to slip in and out quickly. Pick up Terra, then get the hell out of there. That's what Anabelle explained to the soldiers. There weren't many questions.

Anabelle told them to all keep their comms on and be ready for any last-minute announcements. Then she dismissed them and went to take care of her own business. Roy hadn't been at the briefing. That had her worried.

The medbay was much emptier than when Anabelle had visited Roy and Abby earlier. Most of the wounded soldiers had been healed and discharged. They were probably recovering in their barracks. If the mission could have been postponed by a day, there was no doubt that the ranks would have been swollen with volunteers.

Since Terra's arena fights had been broadcast, there had been a groundswell of folks willing to take on the most dangerous missions. That had backfired today. Because so many people had volunteered, everyone had been run ragged.

Anabelle let herself into Roy's room. He was awake, propped up in his bed, reading a holopad. He looked up at Anabelle when she entered the room. "Doesn't look like you need any time to rest," he said gruffly.

Anabelle sat beside Roy and tried to speak as casually as she could. "It's the elf blood. When you live for hundreds of years, you start to appreciate how little you need to sleep."

"Wish I could say the same. Even with everything healed up, my body still feels like it got hit by a fucking tank. Sorry to say, I won't be joining you on the rescue mission. Myrddin won't let me get out of bed. Says if something happened to me, the dragonriders would be toast. First time I've ever been too important to endanger my life."

Anabelle laughed as she thought of how annoyed Roy must be. "So, what happened? I'm assuming you read our debriefing."

Roy put the holopad down and nodded. "Yeah, I got hit with the same crap. They sent a fucking drake after me. Thing damn near tore me to shreds. Still not sure how I ended up here, but living is living. Even if I got treated like a chew toy."

"Not a lot of people would have survived that. You should be proud of yourself. You're a resilient chew toy, at least."

"I'll make sure to put that on my dating profile."

They chuckled nervously. Anabelle avoided Roy's eyes. Even with all the flirting they'd done before, telling Abby she had feelings for Roy had made those feelings much more concrete. She was partially glad Roy wasn't coming on the mission. He looked too messed up for her to do anything other than worry about him. "How long are you going to be on bed rest?" she asked.

"At least a couple of days. I'm not gonna be having any fun for a bit, but that's all right. I'm thinking of it as a vacation. Shame that the only time I get a vacation is when I'm knocking on death's door. Glad that bastard didn't answer."

"I don't think anyone takes a vacation when you're in the middle of a war."

"Point taken. So, about that whole dinner date thing. You know I was just messing with you about that. I mean, not that I wouldn't, you know, want to go out or something some time, but I know how shit is. Sorry for bringing it up. That was unprofessional."

Anabelle waved away Roy's words as she leaned back in her chair. "Don't be stupid," she said, and she left it at that. She still wasn't sure what to make of the whole situation with Roy. Maybe if they weren't risking their lives every day. How did anyone even think of having a relationship when that kind of madness was going on? How the hell did Sarah and Kravis pull it off?

Anabelle looked around the room so she had something to do rather than just sit in awkward silence. "The drow who was in here. Where did she go?"

Roy picked the holopad back up and scrolled through it aimlessly. "Got to have a real nice, personal conversation with Myrddin soon as she woke up. Don't think the old man was happy about bringing in someone who was under the Dark One's control. Can't say I thought it was the smartest idea either. But the guys said they checked her for a chip, and it was burned out, so guess that means she's okay."

Anabelle didn't know where she stood on the topic. She thought it was extremely dangerous to be dealing with anyone who had ever been under the Dark One's control. How did you tell if someone was not in control of their own mind? The drow could easily be a double agent. At the same time, anyone who'd experienced what the Dark One was responsible for was a needed ally.

On top of that, Abby was pretty certain Persephone had been the assassin who was meant to kill Abby.

Either way, that decision was beyond Anabelle's pay grade. That didn't mean she couldn't find out. She hit her comm, patching to Myrddin. "Hey, where's the drow?" she asked.

Myrddin answered instantly. "I assumed you would want to speak with her. She's been provided a room for the time being."

"You think she's actually free of the Dark One's influence?"

"We put her through several tests. Passed every one. If she is under his mind control, it is a sort we haven't seen yet. I believe that is enough reason to keep her close."

Anabelle laughed. Myrddin was always thinking of the long game. He didn't ever seem to be caught up in small details. Even if the drow was under the Dark One's control, he saw this as a chance to learn something. Maybe something that could tip the tide of the war in their favor. "Can she receive visitors?" Anabelle asked.

"She would no doubt appreciate some."

Anabelle clicked off her comm and stood. "I'm gonna go introduce myself to our new guest," she said.

Roy had returned to his usual stoic self. "Sounds good. Let me know if you find anything interesting. I'll see you in a little bit. Be safe out there."

Anabelle reached down and squeezed Roy's hand. "Get some rest. And I will."

CHAPTER SIXTY-ONE

Persephone was kept on the far side of the barracks, away from the other soldiers and staff. Anabelle assumed it was a security precaution. If Persephone turned out to still be under the Dark One's influence, if she were to try something, she'd be a good ways from anyone to harm.

Anabelle knocked on the door twice and waited for an answer. The door creaked open slightly, and a pair of dark brown eyes stared out of the crack between the door and its frame. "Hello," Persephone squeaked.

"My name is Anabelle. Just wanted to stop by and say hi. Welcome you to HQ. Do you mind if I come in?"

Persephone opened the door wider and retreated farther into the room. It was hard to see her as the assassin that had been sent to dispatch Abby. The drow who was in front of her was a mousy, scared thing. She didn't have any of the drow confidence Anabelle had often seen among Persephone's people.

Anabelle sat at the desk and tried to make herself look less intimidating. It was something she'd grown accustomed to in her previous position, but it had been so long since she'd had tried to diminish herself, she wasn't sure if she was still capable of it.

Apparently, her efforts were appreciated because Persephone relaxed. Her cool demeanor softened, and she forced a smile, her sharp incisors glinting. She held her right arm close to her body as if it had been injured. "You okay?" Anabelle asked.

Persephone followed Anabelle's eye line to her arm and laughed nervously. "Oh, this? Yeah, I'm all right. So, you just stopped by to say hi?"

"Not entirely. I haven't ever had a chance to talk to anyone who used to be under the Dark One's mind control. If it isn't too early, I'd like to ask you a few questions. I know you haven't had time to rest, but the more information we have, the better."

Persephone didn't hesitate to answer. "I'll answer whatever you want. Anything to help."

"Okay, so, I guess first, how does it feel? Are you in control of yourself? Are you hearing voices, like him commanding you or anything like that?"

Persephone thought for a while before answering. "No, it's nothing like that. It's like…almost like falling in love. You have these feelings for someone and you don't know why, but they keep getting stronger. Then it stops being like love and becomes something else, but you always feel like yourself. Sort of. I rarely felt like I was doing something I didn't want to."

"What changed when you met Abby?"

Persephone looked as if she were genuinely perplexed. "I don't know. When she was talking to me, I felt something…and I didn't want to kill her. It wasn't a whole lot. There was just a moment when I felt like I actually wanted something again, and it wasn't to hurt her."

"Hm. And then what happened?"

"Then that feeling went away, almost as quickly as I had it. But Abby did something. She broke the microchip the Dark One had put in me, and then I woke up."

Anabelle had suspected something like that. She had seen Abby and Martin disable the microchip of an orc in the arena. This was the second time she'd broken someone out of the Dark One's control—this time, in a much more positive way.

It wasn't feasible to think that Abby could do that with each of the Dark One's servants, but if it could be used on one person, there was the potential to develop something that could work on a large scale. It would take time, but it was an idea. "Thank you," she said. "That's it. You get some rest."

Anabelle had stood to leave when Persephone jumped up as well. "Wait, what's going to happen to me? Am I a prisoner, or something?"

"No, you aren't. I don't know what happens to you now. We aren't going to keep you here against your will. I think you're the only person who can answer that. You should take your time and think about it. Appreciate being able to make your own decisions."

"Where's Abby?"

Anabelle sighed. She recognized that tone of voice. She'd heard it in Abby as well. "She's coming on a mission with me. She should be back within a few hours."

Persephone hung her head as nodded. "Oh, okay. I understand."

Before she left, Anabelle said, "I'll let her know you were asking about her."

The orc guards led Terra down the hallway for what felt like the last time. They had come for Terra in her sleep, pulled her out of bed before she could utter a word. Her weapons had been thrust upon her with little ceremony.

As Terra was pushed down the hall, she stumbled, and one of the orcs grabbed her arm to keep her from falling. When she returned to her feet, she leaned against the wall. "I don't need your fucking help," she spat as she straightened.

"You'd do well not to anger us, human. Just because you've been doing well doesn't mean—"

"I am Terra, She Who was Hewn from Orc Bone," she said quietly, her face glowing with the mark of the chieftain.

The orcs stopped walking for a moment, perhaps remembering the heritage deep within them that had been covered by the Dark

One's influence. They looked at each other as if to say, *"This was something that we once understood. This a sign that bore meaning to us in a distant and far off time."* Then the moment of reflection was gone. Dried up as if it were never there.

Yet there was one orc whose face still looked as if he remembered. He walked slower than the others, trailing behind Terra, his face reflecting thoughts that were difficult to define.

Terra did not notice the orc. The only thing she paid attention to was the light at the far end of the hallway. It reminded her of those old stories about not going toward the light when you were dying. You always avoided the light. Terra had applied that to all aspects of her life in the past.

The orcs and Terra stood at the end of the hallway, silently staring at the gates ahead of them. After enough time passed, the orc who continued to have a twinkle in his eye turned to Terra. "This is meant to be your last battle. I am sorry that it will end like this, but I hope you bring glory to yourself and all others like you."

Something about the way the orc spoke put Terra at ease. He didn't behave like the other orcs. She thought it might be just in her head, but she felt like he was at least trying to continue being an orc. That could have just been wishful thinking.

Terra stared at the stone gates in front of her, wondering what was behind them. She'd survived more than she was capable of since she'd arrived at the arena. Who were these assholes to think this match was going to be her last? She would decide what was her last. Today wasn't going to be an exception. "This isn't my last fight," she said.

None of the orcs responded. She repeated herself if only to hear it one more time.

As Terra waited for the gates to open, Abby's tracker landed behind her right ear. "We're coming for you," the girl said through the tracker.

Terra's heart raced, and she had to hide her smile. She had forgotten there were people outside the ring trying to help her, trying to bring her back home. They hadn't forgotten, even if she had. "All you have to do is stay alive for a little bit. We're coming soon."

Terra showed no outward sign of appreciation, but on the inside, she was screaming with joy. This wasn't going to be her last fight, but it was going to be a good one.

CHAPTER SIXTY-TWO

The extraction party gathered at the hadron collider around two. Abby had only just informed Anabelle that Terra was being taken to what was billed as her final fight. She'd also drawn up a statement of intention that was emailed to the vast majority of news outlets throughout the world, letting them know what Terra was about to experience.

They would still have the option of viewing the fight, but Abby believed broadcasting it posed ethical questions she didn't feel comfortable assuming about others.

Abby would have preferred not to have broadcast the fight. She wasn't sure if this was all going to work out as planned. If something went wrong, she would basically be making an intergalactic snuff film. That wasn't something she'd be proud of.

Anabelle had been the one to suggest leaving the decision up to the media. Whatever they decided, it would be on their heads. She believed the world should see it like back in the good old days of propaganda, the only difference being that this war actually threatened to destroy all of humanity. This wasn't a question of being too sensitive for the viewers. If people didn't see what was happening, there was a good chance they would stop caring.

Anabelle was quite cunning in this regard. It was something Abby respected, but it also kind of scared her. If such a kind and sweet person had the capacity to ignore the value of human life for their own gain, what else was she capable of? And was that going to be expected of her at some point?

As Abby pondered the end product of her time with HQ and its ramifications, the other soldiers assembled. Blackwell and Naota were speaking quietly together. They seemed to have quickly formed a bond of friendship. Anyone who didn't look closely would have been confused. Blackwell seemed to be annoyed with Naota, and Naota confused by Blackwell.

Yet they searched each other out during the day, and there was often laughter between the two, but at what, no one knew.

The seven other recruits and soldiers were folks Abby had not seen before. She wondered how the other soldiers who had been in her squad were doing now. She would have assumed more would have come along. But few, if any, of those soldiers were fused with nanobots and an AI on a genetic level. The humans probably needed a lot more rest.

That was the first time Abby had ever thought of it like that. "The humans." As if she weren't one of them. Maybe she wasn't anymore.

Creon prepared the hadron collider as he and Anabelle explained the way human physics and strength worked on other worlds throughout the nine realms. Anabelle said they were going to get an increase in strength and endurance, but it was dependent on factors that weren't always easy to understand. Even though Terra didn't seem to have any military or weight training, she had managed to kill a balrog.

Creon and Anabelle suggested the recruits not assume they would be that strong. A proper estimate would be Captain America, not the Hulk. She asked if the soldiers would prefer to go in with exosuits.

Blackwell suggested without suits, citing that the suits were only designed to help them compensate. Even with all the upgrades Abby had performed, there was still a chance they would just slow them down. If they could hold their own without the exosuits, they should be abandoned.

There were no disagreements, though Naota made sure to point out that he'd never used an exosuit, nor had he needed one. At those words, Blackwell looked as if he were ready to punch Naota. The bickering between the two quickly dissipated.

Once the soldiers were briefed, Anabelle turned her attention to Blackwell and Naota, speaking to them privately. As the final preparations were being put into place, Abby walked back and forth, wishing she had something to do other than think about how badly everything could go.

She had formulated nearly the entirety of the plan. Creon and Martin had helped a lot with the math she had to learn for the formulas, but Abby had done most of the work. There was a chance that they wouldn't be transported anywhere, that the frequencies Abby had tuned the collider to simply weren't strong enough.

Or their coordinates could be wrong, and Abby could end up sending the entire squad into space. That would be a great way to die —suffocating while being reminded you weren't nearly as smart as you or anyone else thought you were.

Abby's favorite option of what could happen was getting to the arena and not being able to get back.

Abby had never had to deal with the fear of failure before. She'd always understood that sometimes you failed and sometimes you didn't, but she'd never faced stakes as high as these. Failure meant death. Maybe not for her, but for someone else.

"Hey," a voice said from behind Abby.

Abby turned. Persephone was standing behind her, cradling her tentacle. Persephone's biomechanical aspects seemed to have disappeared. Except for that, she looked like a normal drow. "I heard you were all meeting down here," she said. "I wasn't sure if you were going to be here. I just wanted to thank you, you know, for helping me."

The solid lump in Abby's throat kept her from speaking. The only sound that came out was a loud squeak. When she tried again, the sound was sort of a squeal, the muffled sound a mouse makes when it has no other option. Finally, Abby managed to swallow and choked out, "You're welcome."

The human and the drow stood there awkwardly, each seemingly afraid to meet the other's eyes, finding anything and everything else to look at. Finally, the drow leaned forward and kissed Abby on the cheek. "Thanks," she said again before turning to run away.

Anabelle's voice rang out above the clamor of the area. "Hey!" she shouted. "You here because you're combat-ready?"

Persephone stopped in her tracks, turned, and pointed at herself. "Me?"

"You're the only person who doesn't seem to have a reason for being here otherwise."

Persephone looked down at her tentacle. "I don't know if it's safe," she said finally.

"All right, if you're not feeling—"

"For any of you."

Anabelle, along with everyone else in the hangar, stopped what they were doing and turned to Persephone. "Not that I would... It's just, I can get out of control easily," the drow said.

Abby had expected Anabelle to call an end to the conversation, but for some reason, Anabelle smiled widely as she stepped closer to Persephone. "What kind of control?"

Persephone looked around uncomfortably, then peeked around Anabelle to see if Abby could help her. Abby shrugged, just as uncomfortable as Persephone. "It's not quite magic that I use," Persephone said. "And I...kinda lose myself...in a fight."

Anabelle clapped her hands together excitedly. "Perfect. You cover Abby. Stick to her like glue. It's imperative that Abby remains alive. That goes for the rest of you, too. None of us is getting home if Abby doesn't stay alive. Got it?"

There was a chorus of hurrahs as Persephone stepped closer to Abby, then the other soldiers started to make their way toward the hadron collider's teleportation pad. "Creon, send us through," Anabelle shouted.

There was a sudden discharge of energy, the air growing hot, electricity snapping as the collider roared to life. And then they were gone, leaving Creon alone, staring at the space Terra's final hope had once occupied, praying to his gods that they would all return safely.

CHAPTER SIXTY-THREE

The gates separating Terra from the arena rose. She inhaled slowly, trying to understand her mortality. Never one for dwelling on such things, the thoughts passed through her quickly and without much regard to their enormity. For the first time, she understood the finality and frailty of life in a fashion many philosophers had spent lifetimes attempting to discover.

One of the orcs pushed Terra, and she stumbled out into the arena. There were even more orcs in the crowd than before. It looked as if additional seats had been built into the stands for the spectacle of her death. She felt ironically flattered as she walked out into the pit.

Terra's opponent had not been released yet. She was curious to know what the Game Master thought was going to be strong enough to take her down. Apparently, trolls, balrogs, and whatever the hell she had fought last time weren't nearly enough for her. Maybe it was time they busted out the dragons.

The crowd's cheers were deafening. Terra could hardly hear herself think. Not that there was much to think about. Until her foe made themselves visible, nothing else mattered.

As Terra positioned her shield and *katar*, there was a popping sound near her. Suddenly the air got hot, filling with energy that made Terra think this was going to be the attack. The Game Master was probably just going to zap her with a cannon from outer space or something. It would definitely make for a good light show.

Instead, a portal opened in the middle of the arena. It looked as if reality were folding in on itself, showing that there was another world beneath the world which she regularly interacted with.

The crowd went wild at this sudden development. When they saw what stepped out of the portal, they instantly fell silent.

Anabelle, Abby, Persephone, and the rest of the rescue squad stood in the middle of the arena. They all looked confused by their appearance in the fighting pit.

Abby whirled, staring around her as if she'd taken a wrong turn on a road. "No, this ain't where we're supposed to come out," she shouted. "Where's the Dark Gate? This is the arena."

Anabelle grabbed Abby and gave her two quick shakes. "Get your shit together. We're not where we're supposed to be, all right? Where are we?"

Abby looked around until her eyes fell on Terra, who was standing a little ways behind them. "Holy shit, we're in the arena!"

Terra watched the newcomers with a sense of confusion. She was fairly certain these weren't her opponents. They didn't seem like they'd been prepared to fight. Then Terra recognized one of the voices. "Abby?"

Abby waved at Terra before running to her and throwing her arms around her.

Terra was taken aback by the hug from what seemed like a complete stranger, but it felt good to be acknowledged. She hugged Abby back. "Yeah, that's me."

Abby looked as if she were ready to cry, and her voice trembled. "We were coming to bust you out, but something went wrong. We weren't supposed to come into the arena with you."

A voice boomed over the silence of the crowd. Up on the podium, observing the entirety of arena, was the Game Master, strapped to the body of a massive orc. "Ah, you've finally arrived, Earthlings," the Game Master shouted. "We've been watching your progress. The hacking and tech you've been using leaves a very unique energy signature."

The middle of the arena opened, and a platform rose from the crack in the ground. On top of the platform was a small EMP bomb. It lit up for a second and then fired, sending an electromagnetic pulse throughout the arena.

Abby's drones, along with her tracker, short-circuited and fell to the ground.

"Now that we're certain you won't be leaving before you've been given a proper greeting, allow me to introduce you to your deaths."

On the other side of the arena, the gates rose. A horde of orcs marched out. They were followed by four balrogs and a cadre of goblins. Then there was a sudden roar, followed by another, even more high-pitched and fierce.

From the darkness stepped two full-grown red dragons. They both stood at least twelve feet at the shoulder, shooting fire from their gullets as they reared up on their back legs, screeching and flapping their wings.

Terra took a step back, stricken with fear at the sight of the dragons. She was backing away, but the slim elf with the ice-cold eyes didn't seem to be fazed by their odds.

Anabelle turned back to Terra. "You're the human we came to save," she said. "Looks like we're going to have to fight our way out of this. You in?"

"Of course," Terra said without even thinking.

"All right, angels," Anabelle cried. "Let's get ready to kick some serious ass."

Abby chuckled as she shook her head. "That's a much better name than SWARRMT," she muttered.

"Wait, what is?"

"Dark Gate Angels. Like Charlie's Angels except, you know, not as dumb. That should have been our name."

Anabelle laughed. It was a hearty sound, as if she were unaware of the dragons, balrogs, and a small orc army. "Holy shit, you're right. Well, fuck it, that's our name." She raised her hand and pointed at the

Game Master, shouting, "You hear that, fuckface? You're about to get seventeen new assholes, courtesy of the Dark Gate Angels."

The Game Master laughed, his voice echoing throughout the arena. "Very well, angels. Let the games begin."

End of Part 2

PART III

CHAPTER SIXTY-FOUR

The arena had stood for thousands of years. It was one of the first the orcs built when they began the steady expansion of their realm. Each arena was built to be a testament to orcish values.

First among all was resilience. An orc who could easily be put in the ground was hardly an orc. An orc who died on its knees couldn't be called an orc.

Secondly, strength. If it could hit you, then you could hit it harder.

Thirdly, wisdom—an attribute that many did not apply to the orcs for a long period of time. But through watching their ways of warfare, you could discern the amount of wisdom that ran through orcish culture. They were measured by their fights. Nothing was gambled. Everything was multiplied. The nine realms had worried what would have happened if the orcs had ever grown discontent with fighting each other.

Anabelle, Abby, and Terra stood in this ancient arena where orcs had fought until they achieved a level of praise and worship most cultures only give to their gods. The three women had each been fighting their own battles to come to this place.

Behind them stood an army of old and new allies. Blackwell, a soldier of Middang3ard's HQ, who had proved himself on the battlefield multiple times. Naota, a former security guard at an amusement park who was conscripted due to an obscene and unnatural amount of heart. And Persephone, a young drow recently removed from the Dark One's influence. There were also ten other soldiers, the only operatives who weren't totally broken from the last attempted invasion.

Across from the rescue party that had been sent to save Terra was the opposition: enough orcs to be considered a horde, four balrogs, a smattering of goblins, and two full-grown red dragons.

The groups stared at each other from across the arena, neither ready to take the first step into battle. It was obvious why Anabelle and her Dark Angels would be hesitant to start the fight. They were heavily outnumbered. Yet their opponents seemed just as wary to throw themselves into the fray.

Anabelle turned from staring down her enemies. She had the look of a commander in her eyes, a look she must have only just discovered, for it wavered for a moment before righting itself. "We're not going to win this if we go at it like a bunch of idiots. I'll take care of the orcs. Abby and Persephone, I want you on one of the dragons. Terra, I want you on the other. Blackwell—"

Both Abby and Persephone interrupted Anabelle with fairly similar declarations of disbelief. Anabelle didn't hear them out, raising her hand to silence them both. "Abby, I know you can do this, and if Persephone was supposed to be strong enough to kill you, she should be able to do this as well. Any other objections?"

Anabelle waited for Terra to say something, but the human remained silent, only staring at the dragon she had chosen, sizing the creature up. "All right," the elf continued, "Blackwell, Naota, and the rest of you, the balrogs are yours. That sound doable?"

Naota pulled a pair of sunglasses from his pocket and put them on. "Not only doable but feasible."

Blackwell scoffed, his eyes full of irritation as his upper lip curled. "Those are the same thing, you ass."

Naota whipped around, pulling his two trusty tasers out. "Are we going to have a go at this right now? Because I'm itching for a rippin'."

Anabelle stepped between the two and shook her head. "Could you two please keep your shit together for a minute and focus on what we need to do?"

Naota nodded, sheathing his tasers. "Just kidding, boss. Juicing up the morale, that's all."

"That better be what you were doing. Now, who the hell else is sick of waiting around for those assholes to bring the fucking fight?"

Anabelle whipped around, drawing all of the manna in her body and pushing it down to her feet. She didn't have time to worry about the rest of her squad. Taking out the orcs was going to require her complete and utter focus. She sprinted forward, quickly closing the gap between the orc horde and her.

The orcs hadn't even had time to respond by the time Anabelle was in front of them. She was too fast. Anabelle tossed off a little bit of manna from her hands, letting it drop on the ground as what could only have been described as an energy mine. She wove through the horde, tossing off manna here and there as the orcs began to draw their weapons.

Anabelle ran around an orc as a balrog lunged and cracked its whip against her chest, sending her flying, screaming in pain. She hit the ground, rolled twice, and was on her feet, taking the pain, pulling the fire into herself, and converting the dead energy into manna. Then she clenched her fists and exploded her manna mines.

Orcs went flying through the air as energy ripped through their ranks. Anabelle wasn't sure of how many she took out, but she didn't think it was a lot. It was mostly a flashy attack to draw their attention, to challenge them, to let them know this wasn't their fight.

The Middang3ard Marines jumped into action, drawing out their weapons and leaping toward their targets, already acquainted with their newfound strength and agility. They were right to leave behind the exosuits. First among them, although he was not a Marine, was Naota. He flung himself forward as if he were made of nothing, heading toward a balrog with his tasers.

Blackwell wasn't far behind him, shouting, "You idiot! You can't fight a balrog with tasers! That thing is going to rip you to shreds!"

Naota wasn't listening. He slammed into one of the balrogs, scampered up its back, and held his tasers high while screaming, "For humanity!" He plunged his crackling tasers into the balrog's neck.

The balrog screamed in pain, its body jerking wildly as it foamed at the mouth.

Blackwell stopped in his tracks, his jaw nearly touching the ground. "Well, I'll be damned!"

Another balrog snapped Naota on the back with his whip, sending the human flying through the air as he yelled, "Don't let them pass, Blackwell! Don't let them fucking pass!"

Naota skidded across the ground as Blackwell fired his plasma rifle at the balrog that had attacked Naota. Behind him, the other Marines charged.

Terra, Abby, and Persephone were the only ones who hadn't moved. Abby was frozen with indecision. She couldn't take her eyes off the dragon. The same could be said of Terra but for different reasons. Persephone, on the other hand, still stared at her cradled right tentacle. "Are you ready to do this?" she asked Abby.

Abby swallowed hard and cleared her throat. "Uh, guess I have to be." The nanobots slid from her pores, covering her skin in a sleek metallic coating. She floated into the air, her hands burning with energy.

Persephone nodded, closed her eyes, and convulsed as she leaned forward, the skin of her right arm splitting open, dozens of tentacles spilling out in a sloppy mess. White light burned in her eyes. "Then let's go," she growled before running toward the dragon.

As Abby and Persephone headed toward their dragon, Terra looked at her shield and *katar*. "Well, that makes this underwhelming," she muttered to herself. She took off after the others.

Abby fired two blasts from her plasma cannon at one of the dragons as she flew past it. The dragon shot a burst of fire, scattering the energy blasts. It flapped its heavy wings once and rose into the air, nearly closing the distance between itself and Abby.

On the ground, Persephone launched her tentacles, wrapping

them around one of the dragon's legs, then pulled herself into the air and landed on its back.

The dragon rolled, spewing fire at Abby and anything else that was remotely close. She swerved out of the way, dropping to fly under the dragon's stomach. She fired shot after shot of energy at the dragon's soft underbelly.

Roars of pain tore through the air as the dragon slashed at Abby with its front claws. The claws hit Abby hard in the chest, sending her careening away.

Persephone reached out with her tentacles and snagged Abby from the air, pulling her onto the dragon. Once Abby was safe, Persephone raised one of her tentacles, speaking in a language that sounded both dead and dreamy. Her tentacles multiplied and began to wrap around the dragon's body.

Abby started firing into the dragon's backside.

The dragon screeched and rolled again, this time diving toward the ground. It hit on its back, slamming both Persephone and Abby into the arena's sands.

Terra had walked over to meet her dragon head-on. The dragon must have had the same idea. It slowly slunk toward the human, smoke rising from its nose and mouth. The two circled each other.

The dragon loosed a jet of flame, and Terra threw her shield up to avoid being burned. Once the fire stopped, Terra ran toward the dragon, brandishing her *katar* and wondering how anyone with a sword and a shield could beat a dragon.

Terra threw herself into the air, her *katar* raised high. The dragon shot another blast of fire, but Terra whipped her shield up in time, managing to block most of the fire. What remained singed her skin. She connected with the dragon nonetheless, driving her *katar* into the dragon's snout.

First blood had been drawn. The dragon slashed at Terra, throwing her to the ground. She didn't stay on her back long, leaping to her feet, sprinting toward the dragon, and slashing at its front legs.

The dragon pounced on her, its open mouth coming down fast, trying to bite the girl in half. Terra raised her shield, blocking the dragon's lunge. Then she dropped her *katar*, grabbed the dragon by the nose, and pulled as hard as she could.

The crowd went wild, cheering and shouting, "Not-a-Male" as Terra wrestled the dragon to the ground. The dragon frantically tried to back away, its strength matched by Terra's. The two were locked together, and the crowd had never seen or heard of anything such as this happening before in the history of dragons or humanity. No human had ever wrestled a dragon to the ground.

Terra, not wanting to lose any of her momentum, pushed hard, causing the dragon to lose its balance. Then she raised her fist and brought it down on the beast's skull.

The sound of Terra's blow was loud enough that those nearby, orc and human alike, stopped in their tracks. They stood silent, watching the dragon stumble as if it had been hit with a lightning bolt. Terra didn't let up. She picked up her *katar* and ran after the dragon, slashing its face open and blinding its left eye.

The dragon reared up on its hind legs and touched its paw to its eye. It looked down at the blood, then in a low voice that poured through everyone in the arena, said, "Ah, the taste of my blood. I had forgotten such a thing."

The dragon roared, its violent screech sending chills down the spines of all who beheld its awful power. Fire burst over its scales as if hell had been unleashed. The flaming red dragon pounced on Terra, clasped her in its claws, and took to the air, spewing fire as it flew.

Anabelle took advantage of the momentary surprise of the orcs and the rest of those in the arena to launch her own attack. She concentrated on the flow of water, saw it weaving through streams, through rivers, while also focusing her mind on veins of lightning one sees in the sky during a thunderstorm.

She felt her body lose its consistency and she pushed her manna forward, a dazzling display of electricity and water moving as if it had will, spreading through the throng of orcs and goblins, shocking many to death and leaving others spasming, their teeth locked.

Even with the orcs that Anabelle had just dispatched, this wasn't going to cut it. There were too many of them. "Outnumbered" didn't do justice to the balance of this fight. She was going to have to figure something else out very fast.

A mere hundred feet away, Persephone and Abby were struggling with the dragon that had attempted to crush them. Persephone's tentacles were still trying to wrap around the dragon. The dragon suddenly rose to its hind legs, grabbed Persephone's tentacles, and bit down on them.

Persephone screamed in pain as she fell forward, clutching her wounded appendages.

Abby flew out from behind the dragon, constructed a plasma cannon on her shoulder, and fired at the dragon, who nearly tumbled over from the blast. Then she flew to Persephone, scooped the drow up in her arms, and flew to a section of the arena that wasn't overrun with battle. "Are you okay?"

Persephone nodded as she gritted her teeth. The torn tentacles fell out as new smaller tentacles pushed through the open wounds. "Just need a minute," she managed.

Abby looked up to see the red dragon charging toward them. "Not sure if we're gonna get a minute."

Suddenly, the ground burst into flames. A red dragon toppled from the sky, crashing into the ground. It held Terra in its claws, trying to crush her, as Terra hacked at the dragon's chest with her *katar*. They were both covered in blood. When the dragon hit the ground, it threw Terra into the stone wall, which cracked. The dragon got up, swaying as it spat blood.

Terra picked herself up off the ground, hardly able to get to her feet.

The crowd chanted, "Not-a-Male!" over and over.

Terra threw her shield to the ground and slammed her fist to her chest, shouting, "My name is Terra, She Who was Hewn from Orc Bone. My name is Terra!" As she declared her name, the orcish hand-print marking her as a chieftain appeared on her face.

The crowd grew silent as the flaming red dragon launched a jet of fire at the girl, who threw herself to the side to avoid the flames. Terra ran toward the dragon, moving faster than the dragon could turn. She slammed into its side, forcing it onto its back.

Terra ran the length of the dragon's torso, dragging her *katar* down its belly and cutting it open from stomach to neck. She drove her *katar* deep into its throat before moving to its face, then cupped both hands together and drove them into the creature's skull.

The thud of the impact rang out over the entire arena.

Terra stood over the dragon, which lay unmoving. She raised her hands again and slammed them into the dragon's head once more, then keeled over, unconscious on the dragon's chest, which still rose and fell.

Anabelle was making her way out of the throng of orcs. She saw Terra fall, watched as Abby and Persephone fled from the red dragon, witnessed Naota and Blackwell and the Marines fighting a failing battle against the balrogs.

We aren't losing, Anabelle thought. *But we sure as hell aren't winning.*

Anabelle's comm suddenly came to life. Sarah said loud and clear, "Hey! Got an idea for some backup, but I'm going to need Abby's help, all right? Can you get her away from all this?"

"How the hell am I going to do that? Can you see this shit?"

"Hold on." She called up something on her HUD. "Plasma batteries installed. OK, now the whole world can see this. What about those catacombs? Aren't there like a hundred people in there or something? Sounds like enough good fighters to me."

Anabelle thought it over for a second. It didn't matter if it was a good idea. It was an idea. "I'll get Abby, then you two figure out how to help us the fuck out."

CHAPTER SIXTY-FIVE

Back on Earth, Sarah and Kravis stood beside Creon as the goblin ran through frequency after frequency, trying to pinpoint how the Game Master had been able to figure out where the Dark Gate Angels and their troops had come from. That information was extremely dangerous in the hands of one of the Dark One's lieutenants. It would spell doom for Middang3ard HQ.

It was obvious by now that the Dark One's forces greatly outweighed those of any planet's resistance, Earth included. It would be best to keep locational information away from the Dark One.

Creon also had another issue on his hands. The Angels and their squad were being overrun in the arena. The only noticeable victory had been Terra managing to knock out the dragon, but since she had passed out as well, it looked to be more of a draw. There had to be something Creon could use to help the Angels. Otherwise, this was going to be the dreaded snuff film Abby had been so reluctant to broadcast.

Kravis climbed onto a chair while Sarah continued to pace. Kravis pointed at one of the frequencies on the list of thousands Creon was reading through. "That's my homeworld," Kravis said.

Creon absentmindedly nodded and muttered, "Yes, well, we can't get reinforcements from there, can we?"

"But we could get them from somewhere else," Sarah suggested. "Like I did earlier. We could open the Dark Gate we weren't able to use earlier. You could transport Kravis and me back to the gnomish world with coordinates to where we have other troops on other worlds. We could piggyback, back and forth, until we bring them all to the arena."

Creon thought it over for a second. The plan sounded like it would work in practice. The only problem was making sure they could access the Dark Gate at the arena. Everything else was solid. "Go, start prepping the collider right now. Get credentials from Myrddin so you aren't questioned," the goblin said. "I need to get in touch with Abby."

Sarah and Kravis hurried from the room while Creon hit his comm, pinging Abby. "Abby, I have a plan to help you all, but I'm going to need you to do something for me. I'm sending you a copy of the energy signature of the Dark Gate in the arena. I need you to get to it and activate it."

Abby was flying circles around the red dragon, firing when she got a chance, narrowly avoiding the jets of fire that flew past her. She'd received Creon's message and said she was going to do what she could but had no idea how she was going to get the dragon to stop paying attention to her.

Persephone was trying to keep the dragon from getting off the ground with her tentacles, but Abby already knew Persephone was not going to be able to take the dragon on all by herself. However, she had to slip away somehow. "Martin, you remember how you took out Persephone's microchip?"

Martin answered instantly. "It's a sweet idea and all kid, but you're not going to be able to destroy everyone's chip and set them free. That's going to take way more power than you have."

"What if it was just to disrupt them for a bit? Five to ten minutes. Do I have enough juice for that?"

Martin thought about it for a few seconds before answering, "We could build a construct, put it in the middle of the arena, and let it go. You could handle that, but you would need a little bit of time to recover. Probably as much time as it would take for their chips to come back on."

"That will have to do. All right, let's do it."

"Already seventy-five percent done. Just get to the middle of the arena."

Abby didn't waste any time peeling away from the dragon, who seemed confused that Abby suddenly stopped attacking. She made her way to the middle, weaving in and out of the orc horde that Anabelle was thinning out. In there, Abby knelt as nanobots rolled off her hand and into the sand, building up and forming what looked like a small tuning fork.

Martin said, "Just tell me when to set it off."

Abby rocketed off toward Terra, who was still passed out on top of the dragon. She landed and shook Terra awake. "Terra! You have to get up. We need you."

Terra began to rouse, then she jerked up suddenly, looking around as if she had forgotten where she was. When she recognized Abby, she calmed down. "What...what do you need?"

"We need you to go into the tunnels and bring out the other fighters. They'll listen to you. They respect you. Otherwise, we're not going to win this."

Terra looked around the battlefield. Even though some of the orcs and a dragon had fallen, they were not winning the fight. "What are you going to do?"

"I'm going to try to bring even more."

"Let's do it."

Abby nodded and helped Terra stand as she told Martin to fire the microchip scrambler.

An invisible wave of energy flooded through the arena. The dragon and balrogs stopped in their tracks for a second. Then they started back up, fighting as if they were drunk. Still dangerous, but not as much as before. The orcs didn't seem to be affected.

Abby didn't have time to figure out why the orcs seemed immune. She had bigger fish to fry.

Terra returned to her feet, stumbling at first but then steadying, and headed toward the locked gate to the hall where the other fighters were. She kicked it, and the gate buckled under her strength.

Abby was following close behind since her systems were recovering. She might need time to return to fighting mode, but that didn't mean she couldn't move. At the end of the hall, she split off from Terra, going another direction down the halls, following the map she had made from the first time her tracker had followed Terra. She stopped at the room with the Dark Gate and blasted the door open. She reached out, and electric tendrils slipped from her fingers and connected to the Dark Gate.

Martin whistled to himself as he turned the Dark Gate on.

It roared to life, glowing an unearthly purple. "Creon, I got the Gate on. It's all you guys now."

CHAPTER SIXTY-SIX

S arah and Kravis were back on the gnomish world in no time. As soon as Creon relayed that Abby had managed to turn the arena's Dark Gate on, Sarah and Kravis had departed. Time was of the essence. They were making a huge gamble that the Game Master wasn't prepared for another attack. It made sense. The orc seemed smug enough about his first trick.

Overconfidence was the best trait to take advantage of. If Sarah and Kravis worked quickly enough, they'd be able to make sure Game Master never felt anything like it again.

The Dark Gate on the gnomish world opened. Sarah had expected to see Bim-Bop, but he was nowhere to be seen. Maybe the little guy managed to escape after all. That or someone let him out. Either way, he was gone.

Sarah and Kravis stepped through. They had held onto the frequencies that the Gates used just in case. Neither of them had thought they would be useful, but Sarah was glad Kravis had suggested it. Now they got to work setting up the Dark Gates to go to the three different places they needed.

First was the arena. That was the first Gate they opened.

Next was the Red Lion in the Shire of Middang3ard. It was the

MERC bar. There were a handful of powerful fighters there, but Myrddin had recommended the Mundanes specifically. Sarah had heard the name here and there but that was about it.

Third was the Wasp's Nest, the dragonriders' HQ. Boundless was the name of the team Myrddin recommended there. Roy vouched for them as well. Sarah hadn't heard anything about them but figured Myrddin and Roy knew best.

Kravis entered all the frequencies. According to the monitor, the Dark Gates were connected. "I'll go to the legendary MERC HQ on Middang3ard, the Red Lion," Sarah said. "You grab the dragonriders. We'll funnel them straight through the Gates."

"Help me with this one," Kravis said as he tried to push his Gate closer to the Gate leading to the arena. "If they're going to be bringing dragons, we're gonna want to make sure we're going straight from portal to portal. I don't want to end up with five dragons in the room."

Sarah gave Kravis a hand, and when they were satisfied, she jumped through her Gate.

At the Red Lion, Suzuki, the leader of the Mundanes, a nerdy kid with mousy brown hair, serious eyes, and an impressive number of small battle scars, sat at a table with three other humans, drinking mead over a game of cards.

Sandy, a young woman with long black hair, sat to his right. She was absentmindedly circling her wand around her hand of cards, making them dance. Sandy radiated coldness until Beth, a young woman across from her, rolled up a napkin and threw it at her. "Earth to Sandy," she said. "It's your turn to draw."

Beth looked to be the opposite of Sandy. She hardly had any hair, and her face was as vibrant and alive as if she could see the special spark that all things held. If Sandy held herself as if she valued her frailty, Beth looked like she was challenging everyone around her.

At Beth's side was a large teenage boy with the pockmarked face of someone who had once had very severe acne. He was the fittest of the humans, looking as if he'd stepped out of an ad campaign for the original Dungeons and Dragons campaign poster. Stew voraciously ate and drank while he talked loudly.

In the middle of the table, a purple portal opened, dropping Sarah into the middle of the Mundanes' card game. She plopped down on the table, spilling mead and sending cards flying everywhere.

Stew was the first one up, ax drawn, shouting, "What the fuck is this shit?" before bringing his ax down on the table.

Sarah threw herself to the side, barely avoiding getting cut in half. She hadn't been expecting any of the Mundanes to be so trigger-happy. "Hold on, hold on, Myrddin sent me," she muttered as she stood.

The Mundanes collectively watched Sarah as the other patrons in the Red Lion turned back, minding their own business again. A portal opening in the middle of their establishment wasn't enough to rouse them. How jaded this crew was, or how seasoned. These were exactly the kind of warriors they needed right now.

Yet, all of the Mundanes had their hands on their weapons. Seasoned and certainly not naïve. "I'm serious," Sarah said. "He sent me to request you for a mission. He said he'd pay you the bounty himself if there isn't enough loot for you."

Beth and Sandy looked at each other before Sandy showed Beth her wand. "I've been wanting some new equipment. Everything I have has too many bloodstains, and I can't wash them out. Even these," Sandy said as she held up her robes.

Stew sighed loudly as he fell into his seat. "Another quest?" he whined. "Could we get a weekend once? My ass is still sore from the last one."

Suzuki sighed and leaned his head back. "If you stopped trying to smother goblins with your ass, you wouldn't have this problem."

Stew leapt up, pointing at Suzuki. "What do you mean, trying? I ass-smashed six goblins. Beth saw it. She can attest to these glutes."

Beth shrugged as she sat and stole a mead from the table next to her. "I saw it, but Suzy's right. Stop trying to kill things with your butt, and it'll stop hurting all the time."

Sarah listened to the Mundanes bicker. They were children. She couldn't understand how this group of kids could be the legendary MERC squad responsible for nearly squashing the Dark One's plans in the Shire.

She'd never seen such a group of childish warriors.

Suzuki held up his hands, cutting everyone off. "All right, all right, all right. We're doing it," he said. "We could use the practice. The last quest was *rusty*. We need to be keeping ourselves sharp. Plus, if it's from Myrddin, it's probably important."

The Mundanes' leader turned to Sarah. "How can we help?"

CHAPTER SIXTY-SEVEN

Kravis came out of the portal at the Wasp's Nest and landed on a soft bed. He looked around to get his bearings. It looked like he was in a dorm room. Specifically, a young girl's dorm room. This was not the place for him. He scrambled to his feet and headed toward the door.

The door opened, and a teenage girl stepped in. She couldn't have been more than seventeen, which made the bleak look in her eyes all the more disorienting. It was like looking into the eyes of a dragon. She wore a tank top, which allowed Kravis to see the second most interesting thing apart from her dragon-black eyes: a cybernetic arm.

The girl, Alex, and Kravis froze, staring at each other. "Uh, I can explain this," Kravis stammered before making a break for it, trying to slide between Alex and the door.

Alex tried to punch Kravis, missing him by a hair. The impact of her strike tore a noticeable chunk out of the wall.

Kravis ran down the hall, trying to figure out where he was heading. As he turned the corner, he saw Alex run out of her room after him. "Shit, she does not look like she's going to give up," he muttered to himself.

Kravis turned another corner and ran into a gnome. They both fell backward. The younger gnome shook off the fall and started picking up his books. His red beard was very strong for his age. A good grade of red and no patches.

"Hey, Brath! Stop that gnome!" Alex shouted from the rear.

Brath, the teenage gnome Kravis had knocked over, looked at the elder with a bored expression. "We're not in the field," Brath shouted. "You don't get to boss me around unless it's official business."

"Brath, that creep was in my bedroom!"

"Dude, Jaws is going to flip when he hears you had some random-ass gnome in your bedroom."

Kravis was on his feet and running around Brath as Alex was catching up. "I didn't invite him into my room," Alex shouted as she ran past Brath.

"Well, what the hell was he… Oh. OH!"

Brath was up and running after Alex as fast as he could.

Kravis still hadn't figured out where he was going. It seemed like every hallway led to more hallways. He was starting to feel much more lost than before.

"Gotcha!"

Kravis felt his feet lift off the ground, and before he could do anything, Alex had slammed him face-first into a wall. When Kravis managed to open his eyes, Alex had a plasma pistol trained on him. "You better start talking because my trigger finger is getting *real* impatient," she threatened.

Brath leaned over to Alex and whispered, "Your trash-talking is getting better."

"Shut up, Brath. This is not the time."

Kravis held up his hands and pleaded, "Hold on, hold on. This is all a huge misunderstanding. I was sent here by Myrddin to find a team called Boundless. Alex Bound is the leader."

Alex jerked her robotic thumb at herself. "You're looking at her. How do I know you're telling the truth?"

"I have paperwork. And—"

"Anyone could have paperwork. Let me check."

Alex approached the wall, which had a built-in hand-scanning pad jutting out. She pressed her hand to the pad and waited for a moment. Myrddin's face appeared on the wall, slightly distorted by the crystals that made up the Wasp's Nest. "How can I help you, Alex?" Myrddin asked.

Alex pointed at Kravis. "Some pervy gnome appeared in my bedroom and said you sent him here on a secret mission to find Team Boundless. Just wanted to check and see if he was lying before we blasted him."

Myrddin picked up a stack of papers and began to thumb through them. "Hm, let me see. I do believe I have a note for that. Oh, yes. I did send a gnome named—"

"Kravis," the gnome shouted as he stood, catching Myrddin's attention.

"Oh, yes. That would be him. Kravis, what are you doing scaring the children?"

"The Gate was a little less specific than I might have wished."

Alex folded her arms, looking disapprovingly at Kravis and Myrddin. "Next time you guys are planning on opening a portal in my room, you could do me a favor and warn me. An email would have been nice."

Myrddin clicked his tongue and said, "Alex, you know it's your responsibility to check the daily dossier. Or at least have someone in your team take care of that."

Alex blushed bright red and looked at her feet. "All right, all right, Myrddin. Thanks for confirming. Bye."

Myrddin's face disappeared, and Alex leaned toward Kravis, watching him closely. "I'll meet you with the team in the cafeteria after I go over the mission parameters," she said. "Then we'll talk."

Alex turned to return to her room, looking over her shoulder and shouting at Brath, "Get the team together! And we're officially on a mission, so that's an order."

Brath sighed as he gave Kravis one more look and wandered down the hall.

Kravis sat there, caught off-guard by everything that had

happened. He didn't know many operatives who had Myrddin on speed dial, nor did he know any teenagers who had already been given their own squads. They must have been extremely talented for Myrddin to request them by name.

Kravis stood and began the confusing task of finding the cafeteria.

CHAPTER SIXTY-EIGHT

Terra burst into the dining hall, where the other fighters were gathered. Many of them stood around, looking as if they had already lost a battle. Perhaps it was the fight within them that they had forfeited. The only two to look up with anything other than loss in their eyes were Nib-nib and Cire.

Both rose when they saw Terra run in.

Even though Terra's bones ached and she wished to rest, she put on her best face and tried to look as if she were anything other than exhausted. But when Nib-nib came close enough, Terra couldn't help leaning to the side, allowing herself to be supported.

Nib-nib hacked up her healing goop and was pressing it to Terra's body as Cire stepped closer to speak to the other fighters. "We can hear you out there," Cire said. "We've heard the dragons too."

Terra held up one finger and laughed harshly. "Only one dragon at the moment. Managed to knock one of them out."

Nib-nib and Cire looked at each other in disbelief. "You knocked out a dragon?" the orc asked.

"Yep, clocked his punk ass. But, he kinda knocked me out too. So, as long as I'm the spring chicken, we should be good. Those things hit like a motherfucker. Could have sworn I was going to die at least fifteen different times. But I'm not back here to brag. I'm back here to see what the hell all of you are doing just sitting on your asses?"

"Initially, when you were brought out, there were guards keeping your small mantiboid friend and me from following you. Once we returned, we—it would not be unkind to say that we assumed you were dead. The fight above us sounded...it sounded as if you were outnumbered. No one would risk fighting the guards, only to find you dead."

Terra shrugged, obviously surprising Cire. "I thought you would be ashamed of us," he said.

Terra shook her head. "I don't think you can fault people in situations like this. Not being courageous isn't the same thing as cowardice. You guys didn't think you had a fighting chance. Orcs might give you shit about that, but where I come from, people make those decisions all the time. Sometimes it's the only thing that lets you keep going. When you go above that, knowing you might fail, that's a cause to celebrate. But I ain't talking shit about anyone who didn't get there. Shit, I didn't get there for most of my life."

Cire seemed to understand what Terra was talking about. "Is that an invitation for us to be courageous?"

"You were the one who said you'd follow me anywhere. Is that just something you said, or did you mean that?"

Cire pressed his right hand to his chest. "You are my chieftain, and I will follow you to death if you were to ask."

"Well, I'm going to ask you to follow me over there so I can talk to everyone. We'll talk about the whole death thing later, all right?"

Terra made her way to the bulk of the other fighters. She climbed onto the table and grabbed one of the jugs of wine, tossing it back and drinking deeply of it. "Listen up," she shouted. "There's a horde of orcs, a dragon, and one too many balrogs up there. They are not making this easy whatsoever, but I'm out there fighting. There's a shit-ton of people up there I've never met who are fighting to shut this place down. I think it's about time we all went up there and gave it our all."

The fighters looked from one to the other, uncertain of what they should do. Terra could see it in their eyes. Weighing their chances of survival. But then, if they were to stay down here, how much longer until they were forced into a fight that would end their lives?

One of the fighters stepped forward, a human with a scar running down his chest. "Where are the weapons?"

"Oh," Terra said. "I thought I'd have to do more convincing. I have no idea where they keep the weapons, but they can't be too far. We can find them, and then take the fight to the Game Master for a change."

The fighters burst into cheers, chanting Terra's true name.

Terra leapt off of the table and was met by Cire. "I thought that was going to be a lot harder," she admitted. "Was kinda looking forward to giving a huge-ass speech."

"We've been watching you fight against odds that would have crushed any of us," Cire said. "We have been inspired by you for some time, and I know there are more than a few orcs here who want to know if they can survive a Terra-level fight. They were just waiting for a little kick."

"All right, let's go find some weapons."

Terra and the fighters broke apart the chairs and tables in the room, providing each fighter with a club to hold them over until they were able to find something sharp and deadly. From there, they stormed down the halls, tipping over lanterns as they went, setting fire to the arena as they searched for tools to aid them in their vengeance.

By the time they found the weapons cache, the heat from the burning tunnels had nearly forced them out into the openness of the arena. Terra didn't mind. It was about time to get back to the fight.

She really needed to punch something.

CHAPTER SIXTY-NINE

Abby was busy consulting with Creon to get the Dark Gate working for Sarah's new plan. Sending through a couple of people wouldn't have been a problem, but two different squads and dragons presented a complication and they weren't coming through this Dark Gate.

Not in one piece, at least.

Creon was muttering through different solutions while Abby stared warily at the Gate, which was fluctuating between purple and red as if it were angered by the prospect of transporting so many bodies. "Any ideas, Martin?" Abby asked.

Martin was quiet for a few seconds as he tried to process the question. "Well, if you think about it, the Gate is really just a transponder. It grabs the frequency and does something with it. Technically, the Gate isn't the important thing. The frequency is."

Abby nodded, following Martin's train of thought. "I got you. And we have the frequency."

"We could scrap some of the tech from here so it's easier on you—"

"And I could just build my own Gate. In the arena!"

Abby reached behind the Dark Gate and grabbed the frequency

transponder she'd seen in the schematics Sarah had shown them all earlier. Then she returned to the arena, hoping she wasn't too late.

———

By now, the shock from the microchips had worn off. Anyone who was able to stand was fighting.

The horde was growing. Reinforcements had been sent to the arena, and nearly all were focused on Anabelle. The few who could spare their attention were busy trying to aid the balrogs in the destruction of Blackwell and Naota.

The two humans and their squads were doing more damage than anyone would have expected. They hadn't managed to take down any of the balrogs, but they were able to contain the threat. The balrogs weren't able to advance and interfere with anything going on in the ring as long as the humans were suppressing them.

It was a task that both Blackwell and Naota seemed to be quite taken with. Both of them, back to back, firing at anything that moved and wasn't human. They looked like they'd been working together for years. "This the first time you've seen one of these?" Blackwell shouted.

Naota pushed up his sunglasses as he threw his tasers, which were attached by a magical wire courtesy of HQ, at one of the balrogs trying to make a run for it. The tasers chattered through the air, snapping at the balrog before Naota retrieved them. "Everyone who's seen *Lord of the Rings* has seen one of those things before," Naota replied. "I thought they were bigger."

"They usually are. Guess the Game Master was expecting to draw out the fight a little bit. Give the crowd a more entertaining battle. Also, I don't think he was expecting us to bring so much firepower."

The balrogs were backed into a corner, the human squad surrounding them. The humans were laying down fire that, even though it wasn't damaging the balrogs, was too furious to move past. But it was only a matter of time before they ran out of ammo. Granted, it was going to be a long time, but it was going to come eventually. Blackwell didn't want to think about what they were going to do when that happened.

Across from the humans, Anabelle was still trying to take care of the orcs. She had slid back into the Path. Her body was her own to command at the moment, the manna flowing smoothly through her body, easily picking up whatever was cast off by those around her to replenish her own stores.

But there were still too many orcs, more than there had been before. Anabelle wouldn't have been surprised if some of the orcs from the stands had jumped into the arena to join the fight. More likely, the Game Master had a much larger force than he'd initially let on.

Anabelle still hadn't seen any orcs as large as the ones who were guarding the Game Master, so that was something.

Anabelle drew her manna up through her stomach and into her throat as she wove in and out of the orcs, trying to stay on the move and keep from having an individual duel. That would be problematic. If anyone were able to stop her for a second, box her in, there'd be a dozen swords and axes ready to hack her to pieces from every side.

Once the manna was in Anabelle's throat, she concentrated on the heat in her chest, spinning around, blowing fire through the orcish ranks, latching onto the flames with her connection to her manna, and scorching as many orcs as she could.

Much like the human squad, this didn't feel like progress. It felt like holding back a tide at best. If Anabelle had only been fighting the original number of orcs, this would already have been over, but it was obvious the Game Master had the resources to keep throwing at them.

This was a battle of attrition. Anabelle wondered how long she and the team were going to last.

Abby came running out one of the side tunnels of the arena. The scene of chaos was difficult for her to discern. She could tell that one of the dragons was still out cold but couldn't see where Persephone was. The balrogs were still fighting, all four of them. Anabelle was nowhere to be seen. "Creon, is Sarah ready for the transport?"

Creon replied, "She's more than ready. Are you?"

"Gimme a second."

Abby ran toward the middle of the arena, pulling all of the nanobots she could spare out of her body. Her armor began to disappear, revealing the frail human beneath. "How much is this going to take, Martin?" she asked.

"You might want to stay away from anything sharp or life-threatening as the Gate is constructed. I'll see what I can do. Save you a hand cannon and maybe a few thousand for moving defenses, but like I said, maybe sit this one out."

Abby slid into the sand as the nanobots continued to leave her body, separating from her and starting to flow together to build a new Dark Gate. Abby slammed the frequency transponder onto the back of the Dark Gate once it was done. "All right, Creon! Send 'em over," she shouted.

Creon muttered something indistinguishable and then said, "Gotcha. Tilt the Gate toward the sky! The first ones coming through are going to need a big berthing area."

Abby rested the Gate on its back so the portal was facing the sky. A massive purple blast of energy surged from the portal, stretching up into the clouds.

Four dragons soared out of the portal. Abby had never seen anything like them. Each of the dragons was a different color and looked vastly different from the red dragons in the arena. Even more striking, a person sat on each of the dragons.

One of the riders, the one who looked to be the leader, had a robotic arm.

"Abby! Second group is coming through! Get the portal upright again."

Abby grabbed the Gate and began to push it up. It was still heavy, even with the additional strength from being off of Earth, but she got it up.

The portal flashed again, shooting purple and red sparks. Four humans walked out of the portal, each wearing spectacular armor. The one with the wand wore a bone mask and looked to be a wraith. A confusingly muscular young man had on a loincloth and ram's skin shoulder pads. The other two were wearing standardized armor, customized to their design.

The Mundanes had arrived.

Suzuki drew his sword as he looked around the battlefield. "We're here on Myrddin's orders. Who are the enemies?"

Abby fumbled with her words for a second before Beth knelt beside her and repeated the question. "Uh, the orcs and goblins. There are four balrogs, and two dragons," she finally managed to say.

Beth looked at the sky, where the dragonriders were taking stock of the situation. "Ah, looks like Boundless is already here. They should be good with the dragons."

"Boundless?"

"Dragonrider platoon. They're kickass. You might have heard of them?"

Stew shrugged.

"Alex Bound, the first human rider?"

Another shrug.

"Dude, you really need to catch up on your reading."

Stew scoffed loudly as the wraithlike Sandy floated around him. "Whatever. There's four of them and only two dragons. What kind of elite group of riders couldn't handle that?"

"Stop being sore that you don't get to fight a dragon," Sandy giggled as she solidified enough to wrap her arms around Stew. "Let's take the orcs. I want to feel their souls fleeing. I want to feel their blood on my skin. I want—"

"Babe, you're doing that thing again—the one where you sound like a serial killer. Like a really horny serial killer."

Sandy giggled again and floated away from Stew, "I'm just saying, let's get started already."

Suzuki turned to Abby and asked, "Where's the biggest problem? What can we do to help?"

Abby shook her head, trying to keep from getting too stressed out by all the questions and new faces. "I don't know. I haven't seen…"

Suzuki rested his hand on Abby's shoulder and said, "Hey, don't worry about it. We got this." Then he flipped down his HUD, scanned the area, and shouted, "Mundanes, the biggest threat is the orcs. They need to be thinned out, and only one person's taking 'em right now. Let's go rip 'em up!"

The Mundanes took off toward Anabelle and the orcs, leaving Abby alone near the Gate, which was still open. She'd frozen, and she knew why. Whatever security or confidence she'd received from the nanobots was gone. Without the nanobots, she was just a frail human.

Maybe she should listen to Martin and get off the battlefield. The whole reason she'd been picked for Middang3ard HQ was that she was smart. She wasn't supposed to be out here fighting.

A sharp scream interrupted Abby's thoughts. She turned to her left and saw Persephone flying through the air. One of the balrogs had managed to get free of Blackwell and Naota. It had its whip around Persephone's leg and was flinging her through the air.

Abby didn't think. She was already on her feet. The few nanobots left in her body turned her palm into a plasma cannon. She fired at the balrog, catching its attention.

The balrog dropped Persephone and snapped its whip at Abby, who raised her arm, sending the other nanobots into it exactly where the whip wrapped around. She sent a jolt of energy through the bots and up the whip, causing the balrog to release her.

Then Abby felt the comforting weight of tentacles wrap around her and pull her away. Persephone had evaded the balrog and was bringing Abby with her.

Terra ran out of the catacombs, the other slave fighters at her back. She looked out onto the arena. A lot had happened since she disappeared, and a lot more humans were fighting.

A series of roars and screeches tore through the air. Terra looked up and saw dragons fighting each other. "Oh, shit, they definitely weren't here before. Looks like we might have this one in the bag, guys!"

Across from Terra, the Game Master stared down the contents of the arena. A smile lingered on his face as he cleared his throat, his voice booming over the cacophony of violence below. "Finally, our would-be champion has returned," he bellowed. "Just in time for round two to begin!"

The Game Master clapped his hands, the crack echoing through the arena.

The arena gates began to slowly creep open across from Terra. A deep, mysterious growl came from the darkness as the gates all around the arena began to open.

Terra sighed and shook her head before turning to face a gate. "Why are there always more things that need killing?"

CHAPTER SEVENTY

The iron gates of the arena had finally opened. By this time, the crowd was beyond words, beyond cheers. They sat in mute awe, staring down at the spectacle. There had never been a battle such as this in the history of all arenas.

The Game Master's pompous voice continued to boom through the arena. "Let it be seen what power the Dark One commands!" he shouted. "Our warriors have indeed battled as hard as they could. They've even brought in their own reinforcements. Their lives will be cherished, but who are they to stand before the might of the Four Gladiators?"

Terra and Cire were standing beside each other, watching the blackness of the hallways. Cire was breathing heavily as if he were scared. "What is it?" Terra asked.

Cire muttered under his breath, "He can't be serious. The Gladiators have been dead for ages. Dead since the third kingdom fell."

A heavy footstep made the ground jump. Cire and Terra stepped away from the gates, as did the other fighters. "Maybe we should regroup with everyone else."

Cire continued to walk backward, his eyes never leaving the iron gates. The stench of decay wafted from the darkness.

Terra and Cire made their way toward the center of the arena, where the portal was still flashing brightly. Up above, the drag-onriders dipped and dove, fighting the two red dragons, the second one having risen from its involuntary slumber. The sky was alight with fire as if hell had been born of cloud and sun.

The other Dark Gate Angels were also making their way to the center of the arena. They must have all had the idea to regroup. Anabelle and Terra looked worried to see Abby returned to her regular human form. "Where's all the shiny bells and whistles?" Terra asked. "You don't look ready for a fight."

Abby shook her head, embarrassed. "I have enough to fight, but the rest are keeping the portal open," she said. "Can't close it until Creon figures a way for us to get back. Right now, that's our only way out."

Anabelle sighed as the Mundanes, Blackwell, Naota, and the Marines began to back up into the center of the arena as well. "Been relying a lot on that goblin's science," she murmured. "Wish problems like these could just be killed. You'd think they could, you know. Seeing as how they want to kill us."

Terra laughed as she adjusted her shield, Cire at her side, still staring slack-jawed at the iron gates. "You know, I was just complaining about that," she said. "Didn't think there'd be enough to kill. Now it looks like there's going to be too much."

"That fight with the dragon was impressive. I've never seen a human do anything like that. Hell, I've never seen *anyone* do anything like that."

Stew, who had just arrived with the Mundanes, gave a shout of laughter. "Wait, you got to fight one of the dragons?" he asked. "Are you serious? Are you a berserker too?"

Terra nervously looked around for someone to explain it to her. "Uh, can't say I know what you're talking about. I'm just someone who got abducted."

Suzuki snapped at Stew to grab his attention. "Hey, focus! You'll get your dragon eventually."

Stew sulked as he raised his battle-ax.

Terra, Anabelle, and Abby exchanged glances over the Mundanes.

Anabelle leaned close and whispered to Abby, "At least you don't act your age. Glad you're a bit more mature."

The ground shook once more. All of the agents of Middang3ard were silent as they waited to see what was going to come from blackened halls.

Terra said to Cire, "Tell me more about these Gladiators?"

Cire drew a sober breath as he continued to watch the halls. "They were the four finest champions of the arena. Fighting during the third kingdom, the strongest of all orc kingdoms. The four of them were undefeated until they battled each other. That was when they fell. None lived through the battle. They died as champions."

"Is that supposed to be a romantic story?"

"Orcs don't tell romantic stories. We tell stories."

Without warning, the first Gladiator ripped through the stone hallways, sending debris and rocks flying. The creature looked to be an orc but was the size of a mountain troll. Its arms were atrophied, muscles and ligaments hanging from its bones like tattered drapes. Rotting, bony hands gripped a steel club. When the Gladiator breathed, fog emerged from its mouth.

The other three Gladiators tore through their stone entrances as well, looking very much the same as their brethren. Some were larger or smaller than the first but not by much.

Sandy from the Mundanes scoffed loudly at the sight of the Gladiators. "Seriously? That's it? You'd think the necromancer who did this would have at least been a little creative. Nope, just four identical larger versions—"

One of the Gladiators leaned forward, vomiting acidic bile. Another screamed loudly as bony wings erupted from its back. The third's waist erupted into a mass of slithering serpentine bodies.

Sandy laughed nervously. "Looks like I spoke too soon."

"I fucking hate you when you jinx us," Suzuki muttered. Then he turned to Anabelle. "This is your rodeo. What's the game plan?"

Anabelle quickly assessed the situation. More troops were following Terra now, but the orc horde was also beginning to fill out again. Plus, the addition of the four Gladiators had the potential for an entirely different set of problems. At best, the reinforcements that had been brought had only bought them all a little bit more time. "We have to bide our time," Anabelle said. "We're working on a way out of here. Until then, we're—"

Abby interrupted Anabelle. "Wait! I have an idea. We could rig the Gate to explode after we use it. I could put it on a timer, inverting the polarity of the—"

"Skip the nerd talk and tell me what you're going to do!"

Abby bit her lip as she closed one of her eyes, trying to find a quicker way to explain everything. "I can jerry-rig this to explode once we have a clear signal. Two minutes from when Creon gets it fixed. A big enough explosion to take out the entire arena. Dark Gate, orcs, and all. The only thing that'll be here is a crater."

"Assuming we make it to the portal in time. If we stay too close to it, the Game Master is going to expect something. We're going to have to split up and then make sure we get back here in time." Anabelle turned to Suzuki and asked, "You got that?"

Suzuki nodded and asked Sandy, "Okay, which one do you want? I know you probably have some weird thing you wanna get out of the corpse, like a wart-covered spleen or something."

Sandy pointed her wand at the Gladiator with the bone wings. "Could always use more wing bone. And if it comes from an undead orc, that's even better."

Anabelle extended her hand to Suzuki, who grasped and shook it. "Good luck," she said. "Seems kinda—"

"Like a suicide mission?" Suzuki finished. "Yeah, but that's our thing. MERCs say if it has a high likelihood of success, what's the point in getting paid to do it?"

Anabelle gave her commands to Blackwell and Naota. They and their squad were to continue to handle the balrogs. The fighters from the arena were going to concentrate on the orc horde that was slowly approaching. She was going to take one of the gladiators, Terra another. Persephone would handle the last one.

Terra chuckled as she slapped Cire on the back. "You're coming with me. Don't tell me you never dreamed of fighting one of the Gladiators when you were a kid."

Cire looked dubiously at the Gladiator near the gates, staring them down, waiting to be approached. "Can't say I did."

Terra clapped her hand on Abby's shoulder. "Thanks for coming after me. All of you. Sorry I got you into such a big mess."

Abby shook her head, trying to keep the tears out of her eyes. "Don't apologize. It's the least we could do for one of Earth's biggest heroes. Besides, all of our planet is watching. Might as well give them a show, right?"

"All of Earth, huh? Yeah, might as well. So, what are we calling ourselves again?"

Anabelle stepped forward. "The Dark Gate Angels. Best name we've heard so far."

Terra cracked her knuckles as she turned to face her Gladiator. "Sounds good. Let's rough 'em up some, Angels."

The Dark Gate Angels split up, each heading toward a different gladiator.

Anabelle called her manna to her hands as she approached the Gladiator spewing acidic bile. The Gladiator was hunched over its club as if it needed it for support. Anabelle knew it would be a mistake to assume the Gladiator was weak in any way. She was going to hit it with everything she had and put it in the ground as soon as possible.

When Anabelle moved closer, the Gladiator lunged forward, trying to grab her with one hand like a giant drunken baby. Anabelle was easily able to avoid the attack, leaping aside, focusing her manna on hardening and sharpening her skin. She brought her attack down on the Gladiator's shoulder blade, ripping through skin and bone.

The gladiator stumbled backward, grasping its arm, which was leaking the same kind of bile as the gladiator's mouth. Anabelle ripped off the sleeve of her shirt, which was covered in the smoking bile. "Guess that's not the route I'm going to be taking," she muttered to herself.

Across from Anabelle, Terra and Cire were squaring up against the

Gladiator with the multiple snake's tails. "I'm hoping you're like a combat genius or something," Terra said as the two ran toward it.

Cire unsheathed his sword and readied his shield. "I wouldn't say genius, but I can hold my own."

The two went for the gladiator, Cire circling around toward the creature's back while Terra faced it with her *katar*.

The Gladiator slithered forward surprisingly fast, catching Terra off-guard. It swung its heavy mace at Terra, who barely had time to block it with her shield. The force of its attack sent her skidding backward in the sand.

As the Gladiator concentrated on Terra, Cire lunged, preparing to drive his sword into its back. Before the blade could connect, one of the Gladiator's tails whipped up and slapped Cire in the chest, sending him flying.

It swung again at Terra, who stepped to the side and raked her *katar* against its arm, causing it to release its mace. Then she dropped her shield, leaned in, and punched the Gladiator as hard as she could in the face, tearing off its jaw.

A stream of ice shot out of the Gladiator's open face as it reached around, trying to pick up its mace.

Terra stepped back, the ice almost instantly freezing her arm. She continued to retreat as the Gladiator spewed ice everywhere. "Hope he doesn't keep that up for too long," she muttered.

While Terra and Cire fought their Gladiator, Abby and Persephone were closing on the last one, the only one that appeared to be somewhat normal. This Gladiator only looked ancient and rotten.

As Abby's hand converted into a cannon, Creon's voice came through on her comm. "You have seven to ten minutes!" he exclaimed.

Abby fired a shot at the Gladiator, which merely swiped away the blast with his club. "Well, which one is it?" she asked frantically. "Three minutes is a lot of minutes."

"Eight minutes. Eight minutes."

Abby took aim again and fired as Persephone ran from behind her, wrapping her tentacles around the Gladiator's legs. "Let everyone else know!" Abby shouted.

The creature reached down and took hold of the tentacles around its legs. It yanked hard and pulled Persephone into the air.

Abby slid under the drow, lining up her shot and taking it. The blast tore through part of the Gladiator's arm, causing it to drop Persephone. Even before she hit the ground, the wound in its arm was healing.

A screech tore through the air, and Abby looked up as one of the red dragons plowed into the earth on top of the Gladiator, sending rock and sand spewing.

The red dragon tried to get to its feet as Alex on her ether dragon Chine crashed into it. Alex slashed at the dragon with her scythe as Chine fired a jet of black ether at the Gladiator, consuming it within its flames. The red dragon flipped, whipping its tail around to clear space before rising into the air. The force of it threw Alex off Chine.

Persephone reached out with her tentacles, wrapping them around the red dragon's throat to try to keep it on the ground, but the dragon was too strong. It lifted Persephone into the air as it took off. Abby grabbed Persephone's hand and held tight. The drow screamed in pain as she swung Abby up onto the dragon's back.

She held on as tight as she could as the red dragon rose higher.

Alex had gotten back on Chine and they tackled the red dragon in mid-air, sending it careening off its course, while the rest of Team Boundless battled the other red dragon above.

As the red dragon tried to right itself, Persephone pulled herself up next to Abby. They made their way down the dragon's back. Persephone wrapped her tentacles around the dragon's neck and tightened them while Abby continued to the nape of the dragon's neck.

Abby put her hand on the dragon's nape and fired. It screeched in rage and pain, trying to buck Abby and Persephone off, but Persephone tightened her grip. Abby fired again, then again.

The red dragon started losing altitude, then plunged to the ground. It crashed into Terra's Gladiator, sending the ancient creature into the arena's stands.

Abby scampered off of the dragon along with Persephone as the great red beast got to its feet, staring down at the two girls, fire brimming in its mouth. Persephone and Abby were in the dead zone.

The red dragon had opened its mouth to unleash its fire when Terra sprang up and punched the side of the dragon's head. The dragon fell forward, giving Abby and Persephone enough time to move out of the way.

Terra rolled under the dragon and delivered an uppercut with everything she had. Stew, who wasn't too far away, caught Terra's last punch and shouted, "See? Suzy, check it out! Humans can totally go one on one with a dragon," before getting bashed in the head by a flying goblin.

Ether fire scorched the ground as Alex and Chine flew overhead, burning everything they could justify as an enemy.

Creon's words broke through the chaos on everyone's comm. "One minute!" he shouted.

Anabelle exclaimed into her comm, "Humanoids first, then dragons!"

The Mundanes, Dark Gate Angels, and everyone in between dropped what they were doing and headed toward the open Gate in the middle of the arena. Everyone but Abby and Anabelle slipped through. Once they were clear, Anabelle and Abby knocked over the Gate for the dragons, who were racing toward the portal.

The dragonriders passed through without a problem, but by now, the horde of orcs had figured out what was going on. One of the orcs fired a blast that disabled the Dark Gate, weakening the portal. Before Anabelle stepped through, Creon said, "Wait, wait, hold on. The Gate isn't working anymore. I can't send the signal to detonate!"

Abby and Anabelle looked at the horde of monsters approaching. "Uh, any suggestions?" the elf asked.

Abby glanced at her hand, sensing the connection between the nanobots in her blood and those composing the Gate. "I can still detonate it. Get through the portal."

"Are you sure? You don't have—"

Abby grabbed Anabelle and pulled her onto the portal. Their feet didn't sink through; it was like standing on ice. "Ain't got any more time!" Abby shouted as she closed her eyes and focused.

All Abby could hear now was the explosion, all she could feel was an odd energy washing over her, making her body as cold as if she'd been dipped in a frozen lake. Then there was nothing.

CHAPTER SEVENTY-ONE

Roy, along with a dozen other mech riders, hovered in formation above the Pacific Ocean, a couple dozen miles off the Japanese coastline. He was biting his fingernails.

The transport had been successful for the most part. The Mundanes, Persephone, Terra and her fighters, and the dragonriders had all been brought back to Earth, each sent to different coordinates.

Creon had worked magic. He hadn't gone over how difficult the logistics were, but he had managed to split up the transportation three ways. There was no way dragons were going to be able to transport into HQ without tearing everything up. For the most part, it had gone off without a hitch. The dragonriders had been given coordinates to HQ and made their way back. A smaller group of mech riders had picked up Terra, Cire, and the rest.

Roy had watched Anabelle's and Abby's final decision before the portal exploded. He had thought it was going to come to that regardless. The plan had seemed too foolproof. Something had to go wrong.

He was beating himself up for not going on the mission, but Myrddin had anchored him. The wizard said it was for the best. There was no way he was going to throw *every* one of his operatives into this rescue mission. Roy had grudgingly agreed. Then he had watched

Abby and Anabelle blow up the Gate and their only hope to come home.

That was when Creon had gone silent, throwing himself into his work, bouncing between three or four computers while Martin's face flickered back and forth on the holoprojector. When Roy asked Creon what was happening, the goblin had shouted coordinates at Roy and told him to get there as fast as possible.

Once Roy had arrived where he was told, Creon informed him that Anabelle and Abby hadn't killed themselves. They'd been sucked into the portal with its dying breath, sending them flying through some kind of subspace. With the last of Martin's processing power and some quick thinking, Creon was able to redirect the portal to the coordinates provided to Roy.

There was no guarantee that Abby and Anabelle were going to come out alive, though. But at least they would be able to be given a proper burial, a hero's burial like they both deserved.

Roy hadn't allowed himself to think about Anabelle or Abby dying. He wasn't going to entertain the idea until it was in his face. Until then, his mission was to pick the pair up and return them to HQ.

But the thought kept creeping into Roy's head, worming its way through any kind of distraction he could hope to have. It wasn't even a complete thought, just images. Anabelle's head crushed against a stone. Abby's face without any skin. The two agents were too good to die like that. Yeah, they were heroes, but they didn't deserve this.

Roy wondered if this was how Anabelle had felt when she'd pulled him out of his mech a few days ago. *Christ, that was a lifetime ago,* he thought. *Shit needs to slow down after this. Just for a bit.*

Above Roy, the sky opened. It looked as if another sky had forced itself through Earth's. This one was purple and flashed flames that fluctuated between light pink and deep crimson. The portal was nearly the size of an industrial freighter.

Two miniscule specks shot out of the portal. Roy pulled his scanner down and examined them. It was Anabelle and Abby, and their vital signs were faint.

Roy roared forward, the other mechs following him. He swooped beneath Anabelle, flipping over so his belly was facing up and opened his cockpit as another mech swung about and did the same for Abby. He reached out and pulled Anabelle's body out of her freefall.

She lay limp in Roy's lap. She was cold, and her eyes were closed. The veins in her skin were bright blue and looked to have been inked on. If she wasn't dead, she sure as hell felt like it. "Back to HQ ASAP," Roy shouted as he turned his mech around.

There was only one thing to think about at this moment: how fast could his mech move. Roy pushed it harder than he'd ever pushed before, each second feeling like a lifetime. He let his tears fall easily and simply as he whispered over and over, "You're going to make it."

Roy and the mechs headed toward the Japanese Middang3ard base. The medical equipment there wasn't as advanced as what was at HQ, but it was the best bet. Any time wasted could result in Anabelle's and Abby's deaths if it wasn't already guaranteed.

Creon hadn't given Roy a lot of information about where Anabelle and Abby had been traveling. The most he said was that it was not the same kind of portal everyone else had gone through. Abby and Anabelle had gone through some kind of negative space. It was all a little beyond Roy's understanding, and he figured he was wasting time by asking questions.

Now he could see why Creon had been worried. Roy had never seen anyone come through a portal looking this bad before. Japan was definitely the best bet.

As Roy flew, Anabelle turned her face to look at him. Her eyes fluttered open. They were bloodshot, but she was alive. "Hey, there," she muttered. "Wasn't expecting to see you first thing in the morning."

Roy let out a nervous laugh as he leaned forward to kiss Anabelle's forehead. "Holy shit, you made it," he gasped.

"Shh, shh," Anabelle murmured. "It's really loud, and I have a headache. Where's Abby?"

"We picked her up too. We're going to get you both fixed up as soon as possible."

Anabelle yawned and stretched her legs. "That sounds good. I'm just going to take a quick nap. I hate flying, especially in coach. Ugh.

Oh, and get me a martini, please. Thanks, darling." With that, she closed her eyes and went to sleep.

Roy smiled to himself. First-class and martinis? But what really brought a smile to his face was the last thing she'd said.

Darling.

Abby woke up in the late afternoon two days after she'd been brought to the base in Japan, which had all the medical facilities necessary to treat her. The doctors had assured Anabelle and Terra that it was merely because Abby was younger, wasn't used to as much strain, and her body was trying to replenish its nanobots.

The doctors were fascinated by how Abby's white blood cells had been nearly replaced by nanobots. They had a lot of questions, and both Anabelle and Terra were happy that they didn't know the answers. They had taken turns sitting by Abby's bed, waiting for her to wake up.

When Abby did wake up, the first thing she did was throw up a disgusting slew of unusable nanobots. Then she asked for some water and laid back, trying to piece together the events that had led her to being in an unknown hospital bed. She didn't have to think long, though. Both Terra and Anabelle were more than happy to fill her in.

For the first six hours that Abby was conscious, Anabelle, Terra, and she didn't leave the room. They talked incessantly. It was as if they'd known each other their entire lives. Abby had gotten that feeling with Anabelle before, most likely the reason for her early crush, but the same was true of Terra.

There was a bond between the three women, one that was not formed easily or flippantly. It was the sort of thing that transcended friendship or family. When one of the three looked upon the others, they saw an aspect of themselves coupled with something beyond their realm of understanding—something so different that it drew them closer.

At some point, Anabelle was called away by Myrddin to deal with a debriefing and the aftermath of what happened in the arena. This left Terra and Abby alone for some time. Terra couldn't express enough gratitude to Abby. She said she had felt like Abby was her guardian angel, looking out for her the entire time.

Abby, likewise, had come to think of Terra in a very elevated way. She explained that Terra had become a role model for her. She'd never seen anyone fight so hard. If there was anything she wanted to be able to do, it was fight that hard for something she believed in.

When Anabelle returned, she took Terra with her, much to the girl's chagrin. If Terra was going to be part of the Dark Angels, she was going to have to get used to briefings, debriefings, and all of the boring, safe stuff that went into the war efforts of Middang3ard.

When Abby was alone, she watched the Tokyo skyline far into the morning, past the glowing lights of the night. She wasn't tired. She felt like she'd slept for a lifetime.

The phone next to Abby's bed rang, and she picked it up. "This is Abby."

The voice on the other end of the line was crying. Abby recognized those sobs. She a heard them at her father's funeral. "Ma?"

The sobbing quieted, and the voice managed, "Yeah, Abby, it's me."

"Oh, my God, how did you get this number? How are you doing?"

Abby's mother cleared her throat and inhaled so deeply that Abby could hear it clearly over the phone. "You didn't say nothing about flying to other galaxies and fighting dragons when you said you were going to help in a science department," she finally said with a weak laugh.

Abby was hit with a pang of guilt. She had never thought her family would see the broadcast of the last battle. That had slipped her mind. "Ma, I'm so sorry," she said. "They needed things changed...and I have all these abilities...and—"

"Oh, trust me, I know, baby. I ain't ever seen you do anything like that before. It was amazing. Hardly the little girl who left the farm only a few months ago. And I know you couldn't have told me. I know it. You wouldn't want me worrying. And to be honest, I'm glad you didn't. I'm glad I just saw you being able to handle yourself. Your pa would be proud. He always said you were a fighter, even if you were a runt."

Abby sat there quietly, taking in her mother's words. "Thanks, Ma."

"We're all proud of you, Abby. My little girl on the front lines, defending all of humanity. And she's still smart as hell. We couldn't be prouder of you. All of us."

There was a commotion, and Ma shouted something indecipherable. "All right, baby, I got to go. Your sisters wanna get on the line, and I was told you need your rest. I'll give them your love."

"I love you, Ma."

"We love you too, Abby-Lynn. You keep giving 'em hell."

Abby hung up. She had too many emotions going on to get a handle on all of them. There was guilt but also pride. More than anything else, she felt gratitude. Her family understood her. Even if they didn't understand all of what was going on, they understood that Abby was working toward something she believed in.

There was a knock on the door. "Come in," Abby said as she sat up.

The door opened, and Persephone, who had been held up for a few days in debriefings, stepped into the room, cradling her right arm as usual. "Hi! They told me I could come visit if it's okay with you."

"Yeah, yeah, come in."

Persephone slowly walked into the room and sat across from Abby. The pair sat in awkward silence for a little bit before Persephone said, "I heard what you did with the portal. It was very brave. I don't know if I could have done the same. Or if I would have known to."

Abby waved away Persephone's compliment. "I doubt that. Saw the way you went after that dragon. Doubt you would have backed down. But now that all that's over, what are you going to do?"

Persephone bit her bottom lip as she released her arm. There were black cracks running up the drow's skin. "Myrddin is sending me back home in a few days," she said. "My parents are still there, and I've been missing for a long time. We don't know what after that."

Abby got out of bed and walked to the window overlooking

Tokyo. "You know, I'm not good at goodbyes," she said. "But I've always wanted to go to Tokyo. You?"

Persephone came to stand next to Abby. "Never heard of it. I don't know much about the human realm."

"We should check it out. I'll show you some stuff. Martin can translate for us...after we put a disguise on you. Drows ain't exactly welcome on Earth. Not yet."

"Aren't you supposed to be resting? Won't you get in trouble?"

Abby laughed as she opened the window and peeked out. "A few days ago, we fought off an army of orcs and a couple of dragons." She chuckled. "I think I can handle a city of humans. Come on, it'll be fun."

Nanobots covered Abby's body, coating her in a sleek metallic second skin. She stepped out of the window, floating in the air, and reached for Persephone's hand. "Next time, you can show me drow things."

Persephone took Abby's hand. "Promise?"

"Promise."

CHAPTER SEVENTY-TWO

Terra was settling into her new place at Middang3ard HQ. She'd been there for two days, and even if it didn't feel like home, it was starting to seem like a place she could live. A couple of months ago, it would have been overwhelming to come across so many different races from the nine realms. Now she was bummed that more orcs didn't work with Middang3ard.

The orcs who came with Terra were held under supervision until she came to their defense. Myrddin had explained it was a simple precaution, the same thing he had done with Persephone when she arrived. It was only going to last a few days. He knew the role they had played and had no desire to treat them like lower-class citizens.

Until then, Terra could stop by the barracks they were held in and visit with Cire. They'd talk about their plans and what Myrddin was cooking up for the Dark One. Terra was excited to get to work, actual work. Going on missions with a goal sounded much more appealing than fighting in an arena for an unknown amount of time.

Cire, on the other hand, did not know what he was going to do. He had stated multiple times that his vow to Terra was more than just words and he would follow her regardless of where she went. He was just uncertain if he'd be allowed to work within Middang3ard HQ. Even if Myrddin said he wouldn't be treated like a second-class citizen, he had been given an uneasy welcome by HQ's agents.

Terra was sitting on her bed, thinking about what her new life was going to be like. She already missed Abby. Creon, who seemed to get along very well with Nib-nib despite the language barrier, had told Terra that Abby was on an extended stay in Japan until Persephone returned to the drow world.

Terra also hadn't been able to get hold of Anabelle for longer than a few minutes. Anabelle was technically the leader of the Dark Gate Angels, and because of that, she had a score of administrative duties to take care of. Terra wasn't jealous of her.

But that left Terra with a lot of time during the day to fill and no one to fill it with. She wasn't bothered by that. The experiences she'd had in the arena had to be made sense of, and that wasn't going to happen if she was hanging out with folks as much as she could. Quiet time was a necessity.

The arena was something Terra would have never imagined she could have gotten through. Her entire life, she'd balked at challenges. The easiest route was the best route. She had constantly folded under pressure. The Terra she'd left on Earth would have died in the first round.

Where had that strength come from? She had wrestled a dragon to the ground in the arena. How did she have the power to do that? It was deeper than just having more physical strength and endurance. Multiple people had told her they could never have imagined a human going toe to toe with a dragon and coming out alive, let alone besting the creature.

Finally sick of sitting on her bed, Terra got up and headed out. She wandered the corridors of HQ, thinking through things, trying to understand when the switch in her head had happened. Could it have just been being faced with a life and death situation? Had she just never been pushed far enough?

As Terra wandered HQ's halls, she was suddenly curious to know what the rest of humanity was up to. She hadn't thought about Earth since she had been yanked from it. There was bound to be television she hadn't caught up with yet.

Terra went to one of the information kiosks that had been linked to Martin's consciousness. "Hey, Martin, where can I watch some TV?"

Martin popped up on the screen with his usual cup of coffee and sighed. "Are you kidding me?" he retorted. "You've been back for two days, and you're already wanting to veg out on TV? You humans never cease to amaze me. Of all the things to do. You could be out having adventures or—"

"I've been on a nonstop adventure for the last week or two. Give me a break. You telling me you don't ever watch TV to kill time?"

Martin disappeared, replacing himself with a map of HQ with highlights on the rooms with televisions. "I'll also put in a requisition for you to receive your own idiot box," Martin said. "Have fun killing your brain cells."

Terra studied the map, then headed toward the closest common room.

The common room was between the Marines' barracks and the orcs'. Only humans were in it, though. Most of them were playing pool or cards over a beer. The television was open.

As Terra walked past the Marines, she sensed their eyes on the back of her neck. She tried to ignore them and sat on the couch. They didn't have any reason to be staring at her. It didn't make sense to worry about it. Instead, she grabbed the remote and turned the TV on.

The first channel was CNN. They were reporting on the battle in the arena. Terra hadn't seen any of the media coverage since she'd returned. She only vaguely remembered Abby telling her that the fights had been broadcast to Earth.

The interviewer was running a segment where he walked down the street, stopping random people and asking them how they felt about Terra's last fight. The first person was an old man. He had tears in his eyes as he said, "What happened to that poor girl was terrible. Being abducted like that. But she showed them what humans are capable of. She showed them all."

The next interviewee was a middle-aged woman. She replied, "Beat those assholes to a pulp! Ha-ha. Yeah, that Terra, she's a modern hero. Should put her on the dollar bill. Humanity's best."

The one that grabbed Terra by the heart and pummeled her into the ground was a little girl holding a plush doll of Terra. The girl held the doll close to her heart as she said, "I want to be Terra when I grow up. I want to be that strong."

Terra changed the channel after the last interview. She flipped through the channels until she found a cartoon she used to watch as a kid. It was about a group of adventurers traveling through a dungeon, looking for a dragon to fight for its treasure. Terra couldn't help but laugh. "Wow, surprised I didn't see that coming," she said to herself.

CHAPTER SEVENTY-THREE

Anabelle could hardly contain her anger. She'd been back for nearly three days, and all she'd done was sit in meetings hour after hour, listening to Myrddin or Roy or someone else prattle on about this and that. All she could think about was returning to her room, running a hot bath, and polishing off a bottle of elvish wine.

There was a bottle she'd been fantasizing about for some time. Nearly two hundred years old. A nice recollection of a dead Traveler's last battle would play in your mind while you sipped the wine. It would make for a relaxing evening. She could end it with some meditation. Maybe go for a walk. Another bottle of wine.

"Ms. Chase, are you paying attention?"

Anabelle looked up from the pad she'd been doodling on. Myrddin was gazing at her from across the long executive table that Roy and several other old wizards Anabelle had been lucky enough not to be introduced to sat at.

The two locked eyes and it took everything for Anabelle not to slap Myrddin. But this was what she had wanted. Fieldwork involved a lot of meetings. She'd grown to accept this fact of her life. "Of course, I'm listening," she chided. "Even if you're making it impossible to stay awake."

Myrddin didn't look bothered by Anabelle's tone. "Then what did I just say?"

"I'm not on trial here, and this isn't a grade-school classroom. That might be how you talk to your human subordinates, but I am several hundred years older than you."

Myrddin folded his arms crossly before sitting. "Maybe you could act like it," he countered.

Anabelle almost let Myrddin have it, but then she chuckled and nodded. She was glad to be back alive, annoying the hell out of Myrddin while Roy tried to keep from laughing in the corner. A couple of days ago, she'd looked her life in the eye and been prepared to say goodbye to it. Even if Myrddin annoyed the hell out of her, it was better than being dead.

Myrddin started back up with the briefing, and Anabelle felt her eyes getting heavy. Or at least, she hoped it was better than death.

Once the briefing was over, everyone but Myrddin cleared out of the room. As Anabelle prepared to leave, the wizard cleared his throat and motioned for her to come closer. "How I have missed your confrontational nature." He groaned as he stretched his back.

Anabelle tsked and said, "Sarcasm doesn't suit you, old man."

Myrddin smiled sweetly. "That is because I am rarely sarcastic. I was being sincere. Your fiery outbursts have been the most interesting part of my job for years."

"Oh, yeah? Not the part where you're organizing the resistance against the Dark One?"

Myrddin smiled again before conjuring two glasses of wine. "I have been preparing for this for thousands of years. It feels more like a day job than anything else. Dealing with you, though? That's an ongoing struggle. Keeps me young."

Anabelle laughed as she picked up her glass. "What's this?"

"A new batch straight from the elvish realm. The province of Heli-lerth, I believe. Something of a tribute to the last Traveler. I do believe it is a ballad based on your last battle."

Anabelle flushed with honor. There had been countless Travelers who had journeyed the Path before her who had been commemorated in the elvish singing wine. She'd never thought she'd be one of them. The thought hadn't even crossed her mind. "Are you serious?"

Myrddin raised his glass and said, "Why don't you try a taste and find out?"

The two toasted and Anabelle sipped the wine tentatively. It was sweet, almost like honey mixed with elderberry. Anabelle closed her eyes, letting the flavor coat her tongue. In the blackness, she could see the old elvish script with its beautiful and elaborate loops, etching her name in fire against the darkness. *To Anabelle Chase, the Gracious Traveler.*

Anabelle put her glass down and smirked. "Never thought I'd be called gracious in my life."

Myrddin nodded as he took another sip. "Your decision to save Terra at the cost of your own life made quite the impression. As I recall, Travelers are often known for their battle prowess, not their compassion. Also, I think you might want to know, Persephone went back to the drow netherworld this morning."

"And?"

"And what?" Myrddin said, a coy smile painting his face.

"And Abby? Terra?"

"I thought you didn't care for humans?"

Anabelle gave Myrddin a look that would have scared the tide back into the ocean.

"Fine, fine." Myrddin chuckled. "Abby arrived back from Japan today. Terra's here, too. They are both available if you want to spend some time with them."

Anabelle downed the last of her wine and smacked her lips. "Yeah, that sounds right."

Anabelle commed both Terra and Abby and told them to meet in her room in fifteen minutes. Then she turned to Myrddin and said, "I'll see you later. Thanks for the drink."

Abby burst into Anabelle's room with almost uncontainable energy. She threw her arms around Anabelle and then Terra and wouldn't stop talking for nearly fifteen minutes. When she finally did, she sat them both down and showed them all the photos she'd taken in Tokyo. Anabelle ordered drinks to be delivered to the room, and Abby bashfully asked for one. "If I'm old enough to fight for Earth's safety, should I be able to have a drink too?"

Anabelle nodded, "I'm not your mother, but I'm also not gonna be your babysitter, so watch yourself."

Once the drinks arrived, they continued talking, often interrupting each other, all three eager to share what they'd experienced. Before long, they had stopped catching up and had settled on Anabelle's couch, Abby forcing them to watch an anime she'd bought in Japan.

A knock on the door interrupted all the laughter and shouting. Anabelle rushed to the door and opened it. Sarah stood in the doorway, looking at her feet. She held up a bottle of champagne. "I know I didn't get the official invite, but...I was wondering if I could join you."

Anabelle grabbed the bottle of champagne and pulled Sarah into the room. "Of course you can! I've been trying to reach you all day. Is your comm encrypted against messages or something?"

"Oh, yeah. Guess I forgot about that."

Anabelle shoved Sarah over to the couch and forced her to go through introductions with everyone and then made Abby reshow all the photos that had been taken. They poured themselves champagne and turned the show back on, Sarah fidgeting uncomfortably as if she weren't used to sitting with less than five inches between herself and another person.

Toward the end of the movie, Abby yawned and sat on the floor. "So, what's going to happen now? That mission was huge, and it was just a rescue mission."

Anabelle paused the movie, her face turning serious. "It's only a matter of time before the Dark One starts opening other Gates or changes tactics. Either way, we'll be back to work soon enough. Might as well enjoy the break while we have it."

Terra grabbed the remote and the champagne. She took a huge swig and belched before saying, "More fighting. Sounds good." She passed the bottle to Sarah.

Sarah took a small sip and wiped her lips. "Is this the part where we all hold hands and shout 'Go, team?'"

Abby stood, nanobots rolling over her hand, and opened a camera lens in her palm. "How about we settle for a picture?" She plopped down in the middle of the couch, and the other Dark Gate Angels scooted closer. "Say, 'Dead Dark One!'"

The Angels shouted "Dead Dark One" as Abby snapped the photo. She waved her hand and projected a holoversion of the photo. "Yeah, I think that one's good enough."

The End

The Dark Gate Angels are divided ... Terra is most famous person in the world, Abby is home and Anabelle is on her most dangerous mission yet ... a date with Roy.

When more gates start to open up with super warriors unlike anything they've ever seen before, the Angels must band together once more to save the world in *Shades of Dark, Dark Gate Angels 2!*

'

AUTHOR NOTES RAMY VANCE
APRIL 25, 2020

I discovered something very interesting yesterday. Michael reads my author notes. Now, now, I know I shouldn't feel too happy about this … apparently, he reads *everyone's* author notes. Amazing, eh? With everything he has on his plate, he still reads these things.

Whatta guy!

Is my ass kissing too thinly veiled for you? Well, it is for good reason.

I'm trying to fulfill a life-long ambition.

I'm trying to woo him with a new universe idea…a supreme universe with infinite story possibilities, pitting graceful warriors against demonic, blood-sucking monsters. I'm trying to convince him to produce the universe of **Samurai vs. Vampire**.

This mega-cool concept was something I came up with when I was 14. But despite coming up with this the year before I discovered girls, I still believe it stands the test of time. How cool would a fight between skilled swordsmen and demons be? Who would win? What would a war between them even look like?

Who wouldn't want to see that?

Years ago, I convinced a manga artist I know, Ryuta Osada, to do a scene. Seeing them again has awaken the 14-year-old adolescent in my soul.

Regardless of whether or not Samurai vs Vampire will see the light of day, I really wanted to share this scene with the world.

And who knows? Maybe, just maybe, I will awaken the 14-year-old inside Michael, too. (Oh God, how terrifying would that be?)

AUTHOR NOTES MICHAEL ANDERLE
APRIL 28, 2020

THANK YOU for reading our story!

We have a few of these planned, but we don't know if we should continue writing and publishing without your input.

Options include leaving a review, reaching out on Facebook to let us know and smoke signals.

Frankly, smoke signals might get misconstrued as low hanging clouds so you might want to nix that idea...

The Pandemic has messed up Ramy's Brain.

Ramy isn't joking when he says he is trying to persuade me to do the ninja / vampire storyline. He started his effort a couple of weeks ago by leaving little (big) sticky notes in my office. I wrote right back.

'No.'

He then started trying to persuade additional people into his hooliganism and I had to bring up that one word again.

NOW he is trying to push the masses into the effort. I'm afraid the pandemic is started seeping into his brain. Does he have Covid-*V for Vampire*?

Maybe Covid-*Z for Zombies?*

I've already done vampires a bunch of ways... In fact, I've done vampire with katana swords...

That's close enough to samurai warriors, isn't it?

Diary for April 26th - May 2nd 2020

So, it's about six weeks into the stay-home phase, and there are mentions that states are going to slowly open up. A few words (well, a bunch) are slung all across the internet with opinions going both one way or the other.

Then I see a video about Anderson Cooper and the Las Vegas mayor. (Full disclosure, I live on the Strip and am not officially in the Las Vegas city limits but in Clark County. This is something I did not realize until this whole kerfluffle came about, and for some reason, I'm standing just a little bit straighter.)

Now, whether you knew this or not, I think it is interesting to note that the present mayor of Las Vegas is Carolyn Goodman (in office 2012 to 2022 (likely term limit)), the wife of the previous mayor Oscar Goodman (in office 1999-2011 term-limited).

Further, she has been very industrious in the Las Vegas area, working for multiple organizations and leadership roles with the tourism industry, child welfare, and education. So, regardless of the state of the discussion on opening Las Vegas back up and using the citizens in this area (me included) as a science experiment (I'm rather against this notion), I find myself shocked to find out she has a lot of qualifications.

Amazing, I know.

Everyone who knows me through these *Author Notes* realizes I am cynical when it comes to government. In fact, before I reviewed more about the present mayor, I figured there had to be some shenanigans going on for the mayorship to go from spouse to spouse.

However, it seems I should have been paying more attention to the life of Mayor Goodman the First. He has a book (by him as author) published by Hachette titled *Being Oscar: From Mob Lawyer to Mayor of Las Vegas.*

I happen to know that there is a steakhouse he owns downtown at the top of the Plaza Hotel named... Guess? *Guess?....* Oscar's!

He is a brand now.

I have to go.

I might be cynical, but steak covers a lot of cynicism.

I did a good thing...I think.

So my best friend and fellow author Craig Martelle lives in Alaska...inside the North Pole designation, and it costs him an arm and a leg to get decent internet up there in the frozen north.

I happened to ask him how come he loves it up there, and without a beat, he mentioned: "don't have to live near any politicians."

That's hardcore.

So, I received a marketing email from Skyroam about little internet pucks and sent the email to him. I have used Skyroam in the past for internet connectivity while traveling, so I knew how it worked. Apparently, it was working well enough to let him drop a line and save a few hundred bucks a month.

Then, I started looking at shotgunning his internet connections. I'm going to call and see if I can get him on the phone...

Hold on.

.... TALKING ....

I'm back. The short answer is no, it isn't working.

The longer answer is Craig spent an hour and a half playing with his Windows laptop, his Skyroam, and a phone that needed iTunes(??) to make it work. It hasn't so far, and I'm kinda bummed.

He was using some software (of which I can't remember the name), but I think there is just one major reason he is having this trouble.

Windows...He is using *Windows.* (This is complete and utter @#%@@! As it probably has nothing to do with Windows... But, he's on a PC, I'm a Mac guy... We have to carry the ribbing farther, even if I have to do it locked up in my condo thousands of miles away from him. Since Editor Lynne will be checking these author notes, I would not be surprised if she mentions something in here (she's a Windows person as well.)

(Editor's Note: I shall nobly restrain myself, MacMan)

I did the Brownstone Fries...

Short update to the Brownstone Fries idea with Jessie Rae's.

So, I had to speak with Mike Ross (Jessie Rae's BBQ) to explain my Brownstone Fries effort to help support their effort to make free lunches for those in the medical field.

Then, I left a message at their answering machine for call-in orders, but I was too late in the evening to get them to answer.

Bummer.

By the next morning, when I got a return call from Mike's mom, she already knew all about the Brownstone Fries, and it didn't confuse her at all.

Damn.

I was looking forward to explaining the "I need you to charge me for fries, but it's really a gift to help pay for people at the hospitals..." schtick I talked about in my last *Author Notes*.

Oh well, the gift went through, regardless.

Ad Aeternitatem,

Michael Anderle

OTHER BOOKS BY RAMY VANCE

Mortality Bites Series
Keep Evolving Series
Fatebound Series

Other Middang3ard Books

Never Split The Party (01)
Late To the Party (02)
It's My Party (03)
Blue Hell And Alien Fire (04)

Death Of An Author: A Middang3ard Novella

Dragon Approved Series
The First Human Rider
Ascent To The Nest
Defense Of The Nest
Nest Under Siege
First Mission

The Descent
Sacrifices
Love And Aliens
An Alien Affair

BOOKS BY MICHAEL ANDERLE

For a complete list of books by Michael Anderle, please visit:

www.lmbpn.com/ma-books/

All LMBPN Audiobooks are Available at Audible.com and iTunes

To see all LMBPN audiobooks, including those written by Michael Anderle please visit:

www.lmbpn.com/audible

CONNECT WITH THE AUTHORS

Connect with Ramy

Join Ramy's Newsletter

Join Ramy's FB Group: House of the GoneGod Damned!

Connect with Michael Anderle and sign up for his email list here:

Website: http://lmbpn.com

Email List: http://lmbpn.com/email/

Facebook:
www.facebook.com/TheKurtherianGambitBooks

www.ingramcontent.com/pod-product-compliance
Lightning Source LLC
Chambersburg PA
CBHW020227110726
47898CB00004B/1180